DAT

Nebula Awards

32

SFWA's

Choices for the Best Science Fiction and Fantasy of the Year

EDITED BY **JACK DANN**

Harcourt Brace & Company

New York   San Diego   London

The Library of Congress has cataloged this serial as follows:
The Nebula awards.—No. 18—New York [N.Y.]: Arbor House, c1983–v.; 22cm.
Annual.
Published: San Diego, Calif.: Harcourt Brace & Company, 1984–
Published for: Science-fiction and Fantasy Writers of America, 1983–
Continues: Nebula award stories (New York, N.Y.: 1982)
ISSN 0741-5567 = The Nebula awards
1. Science fiction. American—Periodicals.
1. Science-fiction and Fantasy Writers of America.
PS648.S3N38   83-647399
813'.0876'08—dc19
AACR 2 MARC-S
Library of Congress [8709r84]rev

ISBN 0-15-100306-8
ISBN 0-15-600552-2 (pbk.)

Designed by G. B. D. Smith
Printed in the United States of America
First edition
F E D C B A

Permissions acknowledgments appear on page 326, which constitutes a continuation of the
copyright page.

In memory of:
Barbara Doherty
Brian Daley
Carl Sagan
Claudia Peck
David Lasser
Ed Wood
Eleanor Butler Cameron
Elsie Wollheim
Evangeline Walton
Horace L. Gold
Richard Evans
Richard Powers
Sam Merwin, Jr.

The author would like to thank the following people for their help and support:

Justin Ackroyd of Slow Glass Books, Andrew Enstice, Robert Frazier, Mark J. McGarry, Sean McMullen, Christa Malone, Peter Pautz, Steve Paulsen, Bruce Rogers, Jonathan Strahan, Janeen Webb, Eleanor Wood, and special thanks to Pamela Sargent and George Zebrowski, who walked me through the minefields.

Contents

Introduction xi
Jack Dann

**The Year in Science Fiction
and Fantasy: A Symposium** 1
Elizabeth Hand / Lucius Shepard /
Keith Ferrell / Ian Watson /
Terry Dowling / Sean McMullen /
Norman Spinrad / Robert Frazier

Must and Shall 31
Harry Turtledove

In the Shade of the Slowboat Man 62
Dean Wesley Smith

Da Vinci Rising 72
Jack Dann

Rhysling Award Winners 138
Margaret Ballif Simon /
Bruce Boston

A Birthday 146
Esther M. Friesner

The Chronology Protection Case   164
Paul Levinson

Grand Master Jack Vance   189
Robert Silverberg /
Terry Dowling

The Men Return   196
Jack Vance

Yaguara   205
Nicola Griffith

Science Fiction Films of 1996   253
Bill Warren

Five Fucks   267
Jonathan Lethem

Lifeboat on a Burning Sea   287
Bruce Holland Rogers

Appendixes   315
About the Nebula Awards

*Selected Titles from the 1996
Preliminary Nebula Ballot*

Past Nebula Award Winners

*About the Science-fiction
and Fantasy Writers of America*

Introduction

Jack Dann

We seem to be living in an age that has misplaced its history. We're not particularly concerned, though, for history has become something like an old sweater we don't care about wearing anymore. This is the *fin de siècle*, and we're truly into the postmodern pop culture. At the flick of a channel selector we can watch *I Dream of Jeannie* or MTV, *I Love Lucy* or *Murder One*, *The Jack Benny Show* or HBO—or the last fifteen-minute loop of CNN. For those who have grown up in this post-historical era, these programs seem to take on the same value, the same "nowness." *NYPD Blue* and *Bewitched* inhabit the same space.

My graying generation grew up on the nineteenth-century notion of history as a linear construct; the postmodern concept of history is "now" and "not now." "Now" is where it's all happening; "not now" is a muzzy collection of dislocated events. When asked recently what preceded the Industrial Revolution, one university student simply wrote: "prehistoric." History has become a supermarket of sorts, and we can just walk along and collect bits and pieces here and there and put them together in any way we want. Some interesting art and fiction—and a *lot* of advertising copy—uses this supermarket approach to great effect. Humphrey Bogart and *Dragnet*'s detective Jack Webb have been brought back from the grave as "synthespians" to do postmodern product commercials.

But by misplacing history, we lose continuity. We lose our place.

It's difficult to calculate where we are—and why we're here—without knowing where we've been.

I've ceased to be surprised when intelligent science fiction readers tell me they've never heard of—much less read—writers such as Clifford Simak, Edgar Pangborn, Keith Roberts, C. M. Kornbluth, Cordwainer Smith, Theodore Sturgeon—the list goes on and on. Sadly, the culture—and the publishing industry—are geared to the "right now," to what's new and hot.

These Nebula volumes, however, not only represent the cutting edge of "right now"; they also are weighted with history: the "not now" that our genre rests upon. They are a record of where we came from, what we've done, *and* what we're doing. As was said in the science fiction newsmagazine *Locus,* "This series may turn out to be the best record we have of how SF writers have wanted to represent their craft to the world."

I can't resist reaching up to the shelf beside my desk and pulling out the first Nebula Award volume, which was edited by Damon Knight in 1965. In his introduction, Knight describes how these volumes came to be:

"This book is the result of a happy inspiration. When Science Fiction Writers of America was a few months old, Lloyd Biggle, its Secretary-Treasurer, proposed an annual SFWA anthology as a means of raising money. When Doubleday's Lawrence P. Ashmead agreed to publish the book, we realized that with our share of the royalties (ten per cent), we could do something rather handsome in the way of awards for the best stories of the year. The anthology project, first as small as a man's hand, rapidly grew into an annual ballot of SFWA's members to choose the best stories, an annual series of Nebula Awards, and an annual Awards Banquet."

Although the cover of my old Doubleday edition of *Nebula Award Stories* for 1965 is yellowed and cracking, the contents of the book certainly stand up, with milestone stories such as "The Doors of His Face, the Lamps of His Mouth" and "He Who Shapes" by Roger Zelazny; " 'Repent, Harlequin!' Said the Ticktockman" by Harlan Ellison; "Balanced Ecology" by James H. Schmitz; "Computers Don't Argue" by Gordon R. Dickson; "Becalmed in Hell" by Larry Niven; "The Saliva Tree" by Brian W. Aldiss; and the classic "The Drowned Giant" by J. G. Ballard.

I cite the contents because after all these years these stories are undiminished; they still take the breath away; they still evoke the sense of wonder. You'll notice that I didn't tell you up front which were Nebula Award winners and which were "losers" because it's really a moot point. You, the reader, might well have chosen differently. "The Drowned Giant" by J. G. Ballard is a classic in the genre, as important and influential a story as has ever been written. But it didn't win. Philip K. Dick's "We Can Remember It for You Wholesale" and Bob Shaw's "Light of Other Days" were "losers" in 1996. Harlan Ellison's "Pretty Maggie Moneyeyes" and Ballard's "The Cloud-Sculptors of Coral D" lost in 1967, and I think it can be safely said that these stories represent the very best work of each author. I could play this game right up through the years, citing some of the most important and influential stories—and novels—in the genre. This is not to diminish the winners in any way; it *is* to say that in the sense of quality of stories, the terms *winners* and *losers* are often meaningless. (Needless to say, winning awards is certainly meaningful to the *authors*—having lost several handfuls of them, I can attest to that!)

So to continue to balance precariously on my soapbox, I would think of all the stories on the final and preliminary ballots as "SFWA's choices for the best science fiction and fantasy of the year." To that end, I've included the final awards ballot for 1996 (I *have* indicated those that topped the ballot), and you'll also find some selected titles from the 1996 preliminary Nebula ballot in the appendixes.

So, herewith, are *all* the winners:

The 1996 Nebula Awards Final Ballot

FOR NOVEL

°*Slow River* by Nicola Griffith (Del Rey)
The Silent Strength of Stones by Nina Kiriki Hoffman (AvoNova)
Winter Rose by Patricia A. McKillip (Ace)
Expiration Date by Tim Powers (Tor)
Starplex by Robert J. Sawyer (Ace: published in *Analog* July–October 1996)
The Diamond Age by Neal Stephenson (Bantam)

FOR NOVELLA

°"Da Vinci Rising" by Jack Dann (*Asimov's Science Fiction,* May 1995)
"A Woman's Liberation" by Ursula K. Le Guin (*Asimov's Science Fiction,* July 1995)
"Blood of the Dragon" by George R. R. Martin (*Asimov's Science Fiction,* July 1996)
"Time Travellers Never Die" by Jack McDevitt (*Asimov's Science Fiction,* May 1996)
"The Cost to Be Wise" by Maureen F. McHugh (*Starlight 1,* Tor)

°Indicates winner.

"The Death of Captain Future" by Allen Steele (*Asimov's Science Fiction,* October 1995)

FOR NOVELETTE

"Erase/Record/Play" by John M. Ford (*Starlight 1,* Tor)
"Mirror of Lop Nor" by George Guthridge (*Immortal Unicorn,* HarperPrism)
"The Chronology Protection Case" by Paul Levinson (*Analog,* September 1995)
*"Lifeboat on a Burning Sea" by Bruce Holland Rogers (*The Magazine of Fantasy & Science Fiction,* October–November 1995)
"Must and Shall" by Harry Turtledove (*Asimov's Science Fiction,* November 1995)
"The Perseids" by Robert Charles Wilson (*Realms of Fantasy,* December 1995; published in Canada in *Northern Frights 3* [Mosaic Press])
"After a Lean Winter" by Dave Wolverton (*The Magazine of Fantasy & Science Fiction,* March 1996)

FOR SHORT STORY

"In the Pound, Near Breaktime" by Kent Brewster (*Tomorrow SF,* October 1995)
*"A Birthday" by Esther M. Friesner (*The Magazine of Fantasy & Science Fiction,* August 1995)
"The String" by Kathleen Ann Goonan (*The Magazine of Fantasy & Science Fiction,* June 1995)
"Five Fucks" by Jonathan Lethem (*The Wall of the Sky, The Wall of the Eye,* Harcourt Brace)
"These Shoes Strangers Have Died Of" by Bruce Holland Rogers (*Enchanted Forests,* DAW)
"In the Shade of the Slowboat Man" by Dean Wesley Smith (*The Magazine of Fantasy & Science Fiction,* January 1996)

GRAND MASTER NEBULA AWARD

*Jack Vance

The Year in Science Fiction and Fantasy: A Symposium

Elizabeth Hand / Lucius Shepard
Keith Ferrell / Ian Watson
Terry Dowling / Sean McMullen
Norman Spinrad / Robert Frazier

In *Nebula Awards 31,* editor Pamela Sargent wrote: "Science fiction and fantasy are genres that continue to attract a varied and diverse number of writers with very different literary goals. For any one commentator to have a coherent view of the field or to assess the relative importance of individual works is difficult at best. I have instead asked several knowledgeable and gifted writers to point out certain signposts, or to comment on the particular fictional territories they have recently explored."

I elected to follow Sargent's tradition and asked several writers to write about whatever they found interesting in science fiction. I promised to print whatever they wrote. As a result, the essays in the symposium run the gamut from warnings to historical overviews and observations: Elizabeth Hand examines what it is to be a science fiction writer at millennium's end, Lucius Shepard discusses an ominous paradigm shift in science fiction, Keith Ferrell describes the impact of new media on science fiction, and Ian Watson discusses science fiction in Great Britain; Terry Dowling and Sean McMullen give a historical perspective on science fiction in Australia, Norman Spinrad asks who is killing science fiction, and Robert Frazier examines science fiction poetry.

Elizabeth Hand is one of the most important writers to emerge in the '90s. George Alec Effinger called her "a wonderful new talent that's ready to knock the socks off the SF field." And she has done just that! She is the author of the novels *Winterlong, Aestival Tide, Icarus Descending,* and *Waking the Moon,* which won the James Tiptree Jr. Memorial Award and the Mythopoeic Society Fantasy Award. Her novella "Last Summer at Mars Hill" won both the 1995 Nebula and Hugo Awards. Her latest novel is *Glimmering.*

Lucius Shepard has been called "an outrageously talented writer" by Iain Banks, "a dark genius" by Bob Shacochis, and "the rarest of writers, a true artist" by the *Washington Post.* Indeed, Shepard has produced brilliant work, which includes stories such as "R & R," "The Jaguar Hunter," "The Man Who Painted the Dragon Griaule," "Black Coral," "Beast of the Heartland," and "Shades." His novels include *Green Eyes, Life During Wartime, The Scalehunter's Beautiful Daughter, The Golden,* and *The Velt;* and his short-story collections include *The Jaguar Hunter, Kaliman-tan,* and *The Ends of the Earth.* Shepard has won the Clarion Award, the Locus Award, the John W. Campbell Award for Best New Writer, the Science Fiction Chronicle Award, the World Fantasy Award, and the Nebula Award.

Keith Ferrell is the author of over a dozen books; the most recent is the thriller *Passing Judgment,* which E. J. Gorman called "a fascinating and frightening look at where we seem headed as a country no longer certain of its future and vaguely troubled by its past." Ferrell was editor and chief of *Omni* magazine for six years and the senior vice-president and director of General Media International. Now a full-time writer who is in constant demand as a lecturer, he speaks regularly on the future of business, the importance of competitive research, the dangers of censorship, and the future of information technology.

J. G. Ballard has called Ian Watson "the most interesting British SF writer of ideas." Watson has won the Prix Apollo, given annually for the best science fiction novel published in France, the British Science Fiction Association Award, and the Orbit Award. Among his many novels are *The Embedding, The Martian Inca, Alien Embassy, Whores of Babylon, Lucky's Harvest, The Fallen Moon,* and *The Books of the Black Current* trilogy. His short fiction has appeared in *Omni, Asimov's Science Fiction, The Magazine of Fantasy & Science Fiction,* and several best-of-the-year anthologies.

Terry Dowling and Sean McMullen are two of Australia's most important SF writers. Dowling, the recipient of an unprecedented nine Ditmar Awards for Australian science fiction achievement, has been compared with Jack Vance, J. G. Ballard, and Cordwainer Smith, probably because of the rich, variegated worlds and societies he creates, but his vision and layered, sophisticated style are entirely his own. His books include *Rynosseros, Wormwood, Blue Tyson, Twilight Beach,* and *An Intimate Knowledge of the Night.*

Sean McMullen has won the Ditmar Award for science fiction

three times and has also won the Ditmar Award for criticism three times. He is a widely respected authority on the history of Australian science fiction. *Aurealis* magazine has described him as "one of the shining lights of Australian science fiction," and Australia's national newspaper, the *Australian,* has called him "one of our finest writers of hard SF." He is the author of the Greatwinter series of novels, which includes *Voices in the Light* and *Mirrorsun Rising.* He is also the author of the short-story collection *Call to the Edge.* His latest novel is *The Centurion's Empire.*

Ursula K. Le Guin has called Norman Spinrad "one of the best short-story writers in SF, perhaps the best." He has won the Prix Apollo and the Jupiter Award and has been the president of World SF and the Science Fiction Writers of America. His novels include *Bug Jack Barron, The Iron Dream, Riding the Torch, A World Between, Songs from the Stars, The Void Captain's Tale, Child of Fortune, Little Heroes, Russian Spring, Deus X, Passing Through the Flame, The Mind Game, The Children of Hamelin,* and *Pictures at 11.* His short fiction is collected in *The Last Hurrah of the Golden Horde, No Direction Home, The Star-Spangled Future,* and *Other Americas.* His nonfiction includes *Staying Alive: A Writer's Guide* and *Science Fiction in the Real World.* Critic John P. Brennan once wrote that "Spinrad is critically aware of the turbulent unconscious of science fiction, and he has crafted a shelf of SF that rivals anyone's for inventiveness, zestful prose, and hipness."

As a poet and editor, Robert Frazier has made important contributions to science fiction poetry. His own volumes of poetry include *Peregrine, Perception Barriers,* and *Co-Orbital Moons.* He is the editor of *Star*Line,* the newsletter of the Science Fiction Poetry Association, and he has edited *The Rhysling Anthology: Best Science Fiction Poetry of 1982* and *Burning with a Vision: Poetry of Science and the Fantastic.* Frazier has also written short fiction, which includes "Across Those Endless Skies" and "The Summer People." He is the editor of the *Bulletin of the Science-fiction and Fantasy Writers of America.*

Keeping Up
ELIZABETH HAND

"No matter how cynical you get," said Lily Tomlin, "it is impossible to keep up."

She should try being a cynical science fiction writer at millennium's end. You barely get past the Special Doom Issues of *Time* and *Newsweek* (killer cults, asteroids, Olestra, and the usual spate of deranged postal employees) when your virtual rottweiler brings you the *New York Times Online*. Even that stately paper's customary sangfroid seems to be shaken, in pronouncements like "on one day two tropical storms and two hurricanes were moving toward North America" (it's hard to keep up with paranoia, too). This right alongside articles on cloning, antibiotic-resistant bacteria, tidal surges overtaking Indonesia, and Kasparov's slightly wild-eyed accusation that his computer opponent was harboring a soul.

Oh, for the days when one could read the likes of Arthur C. Clarke or Isaac Asimov and be shocked, shocked, by the notion of—well, *anything*.

The gleeful fact is that the future isn't The Future anymore: It's here, it's weird, get used to it. I remember watching *Blade Runner* the day it opened in 1982, being delighted and overwhelmed that somebody had finally been able to capture the look of dystopia on film: neon din, multicultural/corporate advertising, transgressive clothing and bodywork, retro in utero. This morning I drove through town and it's all there, except for the zeppelins urging folks to move offworld—and I live in rural Maine. The only place that actually looks like rural America anymore is Main Street, U.S.A. in Disney World. So, if we're all living in a world resembling outtakes from *The Fire Next Time,* where does that leave those of us who read this stuff, or write it for a living?

How about swimming upstream in the mainstream? Which isn't such a terrible place to be, as long as you can keep your head above the toxic waste being dumped into that river, in the form of absolutely numberless media tie-ins, novelizations, comics, sharecroppings, and "original" novels (as in, An Original Novel by [Insert Famous Person's Name Here]). It used to be that science fiction was universally regarded as a literary ghetto. Now, however, fiction itself has pretty much been relegated to a barrio of the entertainment industry. In the same way that the music and fashion industries (and academe, too, for that matter) have turned to the street for inspiration, so the world of culture—High, Low, Middle—is happily strip-mining science fiction. Is this a Bad Thing?

Well, maybe not. Pop will eat itself, as the saying goes (and a capitalist culture always turns revolt into style); but after devouring its children the revolution can sometimes produce prodigies as well as monsters. So *The X-Files* begets *Millennium,* but it also makes room on the shelves for Scott Spencer's mordant novel *Men in Black* and maybe even Jane Mendelsohn's *I Was Amelia Earhart:* beautiful aviatrix as subject of one of our century's other longstanding conspiracy theories. While Americans' fondness for conspiracy theories may have damned us to endless late-night screenings of *JFK,* it also gives us Don DeLillo, who has a new book forthcoming.

Elsewhere, besieged academics in the Ivory Tower fight off standard-bearers for Idiocy in Our Schools, but somehow find time to reprint Samuel R. Delany's groundbreaking novels *Triton* and *Dhalgren* (Wesleyan University Press), the former with an intro by that po-mo poster girl Kathy Acker. And, right in the middle of the middle of the literary establishment, Random House (under its Vintage imprint) rereleased Alfred Bester's *The Demolished Man* and *The Stars My Destination,* two of the greatest SF novels ever penned, and as cutting edge today as they were over forty years ago.

This continuing gentrification of genre fiction makes possible someone like David Foster Wallace, whose works shot to the top of the best-seller list. Wallace is sort of a literary Beck; his audience includes aging Baby Boomers who cut their teeth on *Gravity's Rainbow,* and also Wallace's own contemporaries, twenty-somethings who know Thomas Pynchon and Harlan Ellison as well as they know the theme from *Green Acres.* In the More Good News Department, the fabulist Steven Millhauser won the Pulitzer Prize for his *Martin Dressler: The Tale of an American Dreamer,* which also crept onto some best-seller lists. Kirsten Bakis's first novel, *Lives of the Monster Dogs,* treads territory staked out by Art Spiegelman in *Maus* and Carol Emshwiller in *Carmen Dog.* The same postmodern centrifuge also allowed Margaret Wander Bonanno to take her well-honed novelizing skills and use them to skewer *Star Trek,* and made William Gibson's pre-Tamagotchi *Idoru* seem more like reportage than confabulation.

Century's end also has managed to produce some homegrown magic realists. Karen Joy Fowler's *The Sweetheart Season,* Bradley Denton's *Lunatics,* Richard Grant's *Tex and Molly in the Afterlife,* and

William Browning Spencer's *Zod Wallop* joined works by people like Alice Munro and Barbara Kingsolver, which give a faint supernatural cast to suburban life. More recently, Arundhati Roy's *The God of Small Things* and Tananarive Due's *My Soul to Keep* have received lavish praise and attention. Diana Vreeland once stated that "Pink is the navy blue of India"; I put my money on Anglo-Indians and Indian writers abroad as making this year's Literary Fashion Statement, and the magical *The God of Small Things* as being This Year's Book.

So. The floodwaters may rise and the sky may fall, but—for the moment, anyway—we can console ourselves that Harold Bloom continues to champion John Crowley, and Paul Park's Jesus received better reviews than Norman Mailer's, and Kim Stanley Robinson is now a Respected Authority. Doesn't that make you feel a little better about the greenhouse effect, flesh-eating bacteria, and the distressing notion that there might be life on Mars, after all?

Must Have Been Something I Ate
LUCIUS SHEPARD

Over the last fifteen years or so, a period that roughly corresponds with my career as a writer, it strikes me that there has been something of a paradigm shift in the genre, one fueled by marketing strategies that pander to the least sophisticated of readers and bolstered by a sensibility propounded by various and sundry suggesting that the writing of strong, clean, beautiful prose is somehow separate from those skills necessary for the creation of science fiction. Of course, this tendency toward exclusion has strong roots in the past—one recalls the rejection of J. G. Ballard's work by certain of his American peers as being subversive, contrary to the moral imperatives of the science fictional status quo. And I myself remember being flabbergasted back in the late seventies on hearing an editor, when asked if facility with the English language was one of his criteria for buying a story, respond by saying that such a facility was absolutely irrelevant.

But it is during the past fifteen years that this aesthetic of the mediocre has hardened from a philosophical stance into a fact of the marketplace. Nowadays some writers are classified as "stylists," while others are considered "storytellers," as if style and narrative were mutually exclusive, as if Gene Wolfe, say, were handicapped in his ability to tell a story by his talent for writing good sentences, and as if storytelling were the sole province of, well, "storytellers," which in my opinion has become something of a buzzword for "hack." Nowadays we have the editor (ex-editor at this point in time) of one of the genre's most prominent magazines proclaiming that nobody wants to read literary science fiction, so why publish it?

It makes you wonder how, during what is commonly referred to as the Golden Age, Bradbury and Sturgeon managed to coexist with Asimov and Heinlein. Was there not then, as now, an intrinsic hostility between these two breeds? Did they not, when brought together, snarl at each other with the instinctual immediacy of cats and dogs? Or was it different then? Was the purpose of writing still perceived to be at least partially an intellectual entertainment rather than, as now, product in the Hollywood sense of the word, attractively packaged stuff designed neither to illuminate nor to stir, but to tranquilize, to satiate, to cause an already stupefied audience to grow ever more torpid and undiscerning?

Back in those balmy days when cyberpunk had not yet been relegated to nostalgia and the *F* in SFWA stood only for *fiction* and not *fantasy*, a member of that organization suggested that anyone who wished to "commit Literature" should be led to the gates of the genre, stripped of his SFWA tie tack, and forced to walk away forever while "Boots and Saddles" played in the background. Well, it appears that our esteemed colleague has gotten her wish to a great degree. New writers who display the dread symptoms of style, writers like Jonathan Lethem and Paul Witcover, flee the precincts of the genre as fast as their feets can carry them, not caring to endure the combative insults of elf-ridden trilogists, and the field has become glutted with multivolume variations on *Lord of the Rings* and Sense of Wonder bug-crushers written with all the passionate élan of tax-instruction booklets. There are, naturally, exceptions to this rule. Literary writers still exist within the bounds of science fiction and fantasy, a good many hiding out much as freedom fighters hide from oppressors, fearful that their identities may become known, surviving in many cases by writing pseudonymous trash. A very few have managed to establish themselves in a secure niche, while others maintain a midlist presence, tolerated for the moment, but viewed with suspicion in the halls of power. Yet others have retreated to the fringes of the field and are prepared to bolt if necessary. Consequently, that portion of the publishing industry that deals with science fiction and fantasy is gradually cutting itself off from new and important influences, from the possibility of revolution and renewal, strangling itself on a homogenous feast of evil trolls and cyberjunk, like a great greedy child jamming a wadded-up bread pill down its throat, face turning red, growing ever shorter of breath, yet continuing to ram the glutinous mass gulletwards in a frenzy of appetite.

As the world dims down, becoming more or less a reflection of the most accurately prophetic story in science fiction history, C. M. Kornbluth's "The Marching Morons," I suppose this simultaneous dimming down of the genre is appropriate. Yet in the millennial twilight, I feel inclined to celebrate the literary traditions of genre if only for a final time, to mention that the two most prominent contributors to the field during the first part of the century, George Orwell and H. G. Wells, were considered literary writers, and to mention further Thomas Disch's *334,* Samuel Delany's *Nevèrijon,* Ray Bradbury's *The Martian Chronicles,* the idiosyncratic work of Brian Aldiss and Keith Roberts, Gene Wolfe's *The Book of the New Sun,* Walter Tevis's *The Man Who Fell to Earth* and *Mockingbird,* Walter Miller's *A Canticle for Leibowitz,* Ursula K. Le Guin's *The Dispossessed*—a list that could go on and on of books that nourished and craftsmen who inspired.

But then nobody wants to read this kind of thing, you know, so why publish it, especially when it's oh so much easier to pry open the public mouth, insert a funnel, and force-feed it another meal of predigested dwarf drool with crunchy bits of faux emotion packaged as little-lame-prince-like heroes and heroines, poor boys who're really kings, and postmodern Cinderellas with prepubescent mental furnishings who speak in dialogue so stilted as to make a sentence like "Hark, I hear a voice" seem naturalistic by comparison.

Of course, I'm just kidding. Nothing floats my boat more buoyantly than a good page-turner about the latest in Dark Lords and Popo the ragged princeling, his nemesis, and some of my absolute best moments on the planet have been spent on far-flung SFWA-created worlds populated by boring dweebs who pass the time conjugating verbs, watching gases combine, and discussing the Meaning of Life, while alien presences do bad things to laboratory humans and the cosmos is saved by a deus ex machina and everyone gets all teary-eyed in the end. And like the rest of you, I cannot help but stand in awe of Janet Crookwaddle's eccentric epic fantasy *Bitch Mage of Lignam Land*. But nonetheless I believe that rather than booting Ursula Le Guin and her ilk out of SFWA we might try to find some dusty corner in which they can practice their considerable craft. Suppose no one had cut these writers sufficient slack back in their youth—would the genre be better off without *The Left Hand of Darkness* and "The Fifth Head of Cerberus" and "The Drowned Giant," without all the marvelous works that inspired a generation of writers? It's a question that demands no answer.

It's clear that what was once called science fiction will soon experience a redefinition, a kind of reduction that will incorporate for the most part only that which can be sold in bulk to underage readers or to readers who rely on the genre for comfort, for that cozy feeling of safe escape they enjoyed as children, and that much of what once would have been published under that label will carve itself out a tiny niche on the edge of the mainstream. Indeed, such a reduction is already occurring. Perhaps it is a good thing, but I don't think so; I don't think that our peculiar literary tradition will thrive unless it is enthusiastically inclusive of its best new writers. Eventually the marketplace, overflowing with rectangular objects the size and shape of Wheaties boxes, sporting bright covers adorned with misted castles and immense astronomical objects and the words *Part 6*—objects that once were called books—eventually that marketplace will shrivel away, as has the horror market, leaving only a few practitioners of this blandly formulaic hoo-ha to ply their insipid trade.

So what is the remedy for this reduction, this decline, this emigration of talent from the already depopulated country of so-called literary science fiction?

There is none . . . at least none that I can see.

Cautionary outcries to the publishing industry will doubtless fall on ears deafened by the ringing of cash registers from the sales of books whose weight in ounces far outstrips their worth as instruments of art or innovation.

For my part, I claim no moral high ground; I simply wanted to express one final bleat of protest before returning to work on my own trilogy, the first volume of which, *The Book of Sentences,* from Gasbag Press, will be followed in quick succession by *The Book of Paragraphs* and *The Book of Chapters,* a rousing 1,500 pages or thereabouts rife with scope, reeking with mutant armies, mixed in with the obligatory sorcerer, Black Demon Kings, an innocent who alone of all mankind can wield the Power—the entire pantheon of cliché, all expressed in prose that would not overstrain an inbred six-year-old.

Art it ain't, but I just know it's going to sell, sell, sell. . . .

Interactive Science Fiction: 1996
KEITH FERRELL

It's a science fiction world on the Web, both in content and in execution. The question is whether or not SF itself should have seen it coming.

In some ways it did, of course, SF anticipates, if not predicts, and anticipations of the global computer network are no exception. Best known remains William Gibson's *Neuromancer,* which in the decade-and-a-third since its publication remains the touchstone for literary explorations of the global computer/communications network. Dozens of literary offspring and responses (not to mention cinematic rip-offs) have explored the consequences—sublime, ridiculous, or both—of the globalization and personalization of computer networks and the electronic world they make available. Gibson himself named that place: cyberspace.

To get a feel, though, for what the Web is like at its best/worst depending on your point of view, take a look at another 1984 novel (what is it about that particular year?): Samuel R. Delany's *Stars in My Pocket like Grains of Sand.* Misunderstood when it first appeared, the novel captures in text what many who surf the Net have experienced firsthand: layer upon layer of information, commingled and contralinear, all flowing everywhere at once. Delany got it just about right.

What Gibson, Delany, and the dozens of others who've explored the phenomenon didn't anticipate—nor for that matter did the computer industry itself—was the speed with which the Internet and World Wide Web have become central to the computer and communications industry, and for that matter to the culture itself. It's a rare advertisement that doesn't contain a Web address. Television news programs hype TV news Web sites. Restaurants have their own Web locations, as do car dealers, astrologers, compost supply companies, and anything else you can imagine. The Web moved in the space of five years from technological marvel to widely hyped fad to a constant, a given, in the communications mix.

All of which is fine and fascinating, but what's out there for science fiction readers?

About what you'd expect. A lot of *Star Trek,* almost as much *Star Wars,* a lot of UFOs, a passel of role-playing games, a ton of fuzzy fantasy, and a little real science fiction.

Often touted as an electronic community, the Web, of course, comprises thousands—perhaps hundreds of thousands—of smaller communities, similar in some ways to what used to be called SIGs—special interest groups. The ease with which a Web site can be created and maintained makes participation in the community ever more accessible to ever more people—a computer and modem, a connection to the Net, and a twenty-dollar programming manual, and you're in business.

The indexing and search engines that make the Web at least ostensibly navigable give a good sense of the various categories of information and the individual sites within those categories. Yahoo!—the biggest and best established of the search engines—yields 54 discrete categories related to science fiction: everything from gay and bisexual SF to categories devoted to long-forgotten TV series. Within those categories are to be found more than 1,100 discrete sites, each focused upon—or foisting off—its creator's interests.

Try a search for *Star Trek.* You get fewer categories—37—but more than 1,600 individual sites. Get the picture?

Do it yourself: broad searches for science fiction topics invariably yield primarily media-related material.

And therein lies much of the truth about science fiction—or what passes for it—on the Web. As in our bookstores, filmed media dominate. While the Internet itself was a primarily text-based medium, a place for readers, the arrival and ascendance of the Web is in some ways turning much of the enterprise into a watcher's medium, perfect for mouse potatoes.

Star Trek, Star Wars, Babylon 5 (fittingly enough, a particularly good site), *Doctor Who, Blake's 7, Lost in Space, Highlander,* and even *Space: Above and Beyond* turn up on the Web far more frequently than written SF or fantasy, just as they increasingly do on publishers' lists. And most of these sites display next to no awareness of SF as a literary medium. Visit these sites—many of them quite well mounted—and you'll find links to other sites where you can find even more material about the same old stuff. Lots of talk, most of it empty, a surprising amount of it in Klingon. Sturgeon's Law applies to cyberspace in spades.

For all the empty talk out there, there is plenty of worthwhile material, if you're willing to take the time to find it. Learning to use search engines, continually narrowing and refocusing your search criteria, can guide you to any number of sites that do take the field and its history seriously. And there are rarities out there: on the Web you can find digital files of Heinlein's voice, indexes to *Asimov's* and other SF magazines, book dealers specializing in rare SF and fantasy, essays on authors famous and obscure.

Fans are using the Web to honor their favorite writers: Asimov, Heinlein, and Herbert seem to dominate the individual author sites, with Clarke and Ellison not far behind. Some of these sites are, to be fair, little more than slavish fan-raves, but others, such as a new Fritz Leiber site, are true labors of love, thoughtful pages that often include valuable biographical information and critical commentary. Look around: you might find something delightful.

Nor should your searches be limited to the flashy graphics of the Web. Text-based newsgroups—organized and, at their best, moderated, discussion groups—focus on virtually every aspect of science fiction, with often-fascinating discussions of authors and topics. There are literally hundreds of such groups: find the ones that match your interests and dive in. The online services also offer plenty of chances to discuss SF in all its forms. America Online hosts several forums, and the otherwise moribund Genie remains a favorite meeting place for science fiction writers and readers.

Fiction itself can be found online, in various formats.

Professional fiction publishing is present but problematic. The Web is viewed as a publishing medium, but mainstream SF publishers have been relatively slow to adapt to it.

There are a couple of exceptions, notable among them the magazine I edited from 1990 until 1996. *Omni* is now an Internet-only publication, having made its final transition from print to electronic media during 1996, after being launched first on America Online a few years earlier. By midyear the shift was complete, with paper *Omnis* (as well as my editorship) a thing of the past. Under the expert guidance of my successor, Pamela Weintraub, *Omni* on the Net continues to publish a wide range of science and speculative science journalism whose quality remains as high as when the magazine came out in monthly paper format.

On the fiction front the formidable Ellen Datlow continues to publish the most literary science fiction and fantasy around. Among the advantages the Web offers Ellen and those who write for her is a certain freedom from the space limitations that paper publication imposes. Indeed, among *Omni's* first online ventures was a series of novellas that would never have fit in the magazine. Additionally, the *Omni* site offers author appearances and promotions, as well as Ellen's delightfully eclectic list of interesting links.

Other magazines are abandoning paper as well. By early 1997, Algis Budrys's *Tomorrow SF* had made the leap to purely electronic publication, with a handsome site that includes not only professional fiction but also quite provocative and insightful (insite-ful?) commentary on the nature of the Web itself.

The appeal is obvious: on the Web you don't have to pay for paper, printing, or distribution. But if it costs less, there's also the other side of the equation: it's harder for a publisher to generate revenues from an electronic publication than from a paper publication. And while Webzines are free from print overhead, they do face the traditional bills for salaries, author payments, etc. While advertising is viewed as the salvation of Web publishing, it has yet to make much of a dent and is likely to find its way to major media publishers long before it reaches the SF sites. Electronic subscriptions are another possibility whose time seems imminent but has not yet arrived.

Amateur fiction is everywhere on the Web, most of it as dreadful as you would expect, and I'll leave it to you to find your way to worthwhile reading. If FAPA had had the Internet . . .

The immediacy of the Web has also made it an important source of breaking and ongoing news, with SF news no exception. While much of that news is media-related (the Webzine *Science Fiction Weekly* is a good source for media-related news, less so for news of print SF), it is possible to track the publication—and occasionally the activities—of print SF authors by way of newsgroups, press releases, and Web sites from the major publishers, and individual author sites.

Locus recently made its long-awaited debut on the Web, with a site that promises to become an important resource for the field, containing excerpts from the print magazine as well as links to related sites.

Authors themselves are using the Web to promote themselves and to make accessible to readers ancillary materials that enhance or enrich their works. The editor of this volume, for example, has a lovely site filled with links that illuminate his *Memory Cathedral* and its wondrous Leonardo. Authors with lively sites include Pat Cadigan, Orson Scott Card, Greg Bear, and others. Again: look around. You never know who's out there.

Not all interactive SF is online. Computer games—and their cousins on Nintendo and other videogame decks—continue to promise science fiction and for the most part continue to fail to deliver it. The evolution of personal computers—vast amounts of computing, graphics, and audio power, despite stable and even declining prices— has enabled game designers and publishers to make their products far more attractive, louder, more colorful, faster, more movielike. Unfortunately these capabilities have yet to be matched by evolution of content. Most SF games are of the blast-the-enemy variety, with a growing subset involving "terraforming" worlds, colonizing them, building up resources, and then blasting the aliens.

Among the largest-selling "SF" games of 1996 was Westwood's Red Alert, a sequel to their phenomenally popular Command & Conquer. Red Alert looks like SF at first glance—Albert Einstein travels through time to assassinate Adolf Hitler, creating a world in which Stalin launches World War II—but upon closer examination can be seen to be a glossy computer war game, its engine based on Dune II, a game of several years ago that turns Frank Herbert's masterpiece into . . . a glossy computer war game. Cyberdreams published Harlan Ellison's I Have No Mouth and I Must Scream and with it came closer to printed fantastic literature. While the game aspects of the product remained a limitation—perhaps unavoidably, computer games require players to solve puzzles—the context of the game gives a deeper sense of character than has been seen in previous computer games, helped no doubt by tens of thousands of words of new Ellison prose.

Some print SF would seem perfectly suited for adaptation to the game format, and near the end of 1996 Sierra published Rama, which took Arthur C. Clarke's novel of alien puzzles and transformed them into a marvelous computer game of alien puzzles. Produced by Gentry Lee, Rama manages to be both a good computer game and good SF. Additionally, the CD-ROM holds interviews with Clarke, and, as a hidden bonus, an excerpt from 3001. Having Arthur accessible in full-motion video on CD-ROM is in itself a science-fictional experience.

Games on the Web are becoming an increasingly popular and sophisticated medium, and we should soon see them achieve critical and profitable mass. Computer gaming is becoming, thanks to the Net, a group activity, albeit an activity that still primarily involves blasting the aliens.

Few media have evolved as rapidly or as widely as the computer and the Web. I've included no Web site addresses here for that very reason: things change too quickly. Here today, gone tomorrow, somewhere else the day after that is all too accurate a description of too many Web sites.

Despite its rapid evolution, the Web is unlikely to lose its centrality in the near future. It's too easy, it's increasingly fast, and it's increasingly televisionlike. More and more games will be linked to Web sites, more and more publishers will be using the Web to promote books, more and more fiction will be published there. Whether or not a culture accustomed to fast, nonlinear graphical information and entertainment will have interest in reading SF is another question.

Should SF have seen it coming? In one sense it didn't have to: Whatever the status—or lack thereof—of worthwhile SF on the Web, the Web is perhaps the most dramatic, and almost certainly the most important, example of just how science fictional our real world has become. Instant access to global information on your desktop? I mean, really!

Could it be that Bill Gates, even now in the process of beginning the launch of hundreds of telecommunications satellites, is the Delos W. Harriman of the real world?

We could probably have done worse.

The British Scene
IAN WATSON

What is perhaps the major British science fiction novel of last year is, in fact, entirely American in theme. Stephen Baxter's *Voyage* recounts at epic length an alternative history of NASA, culminating in a landing on Mars in 1986.

As we all know, in the real world, prestigious, spectacular crewed exploration stopped dead in its tracks after the moon landings, yielding to the space shuttle and to robot missions, and Mars remains a distant dream. Baxter's alternative offers us a genuine geologist on Mars, yet her voyage (together with a black astronaut and a white jet jockey) is still only a one-shot—a flag and footprints merely much farther away, with no subsequent expeditions in sight. So what does any of this encyclopedic chronicle signify, since it never happened and cannot now happen?

Baxter makes it all matter compellingly. Here is the most detailed, and fully felt, account of how a two-year expedition to Mars might be. Here is an urgent dialogue with the whole reality of the space program, complete with all its politics and engineering; and space may yet be our future and our salvation. What's more—and here is what makes all the difference—this is Baxter's most *human* book to date. Not only is it impeccably researched and brilliantly visualized, but in characterization it is streets beyond his previous novels.

Another big British book, hefty in bulk and ambitious, and only the first of triplets, is Peter F. Hamilton's *The Reality Dysfunction*. Hamilton's previous novel, *The Nano Flower*, was slapdash, but this is eloquent and ingenious. By ill fortune a gateway opens into a limbo zone where the souls of the dead drift in boredom. Hungry for existence, the unquiet dead spill through the gateway, taking over the bodies of colonists on a muddy pioneer planet. Ghastly consequences ensue. Not even armed star fleets can stem the tide.

Hamilton ingeniously fuses the horror genre of zombies with the SF genre of brain implants and quantum wormholes, which is no mean feat. His descriptions of worlds and living starships are lavishly inventive. He deploys a legion of believable characters. Special effects run riot, though not implausibly. Ultimately, it all hangs together: the horror, the heroism, even the humour, despite the constant schoolboyish ogling of bosoms, which Hamilton really ought to do something about, and despite outbursts of "spumescent gore" which spill right over the top.

A different eruption into our universe from another dimension comes in Iain M. Banks's *Excession*. As in Banks's other Culture novels (which he alternates with mainstream fiction) we meet artificial intelligence drones-with-attitude, wisecracking superefficient eccentric starships, a lot of self-indulgent people—and to flavour the brew, the Affront, who are really Klingons with tentacles who breathe foul gases and go round torturing furry little animals. As in Vernor Vinge's *A Fire upon the Deep*, elder species sometimes transcend into God-mode, and there is probably a hierarchy of universes—an "excession" being an intrusion from a higher domain. When the Affront, and assorted Culture ships with hidden agendas, scramble to exploit or contain the intrusion, interstellar war breaks out. A trio of quirky Culture ships make it through the withdrawing excession into The Higher Glory, compared with which the very nifty and with-it universe of the Culture is but a lump of lard. The excession itself is a mere youngster from that sublime realm. So, sucks to all *our* highfalutin shenanigans. Ultimately, the book is a game, a tongue-in-cheek caper.

No such games—but much bitter and eloquent irony—when advanced aliens come to Earth in Ian McDonald's *Sacrifice of Fools*. The "Troubles" in Northern Ireland are perhaps epitomised by a joke concerning a Jewish resident of Belfast who is stopped at a paramilitary checkpoint. "Are youse a Protestant or a Catholic?" he is challenged. "I'm a Jew," he replies. "Ah," persists the gunman, "but are youse a *Protestant* Jew, or a *Catholic* Jew?" Onto this scene of sectarian bigotry come 80,000 alien settlers, being one per cent of the interstellar newcomers whom Earth's governments agree to admit in exchange for superior technology.

In this wonderful remix of *Alien Nation,* the off-the-cuff disclosure that it was only by a hair's breadth that the alien Shian voted not to erase human civilization jerks the carpet somewhat from under the narrative scaffolding of cultural concordat. This bit seems to have strayed in from a Niven-Pournelle novel, since McDonald's aliens typically earn their crust as pizza-delivery bikers and manufacturers of customized golf clubs. Yet this is a minor quibble. McDonald's pheromonal aliens are fascinating. In law and sexuality and mind-set and "religion" the Shian differ radically from human beings, and they cast a telling light on human aggression and prejudice, without remotely being angels themselves. The story itself—of a reformed hit man trying to discover who murdered and mutilated his alien "friends"—is harrowing, beautiful, grimly thrilling, and poignantly sardonic.

Memory Seed, a first novel by Stephen Palmer, transposes Jeff Noon's *Vurt* and *Pollen* into "Vert," an attack by the green stuff. Noon wrote about dreamland waging psychotropic pollen attack upon a rainy Manchester. Six thousand years ahead, vegetation wages war—with poisons and spines and tendrils and homicidal pumpkins and pollen—upon the last remnants of the plague of people, embattled in a rainy city full of baroque rituals, botanical computers, prophetic snakes, and such weirdnesses. It was men who first caused Nature's revenge, by raping the planet. Now the few remaining males are kept locked up, and our quirky heroines struggle to survive the final débâcle amidst much cloak and dagger (and rather a lot of "with one bound Jill was free"). A delightfully zany and colourful virtuoso performance, this.

Biology also preoccupies Alison Sinclair in her second novel, *Blueheart,* set on an ocean world, which is unique among Earth's colonies in being habitable without having undergone terraforming—by virtue of humans having adapted to amphibious life. Debate rages regarding whether to terraform, even so. Terraforming would supersede the native marine ecology and the adapted humans, some of whom are illegally going their own metamorphic way. The world building is richly detailed, although the tone is earnest and melancholy.

Meanwhile, Jeff Noon himself—still rooted in his home city of Manchester—playfully sounds a new note by inventing a third Lewis Carroll book. In *Automated Alice,* the Wonderland girl is propelled into an alternative 1998 version of Manchester full of beast-people. She encounters computers composed of termites which calculate with beans—beanery logic, ho ho—and windscreen vipers on cars, a robot version of herself, and murdered filmmakers such as Quentin Tarantula. Some of the plethora of puns which propel the book are delicious. Others are daft. It's all great fun, though finally rather silly. As an artefact, the illustrated *Automated Alice* deserves an award for beautiful book production.

Scotsman Ken Macleod's splendid first novel, *The Star Fraction,* is currently a great success among American Libertarians, despite being slightly left of Trotsky. In *The Stone Canal* Macleod ploughs the same individualistic furrow with bells and hyperboosters on. In the student union bar of Glasgow University in 1975, young militants hold forth about radical politics. Mine's a pint, och aye, have another cigarette. Some centuries later, a robot resurrects one of the militants far away in the galaxy on a planet resembling Mars. Linking the two loci is a cosmic wormhole which artificial intelligences have created—and also a long-lasting rivalry over a lass. Unfortunately, the AIs have become dangerously loony. Many enigmas confront us, about identity and reality and imitation, which are the wellspring of this book. With superb dry wit and acumen and passion—and great alertness to tone of voice—Macleod fuses futuristics and revolutionary activism. Action abounds. Gems of naughty, droll subtext bristle. Next century, *of course* traditional Afghan rug motifs will be AK-47s and MiGs. And everybody smokes cigarettes as often as possible, not to fill in lulls in the narrative (there aren't any) but as a declaration of liberty.

Traditionally, Britain counts within its purview books from its former empire, so although Amitav Ghosh lives in New York, let me mention *The Calcutta Chromosome,* first published last year in New Delhi before its British edition (second prize for lovely production). Here is a wonderfully lively and funny investigation of the mystery of how such a pedestrian person as the real Sir Ronald Ross could, in

1897 in Calcutta, have discovered the cause of malaria—the cold fusion of his day, as regards cutting-edge science—unless he was secretly being manipulated by adepts who had their actual sights set on immortality. The author really is a smarty-pants, and the book does end up as an echo of Eco (Umberto, of that ilk), yet along the way real science is treated very imaginatively and with great comic pizzazz— and Ghosh also invents counter-science, which is the opposite of normal science.

British science fiction is sometimes perceived as downbeat, reflecting post-colonial blues. Actually, it's bubbling with energy.

The Road to 1996
TERRY DOWLING AND SEAN McMULLEN

For the past forty years Australia has been a "lucky" country where science fiction is concerned. In the late fifties a wartime (!) import embargo was lifted, so that by 1962 you could go into Woolworths and find bins of remaindered Digit paperbacks, British editions of books by van Vogt, Kuttner, Williamson, Aldiss, Tubb, Wright, Pohl, and Kornbluth. Some were retitled (which still happens) and many had superb Brian Lewis covers. A few years later there were bins of Ace doubles and singles for around twenty-five cents, bringing the work of Vance, Dick, Zelazny, Herbert, and Delany to precocious young schoolchildren with only lunch money to spend on books. Imprints like Four Square, Gold Medal, Penguin and Panther, Corgi and Arrow were up there with Pyramid and Lancer, Berkley, Ballantine, and Bantam. It didn't matter that you read Asimov's *Foundation and Empire* in the April 1962 Panther paperback or Bradbury's *The October Country* in the British 1961 Ace Books limited edition; they were there to be had, and weren't they just marvellous alongside your Captain W. E. Johns and Simon Black novels, and your Classics Illustrated graphic titles?

On the newsstands, genre magazines became plentiful as well. American magazines such as *Amazing, Fantastic, Analog, Galaxy,* and *If* vied with the top-class British *New Worlds, Science Fiction Adventures, Science Fantasy,* and *Nebula*. They featured stories by the best and most innovative SF storytellers in the business, and you didn't ponder sources, you didn't even think about it much: you just bought and read and thus belonged to that larger world. SF also came out of the comics and British kids' annuals, out of radio shows like *Rocky Starr* and *Captain Miracle,* out of the countless B-movies and monochrome weekly serials. In the wake of television's Australian debut in 1956 came such shows as *Doctor Who, The Twilight Zone, The Outer Limits, Out of the Unknown, Star Trek,* and *Lost in Space.*

Aussie SF writers were thin on the ground as all this SF came flooding in, due to Australia's small population and isolation, and the shortage of suitable markets. Mainstream magazines such as the *Australian Journal, Adam, Man,* and some newspapers published a bit of local SF, but most of our better writers, such as A. Bertram Chandler, John Baxter, Norma Hemming, Lee Harding, Wynne Whiteford, Frank Bryning, and David Rome were establishing themselves overseas. Their stories were going out to wide-ranging American and British magazines and coming back golden and glorious as part of an international scene based on the best that was submitted. What about novels, you ask? There were hardly any.

Throughout the sixties, the seventies, and the eighties, the Australian profile improved. John Baxter first alerted the general mass of Australian readers to the very existence of Australian SF authors with his highly successful landmark anthology *The Pacific Book of Science Fiction.* The short-lived British-Australian magazine *Vision of Tomorrow* also provided a very visible boost. Australian fans hosted a successful Worldcon in 1975, Chandler's output of Rimworlds novels became a steady stream, Australian criticism won Hugo Awards, and the SF world began to recognise that Australia was on the map. By Australia's second Worldcon in 1985, Australian SF was more common, but we were still primarily a nation of readers. It was not until the late eighties and early nineties that the situation really changed.

So what caused the change? It's easy to point to the two Worldcons in Melbourne as pivotal catalysing events behind the change, but in reality the Worldcons were more of a celebration (albeit justified) for those in the know. It was the overseas SF that poured in that gradually changed our attitudes and expectations, but before the world could see our work there was one important issue to tackle: where to publish it?

A spate of small presses and semiprozines grew up in the wake of the 1975 Worldcon, culminating in the professional *Omega Science Digest* in 1981. *Omega* was a big-circulation, glossy *Omni–Science Digest* lookalike which published two stories per issue, and stories published in it were accepted by the SFWA as counting towards Nebula voting rights.

What about quality? As anywhere, it was patchy, but the occasional flashes of brilliance were becoming more frequent. Jack Wodhams and Lee Harding had topped overseas readers' polls in the 1960s, then David Lake's "Re-deem the Time" was republished in Terry Carr's *Best Science Fiction of the Year* anthology for 1980. Damien Broderick's *The Dreaming Dragons* was runner-up in the 1981 Campbell Awards, stories by Sean McMullen and Greg Egan were voted onto the Nebula Awards preliminary ballot in 1989 and 1990 respectively, and George Turner was included in the 1989 final ballot by the committee for *The Drowning Towers*—which also won the Arthur C. Clarke Award. Some of the highlights that followed were: Egan's "Learning to Be Me" winning the *Interzone* readers' poll for 1990, and his "The Infinite Assassin" topping that poll again in 1991; Terry Dowling's *Wormwood* winning the Readercon Small Press Award in 1991, and his *Breaking through to the Heroes* doing it again in 1993; Egan's *Permutation City* winning the Campbell Award in 1995, and ten of his stories being republished in Gardner Dozois's Year's Best Science Fiction series.

And now we reach 1996. Increasingly, Australian works have become serious contenders for overseas awards, local commercial publishers are publishing Australian works and making healthy profits, local semi-professional magazines, such as *Eidolon* and *Aurealis*, are flourishing and thus providing a stable market for short fiction, and very few best-of-the-year reading lists are published without Australian works included. Australians are finally becoming well-known as authors after being primarily customers and critics for decades.

Harlan Ellison gave 1996 a good start in January by asking the audience of a Sydney convention if they realised that they were currently living in the golden age of Australian SF. In fact, the year was not short of highlights. Two Egan stories had Hugo nominations, while the feminist anthology *She's Fantastical* received two nominations for the World Fantasy Awards. The new Aurealis genre awards were inaugurated, and local professionally published SF and fantasy books (including young adult) equalled the previous year's record of fifty, although short fiction publications crashed to sixty-four works, half of the previous year's figure. Dozois's thirteenth *Year's Best Science Fiction* anthology included two of Egan's stories and ten other Australian stories in the honourable mentions list. The companion *Year's Best Fantasy and Horror,* edited by Ellen Datlow and Terri Windling, included yet another of Dowling's stories and listed twenty-nine other Australian works in honourable mentions. Three works by Australian residents made the Nebula preliminary ballot, and Jack Dann's "Da Vinci Rising" won for best novella.

The drop in short fiction output was partly due to authors recognising that there is now a more stable market for books, but the book market itself is not without problems. Much of Australia's recent sales success with genre novels has been based more on marketing than quality, and 1996 sales were reported to be well down in some areas. The boom has also favoured fantasy over SF, and, when isolated, the SF figures are quite low. That longtime champion of Australian SF, Aphelion Publications, decided on a drastic reduction of output, as only two of Aphelion's top authors made the sorts of profits needed to keep the company viable. Henceforth, only occasional anthologies will be published by Aphelion. Finally, as Peter Nicholls pointed out in the *Australian Book Review,* in spite of the boom, Australians still get only a fraction of the books published per head of population that the British and the Americans do. In short, Australia is hardly paradise for a genre author, but people with talent can certainly get somewhere.

The future for Australian SF and fantasy lies in both quality and innovation. *The Interpretaris,* Australia's independently conceived version of *Star Trek,* was first screened only three weeks after the original *Star Trek's* first screening in North America in 1966. It was based on a good and timely idea, but its realisation was underpowered and short on ideas, so it was not a big hit. Now *Spellbinder* and *Ocean Girl* have the originality, quality, and ideas whose lack crippled *The Interpretaris*—so much so that American and British fans e-mail Australians seeking advance copies of these shows. Australia is culturally distinctive enough from the USA and Britain for its SF to be refreshingly different and exciting without being difficult to follow, and overseas readers and editors are waking up to this. The year 1996 was a very good one—but Australians are coming to expect that all years will be very good.

Who Is Killing Science Fiction?
NORMAN SPINRAD

As far as I'm concerned, the most important trend in science fiction in 1996 was one that had been going on for a while beforehand, continued even more strongly into 1997, and threatens to reach condition terminal by the turn of the millennium: the death of SF as a viable publishing mode for anything of literary credibility and as a viable career choice for any writer with ambitions beyond the purely commercial.

Extreme words?

Extreme times.

I'm *not* talking about the death of science fiction as a viable literary form. In 1996, as in the previous few years, many good science fiction novels were published, quite a few fine ones; more in fact than during any so-called Golden Age of the past. Writers of promise continue to enter the field. But in retrospect, it has been quite a while since we have seen a truly great science fiction novel, because, perhaps, few of the excellent writers in the field are stretching toward such greatness.

What I mean by a great science fiction novel is a book that touches both the mind and the heart, that leaves readers with the feeling that the experience of reading the book has evolved their consciousness upward in some small measure, that leaves the communal enterprise we call science fiction with some possibilities that were not there before, that opens creative doors.

From my vantage as a critic, I see that there are perhaps dozens of newer writers in the field capable of seriously aspiring to such a creative level, but few of them seem to be evolving beyond a certain middle level of craftsmanlike excellence. Or if they do, they tend to leave.

Why?

Because there are few if any editors of literary passion in the field encouraging them to do so, and no publishers. And good early novels are being buried by an avalanche of despicable schlock that has no rai-son d'être whatsoever beyond the sacred bottom line.

Star Wars novels. *Star Trek* novels. *X-Files* novels. Writers share-cropping the universes of other writers, living and dead. I used to com-plain that this schlock was creating a false image of what science fiction really was in the mind of the general public. No more. In terms of eco-nomic dominance and rack space, this evil stuff is now what the sci-ence fiction genre has actually become.

Evil?

He said *evil?*

It's about time somebody did. Evil in the sense of morally wrong.

It is not morally wrong to write this schlock if that is what you have to do to survive in the Darwinian piranha-pond that publishing has be-come, any more than it is morally wrong to dig ditches or flip grease-burgers or write episodic TV if it's that or starvation or a life of crime. It's a job.

But that's all that it is. Writers of talent who convince themselves otherwise are collaborating in their own creative destruction.

These writers are victims. They are to be pitied, but they are doing nothing morally wrong. The corporate copyright and trade-mark holders who exploit them are committing evil, but they are soulless decision-making programs running along the sacred bottom line and there is nothing human there to take moral responsibility for the act.

But so-called *senior* writers who lease out their universes or char-acters to so-called *junior* writers for a piece of the action are another matter. What *they* are doing *is* morally wrong. What they are doing is a betrayal of the very community which enabled them to reach a point in their careers where such a temptation could arise.

I'm not talking about genuine collaboration, where two writers plan out a story together and really share the work of writing the book, not necessarily even equally, and one happens to be much more fa-mous than the other.

I'm talking about writers who turn themselves into the corporate equivalent of *Star Trek* or *Star Wars* or *X-Files*—into brand names. Writers who desecrate their own creative oeuvre by franchising it out to others, or who create a format in the manner of a TV "bible" and hire writers to do episodes, or worse still, put their names on novel series put together by packagers or publishers for them.

This is wrong. This is dishonest. This is betrayal. This is killing science fiction.

It is dishonest to accept credit on a book cover for work you have not done. If you have built up a large enough and loyal enough readership to make placing such temptation in your path a commercially viable option, then you are betraying those readers by palming off someone else's work as your own. And you are ripping off whoever does the real work for you.

I have heard all the rationalizations, and I know there are literary fast-food franchisers out there who truly believe them, who truly believe that they are helping more junior writers survive.

And it's true, in a strictly economic sense, they are.

Literary television that SF publishing has become, it's now almost impossible for so-called junior writers to make much of a living doing their own freestanding work. So senior writers who allow them to farm their north forty at a reduced royalty rate are indeed helping them to keep the wolf outside the sharecropper's shack.

But I ask you, colleagues, those of you who *are* colleagues and not book packagers or media entities or the controllers of literary estates, those of you who sincerely really *do* want to do well by doing good, to consider from whence this necessity arose in the first place.

Why has it become necessary for you to rent out your name and/or your "universe" so that the generation behind you can survive economically?

Do you really need to be told?

Do you really need to be told that you are collaborating in the creation of the very conditions that make such "help" necessary and further enriching yourselves at your colleagues' ultimate expense?

For what is being created is a class structure, and already the terms *junior writers* and *senior writers* are being used to formalize it. A handful of senior writers are transforming themselves into brand names like *Star Wars* and *Star Trek,* and more and more writers who should be enriching the literary landscape with the evolution of their own work are being economically forced into permanent junior status.

Macabrely enough, some of the most marketable brand-name senior writers cannot be blamed for this because they are dead.

This, I'm afraid, is the state of "science fiction." I put the term in quotes because so much that is now labeled "science fiction" or "SF" or "sci-fi" isn't even fiction these days. There's a "Sci-Fi Channel" basically devoted to "SF" imagery in its various incarnations. The same imagery that has become a mainstay of advertising. And the toy industry. And the computer industry.

I was a guest a couple of years ago at something in Spain called "La Semana Negra." This event began as a kind of crime novel conference not that dissimilar to the Nebula events of today except that there were no awards and it lasted for a week.

Paco Taibo, the writer and creator of this event, is an incredible ball of fire, and down through the years has secured more and more government and corporate support for the event, and now it has become an immense regional fair, the size of an American state fair, replete with literally dozens of dance pavilions, hundreds of bars and restaurants, carnival rides, hot air balloons, and a sign proclaiming SEMANA NEGRA in letters the size of those on the Hollywood sign.

Buried in the middle of this is a modest-sized tent in which the literary conference still takes place.

Welcome to the Worldcon of the future.

Where somewhere lost in the middle of the "Sci-Fi" corporate fun fair, if we are lucky, there will also be a small tent where a few nostalgic old fans and a few atavistic writers will repair to reminisce about the good old days when sincerely felt, literarily ambitious, real science fiction was written from the heart, when the lunatics controlled the asylum, before it was taken over by the marketeers.

Abandoned Cities
ROBERT FRAZIER

There used to be a vital community of science fiction poets. They argued poetics in print. Argued ideas over the phone. Visited each other outside of the circumstances of a convention hotel. Started small publishing ventures on vapor capital. Collaborated in print. But the community has grown silent as the greater publishing industry conflates and consolidates and gets conservative at the door to a new millennium. I think they're running a bit scared.

Bruce Boston is without a phone number. I heard he moved out of rent control in Berkeley. Anyone know for sure?

Anyone heard a peep from the once-prolific Peter Payack, or Elissa Malcohn?

Seen a poem recently by Roger Dutcher or Steve Tem or Terry A. Garey or Mike Bishop or Gene Van Troyer?

Or for that matter, one by Jack Dann?

I managed to visit the West Coast recently. I didn't find Bruce but did find veterans Andrew Joron and Kathryn Rantala Swindler. In Seattle, Kathy had a broken ankle that was taking forever to mend, and, coincidentally, a collection of science poetry due from a publisher that has promised publication over and over for ten years. She's not just losing her faith; the idea of faith seems lost to her. And after three Rhysling Awards and three impeccable collections, Berkeleyite Andy rarely writes a poem within the genre.

I asked Andy what he thought was going on.

"Speculative poetry is presently heading in the same direction as the rest of the SF genre: toward trivialization. The fact that most major publishers have been swallowed up by a handful of mega-corporations has not only inculcated a climate of aesthetic conservatism but has also led to a generic homogenization. SF texts are now nearly indistinguishable from thrillers or mysteries. Innovative writing in SF—prose or poetry—has been effectively banned by market considerations."

Ouch. Painful to consider, but hard to refute.

"Of course," said Andy, "the fate of speculative poetry is not necessarily tied to that of the SF genre as a whole. SF poetry must *reinvent itself as a community.*"

I can't say I see ahead to that moment, though. Not yet. SF poetry publishers Ocean View Books and Pantograph stand dormant. Venues like *Velocities* have folded. *The Magazine of Speculative Poetry*, which just woke after a long sleep to publish what appears to be its last issue (which *does* include backlog pieces by Garey, Tem, and Joron), sounds like it's giving up. Even the newsletter of the Science Fiction Poetry

Association (*Star★Line*) looks devoid of articles and market reports and poetry workshops and other signs of community activity.

But I admit my faith stands firm, due mostly to the efforts of a handful of poets:

W. Gregory Stewart. His *Blood Like Wine* . . . is a 1996 collection from Preternatural Press.

Denise Dumars. Her *Speaking Bones* is a 1996 collection from Dark Regions Press.

David Lunde. His *Blues for Port City* is a 1995 collection from Mayapple Press.

Steve Sneyd. His *In Coils of Earthen Hold* is a 1994 omnibus collection from the University of Salzburg Press. Steve is not only incredibly prolific but is a historian of SF poetry.

Adam Cornford. His *Decision Forest* is a 1997 collection from Pantograph Press (possibly the last book from a speculative publisher that gave us *Science Fiction* by Joron, *The Stratospheric Canticles* by Will Alexander, and *Phase Language* by Lee Ballentine).

Keith Allen Daniels. Keith is a macabre poet, yet his Anamnesis Press publishes SF: a James Blish poetry book plus scheduled collections by Steven Utley and Joe Haldeman.

Joe Haldeman. *Saul's Death & Other Poems* is proof that his poetry ages well. When Haldeman considers a life in his prose, he worms beneath the person's gristle, probes a wire between their lobes. When he employs scientific wit, it cuts with the same personal abandon. But when Joe commits these to poetry, we share in his act of distillation, in his preservation of such revelatory moments as "frozen like a murderer's heart in a jar." His voice is a true voice at the height of its powers.

David Memmott. David's cycle of poems *The Larger Earth: Descending Notes of a Grounded Astronaut* was published in 1996 by Permeable Press, San Francisco, and his own Oregon imprint, Jazz Police Books, has recently published a science poetry collection that is a *Small Press Review* pick-of-the-month—*A Celebration of Bones,* by Sandra Lindow (1996).

Sandra Lindow. Just check out "On Distance" from the June 1997 issue of *Asimov's.*

Gardner Dozois and *Asimov's.* Who in the last year or so printed such superb works as Wendy Rathbone's "Astronaut Boneyard," Utley's evolution poems "Dodoes" and "The Impatient Ape" (the title poem to his upcoming collection), Stewart's "The Ice Blue Heart," Lunde's "Anguish" and "In Which Gravity Is a Function of the Fall," and William John Watkins.

William John Watkins. Speaking of a poet who scales the height of his powers, consider "In Kafkaville the Funerals Run on Time" (1995), then "The Robot's *Wasteland*" (1996), then "17 Questions the Judges at Nuremberg Forgot to Ask" (1997).

Seek out these works, and you will see what I mean. There may not be a community in evidence, but these individuals rage together against the dying of the light.

Bless them all.

Must and Shall

Harry Turtledove

Although Harry Turtledove has published hard SF, high fantasy, humorous fantasy, and mainstream fiction, he is perhaps most well-known for his alternate histories, such as his brilliant novel *The Guns of the South,* which the Pulitzer Prize–winning historian James M. McPherson called "must reading for every Civil War student. . . . It is absolutely unique—without question the most fascinating Civil War novel I have ever read." Critic M. Hammerton believes that Turtledove has created a genuinely new genre: "a combination of 'straight' SF and alternative history." Turtledove's novels include the Worldwar and Videssos Cycle series, *Agent of Byzantium,* and, most recently, *Thessalonica.* His short-story collections include *Kaleidoscope* and *Departures.* His alternate history novella "Down in the Bottomlands" won a Hugo in 1994, and the novelette "Must and Shall" was also a Hugo finalist.

About "Must and Shall," he writes:

"The Civil War is the great choke point through which American history flows. For better and for worse, the United States is what it is today because of what happened in 1861 to 1865 and how it happened.

"Because of this, the Civil War is endlessly attractive to people who like to play the what-might-have-been game. Those four crowded years offer so many ways in which the course of American history might have been changed. The biggest of these changes, of course, is to have the Confederacy win the war and gain its independence. I've played with that one myself in *Guns of the South,* and will play it again in a different way (without the deus ex machina of the AK-47) in my upcoming *How Few Remain.*

"But if the Civil War were fought a hundred different times on a hundred nearly identical time lines, my guess is that the Union would win about ninety of those wars. One afternoon, I got to thinking that not all Union victories would be identical in outcome. 'Must and Shall' is the result of that speculation.

"In real history, Abraham Lincoln advocated a relatively mild reconstruction for the Southern states after a Union victory. After he was assassinated, Andrew Johnson pursued this policy, though far less smoothly and less successfully than Lincoln might well have managed. But there was a strong faction in the Republican Party that wanted to treat the regained Confederate states as conquered provinces, harshly punishing all the rebel leaders, and defining 'leaders' very broadly. 'Must and Shall' looks at what might have happened had the radical Republicans come to power near the end of the Civil War and taken their revenge on the South.

"Otto von Bismarck is supposed to have said, 'God loves children, drunkards, and the United States of America.' We have only to look at the nearly endless aftermaths to civil wars in Ireland and Yugoslavia, among other places, to conclude that Bismarck had a point. Dreadful as it was, our own Civil War did not make the losers take to the hills and start bushwhacking the victorious occupiers, though it came closer to doing that than many people—especially outside the former Confederacy—realize. We might well have had Northern Ireland writ large across our Southern states. In the world of 'Must and Shall,' we do.

" 'Must and Shall,' like a lot of the work I do, might be thought of as historical fiction with an SFnal twist: change one thing, extrapolate as rigorously as possible, and see what happens. I'm just as well pleased this particular change remains fictional."

12 July 1864—Fort Stevens, north of Washington, D.C.

General Horatio Wright stood up on the earthen parapet to watch the men of the Sixth Corps, hastily recalled from Petersburg, drive Jubal Early's Confederates away from the capital of the United States. Down below the parapet, a tall, thin man in black frock coat and stovepipe hat asked, "How do we fare, General?"

"Splendidly." Wright's voice was full of relief. Had Early chosen to attack the line of forts around Washington the day before, he'd have faced only militiamen and clerks with muskets and might well have broken through to the city. But Early had been late, and now the veterans from the Sixth Corps were pushing his troopers back. Washington City was surely saved. Perhaps because he was so relieved, Wright said, "Would you care to come up with me and see how we drive them?"

"I should like that very much, thank you," Abraham Lincoln said, and climbed the ladder to stand beside him.

Never in his wildest nightmares had Wright imagined the president accepting. Lincoln had peered over the parapet several times already and drawn fire from the Confederates. They were surely too far from Fort Stevens to recognize him, but with his height and the hat he made a fine target.

Not far away, a man was wounded and fell back with a cry. General Wright interposed his body between President Lincoln and the Confederates. Lincoln spoiled that by stepping away from him. "Mr. President, I really must insist that you retire to a position of safety," Wright said. "This is no place for you; you must step down at once!"

Lincoln took no notice of him, but continued to watch the fighting north of the fort. A captain behind the parapet, perhaps not recognizing his commander in chief, shouted, "Get down, you damn fool, before you get shot!"

When Lincoln did not move, Wright said, "If you do not get down, sir, I shall summon a body of soldiers to remove you by force." He gulped at his own temerity in threatening the President of the United States.

Lincoln seemed more amused than anything else. He started to turn away, to walk back toward the ladder. Instead, after half a step, he crumpled bonelessly. Wright had thought of nightmares before. Now one came to life in front of his horrified eyes. Careless of his own safety, he crouched by the president, whose blood poured from a massive head wound into the muddy dirt atop the parapet. Lincoln's face wore an expression of mild surprise. His chest hitched a couple of times, then was still.

The captain who'd shouted at Lincoln to get down mounted to the parapet. His eyes widened. "Dear God," he groaned. "It is the president."

Wright thought he recognized him. "You're Holmes, aren't you?" he said. Somehow it was comforting to know the man you were addressing when the world seemed to crumble around you.

"Yes, sir, Oliver W. Holmes, 20th Massachusetts," the young captain answered.

"Well, Captain Holmes, fetch a physician here at once," Wright said. Holmes nodded and hurried away. Wright wondered at his industry—surely he could see Lincoln was dead. Who, then, was the more foolish, himself for sending Holmes away, or the captain for going?

21 July 1864—Washington, D.C.

From the hastily erected wooden rostrum on the east portico of the capitol, Hannibal Hamlin stared out at the crowd waiting for him to deliver his inaugural address. The rostrum was draped with black, as was the capitol, as had been the route his carriage took to reach it. Many of the faces in the crowd were still stunned, disbelieving. The United States had never lost a president to a bullet, not in the eighty-eight years since the nation freed itself from British rule.

In the front row of dignitaries, Senator Andrew Johnson of Tennessee glared up at Hamlin. He had displaced the man from Maine on Lincoln's reelection ticket; had this dreadful event taken place a year later (assuming Lincoln's triumph), he now would be president. But no time for might-have-beens.

Hamlin had been polishing his speech since the telegram announcing Lincoln's death reached him up in Bangor, where, feeling useless and rejected, he had withdrawn after failing of renomination for the vice presidency. Now, though, his country needed him once more. He squared his broad shoulders, ready to bear up under the great burden so suddenly thrust upon him.

"Stand fast!" he cried. "That has ever been my watchword, and at no time in all the history of our great and glorious republic has our heeding it been more urgent. Abraham Lincoln's body may lie in the grave, but we shall go marching on—to victory!"

Applause rose from the crowd at the allusion to "John Brown's Body"—and not just from the crowd, but also from the soldiers posted on the roof of the capitol and at intervals around the building to keep the accursed rebels from murdering two presidents, not just one. Hamlin went on, "The responsibility for this great war, in which our leader gave his last full measure of devotion, lies solely at the feet of the Southern slavocrats who conspired to take their states out of our grand Union for their own evil ends. I promise you, my friends—Abraham Lincoln shall be avenged, and those who caused his death punished in full."

More applause, not least from the Republican senators who proudly called themselves Radical: from Thaddeus Stevens of Pennsylvania, Benjamin Wade of Ohio, Zachariah Chandler of Michigan, and bespectacled John Andrew of Massachusetts. Hamlin had been counted among *their number when he sat in the Senate before assuming the duties, such as they were, of the vice president.*

"Henceforward," Hamlin declared, "I say this: let us use every means recognized by the Laws of War which God has put in our hands to crush out the wickedest rebellion the world has ever witnessed. This conflict is become a radical revolution—yes, gentlemen, I openly employ the word, and, what is more, I revel in it—involving the desolation of the South as well as the emancipation of the bondsmen it vilely keeps in chains."

The cheers grew louder still. Lincoln had been more conciliatory, but what had conciliation got him? Only a coffin and a funeral and a grieving nation ready, no, eager for harsher measures.

"They have sowed the wind; let them reap the whirlwind. We are in earnest now, and have awakened to the stern duty upon us. Let that duty be disregarded or haltingly or halfway performed, and God only in His wisdom can know what will be the end. This lawless monster of a Political Slave Power shall forevermore be shorn of its power to ruin a government it no longer has the strength to rule.

"The rebels proudly proclaim they have left the Union. Very well: we shall take them at their word and, once having gained the victory Providence will surely grant us, we shall treat their lands as they deserve: not as the states they no longer desire to be, but as conquered provinces, won by our sword. I say we shall hang Jefferson Davis, and hang Robert E. Lee, and hang Joe Johnston, yes, hang them higher than Haman, and the other rebel generals and colonels and governors and members of their false Congress. The living God is merciful, true, but He is also just and vengeful, and we, the people of the United States, we shall be His instrument in advancing the right."

Now great waves of cheering, led by grim Thaddeus Stevens himself, washed over Hamlin. The fierce sound reminded him of wolves baying in the backwoods of Maine. He stood tall atop the rostrum. He would lead these wolves, and with them pull the rebel Confederacy down in ruin.

11 August 1942—New Orleans, Louisiana

Air brakes chuffing, the Illinois Central train pulled to a stop at Union Station on Rampart Street. "New Orleans!" the conductor bawled unnecessarily. "All out for New Orleans!"

Along with the rest of the people in the car, Neil Michaels filed toward the exit. He was a middle-sized man in his late thirties, most of his dark-blond hair covered by a snap-brim fedora. The round, thick, gold-framed spectacles he wore helped give him the mild appearance of an accountant.

As soon as he stepped from the air-conditioned comfort of the railroad car out into the steamy heat of New Orleans summer, those glasses fogged up. Shaking his head in bemusement, Michaels drew a handkerchief from his trouser pocket and wiped away the moisture.

He got his bags and headed for the cab stand, passing on the way a horde of men and boys hawking newspapers and rank upon rank of shoeshine stands. A fat Negro man sat on one of those, gold watch chain running from one pocket of his vest to the other. At his feet, an Irish-looking fellow plied the rag until his customer's black oxfords gleamed.

"There y'are, sir," the shoeshine man said, his half-Brooklyn, half-Southern accent testifying he was a New Orleans native. The Negro looked down at his shoes, nodded, and, with an air of great magnanimity, flipped the shoeshine man a dime. "Oh, thank you very much, sir," the fellow exclaimed. The insincere servility in his voice grated on Michaels's ears.

More paperboys cried their trade outside the station. Michaels bought a *Times-Picayune* to read while he waited in line for a taxi. The war news wasn't good. The Germans were still pushing east in Russia and sinking ship after ship off the American coast. In the South Pacific, Americans and Japanese were slugging away at each other, and God only knew how that would turn out.

Across the street from Union Station, somebody had painted a message: YANKS OUT! Michaels sighed. He'd seen that slogan painted on barns and bridges and embankments ever since his train crossed into Tennessee—and, now that he thought about it, in Kentucky as well, though Kentucky had stayed with the Union during the Great Rebellion.

When he got to the front of the line at the cab stand, a hackman heaved his bags into the trunk of an Oldsmobile and said, "Where to, sir?"

"The New Orleans Hotel, on Canal Street," Michaels answered.

The cabbie touched the brim of his cap. "Yes, sir," he said, his voice suddenly empty. He opened the back door for Michaels, slammed it shut after him, then climbed into the cab himself. It took off with a grinding of gears that said the transmission had seen better days.

On the short ride to the hotel, Michaels counted five more scrawls of YANKS OUT, along with a couple of patches of whitewash that probably masked others. Servicemen on the street walked along in groups of at least four; several corners sported squads of soldiers in full combat gear, including, in one case, a machine-gun nest built of sandbags.

"Nice quiet little town," Michaels remarked.

"Isn't it?" the cabbie answered, deadpan. He hesitated, his jaw working as if he were chewing his cud. After a moment, he decided to go on: "Mister, with an accent like yours, you want to be careful where you let people hear it. For a damnyankee, you don't seem like a bad fellow, an' I wouldn't want nothin' to happen to you."

"Thanks. I'll bear that in mind," Michaels said. He wished the Bureau had sent somebody who could put on a convincing drawl. Of course, the last man the FBS had sent ended up floating in the Mississippi, so evidently his drawl hadn't been convincing enough.

The cab wheezed to a stop in front of the New Orleans Hotel. "That'll be forty cents, sir," the driver said.

Michaels reached into his trouser pocket, pulled out a half-dollar. "Here you go. I don't need any change."

"That's right kind of you, sir, but—you wouldn't happen to have two quarters instead?" the cabbie said. He handed the big silver coin back to his passenger.

"What's wrong with it?" Michaels demanded, though he thought he knew the answer. "It's legal tender of the United States of America."

"Yes, sir, reckon it is, but there's no place hereabouts I'd care to try and spend it even so," the driver answered, "not with *his* picture on it." The obverse of the fifty-cent piece bore an image of the martyred Lincoln, the reverse a Negro with his manacles broken and the legend SIC SEMPER TYRANNIS. Michaels had known it was an unpopular coin with white men in the South, but he hadn't realized how unpopular it was.

He got out of the cab, rummaged in his pocket, and came up with a quarter and a couple of dimes. The cabbie didn't object to Washington's profile, or to that of the god Mercury. He also didn't object to seeing his tip cut in half. That told Michaels all he needed to know about how much the half-dollar was hated.

Lazily spinning ceiling fans inside the hotel lobby stirred the air without doing much to cool it. The colored clerk behind the front desk smiled to hear Michaels's accent. "Yes, sir, we do have your reservation," she said after shuffling through papers. By the way she talked, she'd been educated up in the Loyal States herself. She handed him a brass key. "That's room 429, sir. Three dollars and twenty-five cents a night."

"Very good," Michaels said. The clerk clanged the bell on the front desk. A white bellboy in a pillbox hat and uniform that made him look like a Philip Morris advertisement picked up Michaels's bags and carried them to the elevator.

When they got to room 429, Michaels opened the door. The bellboy put down the bags inside the room and stood waiting for his tip. By way of experiment, Michaels gave him the fifty-cent piece the cabbie had rejected. The bellboy took the coin and put it in his pocket. His lips shaped a silent word. Michaels thought it was *damnyankee,* but he wasn't quite sure. He left in a hurry.

A couple of hours later, Michaels went downstairs to supper. Something shiny was lying on the carpet in the hall. He looked down at the half-dollar he'd given the bellboy. It had lain here in plain sight while people walked back and forth; he'd heard them. Nobody had taken it. Thoughtfully, he picked it up and stuck it in his pocket.

A walk through the French Quarter made fears about New Orleans seem foolish. Jazz blasted out of every other doorway. Neon signs pulsed above ginmills. Spasm bands, some white, some Negro, played on street corners. No one paid attention to blackout regulations—that held true North and South. Clog dancers shuffled, overturned caps beside them inviting coins. Streetwalkers in tawdry finery swung their hips and flashed knowing smiles.

Neil Michaels moved through the crowds of soldiers and sailors and gawking civilians like a halfback evading tacklers and heading downfield. He glanced at his watch, partly to check the time and partly to make sure nobody had stolen it. Half past eleven. Didn't this place ever slow down? Maybe not.

He turned right off Royal Street onto St. Peter and walked southeast toward the Mississippi and Jackson Square. The din of the Vieux Carré faded behind him. He strode past the Cabildo, the old Spanish building of stuccoed brick that now housed the Louisiana State Museum, including a fine collection of artifacts and documents on the career of the first military governor of New Orleans, Benjamin Butler. Johnny Rebs kept threatening to dynamite the Cabildo, but it hadn't happened yet.

Two great bronze statues dominated Jackson Square. One showed the square's namesake on horseback. The other, even taller, faced that equestrian statue. Michaels thought Ben Butler's bald head and rotund, sagging physique less than ideal for being immortalized in bronze, but no one had asked his opinion.

He strolled down the paved lane in the formal garden toward the statue of Jackson. Lights were dimmer here in the square, but not too dim to keep Michaels from reading the words Butler had had carved into the pedestal of the statue: THE UNION MUST AND SHALL BE PRESERVED, an adaptation of Jackson's famous toast, "Our Federal Union, it must be preserved."

Michaels's mouth stretched out in a thin hard line that was not a smile. By force and fear, with cannon and noose, bayonet and prison term, the United States Army had preserved the Union. And now, more than three-quarters of a century after the collapse of the Great Rebellion, U.S. forces still occupied the states of the rebel Confederacy, still skirmished in hills and forests and sometimes city streets against men who put on gray shirts and yowled like catamounts when they fought. Hatred bred hatred, reprisal bred reprisal, and so it went on and on. He sometimes wondered if the Union wouldn't have done better to let the Johnny Rebs get the hell out, if that was what they'd wanted so badly.

He'd never spoken that thought aloud; it wasn't one he could share. Too late to worry about such things anyhow, generations too late. He had to deal with the consequences of what vengeful Hamlin and his like-minded successors had done.

The man he was supposed to meet would be waiting behind Butler's statue. Michaels was slightly surprised the statue had no guards around it; the Johnny Rebs had blown it up in the 1880s and again in the 1920s. If New Orleans today was reconciled to rule from Washington, it concealed the fact very well.

Michaels ducked around into the darkness behind the statue. "Fourscore and seven," he whispered, the recognition signal he'd been given.

Someone should have answered, "New birth of freedom." No one said anything. As his eyes adapted to the darkness, he made out a body sprawled in the narrow space between the base of the statue and the shrubbery that bordered Jackson Square. He stooped beside it. If this was the man he was supposed to meet, the fellow would never give him a recognition signal, not till Judgment Day. His throat had been cut.

Running feet on the walkways of the square, flashlight beams probing like spears. One of them found Michaels. He threw up an arm against the blinding glare. A hard Northern voice shouted, "Come out of there right now, you damned murdering Reb, or you'll never get a second chance!"

Michaels raised his hands high in surrender and came out.

Outside Antoine's, the rain came down in buckets. Inside, with oysters Rockefeller and a whiskey and soda in front of him and the prospect of an excellent lunch ahead, Neil Michaels was willing to forgive the weather.

He was less inclined to forgive the soldiers from the night before. Stubbing out his Camel, he said in a low but furious voice, "Those great thundering galoots couldn't have done a better job of blowing my cover if they'd rehearsed for six weeks, God damn them."

His companion, a dark, lanky man named Morrie Harris, sipped his own drink and said, "It may even work out for the best. Anybody the MPs arrest is going to look good to the Johnny Rebs around here." His New York accent seemed less out of place in New Orleans than Michaels's flat, midwestern tones.

Michaels started to answer, then shut up as the waiter came over and asked, "You gentlemen are ready to order?"

"Let me have the *pompano en papillote*," Harris said. "You can't get it any better than here."

The waiter wrote down the order, looked a question at Michaels.

He said, "I'll take the *poulet chanteclair.*" The waited nodded, scribbled, and went away.

Glancing around to make sure no one else was paying undue attention to him or his conversation, Michaels resumed: "Yeah, that may be true now. But Ducange is dead now. What if those stupid dogfaces had busted in on us while we were dickering? That would have queered the deal for sure, and it might have got me shot." As it hadn't the night before, his smile did not reach his eyes. "I'm fond of my neck. It's the only one I've got."

"Even without Ducange, we've still got to get a line on the underground," Harris said. "Those weapons are somewhere. We'd better find 'em before the whole city goes up." He rolled his eyes. "The whole city, hell! If what we've been hearing is true, the Nazis have shipped enough guns and God knows what all else into New Orleans to touch off four or five states. And wouldn't that do wonders for the war effort?" He slapped on irony with a heavy trowel.

"God damn the Germans," Michaels said, still quietly but with savage venom. "They played this game during the last war, too. But you're right. If what we've heard is the straight goods, the blowup they have in mind will make the Thanksgiving Revolt look like a kiss on the cheek."

"It shouldn't be this way," Harris said, scowling. "We've got more GIs and swabbies in New Orleans than you can shake a stick at, and none of 'em worth a damn when it comes to tracking this crap down. Nope, for that they need the FBS, no matter how understaffed we are."

The waiter came then. Michaels dug into the chicken marinated in red wine. It was as good as it was supposed to be. Morrie Harris made ecstatic noises about the sauce on his pompano.

After a while, Michaels said, "The longer we try, the harder it gets for us to keep things under control down here. One of these days—"

"It'll all go up," Harris said matter-of-factly. "Yeah, but not now. Now is what we gotta worry about. We're fighting a civil war here, we ain't gonna have much luck with the Germans and the Japs. That's what Hitler has in mind."

"Maybe Hamlin and Stevens should have done something different—God knows what—back then. It might have kept us out of—this," Michaels said. He knew that was heresy for an FBS man, but everything that had happened to him since he got to New Orleans left him depressed with the state of things as they were.

"What were they supposed to do?" Harris snapped.

"I already said I didn't know," Michaels answered, wishing he'd kept his mouth shut. What did the posters say?—LOOSE LIPS SINK SHIPS. His loose lips were liable to sink him.

Sure enough, Morrie Harris went on as if he hadn't spoken: "The Johnnies rebelled, killed a few hundred thousand American boys, and shot a president dead. What should we do, give 'em a nice pat on the back? We beat 'em and we made 'em pay. Far as I can see, they deserved it."

"Yeah, and they've been making us pay ever since." Michaels raised a weary hand. "The hell with it. Like you said, now is what we've got to worry about. But with Ducange dead, what sort of channels do we have into the rebel underground?"

Morrie Harris's mouth twisted, as if he'd bitten down on something rotten. "No good ones that I know of. We've relied too much on the Negroes down here over the years. It's made the whites trust us even less than they would have otherwise. Maybe, though, just maybe, Ducange talked to somebody before he got killed, and that somebody will try to get hold of you."

"So what do you want me to do, then? Hang around my hotel room hoping the phone rings, like a girl waiting to see if a boy will call? Hell of a way to spend my time in romantic New Orleans."

"Listen, the kind of romance you can get here, you'll flunk a short-arm inspection three days later," Harris answered, chasing the last bits of pompano around his plate. "They'll take a damnyankee's money, but they'll skin you every chance they get. They must be laughing their asses off at the fortune they're making off our boys in uniform."

"Sometimes they won't even take your money." Michaels told of the trouble he'd had unloading the Lincoln half-dollar.

"Yeah, I've seen that," Harris said. "If they want to cut off their nose to spite their face, by me it's all right." He set a five and a couple of singles on the table. "This one's on me. Whatever else you say about this damn town, the food is hellacious, no two ways about it."

"No arguments." Michaels got up with Harris. They went out of

Antoine's separately, a couple of minutes apart. As he walked back to the New Orleans Hotel, Michaels kept checking to make sure nobody was following him. He didn't spot anyone, but he didn't know how much that proved. If anybody wanted to put multiple tails on him, he wouldn't twig, not in crowded streets like these.

The crowds get worse when a funeral procession tied up traffic on Rampart Street. Two black horses pulled the hearse; their driver was a skinny, sleepy-looking white man who looked grotesquely out of place in top hat and tails. More coaches and buggies followed, and a couple of cars as well. "All right, let's get it moving!" an MP shouted when the procession finally passed.

"They keep us here any longer, we all go in the ovens from old age," a local said, and several other people laughed as they crossed the street. Michaels wanted to ask what the ovens were, but kept quiet since he exposed himself as one of the hated occupiers every time he opened his mouth.

When he got back to the hotel, he stopped at the front desk to ask if he had any messages. The clerk there today was a Negro man in a sharp suit and tie, with a brass name badge on his right lapel that read THADDEUS JENKINS. He checked and came back shaking his head. "Rest assured, sir, we shall make sure you receive any that do come in," he said—a Northern accent bothered him not in the least.

"Thank you very much, Mr. Jenkins," Michaels said.

"Our pleasure to serve you, sir," the clerk replied. "Anything we can do to make your stay more pleasant, you have but to ask."

"You're very kind," Michaels said. Jenkins had reason to be kind to Northerners. The power of the federal government maintained Negroes at the top of the heap in the old Confederacy. With the Sixteenth Amendment disenfranchising most Rebel soldiers and their descendants, blacks had a comfortable majority among those eligible to vote—and used it, unsurprisingly, in their own interest.

Michaels mused on that as he walked to the elevator. The operator, a white man, tipped his cap with more of the insincere obsequiousness Michaels had already noted. He wondered how the fellow liked taking orders from a man whose ancestors his great-grandfather might have owned. Actually, he didn't need to wonder. The voting

South was as reliably Republican as could be, for the blacks had no illusions about how long their power would last if the Sixteenth were ever to be discarded.

Suddenly curious, he asked the elevator man, "Why don't I see 'Repeal the Sixteenth' written on walls along with 'Yanks Out'?"

The man measured him with his eyes—measured him for a coffin, if his expression meant anything. At last, as if speaking to a moron, he answered, "You don't see that on account of askin' you to repeal it'd mean you damnyankees got some kind o' business bein' down here and lordin' it over us in the first place. And you *ain't*."

So there, Michaels thought. The rest of the ride passed in silence.

With a soft whir, the ceiling fan stirred the air in his room. That improved things, but only slightly. He looked out the window. Ferns had sprouted from the mortar between bricks of the building across the street. Even without the rain—which had now let up—it was plenty humid enough for the plants to flourish.

Sitting around waiting for the phone to ring gave Michaels plenty of time to watch the ferns. As Morrie Harris had instructed, he spent most of his time in his room. He sallied forth primarily to eat. Not even the resolute hostility of most of white New Orleans put a damper on the food.

He ate boiled beef at Maylié's, crabmeat *au gratin* at Galatoire's, crayfish bisque at La Louisiane, *langouste* Sarah Bernhardt at Arnaud's, and, for variety, pig knuckles and sauerkraut at Kolb's. When he didn't feel like traveling, he ate at the hotel's own excellent restaurant. He began to fancy his trousers and collars getting tighter than they had been before he came South.

One night, he woke to the sound of rifle fire not far away. Panic shot through him, panic and shame. Had the uprising he'd come here to check broken out? How would that look on his FBS personnel record? Then he realized that, if the uprising had broken out, any damnyankee the Johnnies caught was likely to end up too dead to worry about what his personnel record looked like.

After about fifteen minutes, the gunfire petered out. Michaels took a couple of hours falling asleep again, though. He went from one radio station to another the next morning and checked the afternoon newspapers, too. No one said a word about the firefight. Had anybody tried, prosecutors armed with the Sedition Act would have landed on him like a ton of bricks.

Back in the Loyal States, they smugly said the Sedition Act kept the lid on things down South. Michaels had believed it, too. Now he was getting a feeling for how much pressure pushed against that lid. When it blew, if it blew . . .

A little past eleven the next night, the phone rang. He jumped, then ran to it. "Hello?" he said sharply.

The voice on the other end was so muffled, he wasn't sure whether it belonged to a man or a woman. It said, "Be at the Original Absinthe House for the three A.M. show." The line went dead.

Michaels let out a martyred sigh. "The three A.M. show," he muttered, wondering why conspirators couldn't keep civilized hours like anyone else. He went down to the restaurant and had a couple of cups of strong coffee laced with brandy. Thus fortified, he headed out into the steaming night.

He soon concluded New Orleans's idea of civilized hours had nothing to do with those kept by the rest of the world, or possibly that New Orleans defined civilization as unending revelry. The French Quarter was as packed as it had been when he went through it toward Jackson Square, though that had been in the relatively early evening, close to civilized even by midwestern standards.

The Original Absinthe House, a shabby two-story building with an iron railing around the balcony to the second floor, stood on the corner of Bourbon and Bienville. Each of the four doors leading in had a semi-circular window above it. Alongside one of the doors, someone had scrawled ABSINTHE MAKES THE HEART GROW FONDER. Michaels thought that a distinct improvement on YANKS OUT! You weren't supposed to be able to get real absinthe any more, but in the Vieux Carré nothing would have surprised him.

He didn't want absinthe, anyway. He didn't particularly want the whiskey and soda he ordered, either, but you couldn't go into a place like this without doing some drinking. The booze was overpriced and not very good. The mysterious voice on the telephone hadn't told him there was a five-buck charge to go up to the second story and watch the floor show. Assuming he got out of here alive, he'd have a devil of a time justifying that on his expense account. And if the call had been a Johnny Reb setup, were they trying to kill him or just to bilk him out of money for the cause?

Michaels felt he was treading in history's footsteps as he went up the stairs. If the plaque on the wall didn't lie for the benefit of tourists, that stairway had been there since the Original Absinthe House was built in the early nineteenth century. Andrew Jackson and Jean Lafitte had gone up it to plan the defense of New Orleans against the British in 1814, and Ben Butler for carefully undescribed purposes half a century later. It was made with wooden pegs: not a nail anywhere. If the stairs weren't as old as the plaque claimed, they sure as hell were a long way from new.

A jazz band blared away in the big upstairs room. Michaels went in, found a chair, ordered a drink from a waitress whose costume would have been too skimpy for a burly queen most places up North, and leaned back to enjoy the music. The band was about half black, half white. Jazz was one of the few things the two races shared in the South. Not all Negroes had made it to the top of the heap after the North crushed the Great Rebellion; many still lived in the shadow of the fear and degradation of the days of slavery and keenly felt the resentment of the white majority. That came out in the way they played. And the whites, as conquered people will, found liberation in their music that they could not have in life.

Michaels looked at his watch. It was a quarter to three. The jazzmen were just keeping loose between shows, then. As he sipped his whiskey, the room began filling up in spite of the five-dollar cover charge. He didn't know what the show would be, but he figured it had to be pretty hot to pack 'em in at those prices.

The lights went out. For a moment, only a few glowing cigarette coals showed in the blackness. The band didn't miss a beat. From right behind Michaels's head, a spotlight came on, bathing the stage in harsh white light.

Saxophone and trumpets wailed lasciviously. When the girls paraded onto the stage, Michaels felt his jaw drop. A vice cop in Cleveland, say, might have put the cuffs on his waitress because she wasn't wearing enough. The girls up there had on high-heeled shoes, headdresses with dyed ostrich plumes and glittering rhinestones, and nothing between the one and the other but big, wide smiles.

He wondered how they got themselves case-hardened enough to go on display like that night after night, show after show. They were all young and pretty and built, no doubt about that. Was it enough? His sister was young and pretty and built, too. He wouldn't have wanted her up there, flaunting it for horny soldiers on leave.

He wondered how much the owners had to pay to keep the local vice squad off their backs. Then he wondered if New Orleans bothered with a vice squad. He hadn't seen any signs of one.

He also wondered who the devil had called him over here and how that person would make contact. Sitting around gaping at naked women was not something he could put in his report unless it had some sort of connection with the business for which he'd come down here.

Soldiers and sailors whooped at the girls, whose skins soon grew slick and shiny with sweat. Waitresses moved back and forth, getting in the way as little as possible while they took drink orders. To fit in, Michaels ordered another whiskey and soda and discovered it cost more than twice as much here as it had downstairs. He didn't figure the Original Absinthe House would go out of business any time soon.

The music got even hotter than it had been. The dancers stepped off the edge of the stage and started prancing among the tables. Michaels's jaw dropped all over again. This wasn't just a floor show. This was a— He didn't quite know what it was and found himself too flustered to grope for *le mot juste*.

Then a very pretty naked brunette sat down in his lap and twined her arms around his neck.

"Is that a gun in your pocket, dearie, or are you just glad to see me?" she said loudly. Men at the nearest table guffawed. Since it was a gun in his pocket, Michaels kept his mouth shut. The girl smelled of sweat and whiskey and makeup. What her clammy hide was doing to his shirt and trousers did not bear thinking about. He wanted to drop her on the floor and get the hell out of there.

She was holding him too tight for that, though. She lowered her head to nuzzle his neck; the plumes from her headdress got in his eyes and tickled his nose. But under the cover of that frantic scene, her voice went low and urgent: "You got to talk with Colquit the hearse driver, Mister. Tell him Lucy says Pierre says he can talk, an' maybe he will."

Before he could ask her any questions, she kissed him on the lips.

The kiss wasn't faked; her tongue slid into his mouth. He'd had enough whiskey and enough shocks by then that he didn't care what he did. His hand closed over her breast—and she sprang to her feet and twisted away, all in perfect time to the music. A moment later, she was in somebody else's lap.

Michaels discovered he'd spilled most of his overpriced drink. He downed what was left with one big swig. When he wiped his mouth with a napkin, it came away red from the girl's—Lucy's—lipstick.

Some of the naked dancers had more trouble than Lucy disentangling themselves from the men they'd chosen. Some of them didn't even try to disentangle. Michaels found himself staring, bug-eyed. You couldn't do *that* in public . . . could you? Hell and breakfast, it was illegal in private, most places.

Eventually, all the girls were back on stage. They gave it all they had for the finale. Then they trooped off and the lights came back up. Only after they were gone did Michaels understand the knowing look most of them had had all through the performance: they knew more about men than men, most often, cared to know about themselves.

In the palm of his hand, he could still feel the memory of the soft, firm flesh of Lucy's breast. Unlike the others in the room, he'd had to be here. He hadn't had to grab her, though. Sometimes, facetiously, you called a place like this educational. He'd learned something, all right, and rather wished he hadn't.

Morrie Harris pursed his lips. "Lucy says Pierre says Colquit can talk? That's not much to go on. For all we know, it could be a trap."

"Yeah, it could be," Michaels said. He and the other FBS man walked along in front of the St. Louis Cathedral, across the street from Jackson Square. They might have been businessmen, they might have been sightseers—though neither businessmen nor sightseers were particularly common in the states that had tried to throw off the Union's yoke. Michaels went on, "I don't think it's a trap, though. Ducange's first name is—was—Pierre, and we've found out he did go to the Original Absinthe House. He could have gotten to know Lucy there."

He could have done anything with Lucy there. The feel of her would not leave Michaels's mind. He knew going back to the upstairs room would be dangerous, for him and for her, but the temptation lingered like a bit of food between the teeth that keeps tempting back the tongue.

Harris said, "Maybe we ought to just haul her in and grill her till she cracks."

"We risk alerting the Rebs if we do that," Michaels said.

"Yeah, I know." Harris slammed his fist into his palm. "I hate sitting around doing nothing, though. If they get everything they need before we find out where they're squirreling it away, they start their damn uprising and the war effort goes straight out the window." He scowled, a man in deep and knowing it. "And Colquit the hearse driver? You don't know his last name? You don't know which mortuary he works for? Naked little Lucy didn't whisper those into your pink and shell-like ear?"

"I told you what she told me." Michaels stared down at the pavement in dull embarrassment. He could feel his dubiously shell-like ears turning red, not pink.

"All right, all right." Harris threw his hands in the air. Most FBS men made a point of not showing what they were thinking—Gary Cooper might have been the Bureau's ideal. Not Morrie Harris. He wore his feelings on his sleeve. *New York City,* Michaels thought, with scorn he nearly didn't notice himself. Harris went on, "We try and find him, that's all. How many guys are there named Colquit, even in New Orleans? And yeah, you don't have to tell me we got to be careful. If he knows anything, we don't want him riding in a hearse instead of driving one."

A bit of investigation—if checking the phone book and getting somebody with the proper accent to call the Chamber of Commerce could be dignified as such—soon proved funerals were big business in New Orleans, bigger than most other places, maybe. There were mortuaries and cemeteries for Jews, for Negroes, for French-speakers, for Protestants, for this group, for that one, and for the other. Because New Orleans was mostly below sea level (Michaels heartily wished the town were underwater, too), burying people was more complicated than digging a hole and putting a coffin down in it, too. Some intrepid sightseers made special pilgrimages just to see the funeral vaults, which struck Michaels as downright macabre.

Once they had a complete list of funeral establishments, Morrie Harris started calling them one by one. His New York accent was close enough to the local one for him to ask, "Is Colquit there?" without giving himself away as a damnyankee. Time after time, people denied ever hearing of Colquit. At one establishment, though, the reception-ist asked whether he meant Colquit the embalmer or Colquit the bookkeeper. He hung up in a hurry.

Repeated failure left Michaels frustrated. He was about to suggest knocking off for the day when Harris suddenly jerked in his chair as if he'd sat on a tack. He put his hand over the receiver and mouthed, "Said he just got back from a funeral. She's going out to get him." He handed the telephone to Michaels.

After just over a minute, a man's voice said, "Hello? Who's this?"

"Colquit?" Michaels asked.

"Yeah," the hearse driver said.

Maybe it was Michaels's imagination, but he thought he heard sus-picion even in one slurred word. Sounding like someone from the Loyal States got you nowhere around here (of course, a Johnny Reb who managed to get permission to travel to Wisconsin also raised eye-brows up there, but Michaels wasn't in Wisconsin now). He spoke quickly: "Lucy told me Pierre told her that I should tell you it was OK for you to talk with me."

He waited for Colquit to ask what the hell he was talking about, or else to hang up. It would figure if the only steer he'd got was a bum one. But the hearse driver, after a long pause, said, "Yeah?" again.

Michaels waited for more, but there wasn't any more. It was up to him, then. "You do know what I'm talking about?" he asked, rather desperately.

"Yeah," Colquit repeated: a man of few words.

"You can't talk where you are?"

"Nope," Colquit said—variety.

"Will you meet me for supper outside Galatoire's tonight at seven, then?" Michaels said. With a good meal and some booze in him, Colquit was more likely to spill his guts.

"Make it tomorrow," Colquit said.

"All right, tomorrow," Michaels said unhappily. More delay was the last thing he wanted. No, not quite: he didn't want to spook Colquit, ei-ther. He started to say something more, but the hearse driver did hang up on him then.

"What does he know?" Morrie Harris demanded after Michaels hung up, too.

"I'll find out tomorrow," Michaels answered. "The way things have gone since I got down here, that's progress." Harris nodded solemnly.

The wail of police sirens woke Neil Michaels from a sound sleep. The portable alarm clock he'd brought with him was ticking away on the table by his bed. Its radium dial announced the hour: 3:05. He groaned and sat up.

Along with the sirens came the clanging bells and roaring motors of fire engines. Michaels bounced out of bed, ice running down his back. Had the Rebs started their revolt? In that kind of chaos, the pistol he'd brought down from the North felt very small and useless.

He cocked his head. He didn't hear any gunfire. If the Southern men were using whatever the Nazis had shipped them, that would be the biggest part of the racket outside. OK, it wasn't the big revolt. That meant walking to the window and looking out was likely to be safe. What the devil *was* going on?

Michaels pushed aside the thick curtain shielding the inside of his room from the neon glare that was New Orleans by night. Even as he watched, a couple of fire engines tore down Canal Street toward the Vieux Carré. Their flashing red lights warned the few cars and many pedestrians to get the hell out of the way.

Raising his head, Michaels spotted the fire. Whatever was burning was burning to beat the band. Flames leaped into the night sky, seeming to dance as they flung themselves high above the building that fueled them. A column of thick black smoke marked that building's funeral pyre.

"Might as well find out what it is," Michaels said out loud. He turned on the lamp by the bed and then the radio. The little light behind the dial came on. He waited impatiently for the tubes to get warm enough to bring in a signal.

The first station he got was playing one of Benny Goodman's records. Michaels wondered if playing a damnyankee's music was enough to get you in trouble with some of the fire-eating Johnny Rebs. But he didn't want to hear jazz, not now. He spun the dial.

"—Terrible fire on Bourbon Street," an announcer was saying.

That had to be the blaze Michaels had seen. The fellow sent on, "One of New Orleans' longstanding landmarks, the Original Absinthe House, is going up in flames even as I speak. The Absinthe House presents shows all through the night, and many are feared dead inside. The building was erected well over a hundred years ago, and has seen—"

Michaels turned off the radio, almost hard enough to break the knob. He didn't believe in coincidence, not even a little bit. Somewhere in the wreckage of the Original Absinthe House would lie whatever mortal fragments remained of Lucy the dancer, and that was just how someone wanted it to be.

He shivered like a man with the grippe. He'd thought about asking Colquit to meet him there instead of at Galatoire's, so Lucy could help persuade the hearse driver to tell whatever he knew—and so he could get another look at her. But going to a place twice running . . . That let the opposition get a line on you. Training had saved his life and, he hoped, Colquit's. It hadn't done poor Lucy one damn bit of good.

He called down to room service and asked for a bottle of whiskey. If the man to whom he gave the order found anything unusual about such a request at twenty past three, he didn't show it. The booze arrived in short order. After three or four good belts, Michaels was able to get back to sleep.

Colquit didn't show up for dinner at Galatoire's that night.

When Morrie Harris phoned the mortuary the next day, the receptionist said Colquit had called in sick. "That's a relief," Michaels said when Harris reported the news. "I was afraid he'd call in dead."

"Yeah." Harris ran a hand through his curly hair. "I didn't want to try and get a phone number and address out of the gal. I didn't even like making the phone call. The less attention we draw to the guy, the better."

"You said it." Michaels took off his glasses, blew a speck from the left lens, set them back on his nose. "Now we know where he works. We can find out where he lives. Just a matter of digging through the papers."

"A lot of papers to dig through," Harris said with a grimace, "but yeah, that ought to do the job. Shall we head on over to the Hall of Records?"

Machine-gun nests surrounded the big marble building on Thalia Street. If the Johnny Rebs ever got their revolt off the ground, it would be one of the first places to burn. The Federal army and bureaucrats who controlled the conquered provinces of the old Confederacy ruled not only by force but also by keeping tabs on their resentful, rebellious subjects. Every white man who worked had to fill out a card each year listing his place of employment. Every firm had to list its employees. Most of the clerks who checked one set of forms against the other were Negroes. They had a vested interest in making sure nobody put one over on the government.

Tough, unsmiling guards meticulously checked Harris's and Michaels's identification papers, comparing photographs to faces and making them give samples of their signatures before admitting them to the hall. They feared sabotage as well as out-and-out assault. The records stored here helped down all of Louisiana.

Hannibal Dupuy was a large, round black man with some of the thickest glasses Michaels had ever seen. "Mortuary establishments," he said, holding up one finger as he thought. "Yes, those would be in the Wade Room, in the cases against the east wall." Michaels got the feeling that, had they asked him about anything from taverns to taxidermists, he would have known exactly where the files hid. Such men were indispensable in navigating the sea of papers before them.

Going through the papers stored in the cases against the east wall of the Wade Room took a couple of hours. Michaels finally found the requisite record. "Colquit D. Reynolds, hearse driver—yeah, he works for LeBlanc and Peters," he said. "OK, here's address and phone number and a notation that they've been verified as correct. People are on the ball here, no two ways about it."

"People have to be on the ball here," Morrie Harris answered. "How'd you like to be a Negro in the South if the whites you've been sitting on for years grab hold of the reins? Especially if they grab hold of the reins with help from the Nazis? The first thing they'd do after they threw us damnyankees out is to start hanging Negroes from lampposts."

"You're right. Let's go track down Mr. Reynolds, so we don't have to find out just how right you are."

Colquit Reynolds's documents said he lived on Carondelet, out past St. Joseph: west and south of the French Quarter. Harris had a car, a wheezy Blasingame that delivered him and Michaels to the requisite address. Michaels knocked on the door of the house, which, like the rest of the neighborhood, was only a small step up from the shotgun-shack level.

No one answered. Michaels glanced over at Morrie Harris. FBS men didn't need a warrant, not to search a house in Johnny Reb country. That wasn't the issue. Both of them, though, feared they'd find nothing but a corpse when they got inside.

Just as Michaels was about to break down the front door, an old woman stuck her head out a side window of the house next door and said, "If you lookin' for Colquit, gents, you ain't gonna find him in there."

Morrie Harris swept off his hat and gave a nod that was almost a bow. "Where's he at, then, ma'am?" he asked, doing his best to sound like a local and speaking to the old woman as if she were the military governor's wife.

She cackled like a laying hen; she must have liked that. "Same place you always find him when he wants to drink 'stead of workin': the Old Days Saloon round the co'ner." She jerked a gnarled thumb to show which way.

The Old Days Saloon was painted in gaudy stripes of red, white, and blue. Those were the national colors, and so unexceptionable, but, when taken with the name of the place, were probably meant to suggest the days of the Great Rebellion and the traitors who had used them on a different flag. Michaels would have bet a good deal that the owner of the place had a thick FBS dossier.

He and Harris walked in. The place was dim and quiet. Ceiling fans created the illusion of coolness. The bruiser behind the bar gave the newcomers the dubious stare he obviously hauled out for any stranger: certainly the four or five men in the place had the look of longtime regulars. Asking which one was Colquit was liable to be asking for trouble.

One of the regulars, though, looked somehow familiar. After a moment, Michaels realized why: that old man soaking up a beer off in a corner had driven the horse-drawn hearse that had slowed him up on his way back to the hotel a few days before. He nudged Morrie Harris, nodded toward the old fellow. Together, they went over to him. "How you doin' today, Colquit?" Harris asked in friendly tones. The bartender relaxed.

Colquit looked up at them with eyes that didn't quite focus. "Don't think I know you folks," he said, "but I could be wrong."

"Sure you do," Harris said, expansive still. "We're friends of Pierre and Lucy."

"Oh, Lord help me." Colquit started to get up. Michaels didn't want a scene. Anything at all could make New Orleans go off—hauling a man out of a bar very much included. But Colquit Reynolds slumped back onto his chair, as if his legs didn't want to hold him. "Wish I never told Pierre about none o' that stuff," he muttered, and finished his beer with a convulsive gulp.

Michaels raised a forefinger and called out to the bartender: "Three more High Lifes here." He tried to slur his words into a Southern pattern. Maybe he succeeded, or maybe the dollar bill he tossed down on the table was enough to take the edge off suspicions. The Rebs had revered George Washington even during the Great Rebellion, misguided though they were in other ways.

Colquit Reynolds took a long pull at the new beer. Michaels and Harris drank more moderately. If they were going to get anything out of the hearse driver, they needed to be able to remember it once they had it. Besides, Michaels didn't much like beer. Quietly, so the bartender and the other locals wouldn't hear, he asked, "What do you wish you hadn't told Pierre, Mr. Reynolds?"

Reynolds looked up at the ceiling, as if the answer were written there. Michaels wondered if he was able to remember; he'd been drinking for a while. Finally, he said, "Wish I hadn't told him 'bout this here coffin I took for layin' to rest."

"Oh? Why's that?" Michaels asked casually. He lit a Camel, offered the pack to Colquit Reynolds. When Reynolds took one, he used his Zippo to give the hearse driver a light.

Reynolds sucked in smoke. He held it longer than Michaels thought humanly possible, then exhaled a foggy cloud. After he knocked the coal into an ashtray, he drained his Miller's High Life and looked expectantly at the FBS men. Michaels ordered him another one. Only after he'd drunk part of that did he answer, "On account of they needed a block and tackle to get it onto my hearse an' another one to get it off again. Ain't no six men in the world could have lifted that there coffin, not if they was Samson an' five o' his brothers. An' it *clanked*, too."

"Weapons," Morrie Harris whispered, "or maybe ammunition." He looked joyous, transfigured, likely even more so than he would have if a naked dancing girl had plopped herself down in his lap. *Poor Lucy*, Michaels thought.

He said, "Even in a coffin, even greased, I wouldn't want to bury anything in this ground—not for long, that's for damn sure. Water's liable to seep in and ruin things."

Colquit Reynolds sent him a withering, scornful look. "Damnyankees," he muttered under his breath—and he was helping Michaels. "Lot of the times here, you don't bury your dead, you put 'em in a tomb up aboveground, just so as coffins don't get flooded out o' the ground come the big rains."

"Jesus," Morrie Harris said hoarsely, wiping his forehead with a sleeve, and then again: "Jesus." Now he was the one to drain his beer and signal for another. Once the bartender had come and gone, he went on, "All the aboveground tombs New Orleans has, you could hide enough guns and ammo to fight a big war. God damn sneaky Rebs." He made himself stop. "What cemetery was this at, Mr. Reynolds?"

"Old Girod, out on South Liberty Street," Colquit Reynolds replied. "Don' know how much is there, but one coffinload, anyways."

"Thank God some Southern men don't want to see the Great Rebellion start up again," Michaels said.

"Yeah." Harris drank from his new High Life. "But a hell of a lot of 'em *do*."

Girod Cemetery was hidden away in the railroad yards. A plaque on the stone fence surrounding it proclaimed it to be the oldest Protestant cemetery in New Orleans. Neil Michaels was willing to believe that. The place didn't seem to have received much in the way of legitimate business in recent years, and had a haunted look to it. It was overgrown with vines and shrubs. Gray-barked fig trees pushed up through the sides of some of the old tombs. Moss was everywhere, on trees and tombs alike. Maidenhair ferns sprouted from the sides of the above-ground vaults; as Michaels had seen, anything would grow anywhere around here.

That included conspiracies. If Colquit Reynolds was right, the ghost of the Great Rebellion haunted this cemetery, too, and the Johnnies were trying to bring it back to unwholesome life.

"He'd better be right," Michaels muttered as the Jeep he was riding pulled to a stop before the front entrance to the cemetery.

Morrie Harris understood him without trouble. "Who, that damn hearse driver? You bet he'd better be right. We bring all this stuff here"—he waved behind him—"and start tearin' up a graveyard, then don't find anything . . . hell, that could touch off a revolt all by itself."

Michaels shivered, though the day was hot and muggy. "Couldn't it just?" Had Reynolds been leading them down the path, setting them up to create an incident that would make the South rise up in righteous fury? They'd have to respond to a story like the one he'd told; for the sake of the Union, they didn't dare not respond.

They'd find out. Behind the Jeep, Harris's "all this stuff" rattled and clanked: not just bulldozers, but also light M3 Stoneman tanks and heavy M3 Grants with a small gun in a rotating turret and a big one in a sponson at the right front of the hull. Soldiers—all of them men from the Loyal States—scrambled down from Chevy trucks and set up a perimeter around the wall. If anybody was going to try to interfere with this operation, he'd regret it.

Against the assembled might of the Federal Union (*It must and shall be preserved,* Michaels thought), Girod Cemetery mustered a stout metal gate and one elderly watchman. "Who the devil are y'all, and what d'you want?" he demanded, though the *who* part, at least, should have been pretty obvious.

Michaels displayed his FBS badge. "We are on the business of the federal government of the United States of America," he said. "Open the gate and let us in." Again, no talk of warrants, not in Reb country, not on FBS business.

"Fuck the federal government of the United States of America and the horse it rode in on," the watchman said. "You ain't got no call to come to no cemetery with tanks."

Michaels didn't waste time arguing with him. He tapped the Jeep driver on the shoulder. The fellow backed the Jeep out of the way. Michaels waved to the driver of the nearest Grant tank. The tank man had his head out of the hatch. He grinned and nodded. The tank clattered forward, chewing up the pavement and spewing noxious exhaust into the air. The wrought-iron gate was sturdy, but not sturdy enough to withstand thirty-one tons of insistent armor. It flew open with a scream of metal; one side ripped loose from the stone to which it was fixed. The Grant ran over it, and would have run over the watchman, too, had he not skipped aside with a shouted curse.

Outside the cemetery, people began gathering. Most of the people were white men of military age or a bit younger. To Michaels, they had the look of men who'd paint slogans on walls or shoot at a truck or from behind a fence under cover of darkness. He was glad he'd brought overwhelming force. Against bayonets, guns, and armor, the crowd couldn't do much but stare sullenly.

If the cemetery was empty of contraband, what this crowd did wouldn't matter. There'd be similar angry crowds all over the South, and at one of them . . .

The watchman let out an anguished howl as tanks and bulldozers clanked toward the walls of aboveground vaults that ran up and down the length of the cemetery. "You can't go smashin' up the ovens!" he screamed.

"Last warning, Johnny Reb," Michaels said coldly: "don't you try telling officers of the United States what we can and can't do. We have places to put people whose mouths get out in front of their brains."

"Yeah, I just bet you do," the watchman muttered, but after that he kept his mouth shut.

A dozer blade bit into the side of one of the mortuary vaults—an oven, the old man had called it. Concrete and stone flew. So did chunks of a wooden coffin and the bones it had held. The watchman shot Michaels a look of unadulterated hatred and scorn. He didn't say a word, but he might as well have screamed, *See? I told you so.* A lot of times, that look alone would have been plenty to get him on the inside of a prison camp, but Michaels had bigger things to worry about today.

He and Harris hadn't ordered enough bulldozers to take on all the rows of ovens at once. The tanks joined in the job, too, knocking them down as the first big snorting Grant had wrecked the gate into Girod. Their treads ground more coffins and bones into dust.

"That god damn hearse driver better not have been lying to us," Morrie Harris said, his voice clogged with worry. "If he was, he'll never see a camp or a jail. We'll give the son of a bitch a blindfold; I wouldn't waste a cigarette on him."

Then, from somewhere near the center of Girod Cemetery, a tank crew let out a shout of triumph. Michaels had never heard sweeter music, not from Benny Goodman or Tommy Dorsey. He sprinted toward the Grant. Sweat poured off him, but it wasn't the sweat of fear, not any more.

The tank driver pointed to wooden boxes inside a funeral vault he'd just broken into. They weren't coffins. Each had 1 MASCHINEN-GEWEHR 34 stenciled on its side in neat black letter script, with the Nazi eagle-and-swastika emblem right next to the legend.

Michaels stared at the machine-gun crates as if one of them held the Holy Grail. "He wasn't lying," he breathed. "Thank you, God."

"*Omayn,*" Morrie Harris agreed. "Now let's find out how much truth he was telling."

The final haul, by the time the last oven was cracked the next day, astonished even Michaels and Harris. Michaels read from the list he'd been keeping: "Machine guns, submachine guns, mortars, rifles—including antitank rifles—ammo for all of them, grenades . . . Jesus, what a close call."

"I talked with one of the radiomen," Harris said. "He's sent out a call for more trucks to haul all this stuff away." He wiped his forehead with the back of his hand, a gesture that had little to do with heat or humidity. "If they'd managed to smuggle all of this out of New Orleans, spread it around through the South . . . well, hell, I don't have to draw you a picture."

"You sure don't. We'd have been so busy down here, the Germans and the Japs would have had a field day over the rest of the world." Michaels let out a heartfelt sigh of relief, then went on, "Next thing we've got to do is try and find out who was caching weapons. If we can do that, then maybe, just maybe, we can keep the Rebs leaderless for a generation or so and get ahead of the game."

"Maybe." But Harris didn't sound convinced. "We can't afford to think in terms of a generation from now, anyhow. It's what we were talking about when you first got into town: as long as we can hold the lid on the South till we've won the damn war, that'll do the trick. If we catch the guys running guns with the Nazis, great. If we don't, I don't give a damn about them sneaking around painting 'Yanks Out' on every blank wall they find. We can deal with that. We've been dealing with it since 1865. As long as they don't have the toys they need to really hurt us, we'll get by."

"Yeah, that's true—if no other subs drop off loads of goodies someplace else." Michaels sighed again. "No rest for the weary. If that happens, we'll just have to try and track 'em down."

A growing rumble of diesel engines made Morrie Harris grin. "Here come the trucks," he said, and trotted out toward the ruined entryway to Girod Cemetery. Michaels followed him. Harris pointed. "Ah, good, they're smart enough to have Jeeps riding shotgun for 'em. We don't want any trouble around here till we get the weapons away safe."

There were still a lot of people outside the cemetery walls. They booed and hissed the newly arrived vehicles, but didn't try anything more than booing and hissing. They might hate the damnyankees— they *did* hate the damnyankees—but it was the damnyankees who had the firepower here. Close to eighty years of bitter experience had taught that they weren't shy about using it, either.

Captured German weapons and ammunition filled all the new trucks to overflowing. Some of the ones that had brought in troops also got loaded with lethal hardware. The displaced soldiers either piled into Jeeps or clambered up on top of tanks for the ride back to their barracks, where the captured arms would be as safe as they could be anywhere in the endlessly rebellious South.

Michaels and Harris had led the convoy to the cemetery; now they'd lead it away. When their Jeep driver started up the engine, a few young Rebs bolder than the rest made as if to block the road.

The corporal in charge of the pintle-mounted .50-caliber machine gun in the Jeep turned to Michaels and asked, "Shall I mow 'em down, sir?" He sounded quiveringly eager to do just that.

"We'll give 'em one chance first," Michaels said, feeling generous. He stood up in the Jeep and shouted to the Johnnies obstructing his path: "You are interfering with the lawful business of the Federal Bureau of Suppression. Disperse at once or you will be shot. First, last, and only warning, people." He sat back down, telling the driver, "Put it in gear, but go slow. If they don't move—" He made hand-washing gestures.

Sullenly, the young men gave way as the Jeep moved forward. The gunner swung the muzzle of his weapon back and forth, back and forth, encouraging them to fall back farther. The expression on his face, which frightened even Michaels, might have been an even stronger persuader.

The convoy rattled away from the cemetery. The Johnnies hooted and jeered, but did no more than that, not here, not now. Had they got Nazi guns in their hands . . . but they hadn't.

"We won this one," Morrie Harris said.

"We sure did," Michaels agreed. "Now we can get on with the business of getting rid of tyrants around the world." He spoke altogether without irony.

In the Shade of the Slowboat Man

Dean Wesley Smith

Best-selling author Dean Wesley Smith has written twelve
novels and over eighty short stories. His latest book is *The Abduc-
tors: Conspiracy,* an original mystery/SF novel coauthored with
Jonathan Frakes, a star of the *Star Trek: The Next Generation* TV
series and movies. Smith has won the World Fantasy Award and
the Locus Award and has been nominated four times for the Hugo
Award. With Kristine Kathryn Rusch, he founded the small press
Pulphouse Publishing, which published science fiction, fantasy, and
horror. Together they have written ten novels, both under their own
names and as "Sandy Schofield." The most recent of these collab-
orations appeared in the best-selling *Star Trek: The Next Generation* Invasion! series. Smith is now editing the *Star Trek* anthology
Strange New Worlds. He lives in Lincoln City, Oregon.

"In the Shade of the Slowboat Man" is an evocative and
poignant short story that haunted this reader long after he read it.
Dean Wesley Smith writes:

"Every winter, a bunch of the Eugene professional science fiction writers get together at a wonderful log home overlooking the
Pacific Ocean in a small town called Rockaway. We spend two
days writing short stories, then a wonderful evening sitting in front
of a crackling fire, working the stories over.

"In February 1994, the writers attending, if memory serves,
were Dave Bischoff, Nina Kiriki Hoffman, Ray Vukcevich, Kent Pat-
terson, Jerry and Kathy Oltion, Steve and Chris York, and Kristine
Kathryn Rusch. I had been asked to write a story for a vampire anthology coming out of White Wolf. So I went to Rockaway that
month thinking of that story. A day and a half later, I gave the group
'In the Shade of the Slowboat Man.' My notes from the weekend
show that everyone really liked it, and I made few changes from
the first draft.

"I liked the story, too, so off it went to the anthology editor,
who promptly said it didn't fit his idea of the book. Which was fine.
It actually didn't. 'Slowboat Man' is not a normal vampire story by
any means.

"So when the story came back, I shrugged and tossed it in a file with most of my other short stories. (I have this bad habit of writing stories and never mailing them.) However, this story had already been seen by the people at Rockaway. Kristine [then editor of the *Magazine of Fantasy & Science Fiction*] had also read the story.

"When she learned I didn't plan to send 'Slowboat Man' out to any markets, she badgered me to send it to Ed Ferman at *F&SF.* (He edited my stories for the magazine, since he believed that because Kris was my wife, she couldn't make an honest judgment about my work.)

"After a few days of her pushing me to mail 'Slowboat Man,' I finally sent it to Ed, and he bought it. And now it's here, another prime example of why Kris is such a good editor, even though she didn't actually buy this story. Thanks, Kris.

"The theme and setting of 'Slowboat Man' have appeared in many of my published stories (and even more of the many still in my files). My second professionally published short story (in the very first volume of *Writers of the Future,* fifteen years ago) concerned the topics of love, death, and dying. And that story, 'One Last Dance,' was also set in a nursing home. I have always been concerned with the prisons that growing old puts around us, and I can't imagine getting tired of the continued exploration of those areas with my writing."

Over the long years I had grown used to the sweet smell of blood, to the sharp taste of disgust, to the wide-eyed look of lust. But the tight, small room of the nursing home covered me in new sensations like a mad mother covering her sleeping young child tenderly with a blanket before pressing a pillow hard over the face.

I eased the heavy door closed and stood silently for a moment, my clutch purse tight against my chest. One hospital bed, a small metal dresser, and an aluminum walker were all the furniture. The green drapes were slightly open on the window and I silently moved to stand in the beam of silver moonlight cutting the night. I wanted more than anything else to run. But I calmed myself, took a deep breath, and worked to pull in and study my surroundings as I would on any night on any city street.

As with all of the cesspools of humanity the smell was the most overwhelming detail. The odor of human rot filled the building and the room, not so much different from a dead animal beside the road on a hot summer's day. Death and nature doing their work. But in this building, in this small room, the natural work was disguised by layer after layer of biting poison antiseptic. I suppose it was meant to clean the smell of death away so as not to disturb the sensitive living who visited from the fresh air outside. But instead of clearing, the two smells combined to form a thick aroma that filled my mouth with disgust.

I blocked the smell and focused my attention on the form in the bed.

John, my dear, sweet Slowboat Man, my husband once, lay under the white sheet of the room's only bed. His frame shrunken from the robust, healthy man I remembered from so many short years ago. He smelled of piss and decay. His face, rough with old skin and white whiskers, seemed to fight an enemy unseen on the battleground of this tiny room. He jerked, then moaned softly, his labored breathing working to pull enough air to get to the next breath.

I moved to him, my ex-husband, my Slowboat Man, and lightly brushed his wrinkled forehead to ease his sleep. I used to do that as we lay together in our featherbed. I would need him to sleep so that I could go out and feed on the blood of others. He never awoke while I was gone, not once in the twenty years we were together.

Or at least he never told me he had.

I had never asked.

I was hunting the night we met. The spring of 1946, a time of promise and good cheer around the country. The war was won, the evil vanquished, and the living bathed in the feeling of a wonderful future. I had spent the last thirty years before and during the war in St. Louis, but my friends had aged, as always happened, and it was becoming too hard to answer the questions and the looks. I had moved on many times in the past and I would continue to do so many times in the future. It was my curse for making mortal friends and enjoying the pleasures of the mortal world.

I pleaded to my friends in St. Louis a sick mother in a faraway city and booked passage under another name on an old-fashioned Mississippi riverboat named *Joe Henry*. I had loved the boats when they were working the river the first time and now again loved them as they came back again for the tourists and gambling.

For the first few days I stayed mostly to my small cabin, sleeping on the small bed during the day and reading at night. But on the third day hunger finally drove me into the narrow hallways and lighted party rooms of the huge riverboat.

Many soldiers and sailors filled the boat, most still in uniform and most with women of their own age holding on to their arms and laughing at their every word. The boat literally reeked of health and good cheer and I remember that smell drove my hunger.

I suppose events could have turned another way and I might have met Johnny before feeding. But almost immediately upon leaving my cabin I had gotten lucky and found a young sailor standing alone on the lower deck.

I walked up to the rail and pretended to stare out over the black waters of the river and the lights beyond. The air felt alive, full of humidity and insects, thick air that carried the young sailor's scent clearly to me.

He moved closer and struck up a conversation. After a minute I stroked his arm, building his lust and desire while at the same time blocking his mind of my image. I asked him to help me with a problem with the mattress on my bed in my cabin and even though he kept a straight face the smell of sexual lust almost choked me.

Within two minutes he was asleep on my bed and I was feeding, drinking light to not hurt him, but getting enough of his blood to fill my immediate hunger.

After I finished I brushed over the marks on his neck with a lick so that no sign would show and then cleaned myself up while letting him rest. Then I roused him just enough to walk him up a few decks, where I slipped away, happy that I might repeat the same act numbers of times during this voyage. It was an intoxicating time and I felt better than I had ever remembered feeling in years.

I decided that an after-dinner stroll along the moonlit deck would be nice before returning to my cabin. I moved slowly, drinking in the warmth of the night air, listening to the churning of the paddle wheel, feeling the boat slice through the muddy water of the river.

Johnny leaned against the rail about midship, smoking a pipe. Under the silver moon his Navy officer's white uniform seemed to glow with a light of its own. I started to pass him and realized that I needed to stop, to speak to him, to let him hold me.

He affected me as I imagined I affected my prey when I fed. I was drawn to him with such intensity that resisting didn't seem possible.

I hesitated and he glanced over at me and laughed, a soft laugh as if he could read my every thought, as if he knew that I wanted him with me that instant, without reason, without cause. He just laughed, not at me, but in merriment at the situation, at the delight, at the beauty of the night.

He laughed easily and for the next twenty years I would enjoy that laugh every day.

I turned and he was smiling, a smile that I will always remember. I learned over the years that he had the simple ability to smile and light up the darkest place. He had a smile that many a night I would lose myself in while he told me story after story after story. I never tired of that smile and that first exposure to it melted my will. I would be his slave and never care as long as he kept smiling at me.

"Beautiful evening, isn't it?" he said, his voice solid and genuine, like his smile.

"Now it is," I said. I had to catch my breath even after something that simple.

Again he laughed and made a motion that I should join him at the rail gazing out over the river and the trees and farmland beyond.

I did, and for twenty years, except to feed on others while he slept, I never left his side.

The smell of the room pulled me from the past and back to my mission of the evening. I looked at his weathered, time-beaten form on the bed and felt sadness and love. A large part of me regretted missing the aging time of his life, of not sharing that time with him, as I had regretted missing the years before I met him. But on both I had had no choice. Or I had felt I had had no choice. I might have been wrong, but it was the choice I had made.

Since the time I left him I had never found another to be my husband. Actually I never really tried, never really wanted to fill that huge hole in my chest that leaving him had caused.

But now he was dying and now I also had to move on, change cities and friends again. I had always felt regret with each move, yet the regret was controlled by the certainty that the decision was the only right one, that I would make new friends, find new lovers. But this time it was harder. Much harder.

I sat lightly on the side of his bed and he stirred, moaning softly. I again brushed his forehead, easing his pain, giving him a fuller rest, a more peaceful rest. It was the least I could do for him. He deserved so much more.

This time he moaned with contentment and that moan took me back to those lovely nights on the *Joe Henry,* slowly making our way down the river, nestled in each other's arms. We made love three, sometimes four times a day and spent the rest of the time talking and laughing and just being with each other, as if every moment was the most precious moment we had.

During those wonderful talks I had wanted to tell him of my true nature, but didn't. The very desire to tell him surprised me. In all the years it had not happened before. So I only told him of the thirty years in St. Louis, letting him think that was where I had been raised. As our years together went by that lie became as truth between us and he never questioned me on it.

He was born in San Francisco and wanted to return there where his family had property and some wealth. I told him I was alone in the world, as was the true case, just drifting and looking for a new home. He seemed to admire that about me. But he also knew I was free to move where he wanted.

I had so wanted him to know that.

The day before we were to dock in Vicksburg I mentioned to him that I wished the boat would slow down so that our time together would last. The days and nights since I met him had been truly magical, and in my life that was a very rare occurrence.

He had again laughed at my thought, but in a good way. Then he hugged me. "We will be together for a long time," he had said, "but I will return in a moment."

With that he had dressed and abruptly left the cabin, leaving me surrounded by his things and his wonderful life-odor. After a short time he returned, smiling, standing over me, casting his shadow across my naked form. "Your wish is granted," he had said. "The boat has slowed."

I didn't know how he had managed it and never really asked what it had cost him. But somehow he had managed to delay the boat into Vicksburg by an extra day. A long, wonderful extra day that turned into a wonderful marriage.

From that day forward I called him my Slowboat Man and he never seemed to tire of it.

"Beautiful evening, isn't it?" he said hoarsely from the bed beside me. His words yanked me from the past and back to the smell of death and antiseptic in the small nursing-home room. Johnny was smiling up at me lightly, his sunken eyes still full of the light and the mischief that I had loved so much.

"It is now," I said, stroking him, soothing him.

He started to laugh but instead coughed, and I soothed him with a touch again.

He blinked a few times, focusing on me, staring at me, touching my arm. "You are as beautiful as I remembered," he said, his voice clearing as he used it, gaining more and more power. "I've missed you."

"I've missed you, too," I somehow managed to say. I could feel his weak grip on my arm.

He smiled and then his eyes closed.

I touched his forehead and again he was dozing. I sat on the bed beside him and thought back to that last time I had sat beside him on our marriage bed, almost thirty years earlier.

That last night, as with any other night I went out to feed, I had put him to sleep with a few strokes on the forehead and then stayed with him to make sure his sleep was deep. But that last night I had also packed a few things, very few, actually, because I had hoped to take very little of our life together to remind me of him. It had made no difference. I saw his face, his smile, heard his laugh and his voice every-- where I went.

I had known for years that the day of leaving was coming. And many times over the years we were together I thought of telling him about my true nature. But I could never overcome the fear. I feared that if he knew he would hate me, fight me, even try to kill me. I feared that he would find a way to expose those of us like me in the city and around the country. But my biggest fear was that he would never be able to stand my youth as he aged.

I could not have stood the look of hate and disgust in his eyes.

At least that was what I told myself. As the years passed since I left him I came to believe that my fear had been a stupid one. But I never overcame that fear, at least not until now.

I know my leaving to him must have felt sudden and without reason. I know he spent vast sums of money looking for me. I know he didn't truly understand.

But for me I had no choice. During the month before I left, comments about my youth were suddenly everywhere. Johnny and our friends had aged. I hadn't. I even caught Johnny staring at me when he thought I wouldn't notice.

Three nights before I left, one waitress asked him, while I was in the ladies' room, what his daughter, meaning me, wanted for dessert. He had laughed about it, but I could tell he didn't understand and was bothered. As he should have been.

The night I left, I found a book about vampires hidden in a pile of magazines from his office. A well-read book.

I could wait no longer and I knew then that I could never talk to him about it. I had to go that night and I did so, leaving only a note to him that said I would always love him.

I moved quickly, silently, in an untraceable fashion, to the East Coast. But less than a year later, no longer able to even fight the fight of keeping him out of my mind, I returned to San Francisco under a new name and began to watch him from afar.

As with me, he never remarried. Many nights he would walk the streets of the city alone, just smiling, almost content. I paced him, watching him, protecting him from others of my kind and from the mortal criminals. I imagined that he knew I was watching him. Pacing him. Walking with him. Protecting him. I pretended that knowing I was there made him happy. Many nights I even thought of actually showing myself to him, of holding him again.

But I never did.

I never had the courage.

He stirred under the nursing-home sheet and I watched him as he awoke. He opened his eyes, saw me, and then smiled. "Good. I was hoping you were more than a dream."

"No, Slowboat Man, you aren't dreaming."

He laughed and gripped my hand and I could feel the warmth flowing between us. I leaned down and kissed him on the cheek, his rough skin warm against my face. As I pulled back I could see a single tear in the corner of his right eye. But in both eyes the look was love. I was amazed.

And very glad.

I had feared he would hate me after I had left him without warning. I had feared that when I came to visit tonight he would ask the questions about my youth and how I had stayed so young, questions that I had always been so afraid to answer. I had feared most of all that he would send me away.

But he didn't. And the relief flooded through my every cell. Even after almost thirty years he still loved me. I wanted to shout it to the entire world. But instead I just sat there grinning at him.

In the hundreds of years that I had been alive I had never felt or seen a love so complete and total as his love for me.

It saddened me to think that in the centuries to come I might never find it again.

"I'm glad you decided to come and say good-bye," he said. "I was hoping you would."

I gently touched his arm. "You know I wanted to when—"

He waved me quiet. "Don't. You did what you had to do."

My head was spinning and I wanted to ask him a thousand questions: How he knew? What he knew?

But instead I just sat beside him on the bed and stared at him. After a moment he laughed.

"Now say good-bye properly," he said. "Then be on your way. I overheard the doctor telling one of the nurses that I might not make it through the night and I don't want you here when I leave. Might not be a pretty sight."

I just shook my head at him. I had seen more death than he could ever imagine, but I didn't want to tell him that.

A long spell of coughing caught him and he half sat up in bed with the pain. I stroked his forehead and he calmed and worked to catch his breath. After a moment he said, "I loved it when you used to do that to me. Always thought it was one of your nicer gifts to me, even though I never understood just how or what you did."

Again he laughed lightly at what must have been my shocked look. Even after all these years, even with very little force behind it, his laugh could still gladden my heart, make me smile, ease my worries. Again this time it took only a moment before I smiled and then laughed with him.

"Now be on your way," he said. "The nurse will be here shortly and I have a long journey to make into the next world. I'm ready to go, you know? Actually looking forward to it. You would too if you had an old body like this one."

I nodded and stood. "Good-bye, my Slowboat Man." I leaned down and kissed him solidly on his rough, chapped lips.

"Good-bye, my beautiful wife."

He smiled at me one last time and I smiled back, as I always had.

Then I turned and headed for the door. I knew that I had to leave immediately because if I didn't, I never would. But this time he wanted me to go. I wasn't running away.

As I pulled the handle open to the dimly lit hallway, he called out to me. "Beautiful?"

I stopped and turned.

"I'm sorry I couldn't slow the boat down this time."

"That's all right," I said, just loud enough for him to hear. "No matter how long or how short the lifetime, sometimes once is enough. Sleep well, my Slowboat Man. Sleep well."

And as the door to his final room closed behind me, I added to myself, "And thank you."

Da Vinci Rising

Jack Dann

Jack Dann is the author or editor of over forty-five books. His short fiction has appeared in *Asimov's Science Fiction, The Magazine of Fantasy & Science Fiction, Omni, Playboy,* and other magazines and anthologies. Some of his short fiction has been collected in *Timetipping* and *Slow Dancing through Time* (with Gardner Dozois, Michael Swanwick, Susan Casper, and Jack C. Haldeman II). His novels include *Junction, Starhiker, High Steel* (with Jack C. Haldeman II), and *The Man Who Melted.* His latest novel, *The Memory Cathedral: A Secret History of Leonardo da Vinci,* won Australia's Aurealis Award for Best Fantasy Novel and was number one on the best-seller list in Australia. To date, *The Memory Cathedral* has been translated into eight languages. Dann also edits the multivolume Magic Tales series with Gardner Dozois and the White Wolf Rediscovery Trios series with Pamela Sargent and George Zebrowski. He is a consulting editor for Tor Books. His anthologies include *Wandering Stars, More Wandering Stars, Immortal, In the Field of Fire* (with Jeanne Van Buren Dann), *Faster Than Light* (with George Zebrowski), and *Future Power* (with Gardner Dozois). Dann's latest novel, *The Silent,* is about the Civil War. Based in Melbourne, Australia, he continues to "commute" to New York.

The 1996 Nebula Award–winning novella "Da Vinci Rising" is based on *The Memory Cathedral.* Dann writes:

"In the olden days, when I was a lad and dinosaurs still roamed the upstate reaches of New York, I used to visit Gardner Dozois and Susan Casper in Philadelphia. Before Gardner had become the most influential editor since John W. Campbell, I selfishly thought of him as *my* editor. My Machiavellian strategy was simple: I would arrive at their apartment with a story—or a 100,000-word novel!—under my arm and wouldn't leave until Gardner had read my manuscript and told me how to fix it. I'd sleep on the couch with the cats and skulk around during the day (with the cats) until he'd finally appear, bleary-eyed with fatigue, with my manuscript in hand.

" '*Amnesia* is a boring title,' he said during one of my long stays. 'How about something like *The Man Who Melted*? That sounds more interesting. And you need to open the book up with some action; why not try something like this. . . .'

"I took notes, reworked *The Man Who Melted,* and sold it.

"Oh, yes, I also went back home. Finally.

"And so it was with novels and novellas and novelettes and short stories. Gardner had an unerring eye for plot and pacing and structure.

"He was *my* story doctor.

"[Then] It was 1994, and I had just finished *The Memory Cathedral,* my 200,000-word opus about the secret life of Leonardo da Vinci. I had just moved to Melbourne, Australia, but I came back to Philadelphia to see Gardner and Susan. I must admit I had considered using my old tactic of giving him a manuscript and staying until he read it, but I knew he was too smart for that. He was up to his eyeballs in manuscripts for *Asimov's.* I couldn't selfishly push my way in with a 200,000-word manuscript and ask him to cut out a story.

"He'd rally and retaliate with irrefutable excuses.

"So I took 30,000 words out of *The Memory Cathedral* and told him I thought there was a science fiction story here about Leonardo da Vinci's flying machine. We hung out, went shopping on South Street, went out to dinner; I slept on the couch with the cats and skulked around during the day (with the cats) until Gardner finally appeared, bleary-eyed with fatigue, with my manuscript in hand.

" 'Yeah, there's some interesting stuff here,' he said, 'but you need to . . .'

"I added 5,000 words to the manuscript, cut out whole sections, wrote new transitions, and reworked the entire draft until I had transformed secret history into alternate history.

" 'And you need a title. . . .

" 'How about 'Da Vinci Rising'?' "

One

Dressed as if he were on fire—in a doublet of heliotrope and crimson over a blood-red shirt—Leonardo da Vinci entered the workshop of his master, Andrea Verrocchio.

Verrocchio had invited a robust and august company of men to what had become one of the most important salons in Florence. The many conversations were loud and the floor was stained with wine. Leonardo's fellow apprentices stood near the walls, discreetly listening and interjecting a word here and there. Normally, Master Andrea cajoled the apprentices to work—he had long given up on Leonardo, the best of them all, who worked when he would—but tonight he had closed the shop. The aged Paolo dal Pozzo Toscanelli, who had taught Leonardo mathematics and geography, sat near a huge earthenware jar and a model of the lavabo that would be installed in the Old Sacristy of San Lorenzo. A boy with dark intense eyes and a tight accusing mouth stood behind him like a shadow. Leonardo had never seen this boy before; perhaps Toscanelli had but recently taken this waif into his home.

"I want you to meet a young man with whom you have much in common," Toscanelli said. "His father is also a notary, like yours. He has put young Niccolo in my care. Niccolo is a child of love, also like you, and extremely talented as a poet and playwright and rhetorician. He is interested in everything, and he seems unable to finish anything! But unlike you, Leonardo, he talks very little. Isn't that right, Niccolo?"

"I am perfectly capable of talking, Ser Toscanelli," the boy said.

"What's your name?" Leonardo asked.

"Ach, forgive me my lack of manners," Toscanelli said. "Master Leonardo, this is Niccolo Machiavelli, son of Bernardo de Niccolo and Bartolomea Nelli. You may have heard of Bartolomea, a religious poetess of great talent."

Leonardo bowed and said with a touch of sarcasm, "I am honored to meet you, young sir."

"I would like you to help this young man with his education," Toscanelli said.

"But I—"

"You are too much of a lone wolf, Leonardo! You must learn to give generously of your talents. Teach him to see as you do, to play the lyre, to paint. Teach him magic and perspective, teach him about the streets, and women, and the nature of light. Show him your flying machine and your sketches of birds. And I guarantee, he will repay you."

"But he's only a boy!"

Niccolo Machiavelli stood before Leonardo, staring at him expectantly, as if concerned. He was a handsome boy, tall and gangly, but his face was unnaturally severe for one so young. Yet he seemed comfortable alone here in this strange place. Merely curious, Leonardo thought.

"What are you called?" Leonardo asked, taking interest.

"Niccolo," the boy said.

"And you have no nickname?"

"I am called Niccolo Machiavelli, that is my name."

"Well, I shall call you Nicco, young sir. Do you have any objections?"

After a pause, he said, "No, Maestro," but the glimmer of a smile compressed his thin lips.

"So your new name pleases you somewhat," Leonardo said.

"I find it amusing that you feel it necessary to make my name smaller. Does that make you feel larger?"

Leonardo laughed. "And what is your age?"

"I am almost fifteen."

"But you are really fourteen, is that not so?"

"And you are still but an apprentice to Master Andrea, yet you are truly a master, or so Master Toscanelli has told me. Since you are closer to being a master, wouldn't you prefer men to think of you as such? Or would you rather be treated as an apprentice such as the one there who is in charge of filling glasses with wine? Well, Master Leonardo . . . ?"

Leonardo laughed again, taking a liking to this intelligent boy who acted as if he possessed twice his years, and said, "You may call me Leonardo."

At that moment, Andrea Verrocchio walked over to Leonardo with Lorenzo de' Medici in tow. Lorenzo was magnetic, charismatic, and ugly. His face was coarse, overpowered by a large, flattened nose, and he was suffering one of his periodic outbreaks of eczema; his chin and cheeks were covered with a flesh-colored paste. He had a bull neck and long, straight brown hair, yet he held himself with such grace that he appeared taller than the men around him. His eyes were perhaps his most arresting feature, for they looked at everything with such friendly intensity, as if to see through things and people alike.

"We have in our midst Leonardo da Vinci, the consummate conjurer and prestidigitator," Verrocchio said, bowing to Lorenzo de' Medici as he presented Leonardo to him; he spoke loud enough for all to hear. "Leonardo has fashioned a machine that can carry a man in the air like a bird. . . ."

"My sweet friend Andrea has often told me about your inventiveness, Leonardo da Vinci," Lorenzo said, a slight sarcasm in his voice; ironically, he spoke to Leonardo in much the same good-humored yet condescending tone that Leonardo had used when addressing young Machiavelli. "But how do you presume to effect this miracle of flight? Surely not by means of your cranks and pulleys! Will you conjure up the flying beast Geryon, as we read Dante did, and so descend upon its neck into the infernal regions? Or will you merely *paint* yourself into the sky?"

Everyone laughed at that, and Leonardo, who would not dare to try to seize the stage from Lorenzo, explained, "My most illustrious Lord, you may see that the beating of its wings against the air supports a heavy eagle in the highest and rarest atmosphere, close to the sphere of elemental fire. Again, you may see the air in motion over the sea fill the swelling sails and drive heavily laden ships. Just so could a man with wings large enough and properly connected learn to overcome the resistance of the air and, by conquering it, succeed in subjugating it and rising above it.

"After all," Leonardo continued, "a bird is nothing more than an instrument that works according to mathematical laws, and it is within the capacity of man to reproduce that instrument with all its movements."

"But a man is not a bird," Lorenzo said. "A bird has sinews and muscles that are incomparably more powerful than a man's. If we were constructed so as to have wings, we would have been provided with them by the Almighty."

"Then you think we are too weak to fly?"

"Indeed, I think the evidence would lead reasonable men to that conclusion," Lorenzo said.

"But surely," Leonardo said, "you have seen falcons carrying ducks, and eagles carrying hares; and there are times when these birds of prey must double their rate of speed to follow their prey. But they only need a little force to sustain themselves, and to balance themselves on their wings, and flap them in the pathway of the wind and so direct the course of their journeying. A slight movement of the wings is sufficient, and the greater the size of the bird, the slower the movement. It's the same with men, for we possess a greater amount of strength in our legs than our weight requires. In fact, we have twice the amount of strength we need to support ourselves. You can prove this by observing how far the marks of one of your men's feet will sink into the sand of the seashore. If you then order another man to climb upon his back, you can observe how much deeper the foot marks will be. But remove the man from the other's back and order the first man to jump as high as he can, and you will find that the marks of his feet will now make a deeper impression where he has jumped than in the place where he had the other man on his back. That's double proof that a man has more than twice the strength he needs to support himself . . . more than enough to fly like a bird."

Lorenzo laughed. "Very good, Leonardo. But I would have to see with my own eyes your machine that turns men into birds. Is *that* what you've been spending your precious time doing, instead of working on the statues I commissioned you to repair?"

Leonardo let his gaze drop to the floor.

"Not at all," Verrocchio interrupted, "Leonardo has indeed been with me in your gardens applying his talent to the repair of—"

"Show me this machine, painter," Lorenzo said to Leonardo. "I could use such a device to confound my enemies, especially those wearing the colors of the south." The veiled reference was to Pope Sixtus IV and the Florentine Pazzi family. "Is it ready to be used?"

"Not just yet, Magnificence," Leonardo said. "I'm still experimenting."

Everyone laughed, including Lorenzo. "Ah, experimenting is it? . . . Well, then I'll pledge you to communicate with me when it's finished. But from your last performance, I think that none of us need worry."

Humiliated, Leonardo could only avert his eyes.

"Tell me, how long do you anticipate that your . . . experiments will take?"

"I think I could safely estimate that my 'contraption' would be ready for flight in two weeks," Leonardo said, taking the advantage, to everyone's surprise. "I plan to launch my great bird from Swan Mountain in Fiesole."

The studio became a roar of surprised conversation.

Leonardo had no choice except to meet Lorenzo's challenge; if he did not, Lorenzo might ruin his career. As it was, his Magnificence obviously considered Leonardo to be a dilettante, a polymath genius who could not be trusted to bring his commissions to fruition.

"Forgive my caustic remarks, Leonardo, for everyone in this room respects your pretty work," Lorenzo said. "But I will take you up on your promise; in two weeks we travel to Fiesole!"

Two

One could almost imagine that the Great Bird was already in flight, hovering in the gauzy morning light like a great, impossible hummingbird. It was a chimerical thing that hung from the high attic ceiling of Leonardo's workshop in Verrocchio's *bottega:* a tapered plank fitted with hand-operated cranks, hoops of well-tanned leather, pedals, windlass, oars, and saddle. Great ribbed batlike wings made of cane and fustian and starched taffeta were connected to the broader end of the plank. They were dyed bright red and gold, the colors of the Medici, for it was the Medici who would attend its first flight.

As Leonardo had written in his notebook: *Remember that your bird must imitate only the bat because its webbing forms a framework that gives strength to the wings. If you imitate the birds' wings, you will discover the feathers to be disunited and permeable to the air. But the bat is aided by the membrane which binds the whole and is not pervious.* This was written backward from right to left in Leonardo's idiosyncratic "mirror" script that was all but impossible to decipher. Leonardo lived in paranoid fear that his best ideas and inventions would be stolen.

Although he sat before a canvas he was painting, his eyes smarting from the miasmas of varnish and linseed oil and first-grade turpentine, Leonardo nervously gazed up at his invention. It filled the upper area of the large room, for its wingspan was over fifteen ells—more than twenty-five feet.

For the past few days Leonardo had been certain that something was not quite right with his great bird, yet he could not divine what it might be. Nor could he sleep well, for he had been having nightmares; no doubt they were a consequence of his apprehensions over his flying machine, which was due to be flown from the top of a mountain in just ten days. His dream was always the same: he would be falling from a great height . . . without wings, without harness . . . into a barely luminescent void, while above him the familiar sunlit hills and mountains that overlooked Vinci would be turning vertiginously. And he would awaken in a cold sweat, tearing at his covers, his heart beating in his throat as if to choke him.

Leonardo was afraid of heights. While exploring the craggy and dangerous slopes of Monte Albano as a child, he had fallen from an overhang and almost broken his back. But Leonardo was determined to conquer this and every other fear. He would become as familiar with the airy realms as the birds that soared and rested on the winds. He would make the very air his ally, his support and security.

There was a characteristic knock on the door: two light taps followed by a loud thump.

"Enter, Andrea, lest the dead wake," Leonardo said without getting up.

Verrocchio stormed in with his foreman Simone di Francesco, a burly, full-faced, middle-aged man whose muscular body was just beginning to go to seed. Francesco carried a silver tray, upon which were placed cold meats, fruit, and two cruses of milk; he laid it on the table beside Leonardo. Both Verrocchio and Francesco had been at work for hours, as was attested by the lime and marble dust that streaked their faces and shook from their clothes. They were unshaven and wore work gowns, although Verrocchio's was more a frock, as if, indeed, he envisioned himself as a priest to art—the unblest "tenth muse."

Most likely they had been in one of the outer workshops, for Andrea was having trouble with a terra-cotta *risurrezione* relief destined for Lorenzo's villa in Careggi. But this *bottega* was so busy that Andrea's attention was constantly in demand. "Well, at least *you're* awake," Andrea said to Leonardo as he looked appreciatively at the painting-in-progress. Then he clapped his hands, making such a loud noise that Niccolo, who was fast asleep on his pallet beside Leonardo's, awakened with a cry, as if from a particularly nasty nightmare. Andrea chuckled and said, "Well, good morning, young ser. Perhaps I could have one of the other apprentices find enough work for you to keep you busy during the spine of the morning."

"I apologize, Maestro Andrea, but Maestro Leonardo and I worked late into the night." Niccolo removed his red, woolen sleeping cap and hurriedly put on a gown that lay on the floor beside his pallet, for, like most Florentines, he slept naked.

"Ah, so now it's Maestro Leonardo, is it?" Andrea said good-naturedly. "Well, eat your breakfast, both of you. Today I'm a happy man; I have news."

Niccolo did as he was told, and, in fact, ate like a trencherman, spilling milk on his lap.

"One would never guess that he came from a good family," Andrea said, watching Niccolo stuff his mouth.

"Now tell me your news," Leonardo said.

"It's not all that much to tell." Nevertheless Andrea could not repress a grin. "*Il Magnifico* has informed me that my *David* will stand prominently in the Palazzo Vecchio over the great staircase."

Leonardo nodded. "But, certainly, you knew Lorenzo would find a place of special honor for such a work of genius."

"I don't know if you compliment me or yourself, Leonardo," Andrea said. "After all, you are the model."

"You took great liberties," Leonardo said. "You may have begun with my features, but you have created something sublime out of the ordinary. You deserve the compliment."

"I fear this pleasing talk will cost me either money or time," Andrea said.

Leonardo laughed. "Indeed, today I must be out of the city."

Andrea gazed up at Leonardo's flying machine and said, "No one would blame you if you backed out of this project, or, at least, allowed someone else to fly your contraption. You need not prove yourself to Lorenzo."

"I would volunteer to fly your mechanical bird, Leonardo," Niccolo said earnestly.

"No, it must be me."

"Was it not to gain experience that Master Toscanelli sent me to you?"

"To gain experience, yes; but not to jeopardize your life," Leonardo said.

"You are not satisfied it will work?" Andrea asked.

"Of course I am, Andrea. If I were not, I would bow before Lorenzo and give him the satisfaction of publicly putting me to the blush."

"Leonardo, be truthful with me," Verrocchio said. "It is to Andrea you speak, not a rich patron."

"Yes, my friend, I am worried," Leonardo confessed. "Something is indeed wrong with my Great Bird, yet I cannot quite put my finger on it. It is most frustrating."

"Then you must not fly it!"

"It will fly, Andrea. I promise you that."

"You have my blessing to take the day off," Verrocchio said.

"I am most grateful," Leonardo said; and they both laughed, knowing that Leonardo would have left for the country with or without Andrea's permission.

"Well, we must be off," Leonardo said to Andrea, who nodded and took his leave.

"Come on, Nicco," Leonardo said, suddenly full of energy. "Get yourself dressed"; and as Niccolo did so, Leonardo put a few finishing touches on his painting, then quickly cleaned his brushes, hooked his sketchbook onto his belt, and once again craned his neck to stare at his invention that hung from the ceiling. He needed an answer, but he had not yet formulated the question.

When they were out the door, Leonardo felt that he had forgotten something. "Nicco, fetch me the book Maestro Toscanelli loaned to me . . . the one he purchased from the Chinese trader. I might wish to read in the country."

"The country?" Niccolo asked, carefully putting the book into a sack, which he carried under his arm.

"Do you object to nature?" Leonardo asked sarcastically. "*Usus est optimum magister* . . . and in that I agree wholeheartedly with the ancients. Nature herself is the mother of all experience; and experience must be your teacher, for I have discovered that even Aristotle can be mistaken on certain subjects." As they left the *bottega*, he continued: "But those of Maestro Ficino's Academy, they go about all puffed and pompous, mouthing the eternal aphorisms of Plato and Aristotle like parrots. They might think that because I have not had a literary education, I am uncultured; but *they* are the fools. They despise me because

I am an inventor, but how much more are they to blame for *not* being inventors, these trumpeters and reciters of the works of others! They considered my glass to study the skies and make the moon large a conjuring trick, and do you know why?" Before Niccolo could respond, Leonardo said, "Because they consider sight to be the most untrustworthy of senses, when, in fact, it is the supreme organ. Yet that does not prevent them from wearing spectacles in secret. Hypocrites!"

"You seem very angry, Maestro," Niccolo said to Leonardo.

Embarrassed at having launched into this diatribe, Leonardo laughed at himself and said, "Perhaps I am, but do not worry about it, young friend."

"Maestro Toscanelli seems to respect the learned men of the Academy," Niccolo said.

"He respects Plato and Aristotle, as well he should. But he does not teach at the Academy, does he? No, instead, he lectures at the school at Santo Spirito for the Augustinian brothers. That should tell you something."

"I think it tells me that you have an ax to grind, Master . . . and that's also what Maestro Toscanelli told me."

"What else did he tell you, Nicco?" Leonardo asked.

"That I should learn from your strengths and weaknesses, and that you are smarter than everyone in the Academy."

Leonardo laughed at that and said, "You lie very convincingly."

"That, Maestro, comes naturally."

The streets were busy and noisy; and the sky, which seemed pierced by the tiled mass of the Duomo and the Palace of the Signoria, was cloudless and sapphire-blue. There was the sweet smell of sausage in the air, and young merchants—practically children—stood behind stalls and shouted at every passerby. This market was called *Il Baccano*, the place of uproar. Leonardo bought some cooked meat, beans, fruit, and a bottle of cheap local wine for Niccolo and himself. They continued on into different neighborhoods and markets. They passed Spanish Moors with their slave retinues from the Ivory Coast; Mamluks in swathed robes and flat turbans; Muscovy Tartars and Mongols from Cathay; and merchants from England and Flanders, who had sold their woolen cloth and were on their way to the Ponte Vecchio to purchase trinkets and baubles. Niccolo was all eye and motion as they passed elegant and beautiful "butterflies of the night" standing beside their merchant masters under the shade of guild awnings; these whores and mistresses modeled jeweled garlands and expensive garments of violet, crimson, and peach. Leonardo and Niccolo passed stall after stall—brushing off young hawkers and old, disease-ravaged beggars—and flowed with the crowds of peddlers, citizens, and visitors as if they were flotsam in the sea. Young men of means, dressed in short doublets, wiggled and swayed like young girls through the streets; they roistered and swashbuckled, laughed and sang and bullied, these favored ones. Niccolo could not help but laugh at the scholars and student wanderers from England and Scotland and Bohemia, for although their lingua franca was Latin, their accents were extravagant and overwrought.

"Ho, Leonardo," cried one vendor, then another, as Leonardo and Niccolo turned a corner. Then the screes and cries of birds sounded, for the bird sellers were shaking the small wooden cages packed with wood pigeons, owls, mousebirds, bee-eaters, hummingbirds, crows, blue rock thrushes, warblers, flycatchers, wagtails, hawks, falcons, eagles, and all manner of swans, ducks, chickens, and geese. As Leonardo approached, the birds were making more commotion than the vendors and buyers on the street. "Come here, Master!" shouted a red-haired man wearing a stained brown doublet with torn sleeves. His right eye appeared infected, for it was bloodshot, crusted, and tearing. He shook two cages, each containing hawks; one bird was brown with a forked chestnut tail, and the other was smaller and black with a notched tail. They banged against the wooden bars and snapped dangerously. "Buy these, Maestro Artista, please . . . they are just what you need, are they not? And look how many doves I have, do they not interest you, good Master?"

"Indeed, the hawks are fine specimens," Leonardo said, drawing closer, while the other vendors called and shouted to him, as if he were carrying the grail itself. "How much?"

"Ten denari."

"Three."

"Eight."

"Four, and if that is not satisfactory, I can easily talk to your neighbor, who is flapping his arms as if he, himself, could fly."

"Agreed," said the vendor, resigned.

"And the doves?"

"For how many, Maestro?"

"For the lot."

While Leonardo dickered with the bird vendor, hecklers gathered around to watch, talking openly about him, not seeming to care if Niccolo—or Leonardo himself—could hear them.

"He's as mad as Ajax," said an old man who had just sold a few chickens and doves, and was as animated as the street thugs and young beggars standing around him. "He'll let them all go, watch, you'll see!"

"I've heard tell he won't eat meat," said one matronly woman to another. "He lets the birds go free because he feels sorry for the poor creatures."

"Well, to be safe, don't look straight at him," said the other woman, as she made the sign of the cross. "He might be a sorcerer. He could put evil in your eye, and enter right into your soul!"

Her companion shivered and followed suit by crossing herself.

"Nicco," Leonardo shouted, making himself heard above the din. "Come here and help me." When Niccolo stepped up to him, Leonardo said, "If you could raise your thoughts from those of butterflies"—and by that he meant whores—"you might learn something of observation and the ways of science." He thrust his hand into the cage filled with doves and grasped one. The tiny bird made a frightened noise; as Leonardo took it from its cage, he could feel its heart beating in his palm. Then he opened his hand and watched the dove fly away. The crowd laughed and jeered and applauded and shouted for more. He took another bird out of its cage and released it. His eyes squinted almost shut; and, as he gazed at the dove beating its wings so hard that, but for the crowd, one could have heard them clap, he seemed lost in thought. "Now, Nicco, I want you to let the birds free, one by one."

"Why me?" Niccolo asked, somehow loath to seize the birds.

"Because *I* wish to draw," Leonardo said. "Is this chore too difficult for you?"

"I beg your pardon, Maestro," Niccolo said, as he reached into the cage. He had a difficult time catching a bird. Leonardo seemed impatient and completely oblivious to the shouts and taunts of the crowd around him. Niccolo let go of one bird, and then another, while Leonardo sketched. Leonardo stood very still, entranced; only his hand moved like a ferret over the bleached folio, as if it had a life and will of its own.

As Niccolo let fly another bird, Leonardo said, "Do you see, Nicco, the bird in its haste to climb strikes its outstretched wings together above its body. Now look how it uses its wings and tail in the same way that a swimmer uses his arms and legs in the water; it's the very same principle. It seeks the air currents, which, invisible, roil around the buildings of our city. And there, its speed is checked by the opening and spreading out of the tail. . . . Let fly another one. Can you see how the wing separates to let the air pass?" and he wrote a note in his mirror script below one of his sketches: *Make device so that when the wing rises up it remains pierced through, and when it falls it is all united.* "Another," he called to Niccolo. And after the bird disappeared, he made another note: *The speed is checked by the opening and spreading out of the tail. Also, the opening and lowering of the tail, and the simultaneous spreading of the wings to their full extent, arrests their swift movement.*

"That's the end of it," Niccolo said, indicating the empty cages. "Do you wish to free the hawks?"

"No," Leonardo said, distracted. "We will take them with us," and Leonardo and Niccolo made their way through the crowd, which now began to disperse. As if a reflection of Leonardo's change of mood, clouds darkened the sky; and the bleak, refuse-strewn streets took on a more dangerous aspect. The other bird vendors called to Leonardo, but he ignored them, as he did Niccolo. Instead, he stared intently into his notebook as he walked, as if he were trying to decipher ancient runes.

They passed the wheel of the bankrupts. Defeated men sat around a marble inlay that was worked into the piazza in the design of a cartwheel. A crowd had formed, momentarily, to watch a debtor, who had been stripped naked, being pulled to the roof of the market by a rope.

Then there was a great shout as he was dropped headfirst onto the smooth, cold, marble floor.

A sign attached to one of the market posts read:

> GIVE GOOD HEED TO THE SMALL SUMS THOU SPENDEST
> OUT OF THE HOUSE, FOR IT IS THEY WHICH EMPTY THE PURSE
> AND CONSUME WEALTH; AND THEY GO ON CONTINUALLY. AND
> DO NOT BUY ALL THE GOOD VICTUALS WHICH THOU SEEST, FOR
> THE HOUSE IS LIKE A WOLF: THE MORE THOU GIVEST IT, THE
> MORE DOTH IT DEVOUR.

The man dropped by the rope was dead.

Leonardo put his arm around Niccolo's shoulders, as if to shield him from death. But he was suddenly afraid . . . afraid that his own "inevitable hour" might not be far away; and he remembered his recurring dream of falling into the abyss. He shivered, his breath came quick, and his skin felt clammy, as if he had just been jolted awake. Just now, on some deep level, he believed that the poisonous phantasms of dreams were real. If they took hold of the soul of the dreamer, they could affect his entire world.

Leonardo saw his Great Bird falling and breaking apart. And he was falling through cold depths that were as deep as the reflections of lanterns in dark water . . .

"Leonardo? *Leonardo!*"

"Do not worry. I am fine, my young friend," Leonardo said.

They talked very little until they were in the country, in the high, hilly land north of Florence. Here were meadows and grassy fields, valleys and secret grottos, small roads traversed by ox carts and pack trains, vineyards and cane thickets, dark copses of pine and chestnut and cypress, and olive trees that shimmered like silver hangings each time the wind breathed past their leaves. The deep red tiles of farmstead roofs and the brownish-pink colonnaded villas seemed to be part of the line and tone of the natural countryside. The clouds that had darkened the streets of Florence had disappeared; and the sun was high, bathing the countryside in that golden light particular to Tuscany, a light that purified and clarified as if it were itself the manifestation of desire and spirit.

And before them, in the distance, was Swan Mountain. It rose 1,300 feet to its crest, and looked to be pale gray-blue in the distance. Leonardo and Niccolo stopped in a meadow perfumed with flowers and gazed at the mountain. Leonardo felt his worries weaken, as they always did when he was in the country. He took a deep breath of the heady air and felt his soul awaken and quicken to the world of nature and the *oculus spiritalis:* the world of angels.

"That would be a good mountain from which to test your Great Bird," Niccolo said.

"I thought that, too, for it's very close to Florence. But I've since changed my mind. Vinci is not so far away; and there are good mountains there, too." Then after a pause, Leonardo said, "And I do not wish to die here. If death should be my fate, I wish it to be in familiar surroundings."

Niccolo nodded, and he looked as severe and serious as he had when Leonardo had first met him, like an old man inhabiting a boy's body.

"Come now, Nicco," Leonardo said, resting the cage on the ground and sitting down beside it, "let's enjoy this time, for who knows what awaits us later. Let's eat." With that, Leonardo spread out a cloth and set the food upon it as if it were a table. The hawks flapped their wings and slammed against the wooden bars of the cages. Leonardo tossed them each a small piece of sausage.

"I heard gossip in the piazza of the bird vendors that you refuse to eat meat," Niccolo said.

"Ah, did you, now. And what do you think of that?"

Niccolo shrugged. "Well, I have never seen you eat meat."

Leonardo ate a piece of bread and sausage, which he washed down with wine. "Now you have."

"But then why would people say that—"

"Because I don't usually eat meat. They're correct, for I believe that eating too much meat causes to collect what Aristotle defined as cold black bile. That, in turn, afflicts the soul with melancholia. Maestro Toscanelli's friend Ficino believes the same, but for all the wrong reasons. For him magic and astrology take precedence over reason and experience. But be that as it may, I must be very careful that people do not think of me as a follower of the Cathars, lest I be branded a heretic."

"I have not heard of them."

"They follow the teaching of the pope Bogomil, who believed that our entire visible world was created by the Adversary rather than by God. Thus to avoid imbibing the essence of Satan, they forfeit meat. Yet they eat vegetables and fish." Leonardo laughed and pulled a face to indicate that they were crazy. "They could at least be consistent."

Leonardo ate quickly, which was his habit, for he could never seem to enjoy savoring food as others did. He felt that eating, like sleeping, was simply a necessity that took him away from whatever interested him at the moment.

And there was a whole world pulsing in the sunlight around him; like a child, he wanted to investigate its secrets.

"Now . . . watch," he said to Niccolo, who was still eating; and he let loose one of the hawks. As it flew away, Leonardo made notes, scribbling with his left hand, and said, "You see, Nicco, it searches now for a current of the wind." He loosed the other one. "These birds beat their wings only until they reach the wind, which must be blowing at a great elevation, for look how high they soar. Then they are almost motionless."

Leonardo watched the birds circle overhead, then glide toward the mountains. He felt transported, as if he too were gliding in the empyrean heights. "They're hardly moving their wings now. They repose in the air as we do on a pallet."

"Perhaps you should follow their example."

"What do you mean?" Leonardo asked.

"Fix your wings on the Great Bird. Instead of beating the air, they would remain stationary."

"And by what mode would the machine be propelled?" Leonardo asked; but he answered his own question, for immediately the idea of the Archimedian screw came to mind. He remembered seeing children playing with toy whirlybirds: by pulling a string, a propeller would be made to rise freely into the air. His hand sketched, as if thinking on its own. He drew a series of sketches of leaves gliding back and forth, falling to the ground. He drew various screws and propellers. There might be something useful. . . .

"Perhaps if you could just catch the current, then you would not have need of human power," Niccolo said. "You could fix your bird to soar . . . somehow."

Leonardo patted Niccolo on the shoulder, for, indeed, the child was bright. But it was all wrong; it *felt* wrong. "No, my young friend," he said doggedly, as if he had come upon a wall that blocked his thought, "the wings must be able to row through the air like a bird's. That is nature's method, the most efficient way."

Restlessly, Leonardo wandered the hills. Niccolo finally complained of being tired and stayed behind, comfortably situated in a shady copse of mossy-smelling cypresses.

Leonardo walked on alone.

Everything was perfect: the air, the warmth, the smells and sounds of the country. He could almost apprehend the pure forms of everything around him, the phantasms reflected in the *proton organon:* the mirrors of his soul. But not quite. . . .

Indeed, something was wrong, for instead of the bliss, which Leonardo had so often experienced in the country, he felt thwarted . . . lost.

Thinking of the falling leaf, which he had sketched in his notebook, he wrote: *If a man has a tent roof of caulked linen twelve ells broad and twelve ells high, he will be able to let himself fall from any great height without danger to himself.* He imagined a pyramidal parachute, yet considered it too large and bulky and heavy to carry on the Great Bird. He wrote another hasty note: *Use leather bags, so a man falling from a height of six brachia will not injure himself, falling either into water or upon land.*

He continued walking, aimlessly. He sketched constantly, as if without conscious thought: grotesque figures and caricatured faces, animals, impossible mechanisms, studies of various madonnas with children, imaginary landscapes, and all manner of actual flora and fauna. He drew a three-dimensional diagram of a toothed gearing and pulley system, and an apparatus for making lead. He made a note to locate Albertus Magnus's *On Heaven and Earth*—perhaps Toscanelli had a copy. His thoughts seemed to flow like the Arno, from one subject to another, and yet he could not position himself in that psychic place of languor and bliss, which he imagined to be the perfect realm of Platonic forms.

As birds flew overhead, he studied them and sketched feverishly. Leonardo had an extraordinarily quick eye, and he could discern movements that others could not see. He wrote in tiny letters beside his sketches: *Just as we may see a small imperceptible movement of the rudder turn a ship of marvelous size loaded with very heavy cargo—and also amid such weight of water pressing upon its every beam and in the teeth of impetuous winds that envelop its mighty sails—so, too, do birds support themselves above the course of the winds without beating their wings. Just a slight movement of wing or tail, serving them to enter either below or above the wind, suffices to prevent their fall.* Then he added, *When, without the assistance of the wind and without beating its wings, the bird remains in the air in the position of equilibrium, this shows that the center of gravity is coincident with the center of resistance.*

"Ho, Leonardo," shouted Niccolo, who was running after him. The boy was out of breath; he carried the brown sack, which contained some leftover food, most likely, and Maestro Toscanelli's book. "You've been gone over three hours!"

"And is that such a long time?" Leonardo asked.

"It is for me. What are you doing?"

"Just walking . . . and thinking." After a beat, Leonardo said, "But you have a book, why didn't you read it?"

Niccolo smiled and said, "I tried, but then I fell asleep."

"So now we have the truth," Leonardo said. "Nicco, why don't you return to the *bottega*? I must remain here . . . to think. And you are obviously bored."

"That's all right, Maestro," Niccolo said anxiously. "If I can stay with you, I won't be bored, I promise."

Leonardo smiled, in spite of himself, and said, "Tell me what you've gleaned from the little yellow book."

"I can't make it out . . . yet. It seems to be all about light."

"So Maestro Toscanelli told me. Its writings are very old and concern memory and the circulation of light." Leonardo could not resist teasing his apprentice. "Do you find your memory much improved after reading it?"

Niccolo shrugged, as if it was of no interest to him, and Leonardo settled down in a grove of olive trees to read *The Secret of the Golden Flower*; it took him less than an hour, for the book was short. Niccolo ate some fruit and then fell asleep again, seemingly without any trouble. Most of the text seemed to be magical gibberish, yet suddenly these words seemed to open him up:

> There are a thousand spaces, and the light-flower of heaven and earth fills them all. Just so does the light-flower of the individual pass through heaven and cover the earth. And when the light begins to circulate, all of heaven and the earth, all the mountains and rivers—everything—begins to circulate with light. The key is to concentrate your own seed-flower in the eyes. But be careful, children, for if one day you do not practice meditation, this light will stream out, to be lost who knows where. . . .

Perhaps he fell asleep, for he imagined himself staring at the walls of his great and perfect mnemonic construct: the memory cathedral. It was pure white and smooth as dressed stone . . . it was a church for all his experience and knowledge, whether holy or profane. Maestro Toscanelli had taught him long ago how to construct a church in his imagination, a storage place of images—hundreds of thousands of them—which would represent everything Leonardo wished to re-member. Leonardo caught all the evanescent and ephemeral stuff of time and trapped it in this place . . . all the happenings of his life, everything he had seen and read and heard; all the pain and frustration and love and joy were neatly shelved and ordered inside the colonnaded courts, chapels, vestries, porches, towers, and crossings of his memory cathedral.

He longed to be inside, to return to sweet, comforting memory; he would dismiss the ghosts of fear that haunted its dark catacombs. But now he was seeing the cathedral from a distant height, from the summit of Swan Mountain, and it was as if his cathedral had somehow become a small part of what his memory held and his eyes saw. It was as if his soul could expand to fill heaven and earth, the past and the future. Leonardo experienced a sudden, vertiginous sensation of freedom; indeed, heaven and earth seemed to be filled with a thousand spaces. It was just as he had read in the ancient book: everything was circulating with pure light . . . blinding, cleansing light that coruscated down the hills and mountains like rainwater, that floated in the air like mist, that heated the grass and meadows to radiance.

He felt bliss.

Everything was preternaturally clear; it was as if he was seeing into the essence of things.

And then, with a shock, he felt himself slipping, falling from the mountain.

This was his recurrent dream, his nightmare: to fall without wings and harness into the void. Yet every detail registered: the face of the mountain, the mossy crevasses, the smells of wood and stone and decomposition, the screeing of a hawk, the glint of a stream below, the roofs of farmhouses, the geometrical demarcations of fields, and the spiraling wisps of cloud that seemed to be woven into the sky. But then he tumbled and descended into palpable darkness, into a frightful abyss that showed no feature and no bottom.

Leonardo screamed to awaken back into daylight, for he knew this blind place, which the immortal Dante had explored and described. But now he felt the horrid bulk of the flying monster Geryon beneath him, supporting him . . . this, the same beast that had carried Dante into *Malebolge:* the Eighth Circle of Hell. The monster was slippery with filth and smelled of death and putrefaction; the air itself was foul, and Leonardo could hear behind him the thrashing of the creature's scorpion tail. Yet it also seemed that he could hear Dante's divine voice whispering to him, drawing him through the very walls of Hades into blinding light.

But now he was held aloft by the Great Bird, his own invention. He soared over the trees and hills and meadows of Fiesole, and then south, to fly over the roofs and balconies and spires of Florence herself.

Leonardo flew without fear, as if the wings were his own flesh. He moved his arms easily, working the great wings that beat against the calm, spring air that was as warm as his own breath. But rather than resting upon his apparatus, he now hung below it. He operated a windlass with his hands to raise one set of wings and kicked a pedal with his heels to lower the other set of wings. Around his neck was a collar, which controlled a rudder that was effectively the tail of this bird.

This was certainly not the machine that hung in Verrocchio's *bottega.* Yet with its double set of wings, it seemed more like a great insect than a bird, and—

Leonardo awakened with a jolt, to find himself staring at a horse-fly feeding upon his hand.

Could he have been sleeping with his eyes open, or had this been a waking dream? He shivered, for his sweat was cold on his arms and chest. He shouted, awakening Niccolo, and immediately began sketching and writing in his notebook. "I have it!" he said to Niccolo. "Double wings like a fly will provide the power I need! You see, it is just as I told you: nature provides. Art and invention are merely imitation." He drew a man hanging beneath an apparatus with hand-operated cranks and pedals to work the wings. Then he studied the fly, which still buzzed around him, and wrote: *The lower wings are more slanting than those above, both as to length and as to breadth. The fly, when it hovers in the air upon its wings, beats its wings with great speed and din, raising them from the horizontal position up as high as the wing is long. And as it raises them, it brings them forward in a slanting position in such a way as almost to strike the air edgewise.* Then he drew a design for the rudder assembly. "How could I not have seen that, just as a ship needs a rudder, so, too, would my machine?" he said. "It will act as the tail of a bird. And by hanging the operator below the wings, equilibrium will be more easily maintained. There," he said, standing up and pulling Niccolo to his feet. "Perfection!"

He sang one of Lorenzo de' Medici's bawdy inventions and danced around Niccolo, who seemed confused by his master's strange behavior. He grabbed the boy's arms and swung him around in a circle.

"Perhaps the women watching you free the birds were right," Niccolo said. "Perhaps you *are* as mad as Ajax."

"Perhaps I am," Leonardo said, "but I have a lot of work to do, for the Great Bird must be changed if it is to fly for *Il Magnifico* next week." He placed the book of the Golden Flower in the sack, handed it to Niccolo, and began walking in the direction of the city.

It was already late afternoon.

"I'll help you with your machine," Niccolo said.

"Thank you, I'll need you for many errands."

That seemed to satisfy the boy. "Why did you shout and then dance as you did, Maestro?" Niccolo asked, concerned. He followed a step behind Leonardo, who seemed to be in a hurry.

Leonardo laughed and slowed his stride until Niccolo was beside him. "It's difficult to explain. Suffice it to say that solving the riddle of my Great Bird made me happy."

"But how did you do it? I thought you had fallen asleep."

"I had a dream," Leonardo said. "It was a gift from the poet Dante Alighieri."

"*He* gave you the answer?" Niccolo asked, incredulous.

"That he did, Nicco."

"Then you *do* believe in spirits?"

"No, Nicco—just in dreams."

Three

In the streets and markets, people gossiped of a certain hermit—a champion—who had come from Volterra, where he had been ministering to the lepers in a hospital. He had come here to preach and harangue and save the city. He was a young man, and some had claimed to have seen him walking barefoot past the Church of Salvatore. They said he was dressed in the poorest of clothes, with only a wallet on his back. His face was bearded and sweet, and his eyes were blue; certainly he was a manifestation of the Christ himself, stepping on the very paving stones that modern Florentines walked. He had declared that the days to follow would bring harrowings, replete with holy signs, for so he had been told by both the Angel Raphael and Saint John, who had appeared to him in their flesh, as men do to other men, and not in a dream.

It was said that he preached to the Jews in their poor quarter, and also to the whores and beggars; and he was also seen standing upon the *ringhiera* of the Signoria demanding an audience with the "Eight." But they sent him away. So now there could be no intercession for what was about to break upon Florence.

The next day, a Thursday, one of the small bells of Santa Maria del Fiore broke loose and fell, breaking the skull of a stonemason passing below. By a miracle, he lived, although a bone had to be removed from his head.

But it was seen as a sign, nevertheless.

And on Friday, a boy of twelve fell from the large bell of the Palagio and landed on the gallery. He died several hours later.

By week's end, four families in the city and eight in the Borgo di Ricorboli were stricken with fever and buboes, the characteristic swellings of what had come to be called "the honest plague." There were more reports of fever and death every day thereafter, for the Black Reaper was back upon the streets, wending his way through homes and hospitals, cathedrals and taverns, and whorehouses and nunneries alike. It was said that he had a companion, the hag Lachesis, who followed after him while she wove an ever-lengthening tapestry of death; hers was an accounting of "the debt we must all pay," created from her never-ending skein of black thread.

One hundred and twenty people had died in the churches and hospitals by *nella quidtadecima;* the full moon. There were twenty-five deaths alone at Santa Maria Nuova. The "Eight" of the Signoria duly issued a notice of health procedures to be followed by all Florentines; the price of foodstuffs rose drastically; and although Lorenzo's police combed the streets for the spectral hermit, he was nowhere to be found within the precincts of the city.

Lorenzo and his retinue fled to his villa at Careggi. But rather than follow suit and leave the city for the safety of the country, Verrocchio elected to remain in his *bottega.* He gave permission to his apprentices to quit the city until the plague abated, if they had the resources; but most, in fact, stayed with him.

The *bottega* seemed to be in a fervor.

One would think that the deadline for every commission was to-morrow. Verrocchio's foreman Francesco kept a tight and sure rein on the apprentices, pressing them into a twelve-to-fourteen-hour sched-ule; and they worked as they had when they constructed the bronze *palla* that topped the dome of Santa Maria del Fiore, as if quick hands and minds were the only weapons against the ennui upon which the Black Fever might feed. Francesco had become invaluable to Leo-nardo, for he was quicker with things mechanical than Verrocchio him-self; and Francesco helped him design an ingenious plan by which the flying machine could be collapsed and dismantled and camouflaged for easy transportation to Vinci. The flying machine, at least, was com-plete; again, thanks to Francesco, who made certain that Leonardo had a constant supply of strong-backed apprentices and material.

Leonardo's studio was a mess, a labyrinth of footpaths that wound past bolts of cloth, machinery, stacks of wood and leather, jars of paint, sawhorses, and various gearing devices; the actual flying machine took up the center of the great room. Surrounding it were drawings, insects mounted on boards, a table covered with birds and bats in various stages of vivisection, and constructions of the various parts of the re-designed flying machine—artificial wings, rudders, and flap valves.

The noxious odors of turpentine mixed with the various perfumes of decay; these smells disturbed Leonardo not at all, for they reminded him of his childhood, when he kept all manner of dead animals in his room to study and paint. All other work—the paintings and terra-cotta sculptures—were piled in one corner. Leonardo and Niccolo could no longer sleep in the crowded, foul-smelling studio; they had laid their pallets down in the young apprentice Tista's room.

Tista was a tall, gangly boy with a shock of blond hair. Although he was about the same age as Niccolo, it was as if he had become Nic-colo's apprentice. The boys had become virtually inseparable: Niccolo seemed to relish teaching Tista about life, art, and politics; but then Niccolo had a sure sense of how people behaved, even if he lacked experience. He was a natural teacher, more so than Leonardo. For Leonardo's part, he didn't mind having the other boy underfoot, and had, in fact, become quite fond of him. But Leonardo was preoccupied with his work. The Black Death had given him a reprieve—just enough time to complete and test his machine—for not only did *Il Magnifico* agree to rendezvous in Vinci rather than Pistoia, he himself set the date forward another fortnight.

It was unbearably warm in the studio as Niccolo helped Leonardo remove the windlass mechanism and twin "oars" from the machine, which were to be packed into a numbered, wooden container. "It's get-ting close," Niccolo said, after the parts were fitted securely into the box. "Tista tells me that he heard a family living near the Porta alla Croce caught the fever."

"Well, we shall be on our way at dawn," Leonardo said. "You shall have the responsibility of making certain that everything is properly loaded and in its proper place."

Niccolo seemed very pleased with that; he had, in fact, proven himself to be a capable worker and organizer. "But I still believe that we should wait until the dark effluviums have evaporated from the air.

At least until after the *becchini* have carried the corpses to their graves."

"Then we will leave after first light," Leonardo said.

"Good."

"You might be right about the possible contagion of corpses and *becchini*. But as to your effluviums . . ."

"Best not to take chances," Verrocchio said; he had been standing in the doorway and peering into the room like a boy who had not yet been caught sneaking through the house. He held the door partially closed, so that it framed him, as if he were posing for his own portrait; and the particular glow of the late afternoon sun seemed to transform and subdue his rather heavy features.

"I think it is as the astrologers say: a conjunction of planets," Verrocchio continued. "It was so during the great blight of 1345. But that was a conjunction of *three* planets. Very unusual. It will not be like that now, for the conjunction is not nearly so perfect."

"You'd be better to come to the country with us than listen to astrologers," Leonardo said.

"I cannot leave my family. I've told you."

"Then bring them along. My father is already in Vinci preparing the main house for Lorenzo and his retinue. You could think of it as a business holiday; think of the commissions that might fall your way."

"I think I have enough of those for the present," Andrea said.

"That does not sound like Andrea del Verrocchio," Leonardo said, teasing.

"My sisters and cousins refuse to leave," Andrea said. "And who would feed the cats?" he said, smiling, then sighing. He seemed resigned and almost relieved. "My fate is in the lap of the gods . . . as it has always been. And so is *yours*, my young friend."

The two-day journey was uneventful, and they soon arrived in Vinci.

The town of Leonardo's youth was a fortified keep dominated by a medieval castle and its campanile, surrounded by fifty brownish-pink brick houses. Their red tiled roofs were covered with a foliage of chestnut and pine and cypress, and vines of grape and cane thickets brought the delights of earth and shade to the very walls and windows. The town, with its crumbling walls and single arcaded alley, was situated on the elevated spur of a mountain; it overlooked a valley blanketed with olive trees that turned silver when stirred by the wind. Beyond was the valley of Lucca, green and purple-shadowed and ribboned with mountain streams; and Leonardo remembered that when the rain had cleansed the air, the crags and peaks of the Apuan Alps near Massa and Cozzile could be clearly seen.

Now that Leonardo was here, he realized how homesick he had been. The sky was clear and the air pellucid; but the poignancy of his memories clouded his vision, as he imagined himself being swept back to his childhood days, once again riding with his uncle Francesco, whom they called "*lazzarone*" because he did not choose to restrict his zealous enjoyment of life with a profession. But Leonardo and the much older Francesco had been like two privileged boys—princes, riding from farmstead to mill and all around the valley collecting rents for Leonardo's grandfather, the patriarch of the family: the gentle and punctilious Antonio da Vinci.

Leonardo led his apprentices down a cobbled road and past a rotating dovecote on a long pole to a cluster of houses surrounded by gardens, barns, peasant huts, tilled acreage, and the uniform copses of mulberry trees, which his uncle Francesco had planted. Francesco, "the lazy one," had been experimenting with sericulture, which could prove to be very lucrative indeed, for the richest and most powerful guild in Florence was the *arte della seta:* the silk weavers.

"Leonardo, ho!" shouted Francesco from the courtyard of the large, neatly kept, main house, which had belonged to Ser Antonio. It was stone and roofed with red tile, and looked like the ancient longhouses of the French; but certainly no animals would be kept in the home of Piero da Vinci: Leonardo's father.

Like his brother, Francesco had dark curly hair that was graying at the temples and thinning at the crown. Francesco embraced Leonardo, nearly knocking the wind out of him, and said, "You have caused substantial havoc in this house, my good nephew! Your father is quite anxious."

"I'm sure of that," Leonardo said as he walked into the hall. "It's wonderful to see you, Uncle."

Beyond this expansive, lofted room were several sleeping chambers, two fireplaces, a kitchen and pantry, and workrooms, which sometimes housed the peasants who worked the various da Vinci farmholds; there was a level above with three more rooms and a fireplace; and ten steps below was the cellar where Leonardo used to hide the dead animals he had found. The house was immaculate: how Leonardo's father must have oppressed the less-than-tidy Francesco and Alessandra to make it ready for Lorenzo and his guests.

Piero's third wife, Margherita di Guglielmo, was nursing his first legitimate son; no doubt that accorded her privileges.

This room was newly fitted-out with covered beds, chests, benches, and a closet cabinet to accommodate several of the lesser luminaries in *Il Magnifico's* entourage. Without a doubt, Leonardo's father would give the First Citizen his own bedroom.

Leonardo sighed. He craved his father's love, but their relationship had always been awkward and rather formal, as if Leonardo were his apprentice rather than his son.

Piero came down the stairs from his chamber above to meet Leonardo. He wore his magisterial robes and a brimless, silk berretta, as if he were expecting Lorenzo and his entourage at any moment. "Greetings, my son."

"Greetings to you, Father," Leonardo said, bowing.

Leonardo and his father embraced. Then, tightly grasping Leonardo's elbow, Piero asked, "May I take you away from your company for a few moments?"

"Of course, Father," Leonardo said politely, allowing himself to be led upstairs.

They entered a writing room, which contained a long, narrow clerical desk, a master's chair, and a sitting bench decorated with two octagonally shaped pillows; the floor was tiled like a chessboard. A clerk sat upon a stool behind the desk and made a great show of writing in a large, leather-bound ledger. Austere though the room appeared, it revealed a parvenu's taste for comfort; for Piero was eager to be addressed as *messere*, rather than *ser*, and to carry a sword, which was the prerogative of a knight. "Will you excuse us, Vittore?" Piero said to the clerk. The young man rose, bowed, and left the room.

"Yes, Father?" Leonardo asked, expecting the worst.

"I don't know whether to scold you or congratulate you."

"The latter would be preferable."

Piero smiled and said, "Andrea has apprised me that *Il Magnifico* has asked for you to work in his gardens."

"Yes."

"I am very proud."

"Thank you, Father."

"So you see, I was correct in keeping you to the grindstone."

Leonardo felt his neck and face grow warm. "You mean by taking everything I earned so I could not save enough to pay for my master's matriculation fee in the painters' guild?"

"That money went to support the family . . . your family."

"And now you—or rather the family—will lose that income."

"My concern is not, nor was it ever, the money," Piero said. "It was properly forming your character, of which I am still in some doubt."

"Thank you."

"I'm sorry, but as your father, it is my duty—" He paused. Then, as if trying to be more conciliatory, he said, "You could hardly do better than to have Lorenzo for a patron. But he would have never noticed you, if I had not made it possible for you to remain with Andrea."

"You left neither Andrea nor I any choice."

"Be that as it may, Master Andrea made certain that you produced and completed the projects he assigned to you. At least he tried to prevent you from running off and cavorting with your limp-wristed, degenerate friends."

"Ah, you mean those who are not in *Il Magnifico*'s retinue."

"Don't you dare to be insolent."

"I apologize, Father," Leonardo said, but he had become sullen.

"You're making that face again."

"I'm sorry if I offend you."

"You don't offend me, you—" He paused, then said, "You've put our family in an impossible position."

"What do you mean?"

"Your business here with the Medici."

"It does not please you to host the First Citizen?" Leonardo asked.

"You have made a foolish bet with him and will certainly become the monkey. Our name—"

"Ah, yes, that is, of course, all that worries you. But I shall not fail,

Father. You can then take full credit for any honor I might bring to our good name."

"Only birds and insects can fly."

"And those who bear the name da Vinci." But Piero would not be mollified. Leonardo sighed and said, "Father, I shall try not to disappoint you." He bowed respectfully and turned toward the door.

"Leonardo!" his father said, as if he were speaking to a child. "I have not excused you."

"May I be excused, then, Father?"

"Yes, you may." But then Piero called him back.

"Yes, Father?" Leonardo asked, pausing at the door.

"I forbid you to attempt this . . . experiment."

"I am sorry, Father, but I cannot turn tail now."

"I will explain to *Il Magnifico* that you are my firstborn."

"Thank you, but—"

"Your safety is my responsibility," Piero said, and then he said, "I worry for you!" Obviously, these words were difficult for him. If their relationship had been structured differently, Leonardo would have crossed the room to embrace his father; and they would have spoken directly. But as robust and lusty as Piero was, he could not accept any physical display of emotion.

After a pause, Leonardo asked, "Will you do me the honor of watching me fly upon the wind?" He ventured a smile. "It will be a da Vinci, not a Medici or a Pazzi, who will be soaring in the heavens closest to God."

"I suppose I shall have to keep up appearances," Piero said; then he raised an eyebrow, as if questioning his place in the scheme of these events. He looked at his son and smiled sadly.

Though once again Leonardo experienced the unbridgeable distance between himself and his father, the tension between them dissolved.

"You are welcome to remain here," Piero said.

"You will have little enough room when Lorenzo and his congregation arrive," Leonardo said. "And I shall need quiet in which to work and prepare; it's been fixed for us to lodge with Achattabrigha di Piero del Vacca."

"When are you expected?"

"We should leave now. Uncle Francesco said he would accompany us."

Piero nodded. "Please give my warmest regards to your mother."

"I shall be happy to do so."

"Are you at all curious to see your new brother?" Piero asked, as if it were an afterthought.

"Of course I am, Father."

Piero took his son's arm, and they walked to Margherita's bedroom. Leonardo could feel his father trembling.

And for those few seconds, he actually felt that he was his father's son.

Four

The Great Bird was perched on the edge of a ridge at the summit of a hill near Vinci that Leonardo had selected. It looked like a gigantic dragonfly, its fabric of fustian and silk sighing, as the expansive double wings shifted slightly in the wind. Niccolo, Tista, and Leonardo's stepfather Achattabrigha kneeled under the wings and held fast to the pilot's harness. Zoroastro da Peretola and Lorenzo di Credi, apprentices of Andrea Verrocchio, stood twenty-five feet apart and steadied the wingtips; it almost seemed that their arms were filled with outsized jousting pennons of blue and gold. These two could be taken as caricatures of *Il Magnifico* and his brother Giuliano, for Zoroastro was swarthy, rough-skinned, and ugly-looking beside the sweetly handsome Lorenzo di Credi. Such was the contrast between Lorenzo and Giuliano de' Medici, who stood with Leonardo a few feet away from the Great Bird. Giuliano looked radiant in the morning sun, while Lorenzo seemed to be glowering, although he was most probably simply concerned for Leonardo.

Zoroastro, ever impatient, looked toward Leonardo and shouted, "We're ready for you, Maestro."

Leonardo nodded, but Lorenzo caught him and said, "Leonardo, there is no need for this. I will love you as I do Giuliano, no matter whether you choose to fly . . . or let wisdom win out."

Leonardo smiled and said, "I will fly *fide et amore*."

By faith and love.

"You shall have both," Lorenzo said; and he walked beside Leonardo to the edge of the ridge and waved to the crowd standing far below on the edge of a natural clearing where Leonardo was to land triumphant. But the clearing was surrounded by a forest of pine and cypress, which from his vantage looked like a multitude of rough-hewn lances and halberds. A great shout went up, honoring the First Citizen: the entire village was there—from peasant to squire, invited for the occasion by *Il Magnifico,* who had erected a great, multicolored tent; his attendants and footmen had been cooking and preparing for a feast since dawn. His sister, Bianca, Angelo Poliziano, Pico della Mirandola, Bartolomeo della Scala, and Leonardo's friend Sandro Botticelli were down there, too, hosting the festivities.

They were all on tenterhooks, eager for the Great Bird to fly.

Leonardo waited until Lorenzo had received his due; but then, not to be outdone, he, too, bowed and waved his arms theatrically. The crowd below cheered their favorite son, and Leonardo turned away to position himself in the harness of his flying machine. He had seen his mother, Caterina, a tiny figure nervously looking upward, whispering devotions, her hand cupped above her eyes to cut the glare of the sun. Piero did not speak to Leonardo. His already formidable face was drawn and tight, just as if he were standing before a magistrate awaiting a decision on a case.

Lying down in a prone position on the foreshortened plank pallet below the wings and windlass mechanism, Leonardo adjusted the loop around his head, which controlled the rudder section of the Great Bird, and he tested the hand cranks and foot stirrups, which raised and lowered the wings.

"Be careful," shouted Zoroastro, who had stepped back from the moving wings. "Are you trying to kill us?"

There was nervous laughter, but Leonardo was quiet. Achattabrigha tied the straps that would hold Leonardo fast to his machine and said, "I shall pray for your success, Leonardo, my son. I love you."

Leonardo turned to his stepfather, smelled the good odors of Caterina's herbs—garlic and sweet onion—on his breath and clothes, and looked into the old man's squinting, pale blue eyes; and it came to him then, with the force of buried emotion, that he loved this man who had spent his life sweating by kiln fires and thinking with his great, yellow-nailed hands. "I love you, too, . . . Father. And I feel safe in your prayers."

That seemed to please Achattabrigha, for he checked the straps one last time, kissed Leonardo, and patted his shoulder; then he stepped away, as reverently as if he were backing away from an icon in a cathedral.

"Good luck, Leonardo," Lorenzo said.

The others wished him luck. His stepfather nodded and smiled; and Leonardo, taking the weight of the Great Bird upon his back, lifted himself. Niccolo, Zoroastro, and Lorenzo di Credi helped him to the very edge of the ridge.

A cheer went up from below.

"Maestro, I wish it were me," Niccolo said. Tista stood beside him, looking longingly at Leonardo's flying mechanism.

"Just watch this time, Nicco," Leonardo said, and he nodded to Tista. "Pretend it is you who is flying in the heavens, for this machine is also yours. And you will be with me."

"Thank you, Leonardo."

"Now step away . . . for we must fly," Leonardo said; and he looked down, as if for the first time, as if every tree and upturned face were magnified; every smell, every sound and motion were clear and distinct. In some way the world had separated into its component elements, all in an instant; and in the distance, the swells and juttings of land were like that of a green sea with long, trailing shadows of brown; and upon those motionless waters were all the various constructions of human habitation: church and campanile and shacks and barns and cottages and furrowed fields.

Leonardo felt sudden vertigo as his heart pounded in his chest. A breeze blew out of the northwest, and Leonardo felt it flow around him like a breath. The treetops rustled, whispering, as warm air drifted skyward. Thermal updrafts flowing invisibly to heaven. Pulling at him. His wings shuddered in the gusts; and Leonardo knew that it must be now, lest he be carried off the cliff unprepared.

He launched himself, pushing off the precipice as if he were diving from a cliff into the sea. For an instant, as he swooped downward, he felt euphoria. He was flying, carried by the wind, which embraced him in its cold grip. Then came heart-pounding, nauseating fear. Although he strained at the windlass and foot stirrups, which caused his great, fustian wings to flap, he could not keep himself aloft. His pushings and kickings had become almost reflexive from hours of practice: one leg thrust backward to lower one pair of wings while he furiously worked the windlass with his hands to raise the other, turning his hands first to the left, then to the right. He worked the mechanism with every bit of his calculated two-hundred-pound force, and his muscles ached from the strain. Although the Great Bird might function as a glider, there was too much friction in the gears to effect enough propulsive power; and the wind resistance was too strong. He could barely raise the wings.

He fell.

The chilling, cutting wind became a constant sighing in his ears. His clothes flapped against his skin like the fabric of his failing wings, while hills, sky, forest, and cliffs spiraled around him, then fell away; and he felt the damp shock of his recurring dream, his nightmare of falling into the void.

But he was falling through soft light, itself as tangible as butter. Below him was the familiar land of his youth, rising against all logic, rushing skyward to claim him. He could see his father's house, and there in the distance the Apuan Alps, and the ancient cobbled road built before Rome was an empire. His sensations took on the textures of dream; and he prayed, surprising himself even then, as he looked into the purple shadows of the impaling trees below. Still, he doggedly pedaled and turned the windlass mechanism.

All was calmness and quiet, but for the wind wheezing in his ears, like the sea heard in a conch shell. His fear left him, carried away by the same breathing wind.

Then he felt a subtle bursting of warm air around him.

And suddenly, impossibly, vertiginously, he was ascending.

His wings were locked straight out. They were not flapping. Yet still he rose. It was as if God's hand were lifting Leonardo to Heaven; and he, Leonardo, remembered loosing his hawks into the air and watching them search for the currents of wind, which they used to soar into the highest of elevations, their wings motionless.

Thus did Leonardo rise in the warm air current—his mouth open to relieve the pressure constantly building in his ears—until he could see the top of the mountain . . . it was about a thousand feet below him. The country of hills and streams and farmland and forest had diminished, had become a neatly patterned board of swirls and rectangles: proof of man's work on earth. The sun seemed brighter at this elevation, as if the air itself was less dense in these attenuated regions. Leonardo feared now that he might be drawing too close to the region where air turned to fire.

He turned his head, pulling the loop that connected to the rudder; and found that he could, within bounds, control his direction. But then he stopped soaring; it was as if the warm bubble of air that had contained him had suddenly burst. He felt a chill.

The air became cold . . . and still.

He worked furiously at the windlass, thinking that he would beat his wings as birds do until they reach the wind; but he could not gain enough forward motion.

Once again, he fell like an arcing arrow.

Although the wind resistance was so great that he couldn't pull the wings below a horizontal position, he had developed enough speed to attain lift. He rose for a few beats, but, again, could not push his mechanism hard enough to maintain it, and another gust struck him, pummeling the Great Bird with phantomic fists.

Leonardo's only hope was to gain another warm thermal.

Instead, he became caught in a riptide of air that was like a blast, pushing the flying machine backward. He had all he could do to keep the wings locked in a horizontal position. He feared they might be torn away by the wind; and, indeed, the erratic gusts seemed to be conspiring to press him back down upon the stone face of the mountain.

Time seemed to slow for Leonardo; and in one long second he glimpsed the clearing surrounded by forest, as if forming a bull's-eye. He saw the tents and the townspeople who craned their necks to goggle up at him; and in this wind-wheezing moment, he suddenly gained a new, unfettered perspective. As if it were not he who was falling to his death.

Were his neighbors cheering? he wondered. Or were they horrified and dumbfounded at the sight of one of their own falling from the sky? More likely they were secretly wishing him to fall, their deepest desires not unlike the crowd that had recently cajoled a poor, lovesick peasant boy to jump from a rooftop onto the stone pavement of the Via Calimala.

The ground was now only three hundred feet below. A hawk was caught in the same trap of wind as Leonardo; and as he watched, the bird veered away, banking, and flew downwind. Leonardo shifted his weight, manipulated the rudder, and changed the angle of the wings. Thus he managed to follow the bird. His arms and legs felt like leaden weights, but he held on to his small measure of control.

Still he fell.

Two hundred feet.

He could hear the crowd shouting below him as clearly as if he were among them. People scattered, running to get out of Leonardo's way. He thought of his mother, Caterina, for most men call upon their mothers at the moment of death.

And he followed the hawk, as if it were his inspiration, his own Beatrice.

And the ground swelled upward.

Then Leonardo felt as if he was suspended over the deep, green canopy of forest, but only for an instant. He felt a warm swell of wind; and the Great Bird rose, riding the thermal. Leonardo looked for the hawk, but it had disappeared as if it had been a spirit, rising without weight through the various spheres toward the primum mobile. He tried to control his flight, his thoughts toward landing in one of the fields beyond the trees.

The thermal carried him up; then, just as quickly, as if teasing him, burst. Leonardo tried to keep his wings fixed, and glided upwind for a few seconds. But a gust caught him, once again pushing him backward, and he fell—

Slapped back to earth.

Hubris.

I have come home to die.

His father's face scowled at him.

Leonardo had failed.

Five

Even after three weeks, the headaches remained.

Leonardo had suffered several broken ribs and a concussion when he fell into the forest, swooping between the thick, purple cypress trees, tearing like tissue the wood and fustian of the Great Bird's wings. His face was already turning black when Lorenzo's footmen found him. He recuperated at his father's home; but Lorenzo insisted on taking him to Villa Careggi, where he could have his own physicians attend to him. With the exception of Lorenzo's personal dentator, who soaked a sponge in opium, morel juice, and hyoscyamus and extracted his broken tooth as Leonardo slept and dreamed of falling, they did little more than change his bandages, bleed him with leeches, and cast his horoscope.

Leonardo was more than relieved when the plague finally abated enough so that he could return to Florence. He was hailed as a hero, for Lorenzo had made a public announcement from the *ringhiera* of the Palazzo Vecchio that the artist from Vinci had, indeed, flown in the air like a bird. But the gossip among the educated was that, instead, Leonardo had fallen like Icarus, whom it was said he resembled in hubris. He received an anonymous note that seemed to say it all: *victus honor.*

Honor to the vanquished.

Leonardo would accept none of the countless invitations to attend various masques and dinners and parties. He was caught up in a frenzy of work. He could not sleep; and when he would lose consciousness from sheer exhaustion, he would dream he was falling through the sky. He would see trees wheeling below him, twisting as if they were machines in an impossible torture chamber.

Leonardo was certain that the dreams would cease only when he conquered the air; and although he did not believe in ghosts or superstition, he was pursued by demons every bit as real as those conjured by the clergy he despised and mocked. So he worked, as if in a frenzy. He constructed new models and filled up three folios with his sketches and mirror-script notes. Niccolo and Tista would not leave him, except to bring him food, and Andrea Verrocchio came upstairs a few times a day to look in at his now-famous apprentice.

"Haven't you yet had your bellyful of flying machines?" Andrea impatiently asked Leonardo. It was dusk, and dinner had already been served to the apprentices downstairs. Niccolo hurried to clear a place on the table so Andrea could put down the two bowls of boiled meat he had brought. Leonardo's studio was in its usual state of disarray, but the old flying machine, the insects mounted on boards, the vivisected birds and bats, the variously designed wings, rudders, and valves for the Great Bird were gone, replaced by new drawings, new mechanisms for testing wing designs (for now the wings would remain fixed), and various large-scale models of free-flying whirlybird toys, which had been in use since the 1300s. He was experimenting with inverted cones— Archimedian screws—to cheat gravity, and he studied the geometry of children's tops to calculate the principle of the flywheel. Just as a ruler whirled rapidly in the air will guide the arm by the line of the edge of the flat surface, so did Leonardo envision a machine powered by a flying propeller. Yet he could not help but think that such mechanisms were against nature, for air was a fluid, like water. And nature, the protoplast of all man's creation, had not invented rotary motion.

Leonardo pulled the string of a toy whirlybird, and the tiny four-bladed propeller spun into the air, as if in defiance of all natural laws. "No, Andrea, I have not lost my interest in this most sublime of inventions. *Il Magnifico* has listened to my ideas, and he is enthusiastic that my next machine will remain aloft."

Verrocchio watched the red propeller glide sideways into a stack of books: *De Onesta Volutta* by Il Platina, the *Letters of Filefo,* Pliny's *Historia naturalis,* Dati's *Trattato della sfera,* and Ugo Benzo's *On the Preservation of the Health.* "And Lorenzo has offered to recompense you for these . . . experiments?"

"Such an invention would revolutionize the very nature of warfare," Leonardo insisted. "I've developed an exploding missile that looks like a dart and could be dropped from my Great Bird. I've also been experimenting with improvements on the harquebus, and I have a design for a giant ballista, a crossbow of a kind never before imagined. I've designed a cannon with many racks of barrels that—"

"Indeed," Verrocchio said. "But I have advised you that it is unwise to put your trust in Lorenzo's momentary enthusiasms."

"Certainly the First Citizen has more than a passing interest in armaments."

"Is that why he ignored your previous memorandum wherein you proposed the very same ideas?"

"That was before, and this is now."

"Ah, certainly," Andrea said, nodding his head. Then after a pause, he said, "Stop this foolishness, Leonardo. You're a painter, and a painter should *paint*. Why have you been unwilling to work on any of the commissions I have offered you? And you've refused many other good offers. You have no money; and you've gained yourself a bad reputation."

"I will have more than enough money after the world watches my flying machine soar into the heavens."

"You are lucky to be alive, Leonardo! Have you not looked at yourself in a mirror? And you nearly broke your spine. Are you so intent upon doing so again? Or will killing yourself suffice?" He shook his head, as if angry at himself. "You've become skinny as a rail and sallow as an old man. Do you eat what we bring you? Do you sleep? Do you *paint*? No, nothing but invention, nothing but . . . *this*." He waved his arm at the models and mechanisms that lay everywhere. Then in a soft voice, he said, "I blame myself. I should have never allowed you to proceed with all this in the first place. You need a strong hand."

"When Lorenzo sees what I have—"

Andrea made a *tss*ing sound by tapping the roof of his mouth with his tongue. "I bid thee good night. Leonardo, eat your food before it gets cold. Niccolo, see that he eats."

"Andrea?" Leonardo said.

"Yes?"

"What has turned you against me?"

"My love for you. . . . Forget invention and munitions and flying toys! You are a *painter*. Paint!"

"I cannot," Leonardo answered, but in a voice so low that no one else could hear.

Six

"Stop it, that hurts!" Tista said to Niccolo, who had pulled him away from Leonardo's newest flying machine and held his arm behind him, as if to break it.

"Do you promise to stay away from the Maestro's machine?" Niccolo asked.

"Yes, I promise."

Niccolo let go of the boy, who backed nervously away from him. Leonardo stood a few paces away, oblivious to them, and stared down the mountainside to the valley below. Mist flowed dreamlike down its grassy slopes; in the distance, surrounded by grayish-green hills, was

Florence, its Duomo and the high tower of the Palazzo Vecchio golden in the early sunlight. It was a brisk morning in early March, but it would be a warm day. The vapor from Leonardo's exhalations was faint. He had come here to test his glider, which now lay nearby, its large, arched wings lashed to the ground. Leonardo had taken Niccolo's advice. This flying machine had fixed wings and no motor. It was a glider. His plan was to master flight; when he developed a suitable engine to power his craft, he would then know how to control it. And this machine was more in keeping with Leonardo's ideas of nature, for he would wear the wings, as if he were, indeed, a bird; he would hang from the wings, legs below, head and shoulders above, and control them by swinging his legs and shifting his weight. He would be like a bird soaring, sailing, gliding.

But he had put off flying the contraption for the last two days that they had camped here. Even though he was certain that its design was correct, he had lost his nerve. He was afraid. He just could not do it.

But he *had* to. . . .

He could feel Niccolo and Tista watching him.

He kicked at some loamy dirt and decided that he would do it now. He would not think about it. If he was to die . . . then so be it. Could falling out of the sky be worse than being a coward?

But he was too late, too late by a breath.

Niccolo shouted.

Startled, Leonardo turned to see that Tista had torn loose the rope that anchored the glider to the ground and had pulled himself through the opening between the wings. Leonardo shouted "Stop!" and rushed toward him, but Tista threw himself over the crest before either Leonardo or Niccolo could stop him. In fact, Leonardo had to grab Niccolo, who almost fell from the mountain in pursuit of his friend.

Tista's cry carried through the chill, thin air, but it was a cry of joy as the boy soared through the empty sky. He circled the mountain, catching the warmer columns of air, and then descended.

"Come back," Leonardo shouted through cupped hands, yet he could not help but feel an exhilaration, a thrill. The machine worked! But it was he, Leonardo, who needed to be in the air.

"Maestro, I tried to stop him!" Niccolo cried.

But Leonardo ignored him, for the weather suddenly changed,

and buffeting wind began to whip around the mountain. "Stay away from the slope!" Leonardo called. But he could not be heard; and he watched helplessly as the glider pitched upward, caught by a gust. It stalled in the chilly air, and then fell like a leaf. "Swing your hips forward!" Leonardo shouted. The glider could be brought under control. If the boy were practiced, it would not be difficult at all. But he wasn't, and the glider slid sideways, crashing into the mountain.

Niccolo screamed, and Leonardo discovered that he, too, was screaming.

Tista was tossed out of the harness. Grabbing at brush and rocks, he fell about fifty feet.

By the time Leonardo reached him, the boy was almost unconscious. He lay between two jagged rocks, his head thrown back, his back twisted, arms and legs akimbo.

"Where do you feel pain?" Leonardo asked as he tried to make the boy as comfortable as he could. There was not much that could be done, for Tista's back was broken, and a rib had pierced the skin. Niccolo kneeled beside Tista; his face was white, as if drained of blood.

"I feel no pain, Maestro. Please do not be angry with me." Niccolo took his hand.

"I am not angry, Tista. But why did you do it?"

"I dreamed every night that I was flying. In your contraption, Leonardo. The very one. I could not help myself. I planned how I would do it." He smiled wanly. "And I did it."

"That you did," whispered Leonardo, remembering his own dream of falling. Could one dreamer affect another?

"Niccolo? . . ." Tista called in barely a whisper.

"I am here."

"I cannot see very well. I see the sky, I think."

Niccolo looked to Leonardo, who could only shake his head.

When Tista shuddered and died, Niccolo began to cry and beat his hands against the sharp rocks, bloodying them. Leonardo embraced him, holding his arms tightly and rocking him back and forth as if he were a baby. All the while he did so, he felt revulsion; for he could not help himself, he could not control his thoughts, which were as hard and cold as reason itself.

Although his flying machine had worked—or *would* have worked successfully, if he, Leonardo, had taken it into the air—he had *another* idea for a Great Bird.

One that would be safe.

As young Tista's inchoate soul rose to the heavens like a kite in the wind, Leonardo imagined just such a machine.

A child's kite. . . .

"So it is true, you are painting," Andrea Verrocchio said, as he stood in Leonardo's studio. Behind him stood Niccolo and Sandro Botticelli.

Although the room was still cluttered with his various instruments and machines and models, the tables had been cleared, and the desiccated corpses of birds and animals and insects were gone. The ripe odors of rot were replaced with the raw, pungent fumes of linseed oil and varnish and paint. Oil lamps inside globes filled with water—another of Leonardo's inventions—cast cones of light in the cavernous room; he had surrounded himself and his easel with the brightest of these watery lamps, which created a room of light within the larger room that seemed to be but mere appearance.

"But what kind of painting is *this*?" Andrea asked. "Did the Anti-Christ need to decorate the dark walls of his church? I could believe that only he could commission such work!"

Leonardo grimaced and cast an angry look at Niccolo for bringing company into his room when he was working. Since Tista had died, he had taken to sleeping during the day and painting all night. He turned to Verrocchio. "I'm only following your advice, Maestro. You said that a painter paints."

"Indeed, I did. But a painter does not paint for himself, in the darkness, as you are doing." Yet even as he spoke, he leaned toward the large canvas Leonardo was working on, casting his shadow over a third of it. He seemed fascinated with the central figure of a struggling man being carried into Hell by the monster Geryon; man and beast were painted with such depth and precision that they looked like tiny live figures trapped in amber. The perspective of the painting was dizzying, for it was a glimpse into the endless shafts and catacombs of Hell; indeed, Paolo Uccello, may he rest in peace, would have been proud of such work, for he had lived for the beauties of perspective.

"Leonardo, I have called upon you twice . . . why did you turn me away?" Sandro asked. "And why have you not responded to any of my letters?" He looked like a younger version of Master Andrea, for he had the same kind of wide, fleshy face, but Botticelli's jaw was stronger; and while Verrocchio's lips were thin and tight, Sandro's were heavy and sensuous.

"I have not received anyone," Leonardo said, stepping out of the circle of light. Since Tista was buried, his only company was Niccolo, who would not leave his master.

"And neither have you responded to the invitations of the First Citizen," Verrocchio said, meaning Lorenzo de' Medici.

"Is that why you're here?" Leonardo asked Sandro. Even in the lamplight, he could see a blush in his friend's cheeks, for he was part of the Medici family; Lorenzo loved him as he did his own brother, Giuliano.

"I'm here because I'm worried about *you,* as is Lorenzo. You have done the same for me, or have you forgotten?"

No, Leonardo had not forgotten. He remembered when Sandro had almost died of love for Lorenzo's mistress, Simonetta Vespucci. He remembered how Sandro had lost weight and dreamed even when he was awake; how Pico della Mirandola had exorcised him in the presence of Simonetta and Lorenzo; and how he, Leonardo, had taken care of him until he regained his health.

"So you think I am in need of Messere Mirandola's services?" Leonardo asked. "Is that it?"

"I think you need to see your friends. I think you need to come awake in the light and sleep in the night. I think you must stop grieving for the child Tista."

Leonardo was about to respond, but caught himself. He wasn't grieving for Tista. Niccolo was, certainly. But he, Leonardo, was simply working.

Working through his fear and guilt and . . .

Grief.

For it was, somehow, as if *he* had fallen and broken his spine, as perhaps, he should have when he fell from the mountain ledge as a child.

"Leonardo, why are you afraid?" Niccolo asked. "The machine . . . worked. It *will* fly."

"And so you wish to fly it, too?" Leonardo asked, but it was more a statement than a question; he was embarrassed and vexed that Niccolo would demean him in front of Verrocchio.

But, indeed, the machine *had* worked.

"I am going back to bed," Verrocchio said, bowing to Sandro. "I will leave you to try to talk sense into my apprentice." He looked at Leonardo and smiled, for both knew that he was an apprentice in name only. But Leonardo would soon have to earn his keep; for Verrocchio's patience was coming to an end. He gazed at Leonardo's painting. "You know, the good monks of St. Bernard might just be interested in such work as this. Perhaps I might suggest that they take your painting instead of the altarpiece you owe them."

Leonardo could not help but laugh, for he knew that his master was serious.

After Verrocchio left, Leonardo and Sandro sat down on a cassone together under one of the dirty high windows of the studio; Niccolo sat before them on the floor; he was all eyes and ears and attention.

"Nicco, bring us some wine," Leonardo said.

"I want to be *here*."

Leonardo did not argue with the boy. It was unimportant, and once the words were spoken, forgotten. Leonardo gazed upward. He could see the sky through the window; the stars were brilliant, for Florence was asleep and its lanterns did not compete with the stars. "I thought I could get so close to them," he said, as if talking to himself. He imagined the stars as tiny pricks in the heavenly fabric; he could even now feel the heat from the region of fire held at bay by the darkness; and as if he could truly see through imagination, he watched himself soaring in his flying machine, climbing into the black heavens, soaring, reaching, to burn like paper for one glorious instant, into those hot, airy regions above the clouds and night.

But this flying machine he imagined was like no other device he had ever sketched or built. He had reached beyond nature to conceive a child's kite with flat surfaces to support it in the still air. Like his dragonfly contraption, it would have double wings, cellular open-ended boxes that would be as stable as kites of like construction.

Stable . . . and safe.

The pilot would not need to shift his balance to keep control. He would float on the air like a raft. Tista would not have lost his balance and fallen out of the sky in this contraption.

"Leonardo . . . _Leonardo!_ Have you been listening to anything I've said?"

"Yes, Little Bottle, I hear you." Leonardo was one of a very small circle of friends who was permitted to call Sandro by his childhood nickname.

"Then I can tell Lorenzo that you will demonstrate your new flying machine? It would not be wise to refuse him, Leonardo. He has finally taken notice of you. He needs you now; his enemies are everywhere."

Leonardo nodded.

Indeed, the First Citizen's relationship with the ambitious Pope Sixtus IV was at a breaking point, and all of Florence lived in fear of excommunication and war.

"Florence must show its enemies that it is invincible," Sandro continued. "A device that can rain fire from the sky would deter even the Pope!"

"I knew that Lorenzo could not long ignore my inventions," Leonardo said, although he was surprised.

"He plans to elevate you to the position of Master of Engines and Captain of Engineers."

"Should I thank you for this, Little Bottle?" Leonardo asked. "Lorenzo would have no reason to think that my device would work. Rather the opposite, as it killed my young apprentice."

"God rest his soul," Sandro said.

Leonardo continued. "Unless someone whispered in Lorenzo's ear. I fear you have gone from being artist to courtier, Little Bottle."

"The honors go to Niccolo," Sandro said. "It is he who convinced Lorenzo."

"This is what you've been waiting for, Maestro," Niccolo said. "I will find Francesco at first light and tell him to help you build another Great Bird. And I'll get the wine right now."

"Wait a moment," Leonardo said, then directed himself to Sandro. "How did Nicco convince Lorenzo?"

"You sent me with a note for the First Citizen, Maestro, when you couldn't accept his invitation to attend Simonetta's ball," Niccolo said.

"I told him of our grief over Tista, and then I also had to explain what had happened. Although I loved Tista, *he* was at fault. Not our machine. . . . Lorenzo understood."

"Ah, did he now?"

"I only did as you asked," Niccolo insisted.

"And did you speak to him about my bombs?" Leonardo asked.

"Yes, Maestro."

"And did he ask you, or did you volunteer this information?"

Niccolo glanced nervously at Sandro, as if he would supply him with the answer. "I thought you would be pleased. . . ."

"I think you may get the wine now," Sandro said to Niccolo, who did not miss the opportunity to flee. Then he directed himself to Leonardo. "You should have congratulated Niccolo, not berated him. Why were you so hard on the boy?"

Leonardo gazed across the room at his painting in the circle of lamps. He desired only to paint, not construct machines to kill children; he would paint his dreams, which had fouled his waking life with their strength and startling detail. By painting them, by exposing them, he might free himself. Yet ideas for his great Kite seemed to appear like chiaroscuro on the painting of his dream of falling, as if it were a notebook.

Leonardo shivered, for his dreams had spilled out of his sleep and would not let him go. Tonight, they demanded to be painted.

Tomorrow, they would demand to be *built*.

He yearned to step into the cold, perfect spaces of his memory cathedral, which had become his haven. There he could imagine each painting, each dream, and lock it in its own dark, private room. As if every experience, every pain, could be so isolated.

"Well? . . ." Sandro asked.

"I will apologize to Niccolo when he returns," Leonardo said.

"Leonardo, was Niccolo right? Are you afraid? I'm your best friend, certainly you can—"

Just then Niccolo appeared with a bottle of wine.

"I am very tired, Little Bottle," Leonardo said. "Perhaps we can celebrate another day. I will take your advice and sleep . . . to come awake in the light."

That was, of course, a lie, for Leonardo painted all night and the next day. It was as if he had to complete a month's worth of ideas in a few hours. Ideas seemed to explode in his mind's eye, paintings complete; all that Leonardo had to do was trace them onto canvas and mix his colors. It was as if he had somehow managed to unlock doors in his memory cathedral and glimpse what St. Augustine had called the present of things future; it was as if he were glimpsing ideas he *would* have, paintings he *would* paint; and he knew that if he didn't capture these gifts now, he would lose them forever. Indeed, it was as if he were dreaming whilst awake, and, during these hours, whether awake or slumped over before the canvas in a catnap or a trance, he had no control over the images that glowed in his mind like the lanterns placed on the floor, cassones, desks, and tables around him, rings of light, as if everything were but different aspects of Leonardo's dream . . . Leonardo's conception. He worked in a frenzy, which was always how he worked when his ideas caught fire; but this time he had no conscious focus or goal. Rather than a frenzy of discovery, this was a kind of remembering.

By morning, he had six paintings under way; one was a Madonna, transcendently radiant, as if Leonardo had lifted the veil of human sight to reveal the divine substance. The others seemed to be grotesque visions of hell that would only be matched by a young Dutch contemporary of Leonardo's: Hieronymus Bosch. There was a savage cruelty in these pictures of fabulous monsters with gnashing snouts, bat's wings, crocodile's jaws, and scaly pincered tails, yet every creature, every caricature and grotesquerie, had a single haunting human feature: chimeras with soft, sad human eyes or womanly limbs or the angelic faces of children, taunting and torturing the fallen in the steep, dark mountainous wastes of Hell.

As promised, Niccolo fetched Verrocchio's foreman Francesco to supervise the rebuilding of Leonardo's flying machine; but not at first light, as he had promised, for the exhausted Niccolo had slept until noon. Leonardo had thought that Niccolo was cured of acting independently on his master's behalf, but obviously the boy was not contrite, for he had told Leonardo that he was going downstairs to bring back some meat and fruit for lunch and returned with Francesco.

But Leonardo surprised both of them by producing a folio of sketches, diagrams, plans, and design measurements for kites and for two- and three-winged soaring machines. Some had curved surfaces, some had flat surfaces; but all these drawings and diagrams were based on the idea of open-ended boxes . . . groups of them placed at the ends of timber spars. There were detailed diagrams of triplane and biplane gliders, with wingspan and supporting surface measurements; even on paper, these machines looked awkward and heavy and bulky, for they did not imitate nature. He had tried imitation, but nature was capricious, unmanageable. Now he would *conquer* it. *Vince la natura.* Not even Tista could fall from these rectangular rafts. Leonardo had scribbled notes below two sketches of cellular kites, but not in his backward script; this was obviously meant to be readable to others: *Determine whether kite with cambered wings will travel farther. Fire from crossbow to ensure accuracy.* And on another page, a sketch of three kites flying in tandem, one above the other, and below a figure on a sling seat: *Total area of surface sails 476 ells. Add kites with sails of 66 ells to compensate for body weight over 198 pounds. Shelter from wind during assembly, open kites one at a time, then pull away supports to allow the wind to get under the sails. Tether the last kite, lest you be carried away.*

"Can you produce these kites for me by tomorrow?" Leonardo asked Francesco, as he pointed to the sketch. "I've provided all the dimensions."

"Impossible," Francesco said. "Perhaps when your flying machine for the First Citizen is finished—"

"This *will* be for the First Citizen," Leonardo insisted.

"I was instructed to rebuild the flying machine in which young Tista was . . . in which he suffered his accident."

"By whom? Niccolo?"

"Leonardo, Maestro Andrea has interrupted work on the altarpiece for the Chapel of Saint Bernard to build your contraption for the First Citizen. When that's completed, I'll help you build these . . . kites."

Leonardo knew Francesco well; he wouldn't get anywhere by cajoling him. He nodded and sat down before the painting of a Madonna holding the Christ, who, in turn, was holding a cat. The painting seemed to be movement itself.

"Don't you wish to supervise the work, Maestro?" asked the foreman.

"No, I'll begin constructing the kites, with Niccolo."

"Maestro, Lorenzo expects us—you—to demonstrate your Great Bird in a fortnight. You and Sandro agreed."

"Sandro is not the First Citizen." Then after a pause, "I have better ideas for soaring machines."

"But they cannot be built in time, Maestro," Niccolo insisted.

"Then no machine will be built."

And with that, Leonardo went back to his painting of the Madonna, which bore a sensual resemblance to Lorenzo's mistress Simonetta.

Which would be a gift for Lorenzo.

Seven

After a short burst of pelting rain, steady winds seemed to cleanse the sky of the gray storm clouds that had suffocated the city for several days. It had also been humid, and the air, which tasted dirty, had made breathing difficult. Florentine citizens closed their shutters against the poisonous miasmas, which were currently thought to be the cause of the deadly buboes, and were, at the very least, ill omens. But Leonardo, who had finally completed building his tandem kites after testing design after design, did not even know that a disaster had befallen Verrocchio's *bottega* when rotten timbers in the roof gave way during the storm. He and Niccolo had left to test the kites in a farmer's field nestled in a windy valley that also afforded privacy. As Leonardo did not want Zoroastro or Lorenzo di Credi, or anyone else along, he designed a sled so he could haul his lightweight materials himself.

"Maestro, are you going to make your peace with Master Andrea?" Niccolo asked as they waited for the midmorning winds, which were the strongest. The sky was clear and soft and gauzy blue, a peculiar atmospheric effect seen only in Tuscany; Leonardo had been told that in other places, especially to the north, the sky was sharper, harder.

"I will soon start a *bottega* of my own," Leonardo said, "and be the ruler of my own house."

"But we need money, Maestro."

"We'll have it."

"Not if you keep the First Citizen waiting for his Great Bird," Niccolo said; and Leonardo noticed that the boy's eyes narrowed, as if he were calculating a mathematical problem. "Maestro Andrea will certainly have to tell Lorenzo that your Great Bird is completed."

"Has he done so?" Leonardo asked.

Niccolo shrugged.

"He will be even more impressed with my new invention. I will show him before he becomes too impatient. But I think it is Andrea, not Lorenzo, who is impatient."

"You're going to show the First Citizen *this*?" Niccolo asked, meaning the tandem kites, which were protected from any gusts of wind by a secured canvas; the kites were assembled, and when Leonardo was ready, would be opened one at a time.

"If this works, then we will build the Great Bird as I promised. That will buy us our *bottega* and Lorenzo's love."

"He loves you already, Maestro, as does Maestro Andrea."

"Then they'll be patient with me."

Niccolo was certainly not above arguing with his master; he had, indeed, become Leonardo's confidant. But Leonardo didn't give him a chance. He had been checking the wind, which would soon be high. "Come help me, Nicco, and try not to be a philosopher. The wind is strong enough. If we wait it will become too gusty and tear the kites." This had already happened to several of Leonardo's large-scale models.

Leonardo let the wind take the first and smallest of the kites, but the wind was rather puffy, and it took a few moments before it pulled its thirty pounds on the guy rope. Then, as the wind freshened, he let go another. Satisfied, he anchored the assembly, making doubly sure that it was secure, and opened the third and largest kite. "Hold the line tight," he said to Niccolo as he climbed onto the sling seat and held tightly to a restraining rope that ran through a block and tackle to a makeshift anchor of rocks.

Leonardo reassured himself that he was safely tethered, and reminded himself that the cellular box was the most stable of constructions. Its flat surfaces would support it in the air. Nevertheless, his heart seemed to be pulsing in his throat, he had difficulty taking a breath, and he could feel the chill of his sweat on his chest and arms.

The winds were strong, but erratic, and Leonardo waited until he could feel the wind pulling steady; he leaned backward, sliding leeward on the seat to help wind get under the supporting surface of the largest kite. Then suddenly, as if some great heavenly hand had grabbed hold of the guy ropes and the kites and snapped them, Leonardo shot upward about twenty feet. But the kites held steady at the end of their tether, floating on the wind like rafts on water.

How different this was from the Great Bird, which was so sensitive—and susceptible—to every movement of the body. Leonardo shifted his weight, and even as he did so, he prayed; but the kites held in the air. Indeed, they were rafts. The answer was ample supporting surfaces.

Vince la natura.

The wind lightened, and he came down. The kites dragged him forward; he danced along the ground on his toes before he was swept upward again. Niccolo was shouting, screaming, and hanging from the restraining rope, as if to add his weight, lest it pull away from the rock anchor or pull the rocks heavenward.

When the kites came down for the third time, Leonardo jumped from the sling seat, falling to the ground. Seconds later, as if slapped by the same hand that had pulled them into the sky, the kites crashed, splintering, as their sails snapped and fluttered, as if still yearning for the airy heights.

"Are you all right, Maestro?" Niccolo shouted, running toward Leonardo.

"Yes," Leonardo said, although his back was throbbing in pain and his right arm, which he had already broken once before, was numb. But he could move it, as well as all his fingers. "I'm fine." He surveyed the damage. "Let's salvage what we can."

They fastened the broken kites onto the sled and walked through wildflower-dotted fields and pastures back to the *bottega*. "Perhaps now, Maestro, you'll trust your original Great Bird," Niccolo said. "You mustn't bury it with Tista."

"What are you talking about?" Leonardo asked.

"These kites are too . . . dangerous. They're completely at the mercy of the wind; they dragged you along the ground; and you almost broke your arm. Isn't that right, Maestro?"

Leonardo detected a touch of irony in Niccolo's voice. So the boy was having it up on his master. "Yes," Leonardo said. "And what does that prove?"

"That you should give this up."

"On the contrary, Nicco. This experiment has only proven how safe my new Great Bird will be."

"But you—"

Leonardo showed Niccolo his latest drawing of a biplane based on his idea of open-ended boxes placed at the ends of timber spars.

"How could such a thing fly?" Niccolo asked.

"That's a soaring machine safe enough for Lorenzo himself. If I could show the First Citizen that he could command the very air, do you think he would regret the few days it will take to build and test the new machine?"

"I think it looks very dangerous . . . and I think the kites are very dangerous, Maestro."

Leonardo smiled at Niccolo. "Then at least after today you no longer think I am a coward."

"Maestro, I *never* thought that."

But even as they approached the city, Leonardo could feel the edges of his dream, the dark edges of nightmare lingering; and he knew that tonight it would return.

The dream of falling. The dream of flight.

Tista. . . .

He would stay up and work. He would not sleep. He would not dream. But the dream spoke to him even as he walked, told him *it* was nature and would not be conquered. And Leonardo could feel himself.

Falling.

If Leonardo were superstitious, he would have believed it was a sign.

When the roof of Verrocchio's *bottega* gave way, falling timber and debris destroyed almost everything in Leonardo's studio; and the pelting rain ruined most of what might have been salvaged. Leonardo could rewrite his notes, for they were safe in the altar of his memory cathedral; he could rebuild models and replenish supplies, but his painting of the Madonna—his gift for Lorenzo—was destroyed. The canvas torn, the oils smeared, and the still-sticky varnish surface spackled with grit and filth. Most everything but the three paintings of his nightmare-descent into Hell was destroyed. Those three had been placed against the inner wall of the studio, a triptych of dark canvases, exposed, the varnish still sticky, protected by a roll of fabric that had fallen over them. And in every one of them Leonardo could see himself as a falling or fallen figure.

The present of the future.

"Don't you think this is a sign from the gods?" Niccolo asked after he and Leonardo had salvaged what they could and moved into another studio in Verrocchio's *bottega*.

"Do you now believe in the Greeks' pantheon?" Leonardo asked.

Looking flustered, Niccolo said, "I only meant—"

"I know what you meant." Leonardo smiled tightly. "Maestro Andrea might get his wish . . . he might yet sell those paintings to the good monks. In the meantime we've got work to do, which we'll start at first light."

"We can't build your Great Bird alone," Niccolo insisted.

"Of course we can. And Francesco will allocate some of his apprentices to help us."

"Maestro Andrea won't allow it."

"We'll see," Leonardo said.

"Maestro, your Great Bird is *already* built. It is ready, and Lorenzo expects you to fly it."

"Would that the roof fell upon it." Leonardo gazed out the window into the streets. The full moon illuminated the houses and *bottegas* and shops and palazzos in weak gray light that seemed to be made brighter by the yellow lamplight trembling behind vellum-covered windows. He would make Lorenzo a model of his new soaring machine, his new Great Bird; but he would not see the First Citizen until it was built and tested. Indeed, he stayed up the night, redrawing his designs, reworking his ideas, as if the destruction of his studio had been a blessing. He sketched cellular box kite designs that he combined into new forms for gliding machines, finally settling on a design based almost entirely on the rectangular box kite forms. He had broken away from the natural birdlike forms, yet this device was not unnatural in its simplicity. He detailed crosshatch timber braces, which would keep his cellular wing surfaces tight. He made drawings and diagrams of the cordage. The pilot would sit in a sling below the double wings, which were webbed as the masts of a sailing vessel; and the rudder would be attached to long spars that stretched behind him at shoulder height. A ship to sail into the heavens.

Tomorrow he would build models to test his design. To his mind, the ship was already built, for it was as tangible as the notebook he was staring into.

Notebook in hand, he fell asleep, for he had been but little removed from dreams; and dream he did, dreams as textured and deep and tinted as memory. He rode his Great Bird through the moonlit night, sailed around the peaks of mountains as if they were islands in a calm, warm sea; and the winds carried him, carried him away into darkness, into the surfaces of his paintings that had survived the rain and roof, into the brush-stroked chiaroscuro of his imagined Hell.

Eight

"Tell Lorenzo that I'll have a soaring machine ready to impress the archbishop when he arrives," Leonardo said. "But he's not due for a fortnight."

"You've taken too long already." Sandro Botticelli stood in Leonardo's new studio, which was small and in disarray; although the roof had been repaired, Leonardo did not want to waste time moving back into his old room. Sandro was dressed as a dandy, in red and green, with dags and a peaked cap pulled over his thick brown hair. It was a festival day, and the Medici and their retinue would take to the streets for the Palio, the great annual horse race. "Lorenzo sent me to drag you to the Palio, if need be."

"If Andrea had allowed Francesco to help me—or at least lent me a few apprentices—I would have it finished by now."

"That's not the point."

"That's exactly the point."

"Get out of your smock; you must have something that's not covered with paint and dirt."

"Come, I'll show you what I've done," Leonardo said. "I've put up canvas outside to work on my soaring machine. It's like nothing you've ever seen, I promise you that. I'll call Niccolo, he'll be happy to see you."

"You can show it to me on our way, Leonardo. Now get dressed. Niccolo has left long ago."

"What?"

"Have you lost touch with everyone and everything?" Sandro asked. "Niccolo is at the Palio with Andrea . . . who is with Lorenzo. Only you remain behind."

"But Niccolo was just here."

Sandro shook his head. "He's been there for most of the day. He said he begged you to accompany him."

"Did he tell that to Lorenzo, too?"

"I think you can trust your young apprentice to be discreet."

Dizzy with fatigue, Leonardo sat down by a table covered with books and models of kites and various incarnations of his soaring machine. "Yes, of course, you're right, Little Bottle."

"You look like you've been on a binge. You've got to start taking care of yourself, you've got to start sleeping and eating properly. If you don't, you'll lose everything, including Lorenzo's love and attention. You can't treat him as you do the rest of your friends. I thought you wanted to be his Master of Engineers?"

"What else has Niccolo been telling you?"

Sandro shook his head in a gesture of exasperation and said, "Change your clothes, dear friend. We haven't more than an hour before the race begins."

"I'm not going," Leonardo said, his voice flat. "Lorenzo will have to wait until my soaring machine is ready."

"He will not wait."

"He has no choice."

"He has your Great Bird, Leonardo."

"Then Lorenzo can fly it! Perhaps he will suffer the same fate as Tista. Better yet, he should order Andrea to fly it. After all, Andrea had it built for him."

"Leonardo . . ."

"It killed Tista. . . . It's not safe."

"I'll tell Lorenzo you're ill," Sandro said.

"Send Niccolo back to me. I forbid him to—"

But Sandro had already left the studio, closing the large inlaid door behind him.

Exhausted, Leonardo leaned upon the table and imagined that he had followed Sandro to the door, down the stairs, and outside. There he surveyed his canvas-covered makeshift workshop. The air was hot and stale in the enclosed space. It would take weeks working alone to complete the new soaring machine. Niccolo should be there. Then Leonardo began working at the cordage to tighten the supporting wing surfaces. *This* machine will be safe, he thought; and he worked, even in the dark exhaustion of his dreams, for he had lost the ability to rest.

Indeed, he was lost.

In the distance, he could hear Tista. Could hear the boy's triumphant cry before he fell and snapped his spine. And he heard thunder. Was it the shouting of the crowd as he, Leonardo, fell from the mountain near Vinci? Was it the crowd cheering the Palio riders racing through the city? Or was it the sound of his own dream-choked breathing?

"Leonardo, they're going to fly your machine!"

"What?" Leonardo asked, surfacing from deep sleep; his head ached and his limbs felt weak and light, as if he had been carrying heavy weights.

Francesco stood over him, and Leonardo could smell the man's sweat and the faint odor of garlic. "One of my boys came back to tell me . . . as if *I'd* be rushing into crowds of cutpurses to see some child die in your flying contraption!" He took a breath, catching himself. "I'm sorry, Maestro. Don't take offense, but you know what I think of your machines."

"Lorenzo is going to demonstrate my Great Bird *now*?"

Francesco shrugged. "After his brother won the Palio, *Il Magnifico* announced to the crowds that an angel would fly above them and drop Hell's own fire from the sky. And my apprentice tells me that *inquisitore* are all over the streets and are keeping everyone away from the gardens near Santi Apostoli."

That would certainly send a message to the Pope; the church of Santi Apostoli was under the protection of the powerful Pazzi family, who were allies of Pope Sixtus and enemies of the Medici.

"When is this supposed to happen?" Leonardo asked the foreman as he hurriedly put on a new shirt; a doublet; and *calze* hose, which were little more than pieces of leather to protect his feet.

Francesco shrugged. "I came to tell you as soon as I heard."

"And did you hear who is to fly my machine?"

"I've told you all I know, Maestro." Then after a pause, he said, "But I fear for Niccolo. I fear that he has told *Il Magnifico* that he knows how to fly your invention."

Leonardo prayed that he could find Niccolo before he came to harm. He too feared that the boy had betrayed him, had insinuated himself into Lorenzo's confidence, and was at this moment soaring over Florence in the Great Bird. Soaring over the Duomo, the Baptistery, and the Piazza della Signoria, which rose from the streets like minarets around a heavenly dome.

But the air currents over Florence were too dangerous. He would fall like Tista, for what was the city but a mass of jagged peaks and precipitous cliffs?

"Thank you, Francesco," Leonardo said, and, losing no time, he made his way through the crowds toward the church of Santi Apostoli. A myriad of smells delicious and noxious permeated the air: roasting meats, honeysuckle, the odor of candle wax heavy as if with childhood memories, offal and piss, cattle and horses, the tang of wine and cider, and everywhere sweat and the sour ripe scent of perfumes applied to unclean bodies. The shouting and laughter and stepping-rushing-soughing of the crowds were deafening, as if a human tidal wave was making itself felt across the city. The whores were out in full regalia, having left their district, which lay between Santa Giovanni and Santa Maria Maggiore; they worked their way through the crowds, as did the cutpurses and pickpockets, the children of Firenze's streets. Beggars grasped onto visiting country villeins and minor guildsmen for a denari and saluted when the red carrocci with their long scarlet banners and red dressed horses passed. Merchants and bankers and wealthy guildsmen rode on great horses or were comfortable in their carriages, while their servants walked ahead to clear the way for them with threats and brutal proddings.

The frantic, noisy streets mirrored Leonardo's frenetic inner state, for he feared for Niccolo; and he walked quickly, his hand openly resting on the hilt of his razor-sharp dagger to deter thieves and those who would slice open the belly of a passerby for amusement.

He kept looking for likely places from which his Great Bird might be launched: the dome of the Duomo, high brick towers, the roof of the Baptistery . . . and he looked up at the darkening sky, looking for his Great Bird as he pushed his way through the crowds to the gardens near the Santi Apostoli, which was near the Ponte Vecchio. In these last few moments, Leonardo became hopeful. Perhaps there was a chance to stop Niccolo . . . if, indeed, it was Niccolo who was to fly the Great Bird for Lorenzo.

Blocking entry to the gardens were both Medici and Pazzi supporters, two armies, dangerous and armed, facing each other. Lances and swords flashed in the dusty twilight. Leonardo could see the patriarch of the Pazzi family, the shrewd and haughty Jacopo de' Pazzi, an old, full-bodied man sitting erect on a huge, richly carapaced charger. His sons Giovanni, Francesco, and Guglielmo were beside him, surrounded by their troops, who were dressed in the Pazzi colors of blue and gold. And there, to Leonardo's surprise and frustration, was his great Eminence the Archbishop, protected by the scions of the Pazzi family and their liveried guards. So this was why Lorenzo had made his proclamation that he would conjure an angel of death and fire to demonstrate the power of the Medici . . . and Florence. It was as if the Pope himself were here to watch.

Beside the Archbishop, in dangerous proximity to the Pazzi, Lorenzo and Giuliano sat atop their horses. Giuliano, the winner of the Palio, the ever-handsome hero, was wrapped entirely in silver, his silk stomacher embroidered with pearls and silver, a giant ruby in his cap; while his brother Lorenzo, perhaps not handsome but certainly an overwhelming presence, wore light armor over simple clothes. But Lorenzo carried his shield, which contained "Il Libro," the huge Medici diamond reputed to be worth 2,500 ducats.

Leonardo could see Sandro behind Giuliano, and he shouted his name; but Leonardo's voice was lost in the din of twenty thousand other voices. He looked for Niccolo, but he could not see him with Sandro or the Medici. He pushed his way forward, but he had to pass through an army of the feared Medici-supported Companions of the Night, the darkly dressed Dominican friars who held the informal but hated title of *inquisitore*. And they were backed up by Medici sympathizers sumptuously outfitted by Lorenzo in armor and livery of red velvet and gold.

Finally, one of the guards recognized him, and he escorted Leonardo through the sweaty, nervous troops toward Lorenzo and his entourage by the edge of the garden.

But Leonardo was not to reach them.

The air seemed heavy and fouled, as if the crowd's perspiration was rising like heat, distorting shape and perspective. Then the crowds became quiet, as Lorenzo addressed them and pointed to the sky.

Everyone looked heavenward.

And like some gauzy fantastical winged creature that Dante might have contemplated for his *Paradiso*, the Great Bird soared over Florence, circling high above the church and gardens, riding the updrafts and the currents that swirled invisibly above the towers and domes and spires of the city. Leonardo caught his breath, for the pilot certainly looked like Niccolo; surely a boy rather than a full-bodied man. He looked like an awkward angel, with translucent gauze wings held in place with struts of wood and cords of twine. Indeed, the glider was as white was heaven, and Niccolo—if it was Niccolo—was dressed in a sheer white robe.

The boy sailed over the Pazzi troops like a bird swooping above a chimney, and seasoned soldiers fell to the ground in fright, or awe, and prayed; only Jacopo de' Pazzi, his sons, and the Archbishop remained steady on their horses. As did, of course, Lorenzo and his retinue.

And Leonardo could hear a kind of buzzing, as if he were in the midst of an army of cicadas, as twenty thousand citizens prayed to the soaring angel for their lives as they clutched and clicked black rosaries.

The heavens had opened to give them a sign, just as they had for the Hebrews at Sinai.

The boy made a tight circle around the gardens and dropped a single fragile shell that exploded on impact, throwing off great streams of fire and shards of shrapnel that cut down and burned trees and grass and shrubs. Then he dropped another, which was off mark, and dangerously close to Lorenzo's entourage. A group of people were cut down by the shrapnel, and lay choking and bleeding in the streets. Fire danced across the piazza. Horses stampeded. Soldiers and citizens alike ran in panic. The Medici and Pazzi distanced themselves from the garden, their frightened troops closing around them like Roman phalanxes. Leonardo would certainly not be able to get close to the

First Citizen now. He shouted at Niccolo in anger and frustration, for surely these people would die; and *Leonardo* would be their murderer. He had just killed them with his dreams and drawings. Here was truth! Here was revelation! *He* had murdered these unfortunate strangers, as surely as he had killed Tista. It was as if his invention now had a life of its own, independent of its creator.

As the terrified mob raged around him, Leonardo found refuge in an alcove between two buildings and watched his Great Bird soar in great circles over the city. The sun was setting, and the high, thin cirrus clouds were stained deep red and purple. Leonardo prayed that Niccolo would have sense enough to fly westward, away from the city, where he could hope to land safely on open ground; but the boy was showing off and underestimated the capriciousness of the winds. He suddenly fell, as if dropped, toward the brick and stone below him. He shifted weight and swung his hips, trying desperately to recover. An updraft picked him up like a dust devil, and he soared skyward on heavenly breaths of warm air.

God's grace.

He seemed to be more cautious now, for he flew toward safer ground to the west . . . but then he suddenly descended, falling, dropping behind the backshadowed buildings; and Leonardo could well imagine that the warm updraft that had lifted Niccolo had popped like a water bubble.

So did the boy fall through cool air, probably to his death.

Leonardo waited a beat, watching and waiting for the Great Bird to reappear. His heart was itself like a bird beating violently in his throat. Niccolo. . . . Prayers of supplication formed in his mind, as if of their own volition, as if Leonardo's thoughts were not his own, but belonged to some peasant from Vinci grasping at a rosary for truth and hope and redemption.

Those crowded around Leonardo could not guess that the angel had fallen . . . just that he had descended from the empyrean heights to the man-made spires of Florence where the sun was blazing rainbows as it set; and Lorenzo emerged triumphantly. He stood alone on a porch so that he could be seen by all and distracted the crowds with a haranguing speech that was certainly directed to the Archbishop.

Florence is invincible.

The greatest and most perfect city in the world.

Florence would conquer *all* its enemies.

As Lorenzo spoke, Leonardo saw, as if in a lucid dream, dark skies filled with his flying machines. He saw his hempen bombs falling through the air, setting the world below on fire. Indeed, with these machines Lorenzo could conquer the Papal States and Rome itself; could burn the Pope out of the Vatican and become more powerful than any of the Caesars.

An instant later Leonardo was running, navigating the maze of alleys and streets to reach Niccolo. Niccolo was all that mattered. If the boy was dead, certainly Lorenzo would not care. But Sandro . . . surely Sandro . . .

There was no time to worry about Sandro's loyalties.

The crowds thinned, and only once was Leonardo waylaid by street arabs, who blocked his way. But when they saw that Leonardo was armed and wild and ready to draw blood, they let him pass; and he ran, blade in hand, as if he were being chased by wild beasts.

Empty streets, empty buildings, the distant thunder of the crowds constant as the roaring of the sea. All of Florence was behind Leonardo, who searched for Niccolo in what might have been ancient ruins but for the myriad telltale signs that life still flowed all about here, and soon would again. Alleyways became shadows, and there was a blue tinge to the air. Soon it would be dark. A few windows already glowed tallow yellow in the balconied apartments above him.

He would not easily find Niccolo here. The boy could have fallen anywhere; and in grief and desperation, Leonardo shouted his name. His voice echoed against the high building walls; someone answered in falsetto *voce,* followed by laughter. But then Leonardo heard horses galloping through the streets, heard men's voices calling to each other. Lorenzo's men? Pazzi? There was a shout, and Leonardo knew they had found what they were looking for. Frantic, he hurried toward the soldiers, but what would he do when he found Niccolo wrapped in the wreckage of the Great Bird? Tell a dying boy that he, Leonardo, couldn't fly his own invention because he was afraid?

I was trying to make it safe, Niccolo.

He found Lorenzo's Companions of the Night in a piazza surrounded by tenements. They carried torches, and at least twenty of the well-armed priests were on horseback. Their horses were fitted out in black, as if both horses and riders had come directly from Hell; one of the horses pulled a cart covered with canvas.

Leonardo could see torn fustian and taffeta and part of the Great Bird's rudder section hanging over the red-and-blue striped awning of a balcony. And there, on the ground below, was the upper wing assembly, intact. Other bits of cloth slid along the ground like foolscap.

Several *inquisitore* huddled over an unconscious figure.

Niccolo.

Beside himself with grief, Leonardo rushed headlong into the piazza; but before he could get halfway across the court, he was intercepted by a dozen Dominican soldiers. "I am Leonardo da Vinci," he shouted, but that seemed to mean nothing to them. These young Wolves of the Church were ready to hack him to pieces for the sheer pleasure of feeling the heft of their swords.

"Do not harm him!" shouted a familiar voice.

Sandro Botticelli.

He was dressed now in the thick, black garb of the *inquisitore*. "What are you doing here, Leonardo? You're a bit late." Anger and sarcasm was evident in his voice.

But Leonardo was concerned only with Niccolo, for two brawny *inquisitore* were lifting him into the cart. He pushed past Sandro and mindless of consequences pulled one of the soldiers out of the way to see the boy. Leonardo winced as he looked at the boy's smashed skull and bruised body—arms and legs broken, extended at wrong angles— and then turned away in relief.

This was not Niccolo; he had never seen this boy before.

"Niccolo is with Lorenzo," Sandro said, standing beside Leonardo. "Lorenzo considered allowing Niccolo to fly your machine, for the boy knows almost as much about it as you."

"Has he flown the Great Bird?"

After a pause, Sandro said, "Yes . . . but against Lorenzo's wishes. That's probably what saved his life." Sandro gazed at the boy in the cart, who was now covered with the torn wings of the Great Bird, which, in turn, was covered with canvas. "When Lorenzo discovered what Niccolo had done, he would not allow him near any of your flying machines, except to help train *this* boy, Giorgio, who was in his service. A nice boy, may God take his soul."

"Then Niccolo is safe?" Leonardo asked.

"Yes, the holy fathers are watching over him."

"You mean these cutthroats?"

"Watch how you speak, Leonardo. Lorenzo kept Niccolo safe for you, out of love for you. And how have you repaid him . . . by being a traitor?"

"Don't ever say that to me, even in jest."

"I'm not jesting, Leonardo. You've failed Lorenzo . . . and your country, failed them out of fear. Even a child such as Niccolo could see that."

"Is that what you think?"

Sandro didn't reply.

"Is that what Niccolo told you?"

"Yes."

Leonardo would not argue, for the stab of truth unnerved him, even now. "And you, why are you here?"

"Because Lorenzo trusts me. As far as Florence and the Archbishop are concerned, the angel flew and caused fire to rain from Heaven. And is in Heaven now as we speak." He shrugged and nodded to the *inquisitore,* who mounted their horses.

"So now you command the Companions of the Night instead of the divine power of the painter," Leonardo said, the bitterness evident in his voice. "Perhaps we are on different sides now, Little Bottle."

"*I'm* on the side of *Florence,*" Sandro said. "And against her enemies. *You* care only for your inventions!"

"And my friends," Leonardo said quietly, pointedly.

"Perhaps for Niccolo, perhaps a little for me; but more for yourself."

"How many of my flying machines does Lorenzo have now?" Leonardo asked, but Sandro turned away from him and rode behind the cart that carried the corpse of the angel and the broken bits of the Great Bird. Once again, Leonardo felt the numbing, rubbery sensation of great fatigue, as if he had turned into an old man, as if all his work, now finished, had come to nothing. He wished only to be rid of it all: his inventions, his pain, his guilt. He could not bear even to be in Florence, the place he loved above all others.

There was no place for him now.

───────────

Leonardo could be seen as a shadow moving inside his canvas-covered makeshift workshop, which was brightly lit by several water lamps and a small fire. Other shadows passed across the vellum-covered windows of the surrounding buildings like mirages in the Florentine night. Much of the city was dark, for few could afford tallow and oil.

But Leonardo's tented workshop was bright, for he was methodically burning his notes and papers, his diagrams and sketches of his new soaring machine. After the notebooks were curling ash and smoke rising through a single vent in the canvas, he burned his box-shaped models of wood and cloth; kites and flying machines of various design; and then, at the last, he smashed his partially completed soaring machine . . . smashed the spars and rudder, smashed the boxlike wings, tore away the webbing and fustian, which burned like hemp in the crackling fire.

As if Leonardo could burn his ideas from his thoughts.

Yet he could not help but feel that the rising smoke was the very stuff of his ideas and invention. And that he was spreading them for all to inhale, like poisonous phantasms.

Lorenzo already *had* Leonardo's flying machines.

More children would die. . . .

He burned his drawings and paintings, his portraits and madonnas and varnished visions of fear, then left the makeshift studio like a sleepwalker heading back to his bed; and the glue and fustian and broken spars ignited, glowing like coals, then burst, exploded, shot like fireworks or silent hempen bombs until the canvas was ablaze. Leonardo was far away by then and couldn't hear the shouts of Andrea and Francesco and the apprentices as they rushed to put out the fire.

Niccolo found Leonardo standing upon the same mountain where Tista had fallen to his death. His face and shirt streaked with soot and ash, Leonardo stared down into the misty valley below. There was the Palazzo Vecchio, and the dome of the Duomo reflecting the early morning sun . . . and beyond, created out of the white dressing of the mist itself, was his memory cathedral. Leonardo gazed at it . . . into it. He relived once again Tista's flight into death and saw the paintings he had burned; indeed, he looked into Hell, into the future where he glimpsed the dark skies filled with Lorenzo's soaring machines, raining death from the skies, the winged devices that Leonardo would no longer claim as his own. He wished he had never dreamed of the Great Bird. But now it was too late for anything but regret.

What was done could not be undone.

"Maestro!" Niccolo shouted, pulling Leonardo away from the cliff edge, as if he, Leonardo, had been about to launch himself without wings or harness into the fog. As perhaps he had been.

"Everyone has been frantic with worry for you," Niccolo said, as if he was out of breath.

"I should not think I would have been missed."

Niccolo snorted, which reminded Leonardo that he was still a child, no matter how grown-up he behaved and had come to look. "You nearly set Maestro Verrocchio's *bottega* on fire."

"Surely my lamps would extinguish themselves when out of oil, and the fire was properly vented. I myself—"

"Neighbors saved the *bottega*," Niccolo said, as if impatient to get on to other subjects. "They alerted *everyone*."

"Then there was no damage?" Leonardo asked.

"Just black marks on the walls."

"Good," Leonardo said, and he walked away from Niccolo, who followed after him. Ahead was a thick bank of mist the color of ash, a wall that might have been a sheer drop, but behind which in reality were fields and trees.

"I knew I would find you here," Niccolo said.

"And how did you know that, Nicco?"

The boy shrugged.

"You must go back to the *bottega*," Leonardo said.

"I'll go back with you, Maestro."

"I'm not going back." The morning mist was all around them; it seemed to be boiling up from the very ground. There would be rain today and heavy skies.

"Where are you going?"

Leonardo shrugged.

"But you've left everything behind!" After a beat, Niccolo said, "I'm going with you."

"No, young ser."

"But what will I do?"

Leonardo smiled. "I would guess that you'll stay with Maestro Verrocchio until Lorenzo invites you to be his guest. But you must promise
me you'll never fly any of his machines."

Niccolo promised; of course, Leonardo knew that the boy would
do as he wished. "I did not believe you were afraid, Maestro."

"Of course not, Nicco."

"I shall walk with you a little way."

"No."

Leonardo left Niccolo behind, as if he could leave the past for a
new, innocent future. As if he had never invented bombs and machines
that could fly. As if, but for his paintings, he had never existed at all.

Niccolo called to him . . . then his voice faded away and was gone.

Soon the rain stopped and the fog lifted, and Leonardo looked up
at the red-tinged sky.

Perhaps in hope.

Perhaps in fear.

Rhysling Award Winners

Margaret Ballif Simon / Bruce Boston

The Rhysling Awards are named after the Blind Singer of the Spaceways featured in Robert A. Heinlein's "The Green Hills of Earth." They are given each year by members of the Science Fiction Poetry Association in two categories: best long poem and best short poem.

The 1996 Rhysling Award for Best Long Poem went to Margaret Simon for her poem "Variants of the Obsolete." Her poetry, prose-poems, and stories are included in *Palace Corbie, High Fantastic,* and *Eonian Variations.* Her poems have appeared in *Tomorrow, Magazine of Speculative Poetry, Deathrealm, Noctulpa, Tales of the Unanticipated, Space & Time, Next Phase, Prisoners of the Night, Stygian Vortex* publications, *Dreams & Nightmares, Gaslight, Bizarre Bazarr, Poets of the Fantastic, Pandora, Midnight Zoo, Black Lotus, Xizquil, Niekas, Visions,* and hundreds of other magazines. Simon was raised in Boulder, Colorado. An award-winning artist, she has taught art in Ocala, Florida, for twenty-four years.

Simon describes how she came to write "Variants of the Obsolete":

"It was a personal challenge, inspired because I'd never attempted a long poem (other than one I wrote as Class Poet for Boulder High School in 1960). I'd been reading the works of W. Gregory Stewart, such as 'the button, and what you know,' as well as those of another highly esteemed poet, Bruce Boston: all in the long poem category, and all speculative and delightfully daring mental exploration of the SF genre. So during my December break in 1993, I decided I would write a long poem that would knock my socks off. And it took me three weeks. It virtually wrote itself because it was in segments that I could return to, like tuning into a preset cognitive frequency. I 'lived' the poem to the end which was the whole, which is the time warp of wonder that exists within every poet of speculative poetry. Dare yourself to play your own game, and bet on a winner."

The 1996 Rhysling Award for Short Poem went to Bruce Boston for "Future Present: A Lesson in Expectation." According to *Science Fiction Age:* "If SF were to select a Poet Laureate, the post's most logical first candidate would inarguably be Bruce Boston." *Anatomy of Wonder* describes him as "probably the most fecund and critically acclaimed SF or speculative poet." Boston has won the Rhysling Award a record five times. Both his poetry and fiction have appeared widely in science fiction and mainstream publications. He is the author of the novel *Stained Glass Rain,* the novelette *After Magic,* eight collections of fiction, and twelve books of poetry, most recently *Conditions of Sentient Life* (Gothic Press, 1996). A new book of stories, *Dark Tales & Light,* is forthcoming from Dark Regions Press.

He writes:

"In general terms, 'Future Present: A Lesson in Expectation' is merely a restatement of Robert Burns's most famous couplet, 'The best-laid schemes of mice an' men/Gang aft a-gley.' More specifically, the poem contrasts the utopian visions of the future portrayed in 'golden age' SF with a present which has failed to realize them either materially or spiritually. A present in which we continue to overpopulate, despoil the planet, and embrace leaders who celebrate ignorance, fear, and greed. It also posits a future of worldwide catastrophic proportions. Pessimistic? Yes. Accurate? Prophetic? Apparently in the estimation of some, or the poem would not have won the award."

Variants of the Obsolete
MARGARET BALLIF SIMON

The observer is a gull. Or rather, it once
resembled the Aves, characteristically
retaining beaked nose and skeletal structure
with disproportionate forequarters.

It has positioned itself near a black hole
in the universe, or in time, whichever
you prefer. Sexless, oviparous, yet evolved
as a species capable of interchanging

mating roles. Nothing is impossible,
once certain genes have been successfully
manipulated (your father pooled his talents
in the Collective of '98;) so you know

you are observing the observer,
the telescope you hold trembles
slightly, belying your great interest
in the scene you've trained to capture—

that unfolds too fast for you
to record (though all it takes is a
motion of your right digit)—you
forget—cursing fallibility

a flash of beak, a scalding light
so pure so white—you cannot focus.
In this instant, the gull bends
to the hole, extracting

what you believe is from another
universe. It tears the form to shreds
before your eyes; pauses before the last
morsel is swallowed, turns to face your 'scope.

You can hear it smile.

But you are not smiling. Your mandibles
clench, lock. Sweat beads on your forehead,
drying quickly in the arid breeze. You
reposition 'scope, this time with
shuttle ready for the holograph
record—but even as you

fuss and putter, willing as the human
beast is ever ready to perform—
the candid scene belongs to time; you
spit into the sand, disgruntled. Try

again, beating off the smaller birds
that flock around your equipment,
—sparrows, jays, a flicker—
no admission. Turn on the buzzer, they
freeze, sizzle, fry, fall

build silent compost mounds around your
equipment. You kick the ashes with
plasti-booted heel, their acrid fluid
stains the pristine surface polish. In
disgust, you wipe the flakes

with gloved hand, despairing of
tracing more today, yet from the distant
hill a strident laughter lures you—
surely one more shot at it, you think, you

hope, settling your 'scope again, into the
sunwhite sand, surely this time it will
hold its prey, you'll see the form before
consumption resumes.

There is the land and the sea.
Then there are creatures from the land
and creatures of the sea. Before that
there was vegetation. Before the cycle
began, there were gases . . .

Digestive juices.
Items within the hole.

Your mouth waters. Endorphines can wait,
adrenaline flows, your fingers tighten
on the fulcrum module; it's set, you
sight it there again, hunched expectant

vulturesque above the dark green-blue ball.
Silence. (you are aware of something flying
around your ears—you cuff at it with
the heavy glove, crushing the tiny wings . . .
it falls, distracting you a moment, for

it resembles a hummingbird—you toe it
into the sands with your boot)

Turn back to scanner, there it is—
yes, this time you have it on the
right way is to push this into play and
you'll have that little sucker

in focus what if you get scared what if
it looks like that is human, that thing
being caught like a fish or a worm or a
burp in time?

Yet there you go again. It's only a
piece of what looks like paper. You don't know
what's on the paper. The observer is taking off
becomes too dense to sight in your 'scope

Later, when you go over the recording, you
are able to enlarge the last shot. Your
equipment shows that the observer has a

blank piece of paper in its mouth.
You enlarge that paper ten thousand times.

In the exact center of the paper
you detect a hole.

Possibly, you think, this was made by an ancient
typewriter, for the hole is precisely "O" shaped.

More logically, you surmise, this was a
computer error. So you return to your post
and wait for the return of the observer.

You wipe a few grains of dead sea sands
from your visor, return to view the horizon.
Shattering the still vista, acustualating
organs distinct, distant—the observer

sighted, sandprobes meet tympanic
membrane; you react, this chance
to purloin, document the Origin—
too dear—yet bothersome are

these small birds, who appear to
gather each time you prepare for
record; are they ectogenous, familiar
to their host, now hunched beside the
distant hole? No, you dismiss that—
concentrate on the

scene, the hole, the space where only
one observer finds and sits, where only
we/you/I/the human part of this
totality of organismic world

is attuned to visit, to watch, to
gather and do as it will
with that which comes through
that god damned hole nobody
knows, not even the best
of us they are all dead

your mind is wandering
they swarm about your faceplate
like wingless hummingbirds
faster, harder until

you use the buzzer. Scrape them off,
as bugs on windshield, yet without
a wind (you laugh, for there are
winds no more here) and why
and why again for the observer

is intent—the hole opens:
Slip-sliding from the portal to
infinity, it catches—

your gloved hand, still determinedly
attached to your mechanism.

You scream drowning in a vortex of wounds
wings, wind, whirling down to
meet the brightness not a tunnel
channel no a causeway flocked with
tiny denizens who

grasp you, suspend you above
the hole which is the "O" which is

the last whisperwish of Pharaohs
final gash of a shooting star
a young girl's blush when her
fingers found your erection

someone tunes a fiddle as
guitars duel, drums duet;
the stars are real
you are flying into the "O"

which is the "O" which is the
mouthpiece of your visor. Beside you
sits the observer, the gull-creature

who will laconically
grasp you with dual phalanges
disperse your sight within ebon orbs
desensitize your awareness

confine you to infinite desolation
And will it partake of you—bare essence
of what was once mortal?

You can hear it smile.

Future Present: A Lesson in Expectation
BRUCE BOSTON

The future the past once envisioned is
nothing like the present we now inhabit.
No aerocars. No globed and spired metropoli.
No eccentric rube-goldbergian gadgets that
deliver a cool drink and a *shiatsu* massage
with the casual flick of a single switch.
No passage to the stars or even Mars.

And what of those gently purring walkways
lightly peopled by superior beings who glow
with the logic of a sublime moral grace?

Instead the present through which we slog
and stagger seems raw and tatterdemalion
as the past we expected to trash behind
—the twentieth is the cruelest century—
breeding sex plagues out of ignorance,
rife with demagogues and despoilation.

And while we ponder what roads not taken
have abandoned us to this frantic moment,
this vain dyspepsia of the modern mind
—no one answer, a gross on every side—
the tomorrow we envision is omnivorous:
mushrooming clouds, displacing populations,
devouring civilization with toxic fungal rains.

As those purring walkways recede and fade
into the dimming distance of the mind's eye,
the future, second by ever-rivering second,
oblivious to all expectation, yanks us bodily
into the coagulating rapids of its own design.

A Birthday

Esther M. Friesner

Esther M. Friesner holds a B.A. from Vassar College and a Ph.D. in Spanish from Yale. She has published over twenty novels, which include *The Silver Mountain, Here Be Demons, Harlot's Ruse, Demon Blues, Majyk by Accident, Majyk by Design,* and *Majyk by Hook or Crook;* her most recent titles are *The Psalms of Herod* and *Child of the Eagle.* Her *Star Trek: Deep Space Nine* novel *Warchild* made the *USA Today* best-seller list. Her short fiction and poetry have appeared in *Asimov's Science Fiction, F&SF, Aboriginal SF,* and other magazines and anthologies. With Martin H. Greenberg, she has edited several anthologies, including *Alien Pregnant by Elvis* and *Chicks in Chainmail.* She won the Nebula Award for Best Short Story of 1995 for "Death and the Librarian," and "A Birthday" was a finalist for the 1996 Hugo Award. She lives in Connecticut with her husband, two children, two rambunctious cats, and a fluctuating population of hamsters.

Although Esther Friesner has a reputation of writing some of the funniest and wittiest fantasy in the business, her 1996 Nebula–winning short story "A Birthday" is deadly serious.

She writes:

"If I begin by saying that abortion is a heavily charged political, religious, and emotional subject, I'll probably be knocked off my feet by the sound waves that the rousing 'Well, *duh*!' chorus will generate. This story was not written to be pro-life or pro-choice, just anti-scapegoat.

"With 'A Birthday,' I hoped to remind anyone who needs it that this is one issue where there are no easy choices, no matter what the scope of our available choices may be. While we go on to fight for our beliefs, convictions, and ideals, we mustn't lose sight of the fact that the people being affected most directly by our righteousness-on-parade are neither pawns nor abstract quantities.

"I also confess that I was motivated to write 'A Birthday' when I became a wee tad annoyed by something I'd come to notice: Why is it that in most classics of Western Lit, in cases where a couple engages in pre- or extramarital sex, it's the woman who winds up Paying the Price? And why do so many people believe that this is the way it *ought* to be? Oh, yes, sometimes the man suffers, too—sometimes he even dies—but whatever he suffers, the woman usually suffers the same or worse. And many's the time he escapes unscathed by anything except a touch of bittersweet regret, which makes him even more attractive to the next woman who crosses his path. The woman never gets that option.

"I still recall the big flap over Judy Blume's book *Forever,* in which a teenage girl plans to have sex, obtains birth control, uses it correctly, then eventually breaks up with her boyfriend. The loudest squawks of protest did not arise from the fact that the girl was sexually active, but because she didn't contract an STD, get pregnant, or—the real crowd pleaser—die and become an Object Lesson to other teenage girls everywhere. She just got on with her life. The *nerve*!

"Everything's OK as long as the woman suffers for her sins. And if the erring lass is *seen* to suffer, so much the better: Her public penance allows the spectators thereof to feel comfortably superior, morally smug.

" 'A Birthday' has garnered plenty of feedback. A doctor wrote to me and said that it had affected her deeply; a college instructor chose to use it in the classroom. Still, the comment that's pleased me the most came from someone who said that one could *not* figure out my personal beliefs on the subject of legalized abortion by reading the story.

"Good."

I wake up knowing that this is a special day. Today is Tessa's birthday. She will be six. That means she will start school and I won't see her during the day at all.

My friends will have a party for Tessa and for me. The invitation sits on my bedside table, propped up against the telephone so I can't possibly forget it. I wish I could. There are pink pandas tumbling around the borders of the card and inside my friend Paula has written in the details of time and place in her beautiful handwriting. I get up, get dressed, get ready for the day ahead. Before I leave the apartment I make sure that I haven't locked Squeaker in the closet again. Squeaker is my cat. You'd think it would be hard for a cat to hide in a studio apartment, but Squeaker manages. Tessa loves cats and pandas, just like me. She told me so.

I am almost out the door when I remember the invitation. Tessa hasn't seen it yet. Today will be my last chance to show it to her. I keep forgetting to take it with me, not because I want to deprive my daughter of anything but because of what this birthday means to us both. I don't like to think about it. I tuck the invitation into my purse and go to work.

I arrive a little before nine. Mom always said I never plan ahead, but I do now. There are flowers on my desk at work, six pink fairy roses in a cut glass bud vase with a spill of shiny white ribbon tied around its neck. There is a freedom card propped open on the keyboard in front of my terminal, signed by most of the women in the office. I hang up my jacket and check my IN box for work, but there is nothing there, no excuse to turn on my terminal. Still, a good worker finds work to do even when there's none, and I do so want to touch the keys.

I sit down and reach for a sampler sheet to rub over my thumb and slip into the terminal. Damn, the pad's empty! I know I had some left yesterday; what happened? I can't turn on my terminal without giving it a sample of my cell scrapings so the system knows it's me. Who's been getting at my things? I'll kill her!

No. I mustn't lose my temper like this. I have to set a good example for my girl. It's important for a woman to make peace, to compromise. No one wins a war. Maybe whoever took the last of my sampler sheets needed it more than I do. Maybe she had to stay late, work overtime, and everyone else locked their pads away in their desks so she had to help herself to mine.

"Good morning, Linda." It's my boss, Mr. Beeton. His melon face is shiny with a smile. "I see you've found my little surprise."

"Sir?" I say.

"Now, now, I know what day this is just as well as you do. Do you think the ladies are the only ones who want to wish you the best for the future? Just because there's a door on my office, it doesn't mean I'm sealed inside, ignorant of my girls' lives." He pats me on the back and says, "I'm giving you the day off, with pay. Have fun." And then he is gone, a walrus in a blue-gray suit waddling up the aisle between the rows of terminals.

I don't want to have the day off. What will I do?

Where will I go? The party isn't until six o'clock tonight. There is so much I need to say to her before then. I suppose I could go to the bank, but that's only ten seconds' worth of time. It's nowhere near enough. Here at work I could keep finding excuses to—

Mr. Beeton is at the end of the aisle, staring at me. He must be wondering why I'm still sitting here, staring at a blank screen. I'd better go. I put on my jacket and walk away from my terminal. It will still be here tomorrow. So will part of me.

I hear the murmurs as I walk to the door. The women are smiling at me as I pass, sad smiles, encouraging smiles, smiles coupled with the fleeting touch of a hand on mine. "I'm so happy for you," they say. "You're so strong."

"I've been praying for you."

"Have a good time."

"Have a good life."

"See you tomorrow."

But what will they see? I think about how many sick days I have left. Not enough. I will have to come back tomorrow, and I will have to work as if everything were still the same.

As I walk down the hall to the elevator I have to pass the ladies' room. I hear harsh sounds, tearing sounds.

Someone is in there, crying. I don't have to work today; I can take the time to go in and see who it is, what's wrong. Maybe I can help. Maybe this will kill some time.

The crying is coming from one of the stalls. "Who's there?" I call. The crying stops. There is silence, broken only by the drip of water from a faucet and a shallow, sudden intake of breath from the stall.

"What's wrong?" I ask. "Please, I can help you."

"Linda?" The voice is too fragile, too quavery for me to identify. "Is that you? I thought Beeton gave you the day off."

"He did," I tell whoever it is in there. "I was just on my way out."

"Go ahead, then." Now the voice is a little stronger, a little surer when giving a direct command. "Have fun." Another shudder of breath frays the edges of her words.

I think I know who it is in there now. Anyway, it's worth a guess. "Ms. Thayer?" What is she doing in here? The executives have their own bathrooms.

A latch flicks; the stall door swings open. Ms. Thayer is what I dreamed I'd be someday, back when I was a business major freshman in college: a manager never destined to waste her life in the middle reaches of the company hierarchy, a comer and a climber with diamond-hard drive fit to cut through any glass ceiling her superiors are fool enough to place in her way. Sleekly groomed, tall and graceful in a tailored suit whose modest style still manages to let the world know it cost more than my monthly take-home pay, Ms. Thayer is a paragon. Every plane of expensive fabric lies just so along a body trimmed and toned and tanned to perfection. Only the front of her slim blue skirt seems to have rucked itself a little out of line. It bulges just a bit, as if—as if—

Oh.

"Would you like me to come with you?" I ask her. I don't need to hear confessions. "If it's today, I mean." If I'm wrong, she'll let me know.

She nods her head. Her nose is red and there is a little trace of slime on her upper lip. Her cheeks are streaked with red, her eyes squinched half shut to hold back more tears. "I called," she tells me. "I have a four o'clock appointment. Upstairs, they think I'm going to the dentist."

"I'll meet you in the lobby, then, at three-thirty," I promise. And I add, because I know this is what she needs to hear more than anything, "It's not so bad." She squeezes my hand and flees back into the shelter of the stall. I hear the tears again, but they are softer this time. She is no longer so afraid.

I could take her sorrow from her as I took her fear by telling her there are ways to make what lies ahead a blessing, but I won't do that. She'd never believe me, anyhow. I know I would never have believed anyone when it was me. Besides, I was in college. I knew it all, better than anyone who'd been there, and the evening news was full of stories to back up my conviction that I'd chosen purgatory over hell. You're supposed to be able to survive purgatory.

I should have known better. Surviving isn't living, it's only breath that doesn't shudder to a stop, a heart that keeps lurching through beat after beat after beat long after it's lost all reason to keep on beating. I was wrong. But I was in college, Mom and Dad had given up so much to provide the difference between my meager scholarship and the actual cost of tuition, books, room and board. They said, "Make us proud."

When I dropped out in my junior year and got this job as a secretary, they never said a word.

I think I need a cup of coffee. I know I need a place to sit and think about what I'll do to fill the hours between now and three-thirty, three-thirty and six. There's a nice little coffee shop a block from the office, so I go there and take a booth. The morning rush is over; no one minds.

The waitress knows me. Her name is Caroline. She is twenty-six, just two years older than me. Usually I come here for lunch at the counter when there's lots of customers, but we still find time to talk. She knows me and I know her. Her pink uniform balloons over a belly that holds her sixth baby. She admires me for the way I can tease her about it. "Isn't that kid here *yet*?" I ask.

"Probably a boy," she answers. "Men are never on time." We both laugh.

"So how far along are you?"

"Almost there. You don't wanna know how close."

"No kidding? So why are you still—?"

"Here? Working?" She laughs. "Like I've got a choice!" She takes my order and brings me my food. I eat scrambled eggs and bacon and toast soaked with butter. I drink three cups of coffee, black. I don't want to live forever. I leave Caroline a big tip because it's no joke having five—six—kids to raise at today's prices and a husband who doesn't earn much more than minimum wage.

I get a good idea while I am smearing strawberry jam over my last piece of toast: the Woman's Center. I do weekend volunteer work there, but there's no reason I can't go over today and see if they can use me. I'm free.

I try to hail a cab but all of them are taken, mostly by businessmen. Once I see an empty one sail past, but he keeps on going when I wave. Maybe he is nearsighted and can't see me through the driver's bulletproof bubble. Maybe he is out of sampler sheets for his automatic fare-scan and is hurrying to pick up some more. Maybe he just assumes that because I am a woman of a certain age I really don't want to ride in a cab at all.

I walk a block west and take the bus. Buses don't need fare-scan terminals because it always costs the same for every ride and you don't need to key in the tip. Tokens are enough. I ride downtown across the aisle from a woman with two small children, a boy and a girl. The boy is only two or three years old and sits in his mother's lap, making *rrrum-rrrum* noises with his toy truck. The little girl looks about four and regards her brother scornfully. She sits in her own seat with her hands folded in the lap of her peach-colored spring coat. She wants the world to know that she is all grown up and impatient to leave baby things behind. I wonder if she'll like kindergarten as much as Tessa did? She didn't cry at all when it was time to go, even though it meant I couldn't see her in the mornings.

Things are pretty quiet at the Woman's Center. After all, it is a weekday, a workday. You have to work if you want to live. But Oralee is there. Oralee is always there, tall and black and ugly as a dog's dinner, the way my mom would say. She is the Center manager. It doesn't pay much, but it's what she wants to do. She is seated at her desk—an old wooden relic from some long-gone public school—and when she sees me she is surprised.

Then she remembers.

"Linda, happy freedom!" She rises from her chair and rushes across the room to embrace me. Her skin is very soft and smells like lilacs. I don't know what to do or say. Oralee lives with her lover Corinne, so I don't feel right about hugging her back, no matter how much I like her or how grateful I am for all she's done for me over the years. It would be easier if she hadn't told me the truth about herself. A lesbian is a lesbian, I have no trouble hugging Corinne, but what Oralee is scares me. She clings to Corinne not because she loves her, but because it's safe, because she'll never have to risk anything that way, because her body craves touching. Oralee is always telling us we have to be brave, but she is a coward, pretending she's something she's not, out of fear. I can understand, but I can't like her for it.

Oralee leads me back to her desk and motions for me to sit down. She leans forward, her elbows on the blotter, a pen twiddling through her fingers. "So, to what do we owe the honor?" she asks, a grin cutting through the scars that make her face look like a topographical map with mountains pinched up and valleys gouged in. Today she wears the blue glass eye that doesn't match her working brown one and that startles people who don't know her.

"My boss gave me the day off," I tell her. "With pay."

"Well, of course he did. Soul-salving bastard."

"I have to be somewhere at three-thirty, but I thought that until then you might have something for me to do here."

Oralee pushes her chair a little away from her desk. The casters squeak and the linoleum floor complains. She runs her fingers over her shaven skull in thought. "Well, Joan and Cruz are already handling all the paperwork. . . . Our big fund-raising drive's not on until next week, no need for follow-up phone calls, the envelopes are all stuffed and in the mail . . ."

My heart sinks as she runs down a list of things that don't want doing. I try not to think about the empty hours I'll have to face if Oralee can't use me. To distract myself while I await her verdict, I look at all the things cluttering up her desktop. There is an old soup can covered with yellow-flowered shelving paper, full of paper clips, and another one full of pens and pencils. Three clay figurines of the Goddess lie like sunbathers with pendulous breasts and swollen bellies offered up to the shameless sky. Oralee made the biggest one herself in a ceramics class. She uses Her for a paperweight. Oralee says she is a firm believer in making do with what you've got. Mr. Beeton would laugh out loud if he could see the antiquated terminal she uses. All you need to access it is a password that you type in on the keys so just anyone can get into your files if they discover what it is. At least this way the Woman's Center saves money on sampler pads, even if that's not the real reason.

The photo on the desk is framed with silver, real silver. Oralee has to polish it constantly to keep the tarnish at bay. The young black woman in the picture is smiling, her eyes both her own, her face smooth and silky-looking as the inner skin of a shell, her hair a soft, dark cloud that enhances her smile more beautifully than any silver frame.

At the bottom of the frame, under the glass with the photograph, there is a newspaper clipping. It's just the headline and it's not very big. The event it notes was nothing extraordinary enough to merit more prominent placement on the page: ABORTION CLINIC BOMBED. TWO DEAD, THREE INJURED. The clipping came from a special paper, more like a newsletter for the kind of people who would read TWO DEAD, THREE INJURED and smile. Oralee tells us that most of the papers weren't like that; they used to call them birth control clinics or family planning clinics or even just women's clinics. As if we're none of us old enough to remember when it changed! She talks about those days—the times when the bombings were stepped up and the assaults on women trying to reach the clinics got ugly and the doctors and sometimes their families were being threatened, being killed—as if they'd lasted as long as the Dark Ages instead of just four years. Thank goodness everything's settled down. We're civilized people, after all. We can compromise.

"I know!" Oralee snaps her fingers, making me look up. "You can be a runner. That is—" She hesitates.

"Yes, I can do that," I tell her.

"Are you sure?"

"Just give me what I need and tell me where I have to go. It's all right, really. I need to go to the bank myself anyway."

"Are you *sure*?" she asks again. Why does she doubt me? Do I look so fragile? No. I take good care of my body, wash my hair every day, even put on a little lipstick sometimes. It's not like before, that hard time when I first came to the city, when I was such a fool. I almost lost my job, then, because I was letting myself go so badly. I know better, now. It's my duty to set a good example. Children past a certain age start to notice things like how Mommy looks and how Mommy acts. I've read all the books. You get the child you deserve.

Oralee goes into the back room where they keep the refrigerator. She comes back with a compartmentalized cold pack the size of a clutch purse, a factory-fresh sampler pad, and a slip of paper. "You can put this in your pocketbook if you want," she tells me, giving me the cold pack. "Make sure you only keep it open long enough to take out or put in one sample at a time. And for the love of God, don't mix up the samples!"

I smile at how vehement she sounds. "I've done this before, Oralee," I remind her.

"Sure you have; sorry. Here are the names and addresses. Bus tokens are in the clay pot on the table by the front door. You don't have to bring back the pack when you're done; just drop it off next time you're here." She cocks her head. "If you *are* coming back?"

"Of course I am," I say, surprised that she'd think I wouldn't.

"Oh," she says. "Because I thought—you know—after today's over— Well, whatever. Good luck."

There are five names on the list, most of them in the neighborhood close to the Woman's Center, only one of them farther uptown. It's a glorious spring day. Soon it will be Easter. The holiday came late this year, almost the end of April. I think April is a pretty name to give a girl—April, full of hope and promise, full of beauty. Maybe I should have named my daughter April. I laugh away the thought. What's done is done, too late now to change Tessa's name. Too late.

When I get to the first place I'm surprised by how old the woman is who answers the door. I introduce myself and say that the Woman's Center sent me. I show her the cold pack and the sampler pad, telling her what I'll do for her at the bank. She has black hair that is so shot through with silver threads it looks gray, and her fingers are stained with tobacco. She stands in the doorway, stony-eyed, barring me from the dark apartment beyond, making me stand in the hall while I run through my entire explanation.

After I have finished and I'm standing there, holding out one sampler sheet, she speaks: "I'm not Vicky," she says. "I'm her mother. God will judge you people. You go to hell." And she slams the door in my face.

I feel like a fool, but by the time I reach the next address on the list the feeling has faded. It's better here. The woman's name is Maris and she lives alone. She urges me to come in, to have a cup of tea, some cookies, anything I'd like. Her apartment is small but tasteful, a lot of wicker, a lot of sunlight. "God bless you," she says. "I was just about at my wits' end. I thought if I had to go through that one more time I'd go crazy. It's supposed to get easier with time, but it just gets harder. I've got three more years to go before I'm free. Never again, believe me; never again."

She rubs the sampler sheet over her thumb and watches like a hawk as I fumble it into its thin plastic envelope. The envelope goes into the cold pack and the cold pack goes back into my purse. "Are you sure you remember my password?" she asks as she sees me to the door.

"Yes, but please change it after today," I tell her.

The third and fourth women are not as hospitable as Maris, but there is no one there to tell me to go to hell. One of them is an artist, the other lost her job, and Maris, I recall, told me she'd taken a sick day off from work just on the off chance the Woman's Center could find a runner to come help her. It feels very strange to me, sitting in rooms freckled with spring sunshine, to be talking with strange women when I would normally be at work. In the course of these three visitations I drink three cups of tea and also share a little gin with the woman who has lost her job. My head spins with passwords and special instructions, my hands clasp a pile of three plain brown self-addressed stamped envelopes by the time I teeter out the door in search of my final contact.

I take the bus uptown. Out the window I see new leaves unfurl in blurs of green made more heartstoppingly tender by the gin. It was a mistake to drink, but if I looked into the glass I didn't have to look into the woman's eyes. I decide to get off the bus a few blocks away from my stop. A walk will clear my head.

The blue and red and white lights flash, dazzling me. Two police cars and a crowd have gathered outside a restaurant that's trying to be a Paris sidewalk café. A man is clinging to the curlicued iron fence around one of the trees in front of the place, his face a paler green than the leaves above his head. I smell vomit, sour and pungent. I watch where I step as I try to make my way through the crowd.

One of the policemen is holding a shopping bag and trying to make the crowd back away. The bottom of the shopping bag looks wet. Another one is telling the people over and over that there is nothing here for them to see, but they know better.

A third stands with pad in hand, interviewing a waiter. The waiter looks young and frightened. He keeps saying, "I didn't know, I had no idea, she came in and ordered a Caesar salad and a cup of tea, then she paid the bill and started to go. I didn't even notice she'd left that bag under the table until that man grabbed it and started to run after her." He points to the man embracing the iron girdle of the tree. "I didn't know a thing."

The girl is in the fourth policeman's custody. I think she must be sixteen, although she could be older and small for her age. Her face is flat, vacant. What does she see? The policeman helps her into the back of his squad car and slams the door. "Said she couldn't face it, going to a clinic, having it recorded like a decent woman. Bitch," I hear him mutter. "Murderer."

As I walk past, quickening my step as much as I can without beginning to run, I hear the waiter's fluting voice say, "I don't think it was dead when she got here."

A man answers the door when I ring the bell at my last stop. "Frances Hughes?" I ask nervously. Has a prankster called the Woman's Center, giving a man's name that sounds like a woman's? Oralee says it's happened before. Sometimes a prank call only leads to a wild goose chase, but sometimes when the runner arrives they're waiting for her. Trudy had her wrist broken and they destroyed all the samples she'd collected so far. It was just like those stories about Japanese soldiers lost for years on small islands in the Pacific, still fighting a war that was over decades ago.

The man smiles at me. "No, I'm her husband," he says. "Won't you come in?"

Frances Hughes is waiting for me in the living room. She is one of those women whose face reflects years of breeding and who looks as if she were born to preside over a fine china tea service on a silver tray. If I drink one more cup of tea I think I'll die, but I accept the cup she passes to me because she needs to do this.

"We can't thank you enough," her husband says as he sits down in the Queen Anne armchair across from mine. Frances sits on the sofa, secure behind a castle wall of cups and saucers, sliced lemons and sugar cubes and lacy silver tongs. "I wanted to do it, but Frances insisted we call you."

"You know you couldn't do it, George," says Frances. "Remember how hard it was for you in the clinic, and after?"

"I *could* do it," he insists stubbornly.

"But you don't have to," she tells him softly. "Spare yourself, for me." She reaches over to stroke his hand. There is an old love between them and I feel it flow in waves of strength from her to him.

I leave their building still carrying just three brown envelopes. They don't want me to mail them any cash, like the others; they only want me to close Frances's personal account and transfer the funds into George's.

I also have a check in my wallet from Mr. George Hughes made out to the Woman's Center. He gave it to me when I was leaving the apartment, while I set my purse aside on a miniature bookcase and re-buttoned my jacket. He said, "We were very wrong." I didn't know what he meant. Then, just as I was picking up my purse, my eye lit on the title of one of the volumes in that bookcase.

"No Remorse?"

It is the book that changed things for good, for ill. You can still find it for sale all over. My aunt Lucille gave a copy to my mother. My mother has not spoken to her since. They study it in schools with the same awe they give to *Uncle Tom's Cabin* and *Mein Kampf.* Some say, "It stopped the attacks, the bombings, it saved lives." Others say, "It didn't stop the deaths. So what if they're forced to suffer? It still sanc-tioned murder." Some reply, "It threw those damned extremists a sop, it truly freed women." And others yet say, "It sold out our true freedom for a false peace, it made us terror's slaves." I say nothing about it at all. All I know is what it did to me.

I looked at Frances's husband and I wanted to believe that the book had come there by accident, left behind by a caller who was now no longer welcome under that roof. But when he looked away from me and his face turned red, I knew the truth. I took the check. "You go to hell," I told him, the same way Vicky's mother said it to me.

I will not use Frances Hughes's password and sample to steal. I could, but I won't. I will not betray as I hope not to be betrayed. But George Hughes doesn't know that. Let him call ahead to his bank, change the password. Let him be the one to come down and face the truth of what he's helped to bring about, this dear-won, bloody-minded peace. Let him twist in the wind.

There is almost no line worth mentioning at the bank. It is a small branch office with only one live employee to handle all transactions past a certain level of complexity. All others can be taken care of through the ATMs. There is only one ATM here. As I said, this is a small branch.

I prefer small banks. Larger ones sometimes have live employees on duty whose only job is to make sure that no one uses the ATMs to perform transactions for a third party. That would be cheating.

I stand behind a man who stands behind a woman. She looks as if she is at least fifty years old, but when it is her turn she does not take one of the sampler sheets from the dispenser. Instead she opens her purse and takes out a cold pack like mine, a little smaller. Her hands are shaking as she extracts the sheet, inserts it, and types in the password.

The child is no more than nine months old. It can coo and gurgle. It can paw at the screen with its plump, brown hands. "Hi, sugar," the woman says, her voice trembling. "It's Nana, darlin', hi. It's your nana. Your mama couldn't come here today; she sick. She'll come see you soon, I promise. I love you, baby. I love—"

The screen is dark. A line of shining letters politely requests that the woman go on with her transaction. She stares at the screen, tight-lipped, and goes on. Bills drop one after another into the tray. She scoops them out without even bothering to look down, crams them into her purse, and walks out, seeing nothing but the door.

The man ahead of me dashes a sampler sheet over his thumb, inserts it, and does his business. He looks young, in his twenties. He is handsome. The girls must have a hard time resisting him, especially if he knows how to turn on the charm. He may have the ability to make them think he is falling in love with them, the passion of novels, spontaneous, intense, rapture by accident.

Accidents happen. Accidents can change your life, but only if you let them. While he is waiting for the ATM to process his transaction, he turns his head so that I can see his profile. He looks like a comic book hero, steadfast and noble, loyal and true. If there were an accident, he would accompany her to the clinic. He would hold her hand and stay with her for as long as the doctors allowed. And then it would all be over for him and he could go home, go about his business. No one would insist on making sure he stayed sorry for what was done.

There is no picture on the screen for him.

I am next. I do the other transactions first. Maris has a little three-year-old boy, like the one I saw on the bus. He can talk quite well for his age. He holds up a blue teddy bear to the screen. "T'ank you, Mommy," he says. "I name him Tadda-boy. Give Mommy a big kiss, Tadda-boy." He presses the bear's snout to the glass.

The artist's little girl is still only a few months old. This is easy. I never had any trouble when Tessa was this young. I could pretend I was watching a commercial for disposable diapers on the TV. It got harder after Tessa learned to do things, to roll over, to push herself onto hands and knees, to toddle, to talk . . .

The woman who lost her job has a one-year-old with no hair and the bright, round eyes of the blue teddy bear. I can't tell whether this is a boy or a girl, but I know he or she will be blond. Tessa is blond. She looked like a fuzzy-headed little duckling until she was almost two.

I see why Frances Hughes did not let George handle this. The child lies on its back, staring straight up with dull eyes. It must be more than a year old, judging from its size, but it makes no attempt to move, not even to turn its head. I feel sorry for Frances. Then I remember the book in their house and for a moment I am tempted to believe that there is a just God.

Of course, I know better.

It's my turn. I glance over my shoulder. A line has formed behind me. Four people are waiting. They look impatient. One of them is a woman in her sixties. She looks angry. I guess they have been standing in line long enough to notice that I am not just doing business for myself.

I leave the ATM and walk to the back of the line. As I pass the others I murmur how sorry I am for making them wait, how there was no one waiting behind me when I began my transactions. The three people who were merely impatient now smile at me. The woman in her sixties is at the end of the line. She waits until I have taken my place behind her, then she turns around and spits in my face.

"Slut!" she shouts. "Murdering bitch! You and all the rest like you, baby killers, damned whores, can't even face up to your sins! Get the hell out of—"

"I'm sorry, ma'am, but I'm going to have to ask you to leave." The bank's sole live employee is standing between us. He is a big man, a tall man. I have yet to see one of these small branches where the only live worker is not built like a bodyguard. That is part of the job, too.

"You should toss her out, not me!" the woman snaps. She lunges for me, swatting at me with her purse. I take a step backward, holding the envelopes tight to my chest. I am afraid to drop them. She might get her hands on one and tear it up.

The man restrains her. "Ma'am, I don't want to have to call the police."

This works. She settles down. Bristling, she stalks out of the bank, cursing me loudly. The man looks at me but does not smile. "In the future, please limit yourself to personal transactions," he says.

"Thank you," I say, dabbing the woman's spittle from my cheek with a tissue.

It is my turn again. I want to kiss the sampler sheet before I run it across my thumb, but I know that if I do that, I will not be able to access my account. I wonder how long we will have together? Sometimes it is ten seconds, sometimes fifteen. Maybe they will give us twenty because it's Tessa's birthday. I take a deep breath and insert the sampler sheet, then enter my password.

There she is! Oh my God, there she is, my baby, my daughter, my beautiful little girl! She is smiling, twirling to show off her lovely pink party dress with all the crisp ruffles. Her long blond hair floats over her shoulders like a cloud. "Hi, Mama!" she chirps.

"Hi, baby." My hand reaches out to caress her cheek. I have to hold it back. Touching the screen is not allowed. It either cuts off the allotted seconds entirely, or cuts them short, or extends them for an unpredictable amount of time. Few risk the gamble. I can't; not today.

I take out the invitation and hold it up so that Tessa can see it. "Look, honey," I say. "Pandas!"

"I'm going to school tomorrow," Tessa tells me. "I'm a big girl now. I'm almost all grown up."

"Baby . . ." My eyes are blinking so fast, so fast! Tessa becomes a sweet pink and gold blur. "Baby, I love you so much. I'm sorry, I'm so sorry for what I did, but I was so young, I couldn't— Oh, my baby!"

And I *will* touch her, I *will*! It's all lies they tell us anyway, about how touching the screen will affect how long we may see our children, about how now we are safe to choose, about how our compromise was enough to stop the clinic bombings and the assassinations of doctors and the fear. I don't believe them! I will hold my child!

Glass, smooth and dark.

"I'm sorry, ma'am, but I'm going to have to ask you to leave."

I go with my own business left undone. The man takes a spray bottle of glass cleaner and a cloth from his desk and wipes away the prints of my hands, the image of my lips.

There is another small bank that I like on the east side. I think I'll go there. I start to walk. It's getting late. Paula must be making all kinds of last-minute phone calls, settling the details of my party. They call it freedom. I call it nothing.

At first I hated her, you know. I hated my own child. She was there, always there, on every CRT device I chose to use in college, in public, at home. After the procedure, the college clinic forwarded the development information that the central programming unit needed to establish her birthdate. The tissue was sent along, too, so that they could project a genetically accurate image of my child. She wasn't there until her birthdate, but then—!

Then there was no escaping her. Not if I wanted to use a computer, or an ATM, or even turn on any but the most antiquated model of a television set. I hated her. I hated her the way some hate the children of rape who also live behind the glass, after. But they exult in what they've done, how they've had the last laugh, how they've cheated their assailants of the final insult. I have seen them in the banks, at the ATMs, even at work, once. *Who's got the power now?* they shout at the children, and they laugh until they cry. Sometimes they only cry.

I fled her. I ran away—away from college, away from home, away from so much that had been my life before. Away from Tessa. A mandatory sentence of six years of persecution for one mistake, one accident, seemed like an eternity. She was almost the end of my future and my sanity.

And then, one day, it changed. One day I looked at her and she wasn't a punishment; she was my little girl, my Tessa with her long, silky blond curls and her shining blue eyes and her downy cheeks that must smell like roses, like apples. One day I was tired of hating, tired of running. One day I looked at her and I felt love.

Now they're taking my baby away.

No.

I find a phone booth. "Hello, Ms. Thayer? I'm sorry, something's come up. I can't go with you to the clinic today. . . . Yes, this is Linda. . . . No, really, you'll be all right. No one will bother you; it's against the law. And after, you'll handle it just fine. . . . Sure, you will. I did."

"Hello, Mr. Beeton? This is Linda. I don't think I'll be in tomorrow. . . . Yes, I know you can't give me two days off with pay. That's all right."

"Hello, Paula? Linda. Listen, there's a spare key with my neighbor, Mrs. Giancarlo. Feed Squeaker. . . . No, just do it, I can't talk now. And for God's sake, don't let him hide in the closet. I have to go. Good-bye."

I am walking east. I realize that I am still holding the envelopes full of all the money the women need. Singly they are small sums, but put them all together . . . I could buy a lot of pretty things for Tessa with so much money. I could afford to keep her, if I were rich as Frances Hughes.

There are no mailboxes near the river. I'm letting them all down, all of them except for Frances Hughes and her husband. I'm so sorry. Maybe I should call Oralee—? No. She's a coward. I despise her. If I turn back to find a mailbox, I might turn back forever. Then I'll be a coward, too. It's Tessa who's been so brave, so loving, so alone for so long, and still she smiles for me. Tessa is the only one that matters.

I lean against the railing and see another shore. Gulls keen and dip their wings above the river. Starveling trees claw the sky. The envelopes flutter from my hands, kissing the water. No one is near. I take off my shoes to help me step over the railing. The concrete is cold through my stockings.

There she is. I see her as I have always seen her, smiling up at me through the sleek, shining surface that keeps us apart. She is giggling as she reaches out for the envelopes. Oh, greedy little girl! You can't spend all that. Now that you're six, maybe Mama will give you an allowance, just like the big girls. After all, you're going to school tomorrow. But first, let Mama give you a kiss.

We fly into each other's arms. Oh, Tessa, your lips are so cool! Your laughter rushes against my ears. I breathe in, and you fill my heart.

Happy birthday, my darling.

The Chronology Protection Case

Paul Levinson

Paul Levinson's science fiction and fantasy stories have appeared in *Analog, Amazing,* and in anthologies such as *Xanadu 3.* His nonfiction can be found in *Wired, The New York Review of Science Fiction,* and *Tangent.* He is the editor in chief of the *Journal of Social and Evolutionary Systems.* Levinson is adjunct professor of communications at Hofstra University, and his organization, Connected Education, has been offering graduate courses on the Internet for more than a decade.

About his novelette, "The Chronology Protection Case," which was also a finalist for the Sturgeon Award for best short science fiction of 1995, Paul Levinson writes:

"I've always had a special love for time travel, likely because it's so exquisitely impossible. As I began my professional career as an historian and philosopher of science and technology, I came to realize that most things in science fiction are not as impossible as time travel. Faster-than-light travel, for example, is limited by a series of well-corroborated, interlocking theories—but these theories could someday admit to the same fate as Ptolemy's before Copernicus, or Newton's before Einstein. In contrast, to travel in time is to court extraordinary paradox at every turn, deny the free will that most of us take to be a cornerstone of our existence.

" 'The Chronology Protection Case' began, in effect, with a tiny nonfiction piece I had published in *Wired* in July 1994—'Telnet to the Future?'—in which I argued that literal, immediate communication across time (in contrast to endeavors like time capsules, which do it the hard way) posed an ultimate, unbreachable limit to telecommunication because of the paradoxes mentioned above. I received an avalanche of e-mail in response, some from enraged physicists who wanted to give me mathematical reasons that time travel could indeed be possible (as if mathematics could trump logical paradox). One, in particular, argued his case forcefully, but admitted that Stephen Hawking would agree with me, having postulated a 'chronology protection conjecture' which held that although time travel might be mathematically possible, the universe, in order to avoid paradox, would never permit it.

"Of course, what Hawking had in mind is that physical resistances would always arise in situations in which time travel was mathematically possible. But to my perverse brain, the notion of the universe acting to prevent time travel instantly suggested more intriguing possibilities. . . .

"The other feature of 'The Chronology Protection Case' that gives it its flavor is its hero, Dr. Phil D'Amato, a forensic detective with the New York City Police Department. I've always been a fan of the police procedural, and a guy named Phil who sat next to me when I was a graduate student at the New School went on to become a lieutenant in the NYPD, so I was off and running with Phil D'. As important as 'The Chronology Protection Case' obviously is to me in its own right, its most enduring import may reside in its launching of Phil D'Amato's career. He has since appeared in two other *Analog* novelettes—'The Copyright Notice Case' (April 1996) and 'The Mendelian Lamp Case' (April 1997)—several other stories are percolating, and I am about halfway finished with my first Phil D'Amato novel, presently titled *The Silk Code*."

Carl put the call through just as I was packing up for the day. "She says she's some kind of physicist," he said, and although I rarely took calls from the public, I jumped on this one.

"Dr. D'Amato?" she asked.

"Yes?"

"I saw you on television last week—on that cable talk show. You said you had a passion for physics." Her voice had a breathy elegance.

"True," I said. Forensic science was my profession, but cutting edge physics was my love. Too bad there wasn't a way to nab rapist murderers with spectral traces. "And you're a physicist?" I asked.

"Oh yes, sorry," she said. "I should introduce myself. I'm Lauren Goldring. Do you know my work?"

"Ahm . . ." The name did sound familiar. I ran through the Rolodex in my head, though these days my computer was becoming more reliable than my brain. "Yes!" I snapped my fingers. "You had an article in *Scientific American* last month about some Hubble data."

"That's right," she said, and I could hear her relax just a bit. "Look, I'm calling you about my husband—he's disappeared. I haven't heard from him in two days."

"Oh," I said. "Well, that's really not my department. I can connect you to—"

"No, please," she said. "It's not what you think. I'm sure his disappearance has something to do with his work. He's a physicist, too."

Forty minutes later I was in my car on my way to her house, when I should have been home with pizza and the cat. No contest: a physicist in distress always wins.

Her Bronxville address wasn't too far from mine in Yonkers.

"Dr. D'Amato?" She opened the door.

I nodded. "Phil."

"Thank you so much for coming," she said, and ushered me in. Her eyes looked red, like she suffered from allergies or had been crying. But few people have allergies in March.

The house had a quiet appealing beauty. As did she.

"I know the usual expectations in these things," she said. "He has another woman, we've been fighting. And I'm sure that most women whose vanished husbands *have* been having affairs are quick to profess their certainty that that's not what's going on in *their* cases."

I smiled. "OK, I'm willing to start with the assumption that your case is different. Tell me how."

"Would you like a drink, some wine?" She walked over to a cabinet, must've been turn of the century.

"Just ginger ale, if you have it," I said, leaning back in the plush Morris chair she'd shown me to.

She returned with the ginger ale, and some sort of sparkling water for herself. "Well, as I told you on the phone, Ian and I are physicists—"

"Is his last name Goldring, like yours?"

Lauren nodded. "And, well, I'm sure this has something to do with his project."

"You two don't do the same work?" I asked.

"No," she said. "My area's the cosmos at large—big bang theory, black holes in space, the big picture. Ian's was, is, on the other end of the spectrum. Literally. His area's quantum mechanics." She started to sob.

"It's OK," I said. I got up and put my hand on her shoulder. Quantum mechanics could be frustrating, I know, but not *that* bad.

"No," she said. "It isn't OK. Why am I using the past tense for Ian?"

"You think some harm's come to him?"

"I don't know," her lips quivered. She did know, or thought she knew.

"And you feel this had something to do with his work with tiny particles? Was he exposed to dangerous radiation?"

"No," she said. "That's not it. He was working on something called quantum signaling. He always told me everything about his work—and I told him everything about mine—we had that kind of relationship. And then a few months ago, he suddenly got silent. At first I thought maybe he *was* having an affair—"

And the thought popped into my head: if I had a woman with your class, an affair with someone else would be the last thing on my mind.

"But then I realized it was deeper than that. It was something, something that frightened him, in his work. Something that I think he wanted to shield me from."

"I'm pretty much of an amiable amateur when it comes to quantum mechanics," I said, "but I know something about it. Suppose you tell me all you know about Ian's work, and why it could be dangerous."

What I, in fact, fully grasped about quantum mechanics I could write on a postcard to my sister in Boston and it would likely fit. It had to do with light and particles so small that they were often indistinguishable in their behavior and prone to paradox at every turn. A particularly vexing aspect that even Einstein and his colleagues tried to tackle in the 1930s involved two particles that at first collided and then traveled at sublight speeds in opposite directions: would observation of one have an instantaneous effect on the other? Did the two particles, having once collided, now exist ever after in some sort of mysterious relationship or field, a bond between them so potent that just to measure one was to influence the other, regardless of how far away? Einstein wondered about this in a thought experiment. Did interaction of subatomic particles tie their futures together forever, even if one stayed on Earth and the other wound up beyond Pluto? Real experiments in the 1960s and after suggested that's just what was happening, at least in local areas, and this supported Heisenberg's and Bohr's classic "Copenhagen" interpretation that quantum mechanics was some kind of mind-over-matter deal—that just looking at a quantum or tiny particle, maybe even thinking about it, could affect not only it but related particles. Einstein would've preferred to find another cause—nonmental—for such phenomena. But that could lead to an interpretation of quantum mechanics as faster-than-light action—the particle on Earth somehow sent an instant signal to the particle in space—which of course ran counter to Einstein's relativity theories.

Well, I guess that would fill more than your average postcard. The truth is, blood and semen and DNA evidence were a lot easier to make sense of than quantum mechanics, which was one reason that kind of esoteric science was just a hobby with me. Of course, one way that QM had it over forensics is that it rarely had to do with dead bodies. But Lauren Goldring was wanting to tell me that maybe it did in at least one case, her husband's.

"Ian was part of a small group of physicists working to demonstrate that QM was evidence of faster-than-light travel, time travel, maybe both," she said.

"Not a product of the mind?" I asked.

"No," she said, "not as in the traditional interpretation."

"But doesn't faster-than-light travel contradict Einstein?" I asked.

"Not necessarily," Lauren said. "It seems to contradict the simplest interpretations, but there may be some loopholes."

"Go on," I said.

"Well, there's a lot of disagreement even among the small group of people Ian was working with. Some think the data supports both faster-than-light *and* time travel. Others are sure that time travel is impossible even though—"

"You're not saying that you think some crazy envious scientist killed him?" I asked.

"No," Lauren said. "It's much deeper than that."

A favorite phrase of hers. "I don't understand," I said.

"Well, Stephen Hawking, for one, says that although the equations suggest that time travel might be possible on the quantum level, the Universe wouldn't let this happen . . ." She paused and looked at me. "You've heard about Hawking's work in this area?"

"I know about Hawking in general," I said. "I'm not that much of an amateur. But not about his work in time travel."

"You're very unusual for a forensic scientist," she said, with an admiring edge I very much liked. "Anyway, Hawking thinks that whatever quantum mechanics may permit, the Universe just won't allow time travel—because the level of paradox time travel would create would just unravel the whole Universe."

"You mean like if I could get a message back to JFK that he would be killed, and he believed me and acted upon that information and didn't go to Dallas and wasn't killed, this would create a world in which I would grow up with no knowledge that JFK had ever been killed, which would mean I would have no motive to send the message that saved JFK, but if I didn't send that message then JFK would be killed—"

"That's it," Lauren said. "Except on the quantum level you might achieve that paradox by sending back information just a few seconds in time—say, in the form of a command that would shut down the generating circuit and prevent the information from being sent in the first place—"

"I see," I said.

"And, well, because things like that, if they could happen, if they happened all the time, would lead to a constantly remade, inside-out, self-effacing universe. Hawking promulgated his 'chronology protection conjecture'—the Universe protects the existing time line, whatever the theoretical possibilities of time travel."

"How does your husband fit into this?" I asked.

"He was working on a device, an experiment, to disprove Hawking's conjecture," she said. "He was trying to create a local wormhole with temporal effects."

"And you think he somehow disappeared into this?" Jeez, this was beginning to sound like a bad episode of *Star Trek* already. But she seemed rational, everything she'd outlined made sense, and something in her manner continued to compel my attention.

"I don't know." She looked like she was close to tears again.

"All right," I said. "Here's what I think we should do. I'm going to call in Ian's disappearance to a friend in the Department. He's a precinct captain, and he'll take this seriously. He'll contact all the airports, get Ian's picture out to cops on the beat—"

"But I don't think—"

"I know," I said. "You've got a gut feeling that something more profound is going on. And maybe you're right. But we've got to cover all the bases."

"OK," she said quietly, and I noticed that her lips were quivering again.

"Will you be all right tonight? I'll be back to you tomorrow morning." I took her hand.

"I guess so," she said huskily, and squeezed my hand.

I didn't feel like letting go, but I did.

The news the next morning was terrible. I don't care what the shrinks say: flat-out confirmed death is always worse than ambiguous unresolved disappearance.

I couldn't bring myself to just call her on the phone. I drove to her home, hoping she was in.

She opened the door. I tried to keep a calm face, but I'm not that good an actor.

She understood immediately. "Oh no!" she cried out. She staggered and collapsed in my arms. "Please no."

"I'm sorry," I said, and touched her hair. I felt like kissing her forehead, but didn't. I hardly knew her, yet I felt very close to her, a part of her world. "They found him a few hours ago near Columbia University. Looks like another stupid, senseless, god damned random drive-by shooting. That's the kind of world we live in." I didn't know whether this would in any way lessen her pain. At least his death had nothing to do with his work.

"No, not random," she said, sobbing. "Not random."

"OK," I said, "you need to rest, I'm going to call someone over here to give you a sedative. I'll stay with you till then."

The medic was over in fifteen minutes. He gave her a shot, and she was asleep a few minutes later. "Not random. Not random," she mumbled.

I called the captain, and asked if he could send a uniform over to stay with Lauren for the afternoon. He wasn't happy—his people were overworked, like everyone—but he owed me. Many's the time I'd saved his butt with some piece of evidence I'd uncovered in the back of an orifice.

I dropped by the autopsy. Nothing unusual there. Three bullets from a cheap punk's gun, one shattered the heart, did all the damage, Ian Goldring's dead. No sign of radiation damage, no strange chemistry in the body. No possible connection that I could see to anything Lauren had told me. Still, the coroner was a friend. I explained to him that the victim was the husband of a friend and asked if he could run any and every conceivable test at his disposal to determine if there was anything different about this corpse. He said sure. I knew he wouldn't find anything, though.

I went back to my office. I thought of calling Lauren and telling her about the autopsy, but she'd be better off if I let her rest. I was tired of looking at dead bodies. I turned on my computer and looked at its screen instead. I was on a few physics lists on the Internet. I logged on and did some reading about Hawking and his chronology protection conjecture.

"Lady physicist on the phone for you again," Carl called out. It was late afternoon already. I logged off and rubbed my eyes.

"Hi," Lauren said.

"You OK?" I asked.

"Yeah," she said. "I just got off the phone with one of the other researchers in Ian's group, and I think I've got part of this figured out." She sounded less tentative than yesterday—like she was indeed more on top of what was actually going on, or thought she was—but more worried.

I started to tell her, as gently as I could, about the autopsy.

"Doesn't matter," she interrupted me. "I mean, I don't think the *way* that Ian was killed has any relevance to this. It's the fact that he *was* killed that counts—the reason he was killed."

The reason—everyone wants reasons in this irrational society. Science in the laboratory deals with reason. In the outside world, you're lucky if you can find a reason. "I know it's painful," I said. "But Ian's death had no reason—his killer was likely just a high-flying kid with a gun. Happens all the time. Ian was just in the wrong place. A random victim in the murder lottery."

"No, not random," Lauren said.

She'd said the same thing this morning. I could hear her starting to sob again.

"Look, Phil," she continued. "I really think I'm close to understanding this. I'm going to make a few more calls. I, uh, we hardly know each other, but I feel good talking this out with you. Our conversation last night helped me a lot. Can I call you back in an hour? Or maybe—I don't know, if you're not busy tonight—could you come over again?"

She didn't have to ask twice. "I'll see you at seven. I'll also bring some food in case you're hungry—you have to eat."

I knew even before I drove up that something was wrong. I guess my eyes, after all these years of looking around crime scenes, are especially sensitive to the weak flicker of police lights on the evening sky at a distance. The flicker still turns my stomach.

"What's going on here?" I got out of my car, Chinese food in hand, and asked the uniform.

"Who the hell are you?" he replied.

I fumbled for my ID.

"He's OK." Janny Murphy, the uniform who'd come to stay with Lauren in the afternoon, walked over. "He's forensics."

The food dropped from my hand when I saw the expression on her face. Brown moo-shoo pork juice dribbled down the driveway.

"It's crazy," Janny said. "Doc says it's less than one in ten thousand. Some rare allergy to the shot the medic gave her. It wasn't his fault. It somehow brings out an asthma attack hours later. Fifty percent fatality."

"And Lauren—Dr. Goldring—was in the unlucky part of the curve."

Janny nodded.

"I don't believe this," I said, shaking my head.

"I know," Janny said. "Helluva coincidence. Physicist and his wife, also a physicist, both dying like that."

"Maybe it's not a coincidence," I said.

"What do you mean?" Janny said.

"I don't know what I mean," I said. "Is Lauren—is the body—still here? I'd like to have a look at her."

"Help yourself," Janny gestured inside the house.

I can't say Lauren looked at peace in death. I could almost still see her lips quivering, straining to tell me something, though they were as sealed as the deadest night now. I had an urge to kiss her face. I'd known her all of two days, wanted as many times to kiss her. Now I never would.

I was aware of Janny standing beside me.

"I'm going home now," I said.

"Sure," Janny said. "The captain says he'd like to talk to you tomorrow morning. Just to wrap this whole mess up. Bad karma."

Yeah, karma, like in Fritz Capra's *Tao of Physics*. Like in two entities crossing each other's paths and then nevermore touching each other's destinies. Like me and this soul with the soft, still lips. Except I had no power to influence Lauren, to make things better for her anymore. And the truth is, I hadn't done much for her when she was alive.

I was awake all night. I logged on to a few more fringy physics lists with my computer and did more reading. Finally it was light outside. I thought about calling Stephen Hawking. He was where? California? Cambridge, England? I wasn't sure. I knew he'd be able to talk to me if I could reach him—I'd seen a video of him talking through a special device—but he'd probably think I was crazy when I told him what I had to say. So I called Jack Donovan instead. He was another friend who owed me. I had lots of friends like that in the city. Jack was a science reporter for *Newsday*, and I'd come through for him with off-the-record background on murder investigations in my bailiwick lots of times. I hoped he'd come through for me now. I was starting to get worried. He had lots of connections in the field—he could talk to scientists who'd shy away from me, my being in the Department and all.

It was seven in the morning. I expected to get his answering machine, but I got him. I told him my story.

"OK," he said. "Why don't you go see the captain at the precinct, and then come over to see me? I'll do some checking around in the meantime."

I did what Jack said. I kept strictly to the facts with the captain— no suppositions, no chronological or any other protection schemes— and he took it all in with his customary frown. "Damn shame," he muttered. "Nice lady like that. They oughta take that sedative off the market. Damn drug companies are too greedy."

"Right," I said.

"You look exhausted," he said. "You oughta take the rest of the day off."

"More or less what I had in mind," I said, and left for Jack's.

I thought *my* office was high-tech, but Jack's Hempstead newsroom looked like something well into the next century. Computer screens everywhere you looked, sounds of modems chirping on and off like the patter of tiny raindrops.

Jack looked concerned. "You're not going to like this," he said.

"What else is new?" I said. "Try me."

"Well, you were right about my having better entrée to these physicists than you. I did a lot of checking," Jack said. "There were six people working actively in conjunction with Ian on this project. A few more, of course, if you take into account the usual complement of graduate student assistants. But outside of that, the project was sealed up pretty tightly—not by the government or any agency, but by the re- searchers themselves. Sometimes they do that when the research gets really flaky—like they don't want anyone to know what they're really doing until they're sure they have a reliable effect. You wouldn't be- lieve some of the wild things people have been getting into in the past few years—especially the physicists—now that they have the Internet to yammer at each other."

"I'm tired, Jack. Please get to the point."

"Well, four of the seven—that includes Ian Goldring—are now dead. One had a heart attack—the day after his doctor told him his cholesterol was in the bottom 10 percent. I guess that's not so strange. Another fell off his roof—he was cleaning out his gutters—and sev- ered his carotid artery on a sharp piece of flagstone that was sticking up on his walk. He bled to death before anyone found him. Another was struck by a car—DOA. And then there's Ian. I could write a story on this even without your conjecture—"

"Please don't," I said.

"It's a weird situation, all right. Four out of seven dying like that—and also Goldring's wife."

"How are the spouses of the other fatalities?" I asked.

"All OK," Jack said. "But none are physicists. None knew anything at all about their husbands' work—all of the dead were men. Lauren Goldring is the only one who had any idea what her husband was up to."

"She wasn't sure," I said. "But I think she figured it out just before she died."

"Maybe they all picked up some virus at a conference they attended—something which threw off their sense of balance, caused their heart rate to speed up." Sam Abrahmson, Jack's editor, strolled by and jumped in. Clearly he'd been listening on the periphery of our conversation. "That could explain the two accidents and the heart attack," he added. "Maybe even the sedative death."

"But not the drive-by shooting of Goldring," I said.

"No," Abrahmson admitted. "But it could be an interesting story anyway. Think about it," he said to Jack and strolled away.

I looked at Jack. "Please, I'm begging you. If I'm right—"

"It's likely something completely different," Jack said. "Some completely different hidden variable."

Hidden variables. I'd been reading about them all night. "What about the other three? Have you been able to get in touch with them?" I asked.

"Nope," Jack said. "Hays and Strauss refused to talk to me about it. Both had their secretaries tell me they were aware of some of the deaths, had decided not to do any more work on the local wormhole project, had no plans to publish what they'd already done, didn't want to talk to me about it or hear from me again. Each claimed to be involved now in something completely different."

"Does that sound to you like the usual behavior of research scientists?" I asked.

"No," Jack said. "The ones I know eat up publicity, and they'd hang on to a project like this for decades, like a dog worrying a bone."

I nodded. "And the third physicist?"

"Fenwick? She's in small plane somewhere in the outback of Australia. I couldn't reach her at all."

"Call me immediately if you hear the plane crashes," I said. I really meant "when" not "if," but I didn't want Jack to think I was even more far gone than I was. "Please try to hold off on any story for now," I said, and made to leave.

"I'll do what I can," Jack said. "Try to get some rest. I think there's something going on here all right, but not what you think."

The drive back to Westchester was harrowing. Two cars nearly side-swiped me, and one big-ass truck stopped so suddenly in front of me that I had all I could do to swerve out of crashing into it and becoming an instant Long Island Expressway pancake.

Let's say the QM time-travel people were right. Particles are able to influence each other traveling away from each other at huge distances, because they're actually traveling back in time to an earlier position when they were in immediate physical contact. So time travel on the quantum mechanical level is possible—technically.

But let's say Hawking was also right. The Universe can't allow time travel—for to do so would unravel its very being. So it protects itself from dissemination of information backward in time.

That wouldn't be so crazy. People are saying the Universe can be considered one huge organism—a Gaia writ large. Makes sense then, that this organism, like all other organisms, would have tendencies to act on behalf of its own survival—would act to prevent its dissolution via time travel.

But how would such protection express itself? A physicist figures out a way of creating a local wormhole that can send some information back in time—back to his earlier self and equipment—in some non–blatantly paradoxical way. It doesn't shut off the circuit that sent it. So this information is in fact sent and in fact received—by the scientist. But the Universe can't allow that information transfer to stand. So what happens?

Hawking says the Universe's first line of defense is to create energy disturbances severe enough at the mouths of the wormhole to destroy it and its time-channeling ability. OK. But let's say the physicist is smart or lucky enough to create a wormhole that can withstand these self-disruptive forces. What does the Universe do then?

Maybe it makes the scientist forget this information. Maybe causes a minor stroke in the scientist's brain. Maybe causes the equipment to irreparably break down. Maybe the lucky physicist is really unlucky. Maybe this already happened lots of times.

But what happens when a group of scientists around the world who achieve this time travel transfer reach a critical mass—a mass that will soon publish its findings and make them known, irrevocably, to the world?

Jeez!—I jammed the heel of my hand into my car horn and swerved. The damn Volkswagen driver must be drunk out of his mind—

So what happens when this group of scientists gets information from its own future? Has proof of time travel, information that can't be? The Universe regulates itself, polices its time line, in a more drastic way. All existence is equilibrium—a stronger threat to existence evokes a stronger reaction. A freak fatal accident. A sudden massive heart attack. Another no-motive drive-by shooting that the Universe already dishes out to all too many people in this hapless world of ours. Except in this case, the Universe's motive is quite clear and strong: it must protect its chronology, conserve its current existence.

Maybe this already happened, too. How many physicists on the cutting edges of this science died too young in recent years? Feynman, others . . . Jeez, here was a story for Jack all right.

But why Lauren? Why did she have to die?

Maybe because the Universe's protection level went beyond just those who received illicit future information. Maybe it extended to those who understood just what it was doing, just—

Whamp! Something big had smashed into the rear of my car, and I was skidding way out of control toward the edge of the Throgs Neck Bridge, toward where some workers had removed the barriers to fix some corrosion or something. I was strangely calm, above it all. I told myself to go easy on the brakes, but my leg clamped down anyway and my speed increased. I wrenched my wheel around, but all that did was spin me into a backward skid off the bridge. My car sailed way the hell out over the black-and-blue Long Island Sound.

The way down took a long time. They'd say I was overwrought, overtired, that I lost control. But I knew the truth, knew exactly why this was happening. I knew too much, just like Lauren.

Or maybe there was a way out, a weird little corner of my brain piped up.

Maybe I didn't know the truth. Maybe I was wrong.

Maybe if I could convince myself of that, the Universe wouldn't have to protect itself from me. Maybe it would give me a second chance.

My car hit the water.

I was still alive.

I was a pretty fair swimmer.

If only I could force myself never to think of certain things, maybe I had a shot.

Maybe the deaths of the physicists were coincidental after all. . . .

I lost consciousness thinking no, I couldn't just forget what I already knew so well. . . . How could I will myself not to think of that very thing I was trying to will myself not to think about . . . that blared in my mind now like a broken car horn. . . . But if I died, what I knew wouldn't matter anymore. . . .

I awoke fighting sheets . . . of water. No, these were too white. Maybe hospital sheets. Yeah, white hospital sheets. They smelled like that, too.

I opened my eyes. Hospital rooms were hell—I knew better than most the truth of that—but this was just a hospital room. I was sure of that. I was alive.

And I remembered everything. With a spasm that both energized and frightened me, I realized that I recalled everything I'd been thinking about the Universe and its protective clutch. . . .

But I was still alive.

So maybe my reasoning was not completely right.

"Dr. D'Amato," a female voice, soft but very much in command, said to me. "Good to see you awake."

"Good to *be* awake, Nurse, ah, Johnson." I squinted at her name tag, then her face. "Uhm, what's my situation? How long have I been here?"

She looked at the chart next to my bed. "Just a day and a half," she said. "They fished you out of the Sound. You were suffering from shock. Here." She gave me a cup of water. "Now that you're awake, you can take these orally." She gave me three pills, and turned off the intravenous that I'd just realized was attached to me. She disconnected the tubing from my vein.

I held the pills in my hand. I thought about the Universe again. I envisioned it, rightly or wrongly, as a personal antagonist now. Let's say I was right about the reach of its chronology protection after all? Let's say it had spared me in the water because I was on the verge of willing myself to forget? Let's say it had allowed me to get medicine and nutrition intravenously while I was unconscious because while I was unconscious I posed no threat? But let's say now that I was awake, and remembered, it would—

"Dr. D'Amato. Are you falling back asleep on me?" She smiled. "Come on now, be a good boy and take your pills."

They burned in my palm. Maybe they were poison. Maybe something I had a lethal allergy to. Like Lauren. "No," I said. "I'm OK, now, really. I don't need them." I put the pills on the table and swung my legs out of bed.

"I don't believe this," Johnson said. "It's true—you doctors make the worst god-awful patients. You just stay put now—hear me?" She gave me a look of exasperation and stalked out the door, likely to get the resident on duty, or—who knew?—security.

I looked around for my clothes. They were on a chair, a dried-out crumpled mess. They stank of oil and saltwater. At least my wallet was still inside my jacket pocket, money damp but intact. Good to see there was still some honesty left in this town.

I dressed quickly and opened the door. The corridor was clear. God damn it, I could leave if I wanted to. I was a patient, not a prisoner.

At least insofar as the hospital was concerned. As for the larger realm of being, I couldn't say anymore.

I took a cab straight home.

The most important new piece of evidence—to this whole case, as well as to me personally—was that I was alive. This meant that my assessment of the Universe's vindictiveness was missing something. Or maybe the Universe was just a less effective assassin of forensic scientists than quantum physicists and their knowing wives.

I called Jack to see if there was anything new.

"Oh, just a second, please," the *Newsday* receptionist said. I didn't like the tone of her voice.

"Hello, can I help you?" This was a man's voice, but not Jack's. He sounded familiar, but I couldn't place him.

"Yes, I'm Dr. Phil D'Amato of NYPD Forensics calling Jack Donovan."

Silence. Then, "Hello, Phil. I'm Sam Abrahmson. You still in the hospital?"

Right. Abrahmson. That was the voice. "No. I'm out. Where's Jack?"

Abrahmson cleared his throat. "He was killed with Dave Strauss this morning. He'd talked Strauss into going public with this; Strauss supported your story. He'd picked Strauss up at his summer cottage in Ellenville—Strauss had been hiding out there—and was driving him back to the city. They got blown off a small bridge. Freak accident."

"No freakin' accident," I said. "You know that as well as I do." Another particle who'd danced this sick quantum twist with me. Another particle dead. But this one was completely my fault—I'd brought Jack into this.

"I don't know what I know," Abrahmson said. "Except that at this point the story's on hold. Until we find out more."

I was glad to hear he sounded scared. "That's a good idea," I said. "I'll be back to you."

"Take care of yourself," Abrahmson said. "God knows what that subatomic radiation can do to the body and mind. Or maybe it's all just coincidence. God only knows. Take care of yourself."

"Right." Subatomic radiation. Abrahmson's latest culprit. First it was a virus, now it was radiation. I'd said the same stupid thing to Lauren, hadn't I? People like to latch on to something they know when faced with something they don't know—especially something that kills some physicists here, a reporter there, who knew who else? But radiation had nothing to do with this. Stopping it would take a lot more than lead shields.

I tracked down Richard Hays. I was beginning to get a further inkling of what might be going on, and I needed to talk it out with one of the principals. One of the last remaining principals. It could save both our lives.

I used my NYPD clout to intimidate enough secretaries and assistants to get directly through to him.

"Look, I don't care if you're the bleeding head of the FBI," he said. He was British. "I'm going to talk to you about this just once, now, and then never again."

"Thank you, Doctor. So please tell me what you think is happening here. Then I'll tell you what I know, or think I know."

"What's happening is this," Hays said. "I was working on a project with my colleagues. That's true. But I came to realize the project was a dead end—that the phenomena we were investigating weren't real. So I ceased my involvement in that research. I have no intention of ever picking up that research again—of ever publishing about it, or even talking about it, except to indicate that it was a waste of time. I'd strongly advise you to do the same."

I had no idea how he talked ordinarily, but his words on the phone sounded like each had been chosen with the utmost care. "Why do I feel like you're reading from a script, Dr. Hays?"

"I assure you everything I'm saying is real. As you no doubt already have evidence of yourself," Hays said.

"Now you look," I raised my voice. "You can't just sweep this under the rug. If the Universe *is* at work here in some way, you think you can just avoid it by pretending you don't know about it? The Universe would know about your pretense, too—it's after all still part of the Universe. And word of this will get out anyway—someone will sooner or later publish something. If you want to live, you've got to face this, find out what's really happening here, and—"

"I believe you are seriously mistaken, my friend. And that, I'm afraid, concludes our interview, now and forever." He hung up.

I held on to the disconnected phone, which beeped like a seal, for a long time. I realized that the left side of my body hurt, from my chest up through my shoulder and down my arm. The pain had come on, I thought, at the end of my futile lecture to Hays. Right when I'd talked about publishing. Maybe publishing was the key—maybe talk about dissemination of this information, as opposed to just thinking about it, is what triggered the Universe's backlash. But I was also sure I was right in what I'd said to Hays about the need to confront this, about not running away. . . .

I put the phone back in its receiver and lay down. I was bone tired. Maybe I was getting a heart attack, maybe I wasn't. Maybe I was still in shock from my dip in the Sound. I couldn't fight this all on my own much longer.

The phone rang. I fumbled with the receiver. How long had I been sleeping? "Hello?"

"Dr. D'Amato?" A female voice, maybe Lauren's, maybe Nurse Johnson's. No, someone else.

"Yes?"

"I'm Jennifer Fenwick."

Fenwick, Fenwick—yes, Jennifer Fenwick, the last quantum physicist on this project. I'd wheedled her number from Abrahmson's secretary and left a message for her in Australia—the girl at the hotel wasn't sure if she'd already left. "Dr. Fenwick, I'm glad you called. I, uhm, had some ideas I wanted to talk to you about—regarding the quantum signaling project." I wasn't sure how much she knew and didn't want to scare her off.

She laughed, oddly. "Well, I'm wide open for ideas. I'll take help wherever I can get it. I'm the only damn person left alive from our research group."

"Only person?" So she knew—apparently more than I.

I looked at the clock. It was tomorrow morning already—I'd slept right through the afternoon and night. Good thing I'd called my office and gotten the week off, the absurd part of me that kept track of such trivia noted.

"Richard Hays committed suicide last night," Fenwick's voice cracked. "He left a note saying he couldn't pull it off any longer—couldn't surmount the paradox of deliberately not thinking of something—couldn't overcome his lifelong urge as a scientist to tell the world what he'd discovered. He'd prepared a paper for publication—begged his wife to have it published posthumously if he didn't make it. I spoke to her this morning. I told her to destroy it. And the note, too. Fortunately for her, she had no idea what the paper was about. She's a simple woman—Richard didn't marry her for her brains."

"I see," I said slowly. "Where are you now?"

"I'm in New York," she said. "I wanted to come home—I didn't want to die in Australia."

"Look, you're still alive," I said. "That means you've still got a chance. How about meeting me for lunch"—I looked at the clock again—"in about an hour. The Trattoria Il Bambino on 12th Street in the Village is good. As far as I know, no one there has died from the food as yet." How I could bring myself to make a crack like that at a time like this, I didn't know.

"OK," Fenwick said.

She was waiting for me when I arrived. On the way down, I'd fantasized that she'd look just like Lauren. But in fact she looked a little older and wiser. And even more frightened.

"All right," I said after we'd ordered and gotten rid of the waiter. "Here's what I have in mind. You tell me as a physicist where this might not add up. First, everyone who's attempted to publish something about your work has died."

Jennifer nodded. "I spoke to Lauren Goldring the afternoon she died. She told me she was going to the press."

I sighed. "I didn't know that—but it supports my point. In fact, the two times I even toyed with going public about this, I had fleeting interviews with death. The first time in the water, the second with some sort of pre–heart attack, I'm sure."

Jennifer nodded again. "Same for me. Wheeler wrote about cosmic censorship. Maybe he was on to the same thing as Hawking."

"All right, so what does that tell us?" I said. "Even thinking about publishing this is dangerous. But apparently it's not a capital offense— knowing about this is in itself not fatal. We're still alive. It's as if the Universe allows private, crackpot knowledge in this area—'cause no one takes crackpots seriously, even scientific ones. It's the danger of public dissemination that draws the response—the threat of an objectively accepted scientific theory. Our private knowledge isn't the real problem here. Communication is. The definite intention to publish. That's what kills you. Yeah, cosmic censorship is a good way of putting it."

"OK," Jennifer said.

"OK," I said. "But it's also clear that we can't just ignore this—can't expect to suppress it in our minds. Not having any particular plan to publish won't be enough to save us—not in the long run. Sooner or later after a dark silent night we'd get the urge to shout it out. It's human nature. It's inside of us. Hays's suicide proves it—his note spells it out. You can't just not think of something. You can't just will an idea into oblivion. It's self-defeating. It makes you want to get up on the rooftop and scream it to the world even more—like a repressed love."

"Agreed," Jennifer said. "So what do we do, then?"

"Well, we can't go public with this story, and we can't will ourselves to forget it. But maybe there's a third way. Here's what I was thinking. I can tell you—in strict confidence—that we sometimes do this in forensics." I lowered my voice. "Let's say we have someone who was killed in a certain way, but we don't want the murderer to know that we know how the murder took place. We just deliberately at first publicly interpret the evidence in a different way—after all, there's usually more than one trauma that can result in a given fatal injury to a body—more than one plausible explanation of how someone was killed. Slipped and hit your head on a rock, or someone hit you on the head with a rock—sometimes there's not much difference between the results of the two."

"The Universe is murderous, all right, I can see that, but I don't see how what you're saying would work in our situation," Jennifer said.

"Well, you tell me," I said. "Your group thinks it built a wormhole that allows signaling through time. But couldn't you find another phenomenon to attribute those effects to? After all, we only have time travel on the brain because of H. G. Wells and his literary offspring. Let's say Wells had never written *The Time Machine*? Let's say science fiction had taken a different turn? Then your group would likely have come up with another explanation for your findings. And you can do this now anyway!" I took a sip of wine and realized I felt pretty good. "You can publish an article on your work and attribute your findings to something other than time travel. Indicate they're some sort of other physical effect. Come up with the equivalent of a false phlogiston theory, an attractive bogus conception for this tiny sliver of subatomic phenomena, to account for the time-travel effects. The truth is, few if any serious scientists actually believe that time travel is possible anyway, right? Most think it's just science fiction, nothing else. Who would have reason to suspect a time-travel effect here unless you specifically called attention to it?"

Jennifer considered. "The graduate research assistants worked only on the data acquisition level. Only the project principals, the seven of us"—she caught her breath, winced—"only the seven of us knew this was about time travel. No one else. Ours were supposedly the best minds in this area. Lot of good it did us."

"I know." I tried to be as reassuring as I could. "But then without that time-travel label, all you've got is another of a hundred little experiments in this area per year—jeez, I checked the literature, there are a lot more than that—and your study would likely get lost in the wash. That should shut the Universe up. That should keep it safe from time travel—send the scientific community off on the wrong track, in a different direction—maybe not send them off in any direction at all. Could you do that?"

Jennifer sipped her wine slowly. Her glass was shaking. Her lips clung to the rim. She was no doubt thinking that her life depended on what she decided to do now. She was probably right. Mine, too.

"Exotic matter is what makes the effect possible," she said at last. "Exotic matter keeps the wormhole open long enough. No one knows much about how it works—in fact, as far as I know, our group created this kind of exotic matter, in which weak forces are suspended, for the first time in our project. I guess I could make a case that a peculiar property of this exotic matter is that it creates effects that mimic time travel in artificial wormholes—I could make a persuasive argument that we didn't really see time travel through that wormhole at all, what we have instead is a reversal of processes to earlier stages when they come in contact with our exotic matter, no signaling from the future. You know—we thought the glass was half full, but it was really half empty."

"No," I said. "That's still not going far enough. You've got to be more daring in your deception—come up with something that doesn't invoke time travel at all, even in the negative. Publishing a paper with results that are explicitly said not to demonstrate time travel is akin to someone the police never heard of coming into the station and saying he didn't do it—that only arouses our suspicion. I'm sorry to be so blunt, Jennifer. But you've got to do more. Can't you come up with some effects of exotic matter that have nothing to do with time travel at all?"

She drained her wineglass and put it down, neither half full nor half empty. Completely empty. "This goes against everything in my life and training as a scientist," she said. "I'm supposed to pursue the truth, wherever it takes me."

"Right," I said. "And how much truth will you be able to pursue when you're like Hays and Strauss and the others?"

"Einstein said the Universe wasn't malicious," she said. "This is unbelievable."

"Maybe Einstein was saying the glass was half empty when he knew it was half full. Maybe he knew just what he was doing—knew which side his bread was buttered—maybe he wanted to live past middle age."

"God Almighty!" She slammed her hand on the table. Glasses rattled. "Couldn't I just swear before you and the Universe never to publish anything about this? Wouldn't that be enough?"

"Maybe, maybe not," I said. "From the Universe's point of view, your publishing a paper that explicitly attributes the effects to something other than time travel seems much safer—to you as well as the Universe. Let's say you change your mind, years from now, and try to publish a paper that says you succeeded with time travel after all. You'd already be on record in the literature as attributing those effects to something else—you'd be much less likely to be believed then. Safer for the Universe. Safer for you. A paper with a false lead is not only our best bet now, it's an insurance policy for our future."

Jennifer nodded, very slowly. "I guess I could come up with something—some phenomenon unrelated to time travel—unsuggestive of it. The connection of quantum effects to human thought has always had great appeal, and even though I personally never saw much more than wishful thinking in that direction."

"That's better," I said quietly.

"But how can we be sure no one else will want to look into these effects?" Jennifer asked.

I shrugged. "Guarantees of anything are beyond us in this situation. The best we can hope for are probabilities—that's how the QM realm operates anyway, isn't it—likelihoods of our success, statistics in favor of our survival. As for your effects, well, effects don't have much impact outside of a supportive context of theory. Psalm 51 says 'Purge me with hyssop and I shall be clean'—the penicillin mold was first identified on a piece of decayed hyssop by a Swedish chemist—but none of this led to antibiotics until spores from a mold landed in Fleming's petri dish, and he placed them in the right scientific perspective. Scientists thought they had evidence of spontaneous generation of maggots in old meat until they learned how flies make love. Astronomers saw lots of evidence for a luminiferous ether until Michelson-Morley decisively proved that wrong. You're working on the cutting edge of physics with your wormholes. No one knows what to expect—you said it yourself—yours were the best minds in this area. *You* can create the context. No one's left to contradict you. Let's face it, if you word your paper properly, it will likely go unnoticed. But if not, it will point people in the wrong direction—and once pointed that way, away from time travel, the world could take years, decades, longer, to look at time travel as a real scientific possibility again. The history of science is filled with wrong glittering paths tenaciously taken and defended. That's the path of life for us. I'm not happy about it, but there it is."

Our food arrived. Jennifer looked away from me and down at her veal.

I hadn't completely won her over yet. But she'd stopped objecting. I understood how she felt. To theoretical scientists, pursuit of truth was sometimes more important than life itself. Maybe that's why I went into flesh-and-blood forensics. I pushed on. "The truth is, we've all been getting along quite well without time travel anyway—it could wreak far more havoc in everyone's lives than nuclear weapons ever did. The Universe may not be wrong here."

She looked up at me.

"It's all up to you now," I said. "I'm not a physicist. I can't pull this off. I can take care of the general media, but not the scientific journals." I thought about Abrahmson at *Newsday*. He hadn't a clue which way was up in this thing. He'd just as soon believe this nightmare was all coincidence—the ever popular placeholder for things people didn't want to understand. I could easily pitch it to him in that way.

She gave me a weak smile. "OK, I'll try it. I'll write the article with the mental spin on the exotic effects. *Physics Review D* was given some general info that we were doing something on exotic matter and is waiting for our report. It'll have maximum impact on other physicists there. The human mind in control of matter will be catnip for a lot of them anyway."

"Good." I smiled back. I knew she meant it. I knew because I suddenly felt very hungry and dug into my own veal with a zest I hadn't felt for anything in a while. It tasted great.

Two particles of humanity had connected again. Maybe this time the relationship would go somewhere.

It occurred to me, as I took Jennifer's hand and squeezed it with relief, that maybe this was just what the Universe had wanted all along.

As they say in the department, an ongoing string of deaths is a poor way to keep a secret.

Grand Master Jack Vance

Robert Silverberg /
Terry Dowling

The Grand Master Nebula Award is given to a living writer for a lifetime of achievement, and Jack Vance certainly deserves this honor, for he has produced some of the most interesting and influential work in the fields of science fiction and fantasy. His influence is readily acknowledged by writers as diverse as Gene Wolfe, Robert Silverberg, and Michael Moorcock. He certainly influenced my generation, and that legacy can be easily seen in the rich, atmospheric stories and novels of Gardner Dozois and George R. R. Martin. After reading Vance's short story "The Men Return," I was so electrified by the sheer audaciousness of the ideas and images that I wrote the novel *Junction* as a homage.

In his introduction to the collection *The Best of Jack Vance,* Barry N. Malzberg writes: "Vance is remarkable. His landscapes are wholly imagined, his grasp of the fact that future or other worlds will not be merely extensions of our own but entirely alien has never been exceeded in this field. . . . He is simply one of the best there ever has been at grasping that the material of science fiction will feel differently to those who live through it, and has brought that difference alive."

Like Grand Master Fritz Leiber, Jack Vance's stories and novels have had a profound effect on both modern fantasy and science fiction. Vance's novels and novellas include classics such as *Big Planet,* "The Dragon Masters," "The Last Castle," *To Live Forever, The Languages of Pao,* and *Cugel's Saga.* His short stories can be found in collections such as *The Dying Earth, The Eyes of the Overworld, Eight Fantasms and Magics, The Worlds of Jack Vance, The Best of Jack Vance, Rhialto the Marvelous,* and *The Dark Side of the Moon.* Vance has also written mysteries as John Holbrook Vance and Ellery Queen; and between 1952 and 1953, he wrote six episodes of the television series *Captain Video.* Jack Vance has won the Mystery Writers of America's Edgar Allan Poe Award, two Hugo Awards, a Nebula Award, a Jupiter Award, and the World Fantasy Convention Life Achievement Award.

About his own work, he writes:

"I am aware of using no inflexible or predetermined style.

Each story generates its own style, so to speak. In theory, I feel that the only good style is the style which no one notices, but I suppose that in practice this may not be altogether or at all times possible. In actuality, the subject of style is much too large to be covered in a sentence or two and no doubt every writer has his own ideas on the subject."

The Grand Master Nebula Award was presented to Jack Vance on April 19, 1997, at the Holiday Inn Crown Plaza Hotel in Kansas City, Kansas, where the 1996 Nebula Awards banquet was held.

In this volume Robert Silverberg discusses Jack Vance and his work. Silverberg is one of SF's most honored writers, having won four Hugo Awards, five Nebula Awards, the Jupiter Award, the Prix Apollo, and the Locus Award. His work is complex, richly textured, and elegant; and, as Isaac Asimov said, "Where Silverberg goes today, Science Fiction will follow tomorrow." His novels include *Thorns, Hawksbill Station, The Masks of Time, Nightwings, The Man in the Maze, To Live Again, Tower of Glass, The World Inside, The Book of Skulls, Dying Inside, Shadrach in the Furnace, Lord Valentine's Castle, The Majipoor Chronicles, Valentine Pontifex, Gilgamesh the King, Tom O'Bedlam, Hot Sky at Midnight,* and *The Mountains of Majipoor.* Among his many short-story collections are *The Collected Stories of Robert Silverberg, The Best of Robert Silverberg, Sundance and Other Science Fiction Stories, Unfamiliar Territory,* and the classic *Born with the Dead.* Silverberg has also edited many anthologies, including the influential New Dimensions series, the Alpha series, *The Mirror of Infinity,* and *Dark Stars.* He also writes a monthly column of commentary for *Asimov's Science Fiction.*

Terry Dowling, who also appears in this volume's symposium, offers us a personal glimpse into the life of this very private writer. In addition, it's my pleasure to present one of my all-time favorite Jack Vance stories.

You guessed it in one! It's "The Men Return."

Jack Vance: Grand Master of Science Fiction and Fantasy
ROBERT SILVERBERG

He is a burly, cantankerous, immensely vigorous, and earthy octogenarian with a construction worker's frame and an artist's eye and ear.

For over half a century he has delighted lovers of fantasy and science fiction with a stream of absolutely individual, instantly recognizable work, work which any number of writers can imitate (and have) but only one can create. Mention the name of Jack Vance and any knowledgeable reader thinks immediately of a dozen stories and novels that remain imperishably in memory for their vivid, exotic settings, their ingenious and well-wrought plots, their sly, sardonic characters, and the resonance and poetry of their style.

Though he has been among us all these decades, steadily producing one splendid book after another—his most recent novel, *Night Lamp,* appeared (to enthusiastic reviews) in April of 1996, a few months before his eightieth birthday—he has gone relatively unsung, as that kind of singing goes, until lately. The trophies of our field have been few and far between for him—a niggardly pair of Hugos, in 1963 and 1967, for the novellas "The Dragon Masters" and "The Last Castle," and a solitary Nebula in 1967, also for "The Last Castle." Then came a startling gap of twenty-three years before the novel *Lyonesse: Madouc* brought him the World Fantasy Award in 1990. (There was also an Edgar from the Mystery Writers of America for his 1960 mystery novel, *The Man in the Cage.*)

But, though great popular acclaim, as measured by Hugos and Nebulas and best-seller listings, may have eluded him, he has hardly gone unnoticed over the years. His work has often been honored by those with the capacity to recognize its worth; I speak here of the World Fantasy Award for Lifetime Achievement that he received from the World Fantasy Convention in 1984 and his selection as guest of honor at the World Science Fiction Convention in Orlando, Florida, in 1992. Vance has also been the subject of any number of laudatory monographs and bibliographical studies, going back to Richard Tiedman's pioneering pamphlet, "Jack Vance: Science Fiction Stylist," of 1965. And from that small but valiant publishing firm of Underwood-Miller (and its successor, Underwood Books) has come a virtually complete series of elegantly produced hardcover reprints of the Vancean oeuvre, giving his stories and novels a permanence that mass-market publishing could never provide. Now SFWA caps his long and wondrous career with its Grand Master Award, thus recognizing Jack Vance's place in our pantheon alongside Fritz Leiber, Sprague de Camp, Robert Heinlein, Isaac

Asimov, Clifford Simak, and the rest of that glorious crew that gave modern science fiction its shape and meaning.

He is my neighbor here in Northern California, living just a couple hilltops away in a secluded and rustic house that he built with his own hands, and I have known him for many years: a robust, irreverent, boisterous man, not much like the austere, bookish sort I imagined him to be before we first met in 1964. It was a little difficult at first equating the booming, hearty man who is Jack Vance in person with the fastidious, elegant Vance-persona that I had derived from his stories; but long acquaintance has led me to see that both are contained in one sturdy frame, the jazz-playing, backslapping Jack Vance and the cunning scholar with the oddly medieval way with words, who is just as likely to refer to some shyster publisher as a "jackanapes" or a "coxcomb" as he is to use one of the coarser Angle-Saxonisms that the rest of us might choose.

Vance first turned up in our field in the Summer 1945 issue of the gaudy pulp magazine *Thrilling Wonder Stories* with a story called "The World-Thinker." I have written elsewhere concerning that story that "magazine science fiction in 1945 was pretty primitive stuff, by and large, and so, too, was 'The World-Thinker,' a simple and melodramatic chase story; but yet there was a breadth of vision in it, a philosophic density, that set it apart from most of what was being published then, and the novice author's sense of color and image, his power to evoke mood and texture and sensory detail, was already as highly developed as that of anyone then writing science fiction." A brief autobiographical note appended to the story at the time of its first publication declared, "I am a somewhat taciturn merchant seaman, aged 24. I admit only to birth in San Francisco, attendance at the University of California, interest in hot jazz, abstract physical science, Oriental languages, feminine psychology." The magazine's editor added that Vance had been in the Merchant Marine since 1940, was serving somewhere in the Pacific, and had been torpedoed twice since Pearl Harbor.

I was a little too young to have bought the Summer 1945 *Thrilling Wonder* on the newsstands—I suspect my parents would have been aghast if I had come home with anything so disreputable-looking at that age—but I started reading the SF magazines a couple of years later, despite their flamboyant titles and their shaggy and lurid appearance, and Jack Vance quickly became one of my favorite writers. I learned that his work invariably provided flashes of extraordinary visual intensity and moments of roguish wit, and, more often than not, that sense of peering directly into the unattainable and unknowable future which was the primary thing I desired from science fiction and fantasy.

So it was with immense excitement that I learned, late in 1950, that a Vance novel called *The Dying Earth* would soon be published. I read a preview of it, just a tantalizing snippet, in a little magazine called *Worlds Beyond*—a delicate tale of wizardry and vengeance which whetted my appetite for the actual book, with its images of decay and decline, tumbled pillars, slumped pediments, crumbled inscriptions, the weary red sun looking down on the ancient cities of humanity. I have rarely looked forward to the publication of a novel so keenly. And for months thereafter I searched the magazine shops for Vance's *Dying Earth*, unaware that its ephemeral publisher had gone out of business almost at once and only a few copies had been distributed. But finally a friend who had been lucky enough to find a copy gave me his: I have it still. And treasure that crude-looking little book inordinately, for its rough, badly printed pages unlocked unforgettable realms of wonder for me.

Here we are on an Earth where "ages of rain and wind have beaten and rounded the granite, and the sun is feeble and red. The continents have sunk and risen. A million cities have lifted towers, have fallen to dust. In place of the old peoples a few thousand strange souls live." Vance shows us "a dark blue sky, an ancient sun. . . . Nothing in sight, nothing of Earth was raw or harsh—the ground, the trees, the rock ledge protruding from the meadow; all these had been worked upon, smoothed, aged, mellowed. The light from the sun, though rich, had invested every object of the land, the rocks, the trees, the quiet grasses and flowers, with a sense of lore and ancient recollection."

Thus *The Dying Earth.* And after it came the supremely visionary novel of immortality, *To Live Forever,* and the grand odyssey of *Big Planet,* and the Demon Princes novels, and the Durdane novels, and the Tschai novels, and *Emphyrio,* and *The Blue World,* and "The Gift of Gab," and "The Miracle Workers," and Lyonesse, and Alastor, and . . .

Vance, yes. What a magnificent abundance of sustained inventiveness, decade after decade! We cherish his work; today let us honor its maker.

My Friend Jack
TERRY DOWLING

One of the special joys of my life is to have become close friends with Jack, Norma, and John Vance. Eight visits now, including every Christmas and New Year since 1992. Jack's always at me to go other places but, well, it wouldn't be the same. Theirs is a household of laughter and conviviality, of mischief and grand schemes.

On Tuesday, 14 August 1962, as a fifteen-year-old in Sydney, Australia, I bought that month's issue of *Galaxy* magazine with its cover story "The Dragon Masters." In the schoolboy journal I was keeping at the time I wrote that it was "an excellent story." Soon after there was "The Last Castle" and *Eyes of the Overworld.* During national service in '68–69, I counted myself very lucky indeed when I picked up *The Many Worlds of Magnus Ridolph/The Brains of Earth* Ace Double at the 2RTB base store, and soon after found *The Star King* and *The Killing Machine* in the 3TB camp library. In 1971, I sat by the side of a road and read *The Faceless Man* in *F&SF.*

For the best reasons in the world, sheer enjoyment and admiration, I began writing about Jack's work during the seventies, and when in 1980 Taplinger published *Jack Vance,* a selection of critical essays edited by Tim Underwood and Chuck Miller as part of its Writers of the 21st Century series, Tim included a condensed version of the long article I'd written on Jack's work for an Australian magazine. When I visited Tim in December 1980, he took me to a party at the Vance household over in Oakland so I could meet the man himself.

It went on from there. In April 1982, Jack came down to Australia as guest of honor at Tschaicon. I acted as native guide for him and his son John and gave them a benchmark for the *worst* Mexican food either side of the equator.

In '83 it was the chili cook-off, with Jack and me labouring all day to make the batch of chili that won the evening's prize. We took pirates' oaths in blood and daiquiris never to reveal the recipe. Jack still had the *Hinano* then, his forty-five-foot ketch, and we sat before evening fires talking of sailing from Oakland down to Sydney. For years—long after the *Hinano* was gone—a measure of someone's worth was Jack saying, "We [would/wouldn't] take them on the voyage with us, eh, m'boy?" I counted myself ridiculously lucky to have a berth on this imaginary voyage, but then Jack had taken to calling me "Smuggler" Dowling by this stage, so he must have sensed something of a kindred spirit.

In 1988, it was labouring at the kiln to make a blue faience glaze that kept ending up a moss green—ah, but it was the best moss green in the world. We'd spend hours in the tin pottery shed outside Jack's downstairs writing area, with squirrels dropping pinecones onto the roof from sixty feet overhead, two would-be conspirator alchemists (how it felt) cone-shocked, striving for faience till Norma called us up for a splendid dinner, and we'd sit about embellishing our day's efforts like two highwaymen fresh from a public relations course. Undaunted when my "scarab" paperweights exploded in the test kiln, I set others to firing, and Jack would pause during dinner to say, "What's that I hear?" And when everyone stopped to listen, added, "Can that be the sound of exploding scarabs?"

One year a reference to the ancient scribes of Ebla had us—us!— had *me* scrambling to find all I could about Ebla, since, as Jack always quips, "Vance deposes, Dowling disposes." All we need is a word, a theme, a place name, and I'm off to the bookshelves, searching among the P. G. Wodehouse, Jeffery Farñol, L. Frank Baum titles, among books on English Victorian country houses, ancient weaponry, and the Etruscans, or hauling out the big Webster's, and so the conversation goes, interspersed with Jack on banjo or tunes from the Black Eagle Jazz Band.

I could say more, go on about the "illuminated" Vance manuscripts Jack turned out for his earlier works, the last word of a line a different colour, then the last two words of the next line, and so on, comment on the mischief and merriment, the (for me) quite indescribable thrill of having my own planet given to me in *Throy,* but suffice it to say that Jack is a writer in the grand manner, one with strong views and firm principles, who will take a hard line but always with a twinkle in his eye, who will create the most refined and hilarious business in a tale, then have a character raise a glass to Romance in the true and lasting sense. Let me do that now in words: To Jack and to High Romance, to imaginary voyages and the undying quest for faience blue!

The Men Return

Jack Vance

The Relict came furtively down the crag, a gaunt creature with tortured eyes. He moved in a series of quick dashes, using panels of dark air for concealment, running behind each passing shadow, at times crawling on all fours, head low to the ground. Arriving at the final low outcrop of rock, he halted and peered across the plain.

Far away rose low hills, blurring into the sky, which was mottled and sallow like poor milk-glass. The intervening plain spread like rotten black velvet. A fountain of liquid rock jetted high in the air. In the middle distance a family of gray objects evolved with a sense of purposeful destiny: spheres melted into pyramids, became domes, tufts of white spires, sky-piercing poles; then, as a final *tour de force*, tesseracts.

The Relict cared nothing for this; he needed food and out on the plain were plants. They would suffice in lieu of anything better. They grew in the ground, or sometimes on a floating lump of water, or surrounding a core of hard black gas. There were dank black flaps of leaf, clumps of haggard thorn, pale green bulbs, stalks with leaves and contorted flowers. There were no recognizable species, and the Relict had no means of knowing if the leaves and tendrils he had eaten yesterday would poison him today.

He tested the surface of the plain with his foot. The glassy surface (though it likewise seemed a construction of red and gray-green pyramids) accepted his weight, then suddenly sucked at his leg. In a frenzy he tore himself free, jumped back, squatted on the temporarily solid rock.

Hunger rasped at his stomach. He must eat. He contemplated the plain. Not too far away a pair of Organisms played—sliding, diving, dancing, striking flamboyant poses. Should they approach, he would try to kill one of them. They resembled men, and so should make a good meal.

He waited. A long time? A short time? It might have been either; duration had neither quantitative nor qualitative reality. The sun had vanished, and there was no standard cycle or recurrence. *Time* was a word blank of meaning.

Matters had not always been so. The Relict retained a few tattered recollections of the old days, before system and logic had been rendered obsolete. Man had dominated Earth by virtue of a single assumption: that an effect could be traced to a cause, itself the effect of a previous cause.

Manipulation of this basic law yielded rich results; there seemed no need for any other tool or instrumentality. Man congratulated himself on his generalized structure. He could live on desert, on plain or ice, in forest or in city; Nature had not shaped him to a special environment.

He was unaware of his vulnerability. Logic was the special environment; the brain was the special tool.

Then came the terrible hour when Earth swam into a pocket of noncausality, and all the ordered tensions of cause-effect dissolved. The special tool was useless; it had no purchase on reality. From the two billions of men, only a few survived—the mad. They were now the Organisms, lords of the era, their discords so exactly equivalent to the vagaries of the land as to constitute a peculiar wild wisdom. Or perhaps the disorganized matter of the world, loose from the old organization, was peculiarly sensitive to psychokinesis.

A handful of others, the Relicts, managed to exist, but only through a delicate set of circumstances. They were the ones most strongly charged with the old causal dynamic. It persisted sufficiently to control the metabolism of their bodies, but could extend no further. They were fast dying out, for sanity provided no leverage against the environment. Sometimes their own minds sputtered and jangled, and they would go raving and leaping out across the plain.

The Organisms observed with neither surprise nor curiosity; how could surprise exist? The mad Relict might pause by an Organism, and try to duplicate the creature's existence. The Organism ate a mouthful of plant; so did the Relict. The Organism rubbed his feet with crushed water; so did the Relict. Presently the Relict would die of poison or rent bowels or skin lesions, while the Organism relaxed in the dank black grass. Or the Organism might seek to eat the Relict; and the Relict would run off in terror, unable to abide any part of the world— running, bounding, breasting the thick air; eyes wide, mouth open, calling and gasping until finally he foundered in a pool of black iron or blundered into a vacuum pocket, to bat around like a fly in a bottle.

The Relicts now numbered very few. Finn, he who crouched on the rock overlooking the plain, lived with four others. Two of these were old men and soon would die. Finn likewise would die unless he found food.

Out on the plain one of the Organisms, Alpha, sat down, caught a handful of air, a globe of blue liquid, a rock, kneaded them together, pulled the mixture like taffy, gave it a great heave. It uncoiled from his hand like rope. The Relict crouched low. No telling what deviltry would occur in the creature. He and all the rest of them—unpredictable! The Relict valued their flesh as food; but the Organisms also would eat him if opportunity offered. In the competition he was at a great disadvantage. Their random acts baffled him. If, seeking to escape, he ran, the worst terror would begin. The direction he set his face was seldom the direction the varying frictions of the ground let him move. But the Organisms were as random and uncommitted as the environment, and the double set of disorders sometimes compounded, sometimes canceled each other. In the latter case the Organisms might catch him. . . .

It was inexplicable. But then, what was not? The word *explanation* had no meaning.

They were moving toward him; had they seen him? He flattened himself against the sullen yellow rock.

The two Organisms paused not far away. He could hear their sounds, and crouched, sick from conflicting pangs of hunger and fear.

Alpha sank to his knees, lay flat on his back, arms and legs flung out at random, addressing the sky in a series of musical cries, sibilants, guttural groans. It was a personal language he had only now improvised, but Beta understood him well.

"A vision," cried Alpha. "I see past the sky. I see knots, spinning circles. They tighten into hard points; they will never come undone."

Beta perched on a pyramid, glanced over his shoulder at the mottled sky.

"An intuition," chanted Alpha, "a picture out of the other time. It is hard, merciless, inflexible."

Beta poised on the pyramid, dove through the glassy surface, swam under Alpha, emerged, lay flat beside him.

"Observe the Relict on the hillside. In his blood is the whole of the old race—the narrow men with minds like cracks. He has exuded the intuition. Clumsy thing—a blunderer," said Alpha.

"They are all dead, all of them," said Beta. "Although three or four remain." (When *past, present,* and *future* are no more than ideas left over from another era, like boats on a dry lake—then the completion of a process can never be defined.)

Alpha said, "This is the vision. I see the Relicts swarming the Earth; then whisking off to nowhere, like gnats in the wind. This is behind us."

The Organisms lay quiet, considering the vision.

A rock, or perhaps a meteor, fell from the sky, struck into the surface of the pond. It left a circular hole which slowly closed. From another part of the pool a gout of fluid splashed into the air, floated away.

Alpha spoke: "Again—the intuition comes strong! There will be lights in the sky."

The fever died in him. He hooked a finger into the air, hoisted himself to his feet.

Beta lay quiet. Slugs, ants, flies, beetles were crawling on him, boring, breeding. Alpha knew that Beta could arise, shake off the insects, stride off. But Beta seemed to prefer passivity. That was well enough. He could produce another Beta should he choose, or a dozen of him. Sometimes the world swarmed with Organisms, all sorts, all colors, tall as steeples, short and squat as flowerpots.

"I feel a lack," said Alpha. "I will eat the Relict." He set forth, and sheer chance brought him near to the ledge of yellow rock. Finn the Relict sprang to his feet in panic.

Alpha tried to communicate so that Finn might pause while Alpha ate. But Finn had no grasp for the many-valued overtones of Alpha's voice. He seized a rock, hurled it at Alpha. The rock puffed into a cloud of dust, blew back into the Relict's face.

Alpha moved closer, extended his long arms. The Relict kicked. His feet went out from under him and he slid out on the plain. Alpha ambled complacently behind him. Finn began to crawl away. Alpha moved off to the right—one direction was as good as another. He collided with Beta and began to eat Beta instead of the Relict. The Relict hesitated; then approached and, joining Alpha, pushed chunks of pink flesh into his mouth.

Alpha said to the Relict, "I was about to communicate an intuition to him whom we dine upon. I will speak to you."

Finn could not understand Alpha's personal language. He ate as rapidly as possible.

Alpha spoke on. "There will be lights in the sky. The great lights."

Finn rose to his feet and warily watching Alpha, seized Beta's legs, began to pull him toward the hill. Alpha watched with quizzical unconcern.

It was hard work for the spindly Relict. Sometimes Beta floated; sometimes he wafted off on the air; sometimes he adhered to the terrain. At last he sank into a knob of granite which froze around him. Finn tried to jerk Beta loose, and then to pry him up with a stick, without success.

He ran back and forth in an agony of indecision. Beta began to collapse, wither, like a jellyfish on hot sand. The Relict abandoned the hulk. Too late, too late! Food going to waste! The world was a hideous place of frustration!

Temporarily his belly was full. He started back up the crag, and presently found the camp, where the four other Relicts waited—two ancient males, two females. The females, Gisa and Reak, like Finn, had been out foraging. Gisa had brought in a slab of lichen; Reak a bit of nameless carrion.

The old men, Boad and Tagart, sat quietly waiting either for food or for death.

The women greeted Finn sullenly. "Where is the food you went forth to find?"

"I had a whole carcass," said Finn. "I could not carry it."

Boad had slyly stolen the slab of lichen and was cramming it into his mouth. It came alive, quivered, and exuded a red ichor which was poison, and the old man died.

"Now there is food," said Finn. "Let us eat."

But the poison created a putrescence; the body seethed with blue foam, flowed away of its own energy.

The women turned to look at the other old man, who said in a quavering voice, "Eat me if you must—but why not choose Reak, who is younger than I?"

Reak, the younger of the women, gnawing on the bit of carrion, made no reply.

Finn said hollowly, "Why do we worry ourselves? Food is ever more difficult, and we are the last of all men."

"No, no," spoke Reak. "Not the last. We saw others on the green mound."

"That was long ago," said Gisa. "Now they are surely dead."

"Perhaps they have found a source of food," suggested Reak.

Finn rose to his feet, looked across the plain. "Who knows? Perhaps there is a more pleasant land beyond the horizon."

"There is nothing anywhere but waste and evil creatures," snapped Gisa.

"What could be worse than here?" Finn argued calmly.

No one could find grounds for disagreement.

"Here is what I propose," said Finn. "Notice this tall peak. Notice the layers of hard air. They bump into the peak, they bounce off, they float in and out and disappear past the edge of sight. Let us all climb this peak, and when a sufficiently large bank of air passes, we will throw ourselves on top, and allow it to carry us to the beautiful regions which may exist just out of sight."

There was argument. The old man Tagart protested his feebleness; the women derided the possibility of the bountiful regions Finn envisioned, but presently, grumbling and arguing, they began to clamber up the pinnacle.

It took a long time; the obsidian was soft as jelly and Tagart several times professed himself at the limit of his endurance. But still they climbed, and at last reached the pinnacle. There was barely room to stand. They could see in all directions, far out over the landscape, till vision was lost in the watery gray.

The women bickered and pointed in various directions, but there was small sign of happier territory. In one direction blue-green hills shivered like bladders full of oil. In another direction lay a streak of black—a gorge or a lake of clay. In another direction were blue-green hills—the same they had seen in the first direction; somehow there had been a shift. Below was the plain, gleaming like an iridescent beetle, here and there pocked with black spots, overgrown with questionable vegetation.

They saw Organisms, a dozen shapes loitering by ponds, munching vegetable pods or small rocks or insects. There came Alpha. He moved slowly, still awed by his vision, ignoring the other Organisms. Their play went on, but presently they stood quiet, sharing the oppression.

On the obsidian peak, Finn caught hold of a passing filament of air, drew it in. "Now—all on, and we sail away to the Land of Plenty."

"No," protested Gisa, "there is no room, and who knows if it will fly in the right direction?"

"Where is the right direction?" asked Finn. "Does anyone know?"

No one knew, but the women still refused to climb aboard the filament. Finn turned to Tagart. "Here, old one, show these women how it is; climb on!"

"No, no," Tagart cried. "I fear the air; this is not for me."

"Climb on, old man, then we follow."

Wheezing and fearful, clenching his hands deep into the spongy mass, Tagart pulled himself out onto the air, spindly shanks hanging over into nothing. "Now," spoke Finn, "who next?"

The women still refused. "You go then, yourself," cried Gisa.

"And leave you, my last guarantee against hunger? Aboard now!"

"No. The air is too small; let the old one go and we will follow on a larger."

"Very well." Finn released his grip. The air floated off over the plain, Tagart straddling and clutching for dear life.

They watched him curiously. "Observe," said Finn, "how fast and easily moves the air. Above the Organisms, over all the slime and uncertainty."

But the air itself was uncertain, and the old man's raft dissolved. Clutching at the departing wisps, Tagart sought to hold his cushion together. It fled from under him, and he fell.

On the peak the three watched the spindly shape flap and twist on its way to earth far below.

"Now," Reak exclaimed in vexation, "we even have no more meat."

"None," said Gisa, "except the visionary Finn himself."

They surveyed Finn. Together they would more than outmatch him.

"Careful," cried Finn. "I am the last of the Men. You are women, subject to my orders."

They ignored him, muttering to each other, looking at him from the side of their faces.

"Careful!" cried Finn. "I will throw you both from this peak."

"That is what we plan for you," said Gisa.

They advanced with sinister caution.

"Stop! I am the last Man!"

"We are better off without you."

"One moment! Look at the Organisms!"

The women looked. The Organisms stood in a knot, staring at the sky.

"Look at the sky!"

The women looked; the frosted glass was cracking, breaking, curling aside.

"The blue! The blue sky of old times!"

A terribly bright light burnt down, seared their eyes. The rays warmed their naked backs.

"The sun," they said in awed voices. "The sun has come back to Earth."

The shrouded sky was gone; the sun rode in a sea of blue. The ground below churned, cracked, heaved, solidified. They felt the obsidian harden under their feet; its color shifted to glossy black. The Earth, the sun, the galaxy, had departed the region of freedom; the other time with its restrictions and logic was once more with them.

"This is Old Earth," cried Finn. "We are Men of Old Earth! The land is once again ours!"

"And what of the Organisms?"

"If this is the Earth of old, then let the Organisms beware!"

The Organisms stood on a low rise of ground beside a runnel of water that was rapidly becoming a river flowing out onto the plain.

Alpha cried, "Here is my intuition! It is exactly as I knew. The freedom is gone; the tightness, the constrictions are back!"

"How will we defeat it?" asked another Organism.

"Easily," said a third. "Each must fight a part of the battle. I plan to hurl myself at the sun, and blot it from existence." And he crouched, threw himself into the air. He fell on his back and broke his neck.

"The fault," said Alpha, "is in the air, because the air surrounds all things."

Six Organisms ran off in search of air and, stumbling into the river, drowned.

"In any event," said Alpha, "I am hungry." He looked around for suitable food. He seized an insect which stung him. He dropped it. "My hunger remains."

He spied Finn and the two women descending from the crag. "I will eat one of the Relicts," he said. "Come, let us all eat."

Three of them started off—as usual in random directions. By chance Alpha came face to face with Finn. He prepared to eat, but Finn picked up a rock. The rock remained a rock, hard, sharp, heavy. Finn swung it down, taking joy in the inertia. Alpha died with a crushed skull. One of the other Organisms attempted to step across a crevasse twenty feet wide and was engulfed; the other sat down, swallowed rocks to assuage his hunger and presently went into convulsions.

Finn pointed here and there around the fresh new land. "In that quarter, the new city, like that of the legends. Over here the farms, the cattle."

"We have none of these," protested Gisa.

"No," said Finn. "Not now. But once more the sun rises and sets, once more rock has weight and air has none. Once more water falls as rain and flows to the sea." He stepped forward over the fallen Organism. "Let us make plans."

Yaguara

Nicola Griffith

The 1996 Nebula Award for Best Novel was given to Nicola Griffith's *Slow River*. Griffith was born in Leeds, Yorkshire, England, and has been a laborer, an insurance clerk (for forty-five days), a waitress (forty-five minutes), and a lead singer and songwriter for the women's band Janes Plane. She has also taught self-defense. Her first novel, *Ammonite,* won the Georgia Council for the Arts Individual Artist's Award, the James Tiptree Jr. Memorial Award, and the Lambda Literary Award. To quote from Griffith's entry in the *St. James Guide to Science Fiction Writers:* "Though a relative newcomer, Griffith's mastery of language is exceptional, her settings imaginative and well-drawn, her characters compelling, and her plots fast and finely tuned. Griffith is swiftly earning her place among the vanguard of SF literature." She has also won the National Network of Women Writers Award in England and an artist's project grant from the Atlanta Bureau of Cultural Affairs. She is the coeditor, with Stephen Pagel, of the Bending the Landscape series. Her latest novel, *The Blue Place* (due from Avon in July 1998) is a noir thriller.

Rather than publish an excerpt from Nicola Griffith's *Slow River,* I have chosen to include her 1995 Nebula Award finalist, the disquieting and evocative novella "Yaguara." About this story, the author writes:

"Ellen Datlow was soliciting stories for an anthology of erotic horror. I came up with 'Yaguara.' It was inevitable, really. . . .

"First of all, I was determined that I would not write one of those fuck and die stories so beloved by the writers of bad horror films. You know the ones—where the teenagers are humping in the car/bed/classroom when the Serial Killer gets them. Moral: Sex will kill you, especially if you're female. You're only allowed a boyfriend *after* you've dispatched the Monster (and even then it must be True Love, implying eventual marriage, or you'll end up starring in the next film about Bad Girls Get Theirs. If you're the kind of girl who would rather have a girlfriend, then you're dead meat even before the opening credits).

"Second, much of my work is about the interaction of people and their places. People, fictional and not, are largely the products of their particular time and culture. So what I tend to do is pluck an

unfortunate character from her familiar surrounds, drop her somewhere strange—to herself, and sometimes to the reader—and
watch with interest while she struggles to deal with an alien milieu.
The type and degree of alienness—time, space, culture—don't
matter as long as the details are made utterly real to the character
and, through her, the reader. We should know how the ground
feels underfoot; the level of ambient noise; the taste of the wind
on the back of the tongue.

"Third, I had just read: an article in *Science News* about how
little epigraphers really know about Mayan glyphs; Carl Sagan's
Broca's Brain, on the evolution of the mammalian brain; and a book
by some fool of a zoologist who went to Belize to study jaguars but
ended up killing five of the six animals under observation.

"Fourth, there's a long tradition in lesbian erotica (particularly
that written for straight audiences) that the characters and/or settings are hot, steamy, exotic, sultry, privileged, lush, languorous,
etc., etc., etc.

"The jungle, I thought, is hot, steamy, exotic, sultry, lush, languorous, and so on. It is also a frighteningly alien place for most
of us, full of snakes and spiders and strange diseases. There are
no phones or fax machines, no doctors, no brightly lit bars, just
this vast, moist, breathing thing stretching for miles. No one, no
matter how tightly armored, can venture into the jungle and return
unchanged."

Jane Holford valued her privacy. That is why she became a pho-
tographer: people would look at her pictures and not at her. As an adolescent she had watched a film critic on television. *The gaze of the
camera is not like grammar,* he had said. *After a while there is no difference between subject and object.* He pointed at a still of Marilyn
Monroe, dead for years. *We ate her alive.* Jane had decided then and
there that she would be neither subject nor object but invulnerable
observer. She would keep herself armored, inviolate, safe.

And so Jane did not travel directly from England to Belize. She
packed her cameras and flew to the Yucatan, and from there took a
boat to Ambergris Cay. She would acclimatize to the heat slowly, and
in private.

On Ambergris, Katherine—ex-governor's niece for whom Jane
had once done the favor of losing a roll of incriminating film—was

drunk by ten o'clock in the morning and forgot, most of the time, that she had a guest, and the house servants probably could not have cared less. But Jane still maintained a perfect control. Even when the sun was licking at her shoulders and the Caribbean wove about her its scents of wide open space and hot driftwood, she did not throw back her head and laugh; she did not take off her sandals and squeeze the seaweed between her toes. When a beautiful woman in the market smiled at her, she did not smile back, did not allow herself to blush, to feel the heat building in her belly.

Alone in her room, it was another matter.

After three weeks she no longer felt vulnerable: she could walk outside in the sun without fainting; she knew how much water she needed to drink every day to remain hydrated; and her skin was dark enough to protect her from sunburn. Armor in place, she left for the Maya Mountains in the far south and west of Belize. Dr. Cleis Fernandez and the ruins of Kuchil Balum were waiting.

"Why do you want to take pictures of me?" the epigrapher had asked when Jane had phoned the University of New Mexico a month earlier, at the beginning of March.

"Because I'm putting together a book on women at the top of their professions." *Because you made it, against the odds. Because you haven't let them consume you, yet.* "You're—"

"Get someone else." And the phone had gone dead in Jane's hand.

Jane redialed. "Dr. Fernandez, it's Jane Holford again—"

"Holford? Wait a minute. Holford who did that series last year on the Lascaux paintings? The ones in *Life*?"

"Yes." "And I might excerpt a similar photo-essay from the book in one of the glossies—"

"I'm not interested in that." Her voice was hot and rough, like black glass. "But I do have one condition."

"Go on."

"I want you to photograph the glyphs at Kuchil Balum."

"Tell me about them."

"It's classified as a minor ceremonial site in Belize but it's anything but minor. As for the rest . . . well, you'll come or you won't."

"I'll call you back."

She had checked. Kuchil Balum was in the Maya Mountains, first excavated two years before. Nothing there that could not be found in dozens of other, more accessible ruins in Belize or Guatemala. And yet . . . Apparently Fernandez had been applying for grants all over the place, for money and time to go study these ruins and their glyphs. She had been turned down. Jane read and reread Fernandez's articles in the journals, and *The Long Count*, her single book. The passion and dedication, the need to know, came across loud and clear. Why was Kuchil Balum so important?

She called back four days after their original conversation. "I'll do it."

"You will?" Fernandez sounded challenging. "The jungle isn't a good place just before the rainy season."

"I understand that. Now, my schedule—"

"I'm going there next week and won't be coming out again until the rainy season, May or June. Take it or leave it."

The road was a track torn through the tropical forest by logging skidders, deteriorating to dust and potholes and broken bridges. Leaves brushed the Jeep on both sides and smeared the dusty paintwork with sap, leaving Jane with the feeling that the greenery was closing in behind her and she would be encysted in the forest forever.

Not long after noon, she stopped to drink water from her canteen and eat a banana. It was hot; mosquitoes and bottlas flies whined about her head. Wind, sly as a great cat's breath, stole from banak to ironwood to Santa Maria pine, stirring hot perfumes and the iridescent wings of a blue morpho butterfly. When she turned the key in the ignition, the Jeep's engine roared too loudly, and it seemed to Jane that when she moved, the breath of the forest followed.

Over an hour later, the jungle ahead of her thinned abruptly, melting from dense emerald to sunlit mint. The breeze stiffened and expelled her into a green-sided bowl floored with dirt-brown: a clearing. Adobe huts roofed with thatch stood in an irregular west-east line; a macaw hung in a cage outside the nearest. Chickens scratched in the dirt and a pig rooted in the undergrowth at the edge of the clearing. She turned off the engine and found herself staring into the solemn eyes of a group of thin-armed children.

Stranger, those unblinking camera eyes said, *you cannot hide.*

One child wiped his nose with the back of his hand, another tilted her head at Jane like a bird. Then at some unseen signal they ran back toward the forest and melted into the trees.

Jane climbed down from the Jeep and began to lift an aluminum case from the back.

"Don't do that."

She whirled, found herself facing a lean woman wearing shorts and boots and vest, muscles showing long and tight over knobby bones; neck tendons flat and hard; face planed by heat and hard work; hair in rough curls as black as volcanic rock.

"I'm Cleis Fernandez." When they shook hands, Cleis's long fingers reached past Jane's wrist. "It would be best to leave your things in the Jeep. It's another half mile or so to our shack. We can drive if we go very, very slowly."

Our shack. She had prepared for everything but sharing a room. Jane climbed numbly back into the Jeep.

Jane knew she drove well: poised, unhurried, competent. She glanced in the side mirror, caught the flash of brown eyes studying her in turn, and deliberately looked away. She was the observer, not the observed.

"This is it." It was a square building of breeze block and corrugated aluminum. They climbed down. "It was built by the logging company. Never got used—they went bust. It's more comfortable inside than it looks."

A wooden step led into a single room, low and dark, about eighteen feet square, with plasterboard walls and a dirt floor. There were wooden-framed bunks, each with a blue blanket.

Two bunks. No room into which she could retreat and close the door.

"There's a toilet over here," Cleis pointed, "though I, we, have to fill the cistern from a bucket. The well's in the village; Ixbalum lets me, us, use that at least. The stove uses propane." She lit a match, turned a knob, demonstrated. "I cleared some of the shelf space for your things."

Jane looked at the clothes already on the shelf. New. Aggressively good quality. She had seen clothes like that before, when she shared a room at Cambridge with a scholarship girl.

The windows were holes cut in the wall and screened, the door a flimsy affair. Jane looked for a lock.

"No one will steal anything. Ixbalum won't even let anyone near this place." Jane nodded, wondering who Ixbalum was. "We've got three Coleman lamps. . . ."

Jane closed her eyes. Sharing. The hut smelled of heat and mildew and sweat, and faintly of gas and matches, but behind that lay the must of forest animals and the heavy green scent of ceaseless growth. She felt trapped.

". . . last as long as possible, because I hate the drive to Benque Viejo for more supplies, though if you're willing, we can take turns on that chore. Jane?"

She opened her eyes, smiled her warm, practiced smile. "Thank you for going to so much trouble." *How am I going to survive this?*

The well was at the western edge of the village. Jane wound up the bucket. "Where is everyone?"

"Tending their milpas. Or hunting. Some are hiding in their houses. The children are running wild, or maybe watching us right now."

Jane could see only trees, and the inevitable chickens.

The bucket creaked to the lip of the well. Jane concentrated on pouring from the wooden bucket into the galvanized steel pail. She was fascinated by the cool clear flow, the fact that water could stay cold in one-hundred-degree heat. She dipped her hand in it.

Someone behind her spoke in a throaty Mayan dialect. Jane turned, saw a short, muscular woman with squat powerful limbs and a large jaw.

"Jane, this is Ixbalum."

"What did she say?"

"That rivers are for playing with, well water for drinking."

Ixbalum lifted Jane's left arm, laid it next to her own, pointed to the mahogany brown then the honey, dropped the arm, lifted Cleis's arm, compared the mahogany to teak, spoke for a while, then padded away into the trees.

Jane realized she was wiping her hands on her shorts, stopped. "What did she say?"

"She said you're not made for the mountains."

It was just over a mile from the village to the ruins. The trail was a twisty tunnel through the green. Sweat ran down the underside of Jane's arm, and she felt as though she were breathing sap. Ahead of her, Cleis's shorts whif-whiffed as she walked. Their boots were silent on the thick leaf mold. Insects hummed and whined. Jane slapped at something that landed on her neck.

"Got to be careful of the insects," Cleis said over her shoulder without slowing down. "Especially mosquitoes. They carry botfly eggs and things out of your worst nightmares." Cleis had no idea about her nightmares, Jane thought.

They walked on in silence. The heat pushed its strong fingers under Jane's skin, slicked muscle and bone until she felt slippery inside, like a well-oiled machine. The jungle eased down her throat, sighed in her ears, whispered *You could let go here, and no one would know.*

Jane realized she was stroking her belly, walking with a loose open-hip sway. *Armored, inviolate, safe. . . .* She jerked her hand away from her stomach and laid it on the hard black case hanging down by her hip. She was the only one with a camera here. She was in control.

Cleis stopped abruptly, turned. "We're almost there. You have to remember that this is classified as a minor site, not to be confused with the great centers like Tikal." Cleis's hands moved as she talked, emphasizing phrases with precise gestures like movements distilled from tai chi or wing chun. "There's only one pyramid, and that hasn't been fully excavated. Nothing has. It may not look like much but Kuchil Balum is more important than anyone knows." Her hands stopped, fell back to her sides. "I just wanted you to know that."

They climbed the last few yards up a steep rise and looked down at Kuchil Balum.

Grassy hummocks and walls choked with vines lay scattered around an area the size of a small urban park, perhaps two acres, level, but slightly sunken. It reminded Jane of the huge ruined amphitheaters of Greece, only here it was wood, not stone, that formed the sides of the bowl, great vertigo-producing trunks that spun themselves up and up to bridge earth and heaven.

Over the faint susurrus of leaves a hundred feet from the ground, Jane thought she heard something else, something that she felt as a faint vibration under her feet. "What's that noise?"

Cleis smiled. "We'll save that for last."

Jane clambered over a pile of tumbled stone and to the top of a small mound. It was not hard to envisage this place as it had once been: people coming and going, sun flashing on jade and gold, children playing with a ball. Why had they left?

The northwestern corner of the site was hemmed in by gray rock. In front of that lay a whole complex of ruins. Something just inside the trees caught her attention, something golden that slunk from light to shadow, lifting heavy paws, turning its massive head from side to side. Slowly, heart hammering under her ribs, Jane lifted her camera.

"What is it?"

The golden animal was gone. Perhaps she had imagined it. Jane lowered her camera. "Nothing."

"Over here is the mat house." They walked back down the slope to a small green mound with one side exposed: a few gray stones, beautifully fitted, a doorway and lintel. "I'm particularly interested in the glyphs on the western wall." They squeezed through. Inside it was dim and smelled of animal fur and musk, like a woman's hair after the rain. Cleis ran her hand along the wall. "This section here is vital." She tapped a relief carving, a seated jaguar-headed figure. "The throne indicates temporal power, but other indicators point to the human figure being female. That's very unusual." She looked at Jane. "About as usual as a Latina professor in your Anglo world."

Jane said nothing, refusing to be baited. Cleis smiled slightly, then continued. "Over here," she traced her way across the name glyphs and dates, "another jaguar-human, but this time not in the regalia of the royal house. See the scythe? A peasant. I've seen jaguars as thrones, jaguars as symbols of shamanic and from there royal power, but this is the first time I've seen jaguars as ordinary citizens, or vice versa. I don't know what it means." Frustration deepened the grooves on either side of her mouth for a moment, then she shook her head. "It's dark in here. I hope photographing them won't be a problem."

"No." Jane touched the glyphs lightly with her fingertips.

The strange, bulbous carvings were everywhere she and Cleis went. Cleis's hands were never still as she pointed out the date glyphs and name glyphs, explained the long count and the calendar round. She saved the northwest corner for last.

They climbed up the remains of four huge terraced steps and then through all that remained of what had once been a corridor. The vibration became a thrumming hiss. "See these hinges here? This corridor was once gated on both ends. Very unusual."

They stepped out into sunlight. Cold spray brushed Jane's cheek. "A waterfall. . . ."

But Cleis did not give Jane long to admire the fall, or the pool bobbing with lilies. "This way." They went down steps cut into the stone, underground for five yards, then up again into what had once been a vast courtyard.

Cleis pointed to the wall that ran across the courtyard in six separate sections. It was covered in glyphs. "This is the heart of Kuchil Balum. This is why I'm here."

Jane posed Cleis at the well, at the ruins, outside the shack, trying to catch the intensity that seemed to burn at the woman's center. They stopped when the light faded.

At dusk the air tasted like hot metal. Jane sat on the step outside their shack and sipped at a battered tin cup: rum, lime juice, and well water. Night light, Cleis called it. From inside, the galvanized pail clanked as the epigrapher flushed the toilet. Jane heard the laughter of children float up from the village.

"Not one child in that village has ever seen the inside of a school." Cleis filled her cup, sat next to Jane. "If only Ixbalum were willing to talk, the lack of education could be invaluable to me. . . ."

Jane was glad to keep the conversation impersonal. "In what way?"

"Virtually all the schooling in Belize is done by missionaries: Catholics, Methodists, Seventh Day Adventists, the Assembly of God—you name it, they're here." She sipped meditatively. "There are probably three million people around today who still speak various Mayan tongues, but none of them can read these glyphs. The rituals that gave meaning to all these things were destroyed and discredited by the missionaries."

"But not here?"

"Not here. They probably still tell each other bedtime stories about Queen Jaguar Claw and how she ruled over Mommy and Daddy's great-great-great-to-the-nth-degree grandparents, and how she gave their children jade beads for . . . I don't know . . . maize productivity or something. But they won't talk to me. Ixbalum won't let them."

"I wonder what Ixbalum's afraid of."

Cleis was quiet for a long time. Plum-purple shadows gathered under her cheekbones and in the hollows of her neck. "That I'll make them famous."

Jane nodded slowly in the gathering dark. They had evaded notice for a long time. "How was Kuchil Balum discovered?"

"Three years ago a logger was tracking a jaguar. Came across some funny-looking stones. He didn't think much of them at the time. Apparently he never did find the jaguar, but on the way back, he was bitten by a fer-de-lance. By the time his friends got him to the clinic at Benque Viejo, he was bleeding from the eyes and babbling about a city of stone. He died a few hours later. But one of the nurses remembered what he'd said and told her friend. The friend knew someone who worked for the State Archaeology Department. They sent someone down, some idiot who took a cursory look, labeled it 'Minor Ceremonial Center,' and forgot about it. It was listed, of course, but these sites turn up all the time. Still, I was curious, I'm always curious, so when one of my grad students told me he was planning to spend the summer at Caracol, I asked him to check out this place. He brought back a Polaroid of those jaguar figures I showed you this afternoon. And I knew someone had made a big mistake."

Jane was still thinking about the logger. "It was lucky, for the villagers I mean, that the logging operation went bust when it did, just a mile from the site."

"Luck? I'm not sure I believe in luck." Cleis's long hands hung loosely between her knees. "Look into Ixbalum's face and tell me you still believe it was just bad luck that the skidders kept breaking down, that the bridges collapsed, that every worker who didn't get bitten by a fer-de-lance ran off in ones and twos babbling about the jungle cat that was out to get them."

Jane remembered driving along the logging track, her feeling that the jungle was breathing on the back of her neck, stalking her like a big cat.

Jane listened to the steady, still-awake breathing of Cleis in the other bunk. She could see the next few weeks unrolling before her like sticky flypaper, the jungle whispering to her *Let go, let go, there's no one here to care,* but if she let go now, if she let her armor slip just once, the damage would be permanent: she would have been seen, known. Cleis was always there.

Jane turned on her side, careful not to make any noise or disturb the sheet that was pulled up to her shoulders. She thought about Cleis's toffee-colored eyes, the way they watched her all the time. What did they see?

At mid-afternoon the sun was still strong and heat wrapped around Jane like a thick tongue. A hundred yards away, the waterfall roared, tossing spray into the already humid air. The light was perfect: green-gold and viscous as honey, seeping into every crevice and old chisel cut, easing out details ordinarily invisible. With luck, she would be able to photograph this whole section while the light lasted. She set up her specially adapted tripod and tilted the camera up to the next section of curtain wall. More jaguars, more pictures of the plant that Cleis did not recognize.

"I just don't know what it is," Cleis had said the night before, and pulled out four Polaroids she had taken days earlier. "And it's depicted exactly the same in each glyph, always bent with these six fronds out-ward to show the spiderweb veins. That's significant. It suggests ritual function. And it's always in conjunction with these glyphs here." She tilted the pictures toward the feeble light of the Coleman lamp stream-ing through their doorway, so that Jane could see.

"Jaguars and women?"

"Jaguars, yes, but they're not portrayed symbolically. It's almost as if they're . . . pets or something." She sighed and rubbed her eyes.

"And these women are all young. You can tell by their clothes." Jane took Cleis's word for it. "If I didn't know better, I'd say these glyphs represented some kind of purdah, spent behind the curtain walls. Though what that has to do with the jaguars I don't know. It's so frustrating! If only these people would talk to me!"

Jane looked at the photos again, tapped two glyphs of women covered in what looked like blood. "What does this mean? Some kind of execution?"

"No. Look at them carefully. Both are wounds to the left shoulder, on the muscle: ritual again."

"Scarification?"

"I don't know what the hell it is. I feel as though I should understand, but it's just out of my reach."

Jane touched the limestone carvings, weathered now, and tried to imagine the glyphs fresh and new. The carver had squatted out here in the ninety-degree heat with only soft bronze tools and pieces of dirty string to make sure everything was straight. A labor of months. Years. It was terrible to think that all that effort—the sweat and bruised palms, the pads of fingers callused and permanently white with limestone dust—now meant nothing because no one knew what these enigmatic, bulbous figures represented.

The camera whirred, clicked, whirred again. Jane, stiff after squatting so long, stood and stretched. Froze. Behind her, arms folded, face dappled with tree shadow, stood Ixbalum.

They looked at each other. Jane could not speak Mopan Maya. She lifted a hand in greeting. Ixbalum stared back impassively. Jane cleared her throat. It sounded impossibly loud. She wondered how long Ixbalum had been watching her. "I have to take these pictures," she said, pointing at her camera. "The light won't last forever."

Ixbalum did not move.

She cleared her throat again. She hesitated, then wiped the sweat from her face and doggedly tilted the camera to a different angle. She had a job to do.

Ixbalum's gaze settled on the back of her neck, as hot as the sun. She bent to the viewfinder, focused carfully on a jaguar figure. *All that work.* . . .

She straightened abruptly, turned to Ixbalum.

"Tell me what it means," she said, pointing at the glyphs. "They're your people, Ixbalum. Don't you want the world to hear what they had to say?"

Ixbalum might as well have been carved from the same stone as the glyphs, but the breeze in the trees stirred and the leaf shadow on the Mayan woman's face shifted. Her eyes were yellow, like hammered gold.

Jane stepped back, bumped into her tripod, had to turn quickly to catch it. When she turned back, Ixbalum was gone.

Later, when the sun was slipping behind the trees and the light was more green than gold, when Jane was treading carefully along the trail, camera slung over one shoulder, tripod on the other, she felt that same heat on the back of her neck, as though she was being watched. She stopped, turned slowly. Nothing.

Ten yards farther down, she felt it again. This time she put down her camera, dropped her tripod into her other hand to hold it like a club, and turned.

Six feet away, inside her own bootprint, was a jaguar track so fresh that a piece of dirt tottering on the edge of the heel depression fell inward as she watched.

"Jaguar? You're sure?" Cleis sat cross-legged on her bunk, surrounded by notes.

"It looked like cat to me." Jane leaned her tripod in the corner, began to sort automatically through her film stock. "And the print must have been four or five inches across."

"Ocelot, margay?"

"I didn't think they got that big."

"You heard nothing?"

"Not a thing." Fear made her sound angry. If she had not remembered so clearly touching the spoor with her fingertip, then retrieving her camera, taking a picture, she might be tempted to assume she had imagined the incident. But it was real. A jaguar, a predator, had been a few feet behind her and she had not known it.

Cleis set aside her notes, rubbed her eyes. "The light's terrible in here." Jane remembered the hot gold of Ixbalum's eyes and shivered. Cleis studied her. "Did you know that *jaguar* comes from a South American word, *yaguara,* that means 'wild beast that kills its prey in one bound'? They have very short, powerful limbs and the strength of their jaws is incredible. Pound for pound, they have the most efficient bite of any land-based predator. When I was in the Xingu basin two or three years ago, I saw a tapir that had been killed by a jaguar: the back of its skull was sheared clean off."

All Jane could think of was Ixbalum's short, squat legs, the muscles along her jaw.

"As far as I know, there has only ever been one reported case of a jaguar attacking people, and that was thirty years ago in Guatemala." Cleis, Jane realized, knew she was scared, and was giving her information to deal with because it would help. She was being humored. "Apparently, four men were killed at a convent."

Despite herself, Jane was intrigued. "A convent?"

Cleis grinned. "They probably did something very unchristian to one of the novices and the other nuns banded together and hacked the men to death with machetes, scythes, garden shears. No local doctor is going to argue cause of death with the good sisters, especially when the church probably controls the medical supplies and the hospital." She glanced at her notes, then back to Jane. "Anyway, my point is that jaguars simply don't attack people. Why should they? There's too much to eat around here as it is. Maybe it was following you because you smelled interesting. Maybe it was an adolescent practicing."

Maybe it was trying to intimidate me. But that was ridiculous.

The humidity was thick enough to stand on and the sky low and gray. Cleis threw her knapsack onto the Jeep and climbed behind the wheel. "I'll stay overnight in Benque Viejo," she said. "I've a few things to do."

Jane glanced at the sky. "Think it'll rain?"

Cleis shook her head. "It can't. I can't afford it to."

Jane's clothes were already stuck to her. "Don't forget the beer."

"I won't."

Later, alone on the trail to Kuchil Balum, Jane felt as though she were walking through another world: there was no breeze, and every sound, every smell, was singular and intense.

The air under the trees grew hotter and more damp.

Jane stumbled over a hidden tree limb. She fell to one knee, her nose seven inches from a log over which Azteca ants marched in an endless, silent line. And it was as if she had been looking at the world through a camera and had only just found the right focus. Everywhere she looked life leapt out at her: huge black carpenter bees buzzing around red melastoma flowers the size of roses; a leaf-frog, gaudy and red-eyed, peering from the depths of a sapodilla; the flicker of a gecko's tail. And there were millipedes and rove beetles, silverfish and wood lice, and spiders spinning their silent webs to catch them. The air was luxuriant with rot, like the breath of a carnivore.

She stood up feeling hot and hunted and hemmed in. A snake slithered in the undergrowth. Her heart began to thump like a kettle-drum. She licked salt from her lips, wondered how many different eyes were watching her from behind tree trunks or under leaves. A twig snapped under a heavy paw. Something big was coming toward her. . . . Yaguara, *a South American word meaning "predator that kills its prey in one bound."* She ran.

Night seeped through the trees like tea and gathered under her bunk. She sat on the rough blanket fully clothed, facing the door. A shelf bracket pressed into her shoulder blade but she stayed where she was. The jungle was full of eyes.

She dozed and dreamed she was walking to the ruins in thin moonlight. Sliding earth and metal sounds came from the direction of the purdah house. Cleis was digging feverishly, lips skinned back with effort, teeth glinting like old bone. "It's here somewhere," she was muttering to herself, "I just have to keep digging." Jane wanted her to stop, just for a moment, but she could not seem to get close enough to touch Cleis. She would walk toward her and stretch out her hand only to find that she had gone the wrong way and Cleis was behind her. Then suddenly Cleis was laughing. "Yes!" she shouted, and threw away the shovel, and she was digging with her hands, throwing the dirt back between her legs like a cat. "I've found it!" She looked up at Jane, and her eyes were golden, and suddenly the dirt was piling up around Jane, burying her, and she could not breathe—

Jane surged off the bunk, swallowing, and staggered outside. The night was silent: the four in the morning lull before dawn.

The Jeep bumped into the clearing a little after midday. Jane ran to greet Cleis.

"Well, hello to you, too," Cleis said. "What have I done to deserve this honor?"

Jane stopped abruptly. "Did you bring the beer?"

Cleis nodded. "Though I would have driven faster if I'd known you were so desperate. Give me a hand unloading this stuff."

They lugged the new gas bottles inside. Cleis pulled the cardboard off a six-pack and submerged the bottles in the galvanized pail. "Should cool off quickly." She trundled an empty gas bottle out of the way for Jane. "You get some good pictures yesterday?"

"Yes."

"Any rain?"

"No."

They unloaded foodstuff for a while in silence. "According to Radio Belize, the rains will be late this year."

"That's good."

"I see you've lost none of your talent for conversation." Cleis sighed. "Sorry. That was uncalled for. It's just that I've got things on my mind and I wanted . . ." She shook her head. "Doesn't matter."

Jane watched Cleis slide the orange tubing into place on the gas bottle, turn the knob on the stove, listen for the hiss. She looked different. Something had happened in Benque Viejo.

Cleis opened a beer. "Let's go up to the site. It's cool by the water."

They took the pail and an extra six-pack up the trail and sat on the grassy bank together. Cleis threw stones, opened her second beer, sucked half down without pausing. They listened to the waterfall.

Cleis popped open her third bottle, seemed to come back from wherever she had been. "So, how was your night alone in the jungle?"

Jane wondered if Cleis knew she had been terrified. "I was . . . Well, I felt skittish, had bad dreams."

Cleis nodded. The sun glinted on tiny beads of sweat on her upper lip. "It was like that for me the time I spent four months in the Xingu basin in Brazil. Years ago. Strange place, the jungle. Feels alive sometimes, and then other times . . . you wonder what the hell you were worried about."

Jane started on the second six-pack about mid-afternoon. Despite the weight of the heat, she felt lighter than she had done in a long time.

"How come your first name's Cleis?" she asked. She was sitting next to Cleis who was sprawled out on the turf, hair almost touching Jane's thigh. Jane wondered idly what that hair would feel like wrapped around her fingers.

"My mother was fond of poetry. Read lots of the classics in Colombia, when she was young. Don't look so surprised."

"I'm not surprised."

Cleis did not seem to hear her. "She may have ended up in poverty in East L.A., and I might have had to do everything on scholarship, be twice as good as the Anglos to get what I wanted, but we have a history, a past. The U.S. isn't the only place where people know things."

"Cleis was Sappho's daughter." *Now why did I say that?*

"I know."

A kingfisher flashed blue and green and black across the pool. "Get kingfishers in England," Jane said.

"I know that, too." Cleis climbed to her feet. "Time for a swim." She pulled off her shirt, unzipped her shorts. "Aren't you coming in?"

Fear squeezed Jane's throat. "I'm not sure it's wise to swim after so much to drink."

"Three beers? Besides, look at this place!"

The pool was green and quiet. Damselflies hummed over the surface at the edge away from the fall where water cabbage floated, leaves like huge furry clams. Along the northern bank heliconias with leaves as big as canoe paddles made a dense wall between the forest and water on one side. No one would see.

Jane shook her head. "No. I can't swim."

"Well, you could just paddle a bit." Cleis's body gleamed like polished hardwood. "The floor slopes gently. No danger of falling into a pit. And I'm here."

I know. "I'd rather not."

"The water's cool."

Jane was aware of sweat running over her stomach, trickling down the small of her back, itching behind her knees. Swimming would be lovely. She almost moved. Almost stood up and took off her shirt, but years of habit and training brought her up short just as effectively as a chain around her neck. "No." It came out flat and hard.

Cleis's eyes narrowed. "What is it? You don't think a bare-assed Latina is good enough to swim with?"

"It's not that."

Cleis stood with her hands on her hips. "What then?"

Jane drained the bottle of its last, warm mouthful. *Armored, inviolate, safe.* "You wouldn't understand." Immediately, she knew she had said the wrong thing.

"So. Now I'm stupid as well as inferior. What is your problem, Lady Jane? You drive in here, cool as cut glass, and act like you're queen of the fucking world. You smile at me so politely and ask me questions for your damn article. You take my picture, you listen to me rambling on, but you give me nothing. Not one thing. Why? Because deep down you think you're better than me. Better than everyone."

"No. That's not it. It's just that . . ."

Cleis lifted her eyebrows, waiting, and Jane realized that she was being goaded. For once, she allowed it.

"Why is everyone so eager to show everything to everyone all the time? Everywhere you look there are people being stared at: television, film, video, magazines, newspapers. Close-ups taken from a mile away, such huge scale that pores look like craters. You can't hide anything. Everyone looking, being looked at. Gossip columnists. Stalkers. Tell-all biographies. Desperate actors having their faces sculpted to look like last week's star. It never stops." She was panting.

"What exactly are you afraid of?"

Jane blinked. "What do you mean, what am I afraid of? These people are being eaten alive! Everything they do or say is consumed by a greedy public. A woman's child is mown down on the street and the cameras are there: tracking her tears, recording the snot on her chin, following the way she shifts from foot to foot because she needs the bathroom. Sometimes they follow her *into* the bathroom. Once you start giving them something, once they see the hairline crack in your armor, they're there, driving in, wedging you open, spilling your guts."

"I still don't understand why it bothers you so much." Jane stared at her. "Look, suppose they wired up your bathroom and made a tape of you taking a dump, complete with groanings and strainings, so what? So fucking what. It's something every person on this earth does. Nothing to be ashamed of."

"But it's private! It's my life. . . ."

"You don't have a life. You're so afraid someone will take it away you haven't allowed yourself one."

"No! That's not—"

"Then why are you so scared?"

Cleis gestured at her own nakedness, at Jane in her hot, itchy clothes, the cool lake, the empty jungle. All of a sudden, horrifyingly, Jane did not know why. She was twenty-nine years old and had spent her whole life hiding behind a mask and she did not know why. She had denied herself so much: never had a lover, never been naked in public, never been drunk or screamed out loud with pleasure except in the privacy of her own apartments. She had never had a friend, never had a real argument, never wept over a dead pet.

She looked blindly out over the water. Normal people swam naked and did not care. She was not normal. She did not know what she was, or who. She wanted to lay her head down on the turf and cry: grieve for all those lost years. But even now the habit of privacy was too strong.

"It's never too late to change," Cleis said. And she waded out into the pool and dived underwater.

Jane watched the ripples. She knew she could not swim naked in that pool. Not today. But she could, at least, get drunk.

The sun was sinking when she woke. She sat up, and her head thumped. There were mosquito bites on her legs and one already swelling on her left breast. She looked around. Cleis's clothes were gone.

She knelt down and splashed her face with water, trying to think. Beer bottles clinked. She gathered them up, then felt foolish and put them down; counted them. Twelve. And Cleis had had three, four at most. She swayed and realized that she was still drunk. But she never got drunk.

"Cleis!" She climbed carefully up the western slope to the purdah house. "Cleis!" She listened, walked south toward the glyph-covered walls, stopped. She heard something, a vague scrabbling coming from the tumbled remains of a masonry wall.

Cleis was half lying, half sitting against a stack of newly fallen stone. Her left arm hung useless and bloody. She was swearing, very quietly, and trying to push herself upright.

"Cleis?"

Cleis smiled lopsidedly. "Fucking thing." She sounded cheerful. Shock, Jane decided.

Jane peered at her eyes. They were glassy. "Do you hurt anywhere except your shoulder?"

"Shoulder?" Cleis looked at it. "Oh."

"Yes. Do you hurt anywhere else? Did you fall, bang your head?" Cleis's left arm was broken by the looks of it, and the gashes on her shoulder would need stiches. There was no sign of a head injury, but you could not be too careful.

". . . fucking thing knocked the wall down on purpose. Kill that fucking thing. . . ."

It was getting dark. She needed to get Cleis to a safe place. First she needed to make a sling.

She touched the buttons of her shirt, hesitated. *Does it matter?* Oh, yes, it still mattered. But there was no real choice. She shivered, despite the heat, then wrenched it off, trying not to imagine a grainy telephoto image of her breasts appearing on newsstands around the country. She draped the shirt around Cleis's neck, tied the sleeves together. "Help me, damn it." But Cleis was lost in a world of shock and pain. Jane thrust the arm into the support.

Later, Jane never really knew how she managed to get them both back down the trail safely. She womanhandled Cleis out of the rubble and laid her on the smooth grass. Cleis was too heavy to carry far, Jane could not drag her by the arms. . . . She took off her belt, slid the leather tongue under the small of Cleis's back, under and around Cleis's belt, then threaded it through the buckle. Tugged. It should hold.

The forest was hot and close. The light was going rapidly. Jane plodded along, dragging Cleis behind her like a sled.

Two-thirds of the way down the trail, Ixbalum was there, standing

in the leaf shadow, eyes invisible. *Eyes. Cameras. Don't think about it.*
"Help me." She did not know if Ixbalum understood or, if she did,
whether she cared. "Please."

Ixbalum turned and said something over her shoulder. Two men
with the same sloping foreheads and close-set eyes of figures depicted
in thousand-year-old glyphs stepped from behind her.

"Be careful," Jane said, half to Ixbalum, half to the men. "Her
arm's broken."

Ixbalum gestured for Jane to move aside. Jane stayed where she
was. If she could just keep hold of the belt that connected her to Cleis
she would not feel naked. "She might have hurt her head, too." The
men stepped around her. One gently pried the belt from Jane's hand.

"It was a jaguar," Cleis suddenly said, very clearly.

"What—" But they were picking Cleis up and Jane had to scramble
to follow them down the trail.

The tallow candle flickered and sent shadows dancing over Cleis's
sleeping face. On her chair by the bed, Jane huddled deeper into the
coarse cotton wrap that Ixbalum had held out to her without comment,
and tried to stay awake. She felt feverish with too much sun and alco-
hol and fatigue, and she wondered when Ixbalum would be back.

Cleis opened her eyes. "This isn't our shack."

"You're in Ixbalum's house. How do you feel?"

"I don't know yet. Confused. What happened?"

"A wall fell on you. About eight hours ago. Don't move your arm.
It's splinted."

"Broken?" Jane nodded. Cleis closed her eyes. Opened them.
"Help me sit up." She hissed with pain when Jane lifted her. "Feel like
I've been run over by a truck." She wrinkled her nose. "What's that ter-
rible smell?"

"Some salve or other Ixbalum put on your shoulder. You have some
bad cuts."

"On my left shoulder?" She seemed tense. Jane nodded. That answer did not seem to please her. "Anything else?"

"Just bruises."

"Where?"

"Legs, mainly."

"No . . . blood?"

"Except from your arm, no."

"You're sure?"

"I'm sure."

Tears ran, sudden and silent, down Cleis's cheeks. Jane looked around; there was nothing in Ixbalum's hut that might do as a tissue.

"You're all right." Jane realized she had never had to reassure anyone before; there had always been someone else, someone closer to do the comforting. "Really. No head injury. And your arm should be fine in a few—"

"I'm pregnant."

Jane did not have the faintest idea how to respond.

"I found out for certain in Benque Viejo. Just over three months gone." Jane got up, dipped her a bowl of water from the barrel by the door. "Thank you." She looked up, met Jane's eyes. "Aren't you going to ask me if it's good news?"

Cleis seemed thin and vulnerable, her eyes big, and Jane wished she knew how to comfort her. "Is it?"

Cleis nodded. "I'm forty-one. I've never loved anyone enough to have a child with them. Last year I realized I probably never would. So I decided to have one on my own. It took me ten months of trying. I thought that wall coming down . . ." She was crying again. This time Jane wiped away the tears with her hands.

"You're all right. You're all right."

"I'm sorry." And Jane thought she might be apologizing for more than the tears.

After a while, Cleis looked around at the smooth adobe walls, the herbs hanging from the roof. "Where's Ixbalum?"

"She went out about two hours ago." They had not exchanged a single word. Jane had just watched while the Mayan woman washed Cleis's wounds, slathered them with an already prepared salve, bound them. When Ixbalum had gestured for her to help with the split-branch splints, she had.

"I want to get out of here."

So did Jane. She never wanted to see Ixbalum, and those golden eyes that had seen her naked, again.

————————

Cleis pushed aside the glass of water and the pills that Jane was holding out. "I don't want them. Not yet. I don't know what's going on, but I don't like it." She was flushed, sweaty. Jane wondered if she had made a mistake encouraging Cleis to walk back to their shack so soon. At least she was lying down now.

"Take the pills. You have a fever, and your arm must hurt."

"Of course it hurts. Christ knows what crap she put on it. How do I know my arm's not rotting off?"

They had already been through this. "I watched her wash it. She seemed to know what she was doing." She should have come here and got the first-aid kit, proper antiseptics, antibiotic creams, but she had been too drunk, too shaken up from the conversation by the pool. And Ixbalum had been so . . . competent. She said, again, "I don't know what the salve was but it was fresh—moist, green-smelling—and the bowl looked clean."

"But why was it fresh? How did she know I'd need it?" Cleis was getting more and more fretful.

"Just take these pills. Everything will seem better when you've had some sleep."

Cleis plucked for a moment at the blanket. "Oh, give me the goddamn things then." She swallowed them. "Now will you listen to me?"

Jane sighed. "Go ahead."

"I was looking at the glyph wall, wondering what was under all those vines, thinking maybe I should start clearing them away the next day, when it suddenly struck me how, I don't know, how orderly the vines seemed. So I squatted down and had a closer look: they were growing from the dirt an even eight inches apart. They'd been cultivated. To hide the glyphs. I stood up, thinking maybe I'd tug on them a bit, see how—"

"No wonder the wall came down!" Jane's voice was loud with relief, and it was then that she realized how scared she was.

"But I didn't actually pull on them. I was just thinking about it."

"You'd been drinking. We both had. All that beer . . ." *Go to sleep,* she was thinking. *I don't want to hear this.*

"I didn't touch that damn wall. The jaguar did it."

Jane closed her eyes. Those dreams of danger and golden eyes.

"Did my face look like that when you were telling me about the jaguar that followed you home from the ruins?" Cleis reached out, grasped Jane's wrist. Her hands felt thinner, dry. "Listen to me, Jane. Just listen. Don't think, not yet. A jaguar knocked down that wall, wounding my shoulder, my left shoulder, like those young women in the glyphs. Ixbalum knew we were coming, and that I was hurt. She had to know, there's no other explanation for the salve and her appearance on the trail. How much do you bet that some of those herbs hanging upside down from her roof are the same as the plants pictured on the glyph wall?"

No, Jane thought, and felt the same fear as that day when she had turned around and seen a jaguar print crumbling inside her own tracks. "You're feverish," she said firmly. "Maybe there was a jaguar, yes. Maybe the ruins have become the stamping grounds of some solitary cat. But that doesn't alter the fact that you need to get to sleep. Now. You need to get some rest and get well."

Cleis was pale now, her lids drooping. "You believe me, I know you do. Because you're scared. I'm scared." Her chin was sinking onto her chest now, eyes barely open. "Ritual wounding . . . How did she know?" Her eyes closed. "Fucking thing. You'll see. . . ."

Jane sat where she was for more than half an hour, watching Cleis sleep, telling herself that Cleis was wrong.

Jane half woke in the middle of the night. Her muscles were relaxed, soft; she felt content. Across the room moonlight showed a tangle of blankets pushed back from an empty bed. There was some reason why she should be disturbed by that, but she was already falling back to sleep.

The next time she woke moonlight and shadow patterns had moved farther along the wall, and Cleis's bed was no longer empty. She crept out of bed, padded over to the other bunk. She must have dreamed that Cleis was gone, earlier. Cleis was sleeping soundly, naked as usual. Jane checked to make sure no blood was seeping through the bandages, then simply watched her for a while.

Cleis woke late the next morning. Jane brought her water and fruit, checked her fever. "Not as bad as yesterday, but still too high for you to be out of bed."

Cleis twisted restlessly under her blanket. "You should be out working. Just because I have to spend the damn day in bed wasting precious time doesn't mean the rains are going to come later than planned."

"Your color's better," Jane said.

"Well, I hurt. My legs, my shoulders . . . strange places. All my tendons feel pulled."

"You'd better take some painkillers."

"I don't want any more drugs." She touched her stomach. "Anyway, they give me strange dreams. I feel exhausted from running around the jungle in my dreams." She looked up at Jane crossly. "*Now* what's the matter? I'm fine. I'll take the damn pills. Go do some work."

Work, at least, would mean she would not have to think.

"And before you go, hand me those notes. I can be of *some* use." Jane picked up the nearest camera case, opened the door. "And Jane, I think I was a bit delirious last night. Said some wild things. Just forget it, OK?"

Jane nodded mutely.

Cleis's fever lasted three days. She was up and about before then. "Don't tell me I should rest. I'm fine. Never better. I don't need two good arms to study the glyphs. And the rains won't wait."

The first couple of days at the site, Jane kept a surreptitious eye on Cleis, but gave up when Cleis caught her at it and glared. They worked in silence, Jane moving crabwise with camera and tripod along walls, changing filters, checking light levels; Cleis making notes, taking measurements, staring blankly at the trees and muttering to herself.

On the fourth day, Jane got back to the shack to find Cleis sitting on the bed with her notes, and the remains of the splint piled in a heap on the table. "I took it off," Cleis said. "My arm feels fine. It was probably just a sprain."

There was nothing Jane could say. She cleared away the mess.

Something had changed since Cleis's accident: children now ran past their shack, playing games, and more than once Jane had seen villagers walking through the trees to their milpas, mattocks on their shoulders. They had greeted her with a smile and a wave.

Sometimes, too, she would look up from her camera to see Cleis and Ixbalum together, out of earshot, talking. Jane wondered why Ixbalum was now willing to speak to Cleis; wondered what she was saying, what craziness she was spilling into Cleis's eager ears. But she did not ask. Instead, she tried to push Cleis from her mind by working from first light until last. At night she would lie down, exhausted, and fall into a troubled sleep. Her dreams were vivid and fractured. More than once she woke to find Cleis gone from her bed. *Where do you go?* Jane wanted to ask, *and how?* But she never did. She imagined Cleis and Ixbalum gliding through the jungle, looking into the dark with their golden eyes. . . .

One night her dreams were jumbled images: time running backward while she watched the ruins re-form into a city; vast storms overhead; Cleis talking to her earnestly, explaining. "Ixbalum doesn't care what I know anymore. It doesn't matter what the children tell me. I'm hers now." Jane woke drenched in sweat. She looked over at Cleis's bed: she was sleeping like a baby.

Am I going mad?

She needed to get away. She got out of bed, pulled on her clothes.

She waited until just after dawn to wake Cleis. "The photography is ahead of schedule, and we need supplies. I'm driving to Benque Viejo. I'll be gone two or three days."

Jane had expected to reach Benque Viejo, walk through its streets, loud with traffic and thick with the stink of leaded gasoline, and come slowly out of her nightmare. All the time she was pulling Belize dollars from her wallet for bottled gas and beer and canned food she wondered when it would stop feeling strange and dangerous to be back in the world.

She booked herself into a hotel and took a bath, but the water was only lukewarm and she found herself longing for the lake with its water cabbage and kingfisher.

After weeks of eating fish and fruit and corn, the steak dinner was alien and almost inedible. She left a tip on the table and walked from the restaurant into the street. The sky was dusky pink, streaked with pearl gray clouds. She wished Cleis could be there to see it. And then she knew she did not want to spend three days here in Benque Viejo when she could be at Kuchil Balum. The rains would be coming soon.

There was no time. Because when the rains came, Cleis would go back to New Mexico, and she . . .

What is happening to me? She did not know. All she knew was that she had to get back.

It was mid-afternoon of the next day when she parked in front of their shack. Cleis was not there. *Probably at the site. No matter.* Jane took her time unloading the supplies, nervous about seeing Cleis again.

Then there was nothing left to do; she had even washed the enamel plates that had been lying on the table—the same plates she and Cleis had eaten from the night before she had left for Benque Viejo. She tried not to worry. Cleis had probably been eating straight from a can, too busy to take the time to prepare anything. She checked the shack one last time, then set off for the ruins.

The waterfall fell peacefully, a flock of black-and-orange orioles wheeled about the crown of a tree at the edge of the clearing, but there was no Cleis.

"Cleis!" The call echoed back, and Jane remembered the last time she had called to Cleis here. Had something else happened, something worse?

She ran through the ruins, calling, ducking in and out of half-excavated buildings. Nothing. Maybe she was at the village, talking to Ixbalum.

Two women stood at the well, a man plucked a chicken on his doorstep. They looked up when Jane ran into the clearing. "Cleis?" she asked. They frowned. "Cleis?" she asked again, pantomiming curls falling from her head. "Ah," they said, and shook their heads.

Jane ran to Ixbalum's hut. The door was closed. She banged on it with her fist. No reply. She banged again, then pushed her way in.

Without the candles, the hut was cool and dark. There was no one there. Jane brushed aside bunches of herbs on her way back to the door, then turned around again and plucked a leaf from each bundle. She could look at them later, see if any matched the ritual leaf on the glyphs.

She was just putting them in her pocket when Ixbalum came in.

The Mayan woman stood there with her arms folded, looking at Jane, looking at the floor where one leaf lay in the dirt. Jane picked it up and put it in her pocket with the others. This woman had already seen her naked, and drunk, and she was too concerned for Cleis to feel any shame at being found in Ixbalum's hut. "I want to know where Cleis is."

Ixbalum said nothing. Jane could feel herself being studied. This time she did not cringe.

"If you know where she is, I want to know. She's pregnant, and I think that fall was more of a shock then she knows. I want to take her away from here." *Do I?* "I'm asking for your help."

Ixbalum moved so suddenly that Jane thought she was going to strike her, but Ixbalum reached up past Jane's left ear and drew a leaf from one of the bunches. She held it out to Jane.

"I don't understand." But she did.

Ixbalum shook the leaf in front of Jane's face. The message was unmistakable: Take it. Jane did. Ixbalum nodded, very slightly, then made a *Go now* gesture and turned her back.

Not knowing what else to do, knowing only that it was pointless shouting when neither understood the other, Jane went back out into the sunshine. The leaf was a big one, dull gray-green now, but it would have been bright when fresh, the color of the paste Ixbalum had smeared on Cleis's shoulder. It had six points, and a tracery of veins like a spider's web.

Night came as a rising cloud of living sound. The creaky chorus of thousands of insects rubbing together chitinous legs and wing combs echoed and reverberated through the trees. Fireflies streaked the dark with yellow.

Jane lay on her back on her bunk. Her arms were grazed and scratched from pushing aside branches, being caught by unexpected thorns. She had cut her palm on a frond of razor grass. Her throat was sore from calling. For the first time she was unclothed and not covered with a sheet. She lay naked to the world, as an offering. *Please come back. Just come back safe.*

Cleis returned at dusk the next day. She pushed the door open and walked in slowly. Her hair was filthy, her face drawn. She stopped when she saw Jane. "You're back early." Her voice was flat with exhaustion.

Jane wanted to touch her face, hold her, make sure she was all right. "I got back yesterday. I've been waiting, and worrying. I went out looking." Cleis swayed a little. "It's dangerous to get too tired out there."

Cleis sat down on her bunk, sighed, and closed her eyes as she leaned back against the wall. "I didn't know you'd be here to worry."

"I just . . ." Jane did not know how to explain why she had come back early. "I just wanted to know where you've been."

Cleis's eyes flicked open. Underneath, her skin was dark with fatigue, but the eyes themselves were bright, intense. "Do you? Do you really?"

Jane took a deep breath; she felt very vulnerable. "Yes."

"The simple answer," Cleis said, over a cup of hot tea, "is that I don't know where I've been." They were sitting at the table, a Coleman lamp drawing moths that fluttered against the screen. Jane had insisted that Cleis eat something, rest a little, before talking. "The complex answer. . . . What do you know about dreaming?"

Jane was momentarily thrown off balance. "Not much."

"Dreams are something I researched in my twenties, a long time before becoming interested in Mayan civilization. Simply stated, the human brain exists in three parts, one cobbled onto the other, communicating uneasily, each with different . . . behaviors. There's the first evolutionary stage, the reptile or R-complex, the crocodile brain whose realm is sexual, aggressive, and ritual behavior. Then when mammals evolved from reptiles, they developed the limbic system, which meant they perceived the world differently—in terms of signs and vividly sensory and emotional images. To do this, they had to bypass the crocodile brain, suppress it. They couldn't ignore it altogether, though, because it controlled a lot of the body's physical functions: the urge to fuck and fight and eat."

"What does all this have to do with where you were last night?"

"I'm getting there. Anyway, mammals found a way to turn the R-complex, the crocodile brain back on, harmlessly, during sleep. Which means, of course, that our dreams are the crocodile's dreams: sex and food and fighting." Her eyes were bright. "Haven't you ever wondered why we get clitoral erections during dreams?"

"No."

"Then some mammals developed the neocortex. We became self-conscious. Ever wondered why you can't read or do math in your dreams?"

Jane opened her mouth to say she had never noticed whether or not she could, then remembered countless dreams of opening books only to be frustrated by meaningless squiggles.

Cleis noticed and nodded. "The neocortex handles analytic recollections. It's usually turned off when we dream. That's why dreams are so hard to remember. When I change, I become a mammal with no neocortex. My waking state is like a dream state. When I change back, when I wake, I remember very little. So, in answer to your question: I don't know where I've been."

There was a bubble of unreality around Jane's head, around the whole room. She concentrated on her hands, neatly folded together before her on the table. *My hands are real.* "What are you trying to tell me?"

Cleis reached out and touched those neatly folded hands. "I think you already know."

Jane felt very calm. She pulled the six-fronded leaf from her pocket. "You believe in this."

Cleis said nothing.

"You think . . . you think that those glyphs on the purdah wall are true. That the ritual wounding has purpose." She remembered Ixbalum shaking the leaf in her face. "You think your accident wasn't an accident. That Ixbalum infected you with some kind of, I don't know, changing agent, a catalyst. That you can become . . . that you change into a jaguar."

Now laugh. Tell me it isn't true. But Cleis just nodded. "Yes."

"Do you know how that sounds?" Her voice was very even, but her heart felt as though it was swelling; so big it pushed at her stomach, making her feel ill.

"You've seen the evidence with your own eyes—"

"I've seen nothing! A wall, some pictures, some leaves. You got drunk, pulled the wall on top of you, broke your arm, and probably took a bang on your head. Ixbalum fixed you up. You disappear at night and come back looking like hell, with a pseudo-scientific explanation that basically boils down to this: you can't remember and you're not responsible. All the evidence points not to the fact that you've discovered some mystical Mayan rite, but that something is wrong in your head, and getting worse." She put the leaf down carefully on the table. "Look at it. Look at it hard. It's just a leaf."

"I've read the dates on the stelae, Jane. Kuchil Balum, Place of the Jaguar, was occupied up until the sixteenth century."

"What has that got to do with—"

"Think!" Cleis's voice was thin and hard, bright as wire. "The lowland Mayan culture began to die more than a millennium ago: population pressure, some say, and crop failures, but I'm fairly sure it was more to do with a loss of faith. But not here. Here the power of the gods was tangible. Young girls from every family were sent to the purdah house at puberty. They were ritually wounded, infected. Some changed, most did not." She searched Jane's face. "Every family had the opportunity, the chance to join the elite. That welded the community together in ways we can't even begin to comprehend."

A moth fluttered frantically against the window screen.

"But even jaguar gods can't stand against guns and missionaries," Cleis continued. "So they pulled down their beautiful stone buildings and built themselves a village that appears unremarkable. They hid, but they've kept their culture, the only Mayans who have, because they have people like Ixbalum."

They sat for a moment in silence. Jane stood up. "I'll make some more tea."

She busied herself with the kettle and teapot. There had to be a way to get Cleis to see past this delusion, some way she could persuade Cleis to pack her bags and leave with her and have her head X-rayed. She did not know what to say, but she knew it was important to keep the dialogue open, to keep Cleis anchored as much as possible in the real world.

The kettle boiled. Jane brought the pot to the table. "It's not the same without milk," she said.

Cleis smiled faintly. "Being an ignorant American, I don't think it's the same without ice."

She seemed so normal. . . . Jane asked sharply, "When you change, how do you think it affects your child?"

Cleis looked thoughtful. "I don't know." She leaned forward. Jane could feel Cleis's breath on her face. She wanted to strain across the table, feel that breath hot on her throat, her neck. "You haven't asked me how it feels to change. Don't you want to know?"

Jane did. She wanted to know everything about Cleis. She nodded.

"It's like walking through a dream, but you're never scared, never being chased, because you're the one who's dangerous. I'm not me, I'm . . . other."

"Other?"

"Here, now, I have a sense of self, I know who I am. I can use symbols. It's . . ." She frowned. "It's hard to describe. Look at it this way." She patted the table. "I know this table is made of wood, that wood comes from trees, and that this wood is pine. Underlying all that knowledge is the ability to work in symbols—tree, furniture, wood—the ability to see beyond specifics. When I'm changed, symbols, words . . . they become meaningless. Everything is specific. A barba jalote is a barba jalote, and a chechem is a chechem. They're distinct and different things. There's no way to group them together as 'tree.' The world becomes a place of mystery—unknowable, unclassifiable—and understanding is intuitive, not rational."

She toyed absently with the leaf.

"I'm guided by signs: the feel of running water, the smell of brocket deer. The world is unpredictable." She paused, sighed, laid her hands on the table. "I just am," she said simply.

The rainy season was not far off. The days were hotter, more humid, and Jane worked harder than before because when she was busy she did not have to deal with Cleis, did not have to look at her, think about how her skin might feel, and her hair. She did not have to worry about getting Cleis to a hospital.

The nights were different.

They would sit outside under the silky violet sky, sipping rum, talking about the jungle.

"The jungle is a siren," Cleis said. "It sings to me." Sweat trickled down the underside of her arm. Jane could smell the rich, complex woman smells. "Especially at night. I've started to wonder how it would be during the rains. To pad through the undergrowth and nose at dripping fronds, to smell the muddy fur of a paca running for home and know its little heart is beat beat beating, to almost hear the trees pushing their roots farther into the rich mud. And above, the monkey troops will swing from branch to branch, and maybe the fingers of a youngster, not strong enough or quick enough, will slip, and it'll come crashing down, snapping twigs, clutching at leaves, landing on outflung roots, breaking its back. And it'll be frightened. It'll lie there eyes round, nose wet, fur spattered with dirt and moss, maybe bleeding a little, knowing a killer is coming through the forest." Cleis's nostrils flared.

Jane sipped her rum. She could imagine the jaguar snuffing at the night air, great golden eyes half closed, panting slightly; could taste the thin scent molecules of blood and fear spreading over her own tongue, the anticipation of the crunch of bone and the sucking of sweet flesh. She shivered and sipped more rum, always more rum. When the sun was up and she looked at the world through a viewfinder she did not need the numbing no-think of rum, but when there was just her and Cleis and the forest's nightbreath, there was nowhere to hide.

And so every night she staggered inside and fell across her bed in a daze; she tried not to smell the salty sunshiny musk of Cleis's skin, the sharp scents of unwashed hair, tried not to lean toward the soft suck and sigh of rum fumes across the room. Tried, oh tried so hard, to fall asleep, to hear nothing, see nothing, feel nothing.

But there would be nights when she heard Cleis sit up, when she could almost feel the weight of Cleis's gaze heavy on the sheet Jane kept carefully pulled up to her chin, no matter how hot she was. On those nights she kept her eyes shut and her mind closed, and if she woke in the middle of the night and felt the lack of heat, the missing cellular hum of another human being, she did not look at Cleis's bed, in case it was empty.

But one night, Jane woke sitting up in bed with her eyes open after a dream of sliding oh so gently over another woman, sliding in their mutual sweat, and she saw that Cleis was gone.

I'm alone, she thought, and was suddenly aware of every muscle in her body, plump and hot, of her thighs sliding together, wet and slippery, of her skin wanting to be bare. *There are no cameras here.* She laid her hand on her stomach, felt tendons tighten from instep to groin. And before she could really wake up and realize what she was doing—tell herself that this was not the same as being alone in her room, one she could lock—she was standing naked before Cleis's empty bed, before the wooden corner post. It came to mid-thigh, a four-by-four rounded off at the top and polished. She stroked it with one hand, her belly with the other. Her pubic hair was a foot away from the post; a foot, then eight inches, six. She sank to her knees, rubbed her face on the post, held one breast, then the other. One thick drop of milky juice ran down the inside of her thigh. She pressed her belly to the wood, stood up slowly, feeling the top of the post run between her breasts, down her stomach, her abdomen, then moved away very slightly, oh so very slowly, so the post skipped a beat then skimmed the tops of her thighs.

"Oh yes," she said, imagining Cleis lying face down in front of her, moonlight on her buttocks. "Oh yes."

She crouched down, crooning, leaning over the post, palms resting on the bunk, feet braced on the cool dirt floor. She began to lower herself.

The door creaked open. Jane froze. Something behind her coughed the tight throaty cough of a jaguar; another drop of milky juice ran down her thigh. The animal behind her rumbled deep in its chest. Jane did not dare turn around. It rumbled again: *Don't stop.* Her vulva was hot and slick and her heart thundered. The cough behind her was closer, tighter, threatening: *Do it now.*

Jane licked her lips, felt the golden eyes traveling up her achilles, her calves, the back of her knees, the tendons in her thighs, the cheeks of her bottom. She dare not turn, and she dare not disobey, nor did she want to.

"Ah," she said softly, and laid her cheek on the sheet. *Between Cleis's shoulder blades.* Touched the rumpled blanket above her head. *Cleis's rough curls.* And lowered herself onto the beautifully smooth oh so lovely rounded and rich wood. *The swell and heat of Cleis.* She moved gently. "Oh, I love you." And she felt breath on her own clenching bottom, the close attention of whatever was behind her, and suddenly she knew who, what, was behind her and loved her, it. "Yes, I love you," she said, but it was a gasp as she felt the wood round and slick between her legs slide up and down and her breath caught and "Ah," she said, "ah," and she was grunting, and then she felt a sharp cool pressure against her shoulder where claws unsheathed and rested, possessive, dimpling the skin, and she was pulling herself up and over that wooden corner, *Cleis's soft plump slippery-now cheek,* her face tight with effort, and her breasts flattened on the bed as she thrust and her chin strained forward and the muscles under her skin pumped and relaxed and sweat ran down her legs and the room was full of a rumbling purr. Fur brushed her back and she was pressed into the bed by an enormous weight, a weight with careful claws, and the heat between her and the wood was bubbling up in her bones and "Ah!" she shouted, "ah!" hardly able to breathe, and could not stop, not now not now, and she humped and rocked and grunted and came, curling around the bunk *around Cleis* like a fist. Sweat ran from her in rivers; a pulse in her temple thumped.

Claws slid back in their sheaths, the heat and weight withdrew. A throaty rumble: *Don't move.* And then it was gone.

Jane buried her face in the damp sheets that smelled of Cleis, that smelled of her and Cleis, and cried. *I don't know where I've been,* Cleis had said, *when I change back, I remember very little.*

When Jane woke up, Cleis was fast asleep in her bunk.

The mid-morning sun poured like buttermilk over Jane where she knelt on the turf before the glyph wall.

What is happening to me?

She rested her fingertips on the glyphs. "What do you really say?" she whispered.

She was alone. Cleis had gone into the forest that morning, saying she wanted to examine the area for evidence of fruit tree cultivation.

She found herself standing by the fall, staring into the sheeting water, mind empty.

Wake up! she told herself fiercely. *Think. Don't let this just happen to you. . . .* She jumped fully clothed into the water.

She bobbed back to the surface, gasping. It was cold. *Good.* She swam back to the bank, climbed out just long enough to strip off her sodden clothes.

She did not even think about whether or not anyone might be watching.

She dived back in and swam in a fast crawl to the waterfall, let it thunder on her head for a moment; swam again.

This is real, she told herself. *This: sun, water, air. Not dreams, not Cleis's delusions.*

She swam until she was exhausted, then climbed out onto the bank and lay in the sun. She fell asleep.

When she woke, the memory of the dream, the soreness between her legs, was still vivid. She sighed. Her rational mind told her one thing, all the evidence *All my needs* told her another. Which did she want to be real? She did not know.

Her clothes had dried in a wrinkled pile. Jane shook them out one by one and put them back one.

The inside of the shack was hotter than the outside. Cleis had been cooking.

"Here," she said, and handed Jane a tin plate. "Beans and tortillas and fresh corn. Let's eat outside."

Jane wondered where the food had come from, but obeyed silently. Cleis seemed different. Cheerful. Jane wondered if it was anything to do with last night, felt the world spin a little. A dream. It had been a dream.

They sat very close together on the step, arms brushing against each other as they ate. Jane watched the small muscles along Cleis's forearm ripple as she chased beans with her fork, wiped at the juice with her tortilla. Her arms seemed thicker, the muscles more solid than they had been. Jane wondered if that was a result of pregnancy. Women plumped out a little, didn't they? She studied Cleis. Not long ago her muscles had been long and flat, face hollow as though the intensity of her concentration burned away all subcutaneous fat. Her eyes had peered bright from dark hollows. Now she seemed squarer, stronger, more lithe.

"I'd like to take more pictures of you."

"You already have all the pictures you'll need for that article."

Jane had almost forgotten the reason she had come to Belize. She felt as though she had always been here, always eaten from tin plates and drunk rum with Cleis. "I didn't mean that. I mean of you, as you . . . as your pregnancy develops. I want to document your changes."

Changes. The word hung in the air between them.

"Ow!" A sharp pain shot through Jane's left breast. "Christ!" Another shooting pain jerked her arm sending the tin plate flying, beans spattering on Cleis's shorts. Cleis jumped to her feet. Jane clapped a hand to the fire in her breast.

"Move your hand." All Jane could do was gasp. "Move your hand, Jane. I need to see."

But Jane was scared. She did not know what was happening, was afraid to see. "It hurts!"

"Move your hand." This time Jane let Cleis move her hand away, did not protest as she unbuttoned her shirt. She turned her head away as Cleis sucked in her breath.

"What is it?"

"Botfly. It's eating its way out of your breast."

"Get it out! Get it out!" Jane wanted to rip at her breast, at the thing that was eating her flesh, but Cleis was holding her hands.

"Listen to me. Fasten up your shirt again. It's not big. There won't be any permanent damage, but I have to go get something. Can you do that?"

Jane nodded, thinking Cleis meant to get something from the shack. But Cleis set off down the track that led to the village.

"Wait!"

"I won't be long. Be brave, bonita."

Jane sat with her breast cupped in her hand. *Bonita.*

It must have been from that mosquito bite she got the day Cleis broke her arm. The egg of the botfly had hatched on her skin and burrowed its way down into her breast. Now it was big enough to need food. It would stay in her breast, feeding on her flesh, breathing through the hole it would chew through her skin, until it was large enough to hatch into a botfly. Unless they could get it out. The pain was excruciating.

Bonita.

Cleis returned, slightly out of breath and slick with sweat.

"Chew this." She held out a large dried leaf.

"Where did you get it?" Cleis just looked at her. Ixbalum, of course. "What is it?"

"Tobacco."

"Tobacco? What good will that do? That won't take away the pain!"

"It's not for pain. Just chew it." Cleis tore off a piece, held it out. Jane took it, reluctantly, put it in her mouth, chewed gingerly.

"Tastes terrible."

"Just chew. Don't swallow. No, chew some more." Cleis put down the rest of the leaf and started to unbutton Jane's shirt again. Jane watched her, saw the way the skin around her eyes wrinkled in concentration, the faint sparkle of perspiration on her lip. Jane wondered how those long brown hands would feel wrapped around her breasts. She could feel her color rising. She was afraid that her nipples would harden. She cleared her throat. "How does it look?"

"See for yourself."

Jane, still chewing, looked. There was a hole, no bigger than the knob on her watch, about three inches right of her nipple. So small for so much pain.

Cleis held out her hand. "Spit it out." Jane did, feeling a little self-conscious. Cleis pinched off a tiny clump of soggy pulp and rolled it between the strong fingers of her right hand. "This might hurt." She put her left hand on Jane's breast, one finger on each side of the hole, then spread them slightly, so that the pink under her nails turned white and the larva's breathing hole stretched open. Her fingers were very gentle, very precise. Very human. Cleis plugged the hole neatly with the tobacco. "Very brave, bonita. The nicotine will kill it. Then we'll pull it out with a pin." They watched each other's faces as Cleis began to fasten Jane's shirt again, then hesitated. Cleis's eyes were very dark, and a vein in her throat pulsed.

Jane panicked. "The food was nice. Thank you."

Cleis studied her a moment, then half turned away. "Don't thank me, thank our mysterious benefactor. When I got back this afternoon, I found a little pile of stuff, tortillas, corn, fresh fruit for later, on the doorstep."

Jane closed her eyes against sudden nausea as the real world threatened to come unglued.

Cleis, still not looking at her, did not notice. "They've probably finally figured out we're not burning-eyed fanatics clutching bowdlerized Bibles in one hand and McDonald's franchises in the other."

Jane nodded, as though she agreed, but she knew: the food was a gift, to their new god.

Every afternoon when they got back from the site there was something: sometimes fruit, or a plucked chicken; eggs; once a clay pot full of some sticky alcoholic beverage. They drank that on the night Cleis used a pin to pull the plug of tobacco, black now, from Jane's breast, and then teased out the botfly larva. Jane held the pin with the skewered larva over the gas ring until it was ashes. She had bad dreams that night, dreams of being eaten alive by wriggling maggots, but when she woke up, Cleis was there. "You killed it, Jane. It's dead."

Most nights, Jane woke up to find Cleis gone. She did not speak of it. *Don't reinforce the madness,* she told herself, but sometimes she wondered whose madness. She felt as though she were being sucked into an increasingly angled world, where the beliefs of Cleis and Ixbalum and the villagers, the evidence of forest and ruin, all made sense, if only she would let go of everything that made her sane. Everything that made her human.

The forest is a siren, Cleis had said, and Jane could hear it singing, day and night.

Cleis was changing, spending more and more time in her own world, content to drowse on the warm, sunlit terraces, or stare off into the distance while Jane worked.

Perhaps it was her pregnancy. Jane did not know much about the process, but Cleis grew visibly more pregnant every day, which she did not think was normal.

"We should take you to Benque Viejo for a checkup," she said one afternoon when Cleis was waking from a nap. "You're too big for four months."

Cleis shrugged. "The process is being accelerated. Jaguar gestation is only three months."

For the first time in her life, Jane deliberately broke an expensive piece of equipment: she threw the camera she was using against a rock and did not bother to pick up the pieces.

Now when Jane woke up in the mornings she could taste the damp in the air, a different damp, cold, spelling the end of their time here.

Cleis seemed to smell it, too. She became restless, always moving about, standing up two minutes after she sat down. She was eating less and less, and barely bothered to listen when Jane told her she should eat, for her own health and her child's. Sometimes Jane would come back from the site and find Cleis staring at something—a pen, the stove—as though it were utterly alien.

Cleis began to stay away for longer stretches: all night, then twenty-four hours.

"Why?" Jane wanted to know. "Why are you doing this?"

"I can't help it. It . . . everything is so simple out there. I don't need to worry about always having to be better than everyone else just to stay in place. I smell the green and it's like opium. It makes me forget."

And Jane knew she was losing her.

Four days later, Cleis disappeared.

She did not come home one night, or the next day. One night stretched to two, then a week. Jane thought she would go mad. She searched the jungle by day, left messages on rocks and carved words on trees with a knife. She cooked every night, hoping the smell of food would draw Cleis back.

She still went to the site to take pictures. There were probably a hundred thousand glyphs, some of which would not survive another another rainy season. And there was always wildlife to photograph. If she just kept taking pictures, Cleis would come back. She would. They would go back to New Mexico together, and Jane would alternately help Cleis put together her notes and visual evidence, and work on a book of photographs of Belize. Everything would turn out all right. She just had to make sure she had everything done for when Cleis returned, before the rains.

One day, walking through the trees with her camera in search of a purple-throated hummingbird, Jane heard a strange noise. A pattering. Something cold hit her face, then her leg, her shoulder. All around her leaves started to bounce, and the stem of a bromeliad trembled as it filled. The patter became a rush.

Rain.

Rivulets of the stuff began to run down the trunk at her back and the rush became a hiss. There was too much water for the forest to absorb and within seconds there was a muddy brown stream running past her feet. A leaf floated past, with a spider balanced on it, as though it were a life raft.

One week became two, then three. Jane wandered in the rain, imagining Cleis as a jaguar, drinking from the new pools, licking raindrops from her whiskers. Jane no longer left written messages, only her scent, and still Cleis did not come.

One night, something woke Jane. She sat up, listened: the rain had stopped. She got up, went outside. All around the shack there were jaguar tracks pressed into the mud.

"Cleis?" But she whispered, afraid. The windows of her shack were screen, and the door flimsy. There were many jaguars in the forest.

When she woke again in the morning, the rain was thrumming steadily on the tin roof. She sighed, pulled on a long shirt and opened the door to take a look at the world.

There, curled in the mud, naked and still, was Cleis. Jane stood in the open doorway, unable to move, throat tight. Then she ran down the steps and knelt beside her. Cleis's hair was reddish brown with mud and a large scratch stretched over her ribs. She looked nine months pregnant.

"Cleis?" Jane touched her, hesitantly, then jerked back when she felt cold flesh. But Cleis opened her eyes.

Getting her up the steps and into the shack was harder than dragging her down the trail, but Jane managed, eventually. She stripped the covers from Cleis's bunk so they would not get wet, sat her down. "Now you keep still while I put a kettle on."

Cleis sat like a cold soapstone carving while Jane rubbed her down with a towel and talked about the rain, the hot tea she would make, the photographs she had been taking. After a few minutes, Cleis began to tremble. Jane kept rubbing.

"That's right. You're home now. You're safe with me." The trembling became great rolling shudders. Jane wrapped a clean dry towel around her. "You don't have to worry about anything. I'll take care of you." She stroked Cleis's hair. "While you've been gone I've been at the site every day, taking pictures. It's changed with the rains, got more lush." Cleis's eyes were still blank, uncomprehending. "The waterfall used to be so clear but now it's muddy. The other day I saw a turtle sunning itself on the bank. . . ." She talked on and on, about everything and nothing, until she felt a hot tear splash on her shoulder. Then she made the tea, guided Cleis's hand to the cup. Watched until she was sure Cleis would hold the tea without burning herself.

"Good. Now you drink that all up while I put a fresh sheet on this bunk, and then we'll get you tucked in nice and cozy and you can sleep for a while." Cleis watched her while she made the bed. Her eyes were deep sunk, surrounded by grainy brown circles the color of tannin. "There. Everything will look better after some sleep."

In sleep, Cleis looked fragile. Her eyelids were delicate with purples: lavender, indigo, violet. Her face was drawn, leached of color; a kind of dirty tan. She had kicked the sheet down to her waist and Jane could see that her breasts were a different shape.

She would give birth soon.

But that's impossible.

Jane sighed. She no longer knew what was possible and what was not. All that mattered was that Cleis had come back. She stroked the lean hand lying on top of the sheet. The fingernails were filthy now, and ragged, but Jane only saw the way that hand had opened her shirt, weeks ago, had gently moved away her own hand, had made her feel better.

She lifted the hand and kissed it. "Oh, I have missed you." Cleis slept on. "As soon as you're well enough, we'll leave this place."

She got up and started packing.

Cleis slept for nearly ten hours, then woke up long enough to be fed some soup. When the soup was gone, she went back to sleep.

When it got dark, Jane lit all three Coleman lamps, even though the heat was overwhelming. If Cleis woke up in the middle of the night, the first thing she wanted her to see was light. Bright, artificial light. She stood by Cleis's bed, hesitating: the other bunk was covered in open suitcases and piles of clothes. Moving them would wake her. Jane drew back the sheet and fitted herself carefully around the strange mix of bone and muscle and pregnancy that was Cleis, and fell asleep almost instantly.

When she woke up it was still the middle of the night. Cleis was whimpering, burrowing into her neck. "Sshh, sshh. I'm here. What is it?" But then Cleis was clinging to her and crying and Jane was stroking her side, shoulders arms side of breast ribs belly-bulge hip and back, up and down, telling her it was all right, it was all right, and then the heat Jane felt was more than the hiss and spit of Coleman lamps, more than the warmth of a humid Belize night. And Cleis was no longer sobbing on her neck but kissing it, and the arms wrapped so tightly around her were pulling her in, until their mouths were almost close enough to touch, and Jane's arm was under Cleis's neck, supporting her head, and her leg was wrapped over Cleis's and her other hand stroking her breast, her hips, her thighs.

"Kiss me," Cleis said.

Jane expected her lips to be dry and rough, but they were soft as plums.

At first they made love as though they were underwater: coming together too fast, bumping, drifting apart, but then they were moving together, rising toward the surface, a roaring in their ears, and the muscles in arms and thighs and belly were clenched tight as each breathed the other's breath as though it were the only oxygen available.

"Show me I'm real," said Cleis, and slid her palm up to the hot slick between Jane's thighs. "Come in my hand." And Jane did.

They lay in each other's arms, slippery as newborns, while Jane kissed Cleis's forehead, again and again.

"I've packed almost everything," Jane said as they ate breakfast. Cleis was wearing a long shirt. Nothing else would fit her. "We need to get you to a clinic as soon as possible. You look like you're ready to give birth any minute."

Cleis rested a hand on her belly. She nodded but did not say anything.

"I'll check the Jeep as soon as we've had breakfast." Jane decided not to mention her worries about the passability of the trail in this wet weather. "Will you be all right for the journey?"

Cleis moved her eyes sideways, lifted her shoulders slightly in a *Who knows?* gesture.

"Well . . . do you feel well enough at this moment?"

Cleis nodded, then seemed to realize she would have to give more than that. "Everything is very strange for me. Different. Sitting here, talking to you, is like looking through a kaleidoscope. Someone keeps twisting it out of shape, and then I don't know who you are, or who I am, or what we're doing here. Talking is sometimes . . . difficult."

Jane did not want to ask the next question, because she was scared of the answer. But she had to know. "Do you . . . is leaving what you want to do?"

Cleis hesitated, then laid a hand on her belly and nodded. Jane knew she would get no more from her for a while.

They set off at midday. It was cold, and pouring with rain. Jane helped Cleis to the passenger seat, more because of Cleis's mental state than any physical disability. Cleis moved easily, muscles plainly visible beneath her skin. Once she was in the Jeep Jane wrapped several shirts around her bare legs.

It was slow going. Twice, Jane had to climb out of the Jeep and tuck canvas under rear wheels that could find no traction in mud. But she did not mind the rain or the mud or the cold: she was getting Cleis to safety.

All this time, Cleis sat in her bundle of clothes, silent and distant.

Eight miles down the trail they came upon a tree that had fallen across their path. Jane turned off the engine. "Stay here. I'll go take a look."

The trunk was too big to drive over and the undergrowth on either side of the trail too thick to drive through. Jane walked back to the Jeep. "I'm going to try to hack us a path around this thing." She reached under the driver's seat and pulled out the machete. "Just stay here and keep the windows and doors locked." Cleis did not seem to hear her. Jane rolled up both windows and locked the doors, hesitated, then took the car keys. "It might take a while."

Jane hurried, swinging the machete heedlessly through vines and flowers. Her arms were aching and her face itched with spattered sap by the time she had a path cleared.

She hurried back to the Jeep. "That should—"

Cleis was gone. A pile of empty clothes lay on the passenger seat. "No," Jane said quietly, "not now." She would not let the forest have her. "Do you hear me?" she bellowed. "I won't let you have her!"

She crashed through the undergrowth, smashing past branches, pushing through tangles, the machete forgotten. She had no idea how long she trampled through the forest, blinded by grief and rage, but eventually she found herself by a stream, sobbing. She wiped the tears away from her eyes. Maybe Cleis was already back at the Jeep. Maybe she had just wandered off for a moment then remembered who she was. Yes. She should get back to the Jeep.

But the Jeep was still empty. Jane sat behind the wheel, staring into the trees until it was dark. Then she switched on the lights and drove back to the shack.

She did not unpack the Jeep. For the next five nights she left a Coleman lamp burning on the step, just in case. She barely slept anymore, but wandered through the trees, calling. On the sixth night she did not go back to the shack. Perhaps if she stayed out here, lived as Cleis lived, she could understand. Her back itched; her shirt was filthy. She took it off, left it hanging on a branch.

That night she slept curled up on a tree bough, like a jaguar. Like Cleis. She woke hours later, heart kicking under her ribs. Did jaguars dream of falling?

The next day she wandered aimlessly through the forest, eating fruit where she found it. She ran her hand across the surface of a puddle, wondered what it would be like to have paws heavy enough to break a paca's back, how it would feel to lean down to lap with a great pink tongue, to see the reflection of round golden eyes and white whiskers. She wandered. Time ceased to mean anything much.

Maybe it would not be so bad to walk through the forest on four feet. The world would look very different, but things would become very simple. And she would be with Cleis.

She found herself back at the shack, taking a large knife from the table. It did not take long to get back to the ruins. She knelt by the glyph wall. She would cut open her own shoulder and ask Ixbalum to

give her the change salve. Then she could join Cleis. They could be together. She laid the knife against the muscle of her left shoulder, and
cut. Her blood was shockingly red, the pain incredible.

She blinked at the knife. "What am I doing?"

She had to find a way to get Cleis out, not to lose herself. She
threw the knife away from her, and stood up, holding her arm. The cut
was deep. It needed cleaning up. She had to get back to the shack.

That night, as she lay on her bunk, bandaged shoulder aching, the
endless chorus of frogs and insects fell silent. Jane was suddenly full of
hope. She pulled on her boots and went to the door. Then she heard it,
a low moaning yowl, like a cat in heat. A big cat. The yowl leapt to a
scream, then another. The scream turned into a tight cough. She heard
harsh panting, hissing, and then that terrible scream.

"Cleis!" Cats sometimes fought over territory. Jane snatched up
the lantern and ran out into the dark, following the noise. Fifty yards
into the trees, the screaming stopped, and there was a thrashing in the
undergrowth, then silence. Jane ran harder.

There was no sign of the cat, but it had flattened an area of undergrowth with a diameter of about ten feet, and the grass was covered in
blood. She cast about for tracks, or a trail of blood, anything. There was
nothing. Exhausted, she headed back to the shack and lay down, refusing to imagine what might have happened to Cleis.

Someone was shaking her shoulder. Jane opened her eyes. Cleis stood
before her naked, gaunt, holding something. Must be a dream. Cleis
was pregnant.

The shaking did not stop.

Gaunt. Jane sat bolt upright. Cleis was holding a baby. "Take
her. She can't stay with me." Cleis thrust the child at Jane, then opened
the door.

"Wait!"

"I can't. She's been fed. Take her away from here."

"No. I'm not going anywhere without you." Jane climbed out of
bed, scrunched the blanket into a nest, and laid the child down. "I'll
follow you, leave the baby here."

"You can't."

"I can. I will. You're not well, Cleis. You need to leave with me. I want you to. Please." Cleis stood, uncertain. "Don't you want to?"

"Yes!"

"Then why don't you?"

"I can't!" Cleis backed up against the wall.

Jane sat down. She did not want Cleis to bolt. "Come and sit. Just for a moment. We'll have some tea."

"No. I can't, Jane. I really can't. I have to stay here. Under the trees. It's where I belong now. I need to stay."

"You need to look after your child."

"No. Don't you see? It's stronger even than that. I need to be out there, to live. I need it, like I need water, or air."

"I'll follow you. I'll leave the child here and I'll follow you."

"Then she'll die," Cleis said sadly. And it was that sadness, that resignation that finally told Jane that Cleis would not change her mind. Could not. That Cleis would rather run through the trees than stay here, or anywhere, with Jane. If it was not for the tiny life on the bed . . .

"What if she . . . what if she grows up to be like you?"

"She won't. If you take her away. She won't miss what she's never had."

"I love you."

"I know. I'm sorry." She moved to the bed, picked up the baby, put her in Jane's arms. "Love my child for me."

They did not say good-bye.

She wrapped the child carefully in a clean shirt and walked down to the village. Two women took one look at her face and went back inside their huts. Ixbalum's hut was empty. A bunch of children gathered at the edge of the trees. Jane stood in the middle of the clearing and addressed the air. "Where is Ixbalum?"

A chicken clucked.

"Where is Ixbalum?"

A woman put her head out of a hut and called to one of the children, shouting instructions. The girl listened, looked sideways at Jane, then darted into the forest. Jane waited patiently. The baby in her arms yawned and opened its eyes. They were the color of brand-new copper pennies.

The girl came back with Ixbalum.

"You did this," Jane said finally. She thought she saw pity on Ixbalum's face, but perhaps she imagined it. "I need your help. I'll need milk." She pointed to her breasts, then the child. Ixbalum walked over to her hut and disappeared inside. Jane waited. She did not know what else to do.

Ixbalum came back out holding a pile of soft rags and a gourd. She held them out. The gourd was full of milk. Some spilled on Jane's thumb as she took it. She sucked at it: rich, not cow's milk.

"You knew, didn't you? You knew."

But Ixbalum shook her head wearily and pointed to Jane, to the baby, and made a flicking motion with her hand. It was unmistakable: *Go away.*

"I'll go for now, because that's what she wanted. But you better . . . you keep her safe for me. Just keep her safe."

The journey to Benque Viejo was not difficult. No more trees had fallen across the skidder trail and the baby, whom she called Penny, because of her eyes, slept soundly in the cardboard box Jane had strapped into the passenger seat. She stayed in Benque Viejo only long enough to buy diapers and baby formula and a feeding bottle, fill tanks with enough gas to get her to the capital city, Belmopan, and to make a phone call to the niece of the ex-governor, on Ambergris.

"Katherine, I want someone who will fill out a birth certificate, no questions asked."

"Who on earth for?"

"My adopted child."

Silence. "Well, that's a turn up for the books. Are you sure? What will people think if you get back to England with a baby in tow? . . ."

"I don't care about that anymore." And she did not. She really did not.

She climbed back in the Jeep. Penny opened those startling eyes, stretched. Jane wondered if she would look like Cleis when she was older.

Science Fiction Films of 1996

Bill Warren

What most people know about science fiction, they learn from films. The average person on the street will be more likely to have heard of *Lawnmower Man* than William Gibson's brilliant novel *Neuromancer,* which ignited the cyberpunk movement. Those who have never heard of Doc E. E. Smith's Skylark series or Jack Williamson's *Legion of Space* or Alfie Bester's *The Stars My Destination* will surely be familiar with *Star Wars* and *Star Trek.* Most people have seen Philip K. Dick's dark urban vision of the future . . . on the big screen. Film is the great medium of our time, and it has injected science fiction into the popular culture . . . and into the collective consciousness. As I write this, the seventy-million-dollar *The Fifth Element* is the opening film at the Cannes Film Festival.

Although the SFWA does not presently award a Nebula in the category of film, it is traditional to include a survey of the year's most important science fiction and fantasy films in each volume. Veteran film critic and reviewer Bill Warren analyzes the SF films of 1996. Warren is the author of *Keep Watching the Skies,* which is the definitive survey of SF film from 1950 to 1962. His film criticism has appeared in periodicals such as *Starlog, Fangoria, Cinefantastique,* and *American Film.*

Science fiction and fantasy have become part of the annual output of Hollywood, but while sometimes there's entertainment, there's rarely any originality. The year 1996 was business as usual for science fiction in Hollywood: there were imitations of older movies, sequels, some variations on Jekyll and Hyde, a few superheroes, and the like. One of the best movies of the year was about a fantasy/science fiction writer, Robert E. Howard.

The people who decide which movies get made don't understand that science fiction itself draws in audiences, even though the biggest hit of 1996 was flamboyantly science fiction. Ever since Hugo Gernsback reprinted H. G. Wells's *War of the Worlds* in the 1920s, thrillers about mass alien invasions have turned up in written science fiction but remained rare in filmed SF. In fact, until 1996, there were only two American movies about an all-out alien assault: George Pal's version of Wells's novel itself, and *Earth vs. the Flying Saucers,* both in the precedent-setting 1950s.

Independence Day is all the fireworks of the Fourth of July in one movie, as well as all the patriotism, and all the corn. The movie borrows heavily from alien-invasion movies of the past, using the format of the disaster movies of the early seventies. That is, a lot of separate characters each have their own individual adventure, while joining together at the climax to face the problem together. While there are no major stars in *Independence Day,* it's strongly, if oddly, cast: Jeff Goldblum, Will Smith, Randy Quaid, Bill Pullman, Mary McDonnell, Judd Hirsch, Robert Loggia, and Brent Spiner, among others.

Over a hundred flying saucers fifteen miles in diameter take up positions over the Earth's major cities and, after a countdown, begin blasting the cities with explosive rays. As usual, Earth's weapons are useless against them; however, as in *War of the Worlds,* the aliens prove vulnerable to a virus—but a computer virus this time.

Director-writer Roland Emmerich and cowriter Dean Devlin are cheerfully sanguine about being influenced by movies of the past; they weren't out to make art, but a popcorn movie on a big scale. The two are not exactly masters of dialogue. Though they show improvement over *StarGate,* and, lord knows, *Universal Soldier,* they still can't write memorably; the dialogue in *Independence Day* is utilitarian, prosaic, unimaginative. The same is true of Emmerich's direction. The film is as entertaining as it is specifically because of the premise and some of the performances.

Thanks both to this premise and a shrewd, even witty, advertising campaign, *Independence Day* was phenomenally successful; at last report, it had grossed more than $800 million, making it one of the biggest hits ever. If you don't expect much, and if you see it on the big screen, it is an entertaining movie—just not a very good one.

At Christmas, Tim Burton's alien-invasion comedy, *Mars Attacks!,* was released, and while it's an improvement on *Independence Day* in terms of intelligence and style, it's not Burton's best movie and was a disappointment, both commercially and critically. (Burton fled into the security of another comic-book character; in mid-1997, he signed to do a new version of *Superman*.)

On the other hand, *Mars Attacks!* is often a hoot, the most unusual and distinctive Hollywood movie of 1996. After a slow start, it builds to a wild, imaginative barrage of effects and stunts, with famous actors running madly about, screaming and/or being blasted by the invading Martians. Derived from bubblegum cards, the basic plot could hardly be simpler: a fleet of Martian flying saucers arrives on Earth and soon makes their intentions clear by incinerating Congress and going on a rampage of worldwide destruction. The Martians are as gleeful as children about the whole thing, performing prankish experiments and posing for photos in front of the Taj Mahal as it's blown away.

Like *Independence Day, Mars Attacks!* has a huge cast of familiar faces, though the names are bigger: Jack Nicholson (in two roles), Martin Short, Pierce Brosnan, Rod Steiger (who's remarkably funny), Paul Winfield, Glenn Close, Natalie Portman, Michael J. Fox, Annette Bening, Lukas Haas, Sarah Jessica Parker, Tom Jones, Sylvia Sidney, and Danny DeVito. All reported having a great time on the set, but great times don't always transfer to the screen.

Mars Attacks! was also influenced by older movies. Some of the hardware about the Martian flying saucer seems derived from *Forbidden Planet;* the saucers themselves echo those in *Earth vs. the Flying Saucers;* one shot evokes the climax of *This Island Earth;* and when a Martian saucer first sets down in Washington, it resembles a scene from *The Day the Earth Stood Still,* while Danny Elfman's witty music distantly echoes Bernard Herrmann's themes from that film.

Burton's province is a unique kind of weirdness that can be comical, but isn't necessarily (*Batman* is a case in point). He's quirky, intelligent, and vividly his own person. Not everyone responds to his style, and some even go so far to say that he's a bad director—a preposterous claim. If you aren't in tune with him, then don't bother with his films because you're never likely to click in. But always remember, dark is the slave that mows like a harvest.

While Roland Emmerich and Tim Burton were attacking the Earth with hordes of alien invaders, David Twohy had a more limited agenda in *The Arrival*. Once again, there are ghostly echoes of older movies: *Forbidden Planet, It Came from Outer Space* and *Quatermass II (Enemy from Space)*. Twohy is a clever, intelligent writer and a promising director who knows how to create contemporary variations on themes from the past. If he had paced the last third of *The Arrival* as well as he does the first two-thirds, it would be a minor gem; as it is, it's smart fun, though flawed, partly by an inappropriate death.

Radio astronomer Zane Ziminski (Charlie Sheen) discovers a signal in an unexpected wavelength from a nearby star, but he's fired. Convinced he's onto something, he persists, discovers that same spike in the signal again—only this time it is coming from Earth. His pursuit of this mystery leads him to Mexico, where he meets a global-warming researcher (Lindsay Crouse) who has found poppies blooming above the Arctic Circle. They soon learn that Earth has been infiltrated, rather than invaded, by aliens who can disguise themselves to look like people and who are intent on altering the global climate to better fit them.

The Arrival has fewer gimme-a-break idiocies than almost any SF film in recent years, and when Twohy tosses around the technical terms at the beginning, it's clear he knows what they mean. The dialogue is above average for a medium-budget picture of any genre and, though it's often amusing, is mercifully short on wisecracks. The production notes indicate Twohy's cautious about being "typed" as a science fiction movie writer/director, but while that might not be good for David Twohy, I think it would be just fine for audiences.

Although I suspect some would like to try, you can't beat *Star Trek* to death with a stick. The first *Star Trek: The Next Generation* movie, *Star Trek: Generations,* was third-rate. *Star Trek: First Contact* is far better, a lot of fun for Trekkies and casual Trek-goers alike. Jonathan Frakes (who plays Riker) makes a responsible feature debut as director, the special effects are everything you'd want, most of the regulars get a moment to shine, and the three guest stars play colorful, interesting characters.

The villains of the piece are the Borg, a partly living, partly mechanical race with a collective consciousness, intent on "assimilating"—Borgizing—the entire universe one planet at a time. This is the kind of obvious, unimaginative idea conceived by someone who has little familiarity with science fiction. The Borg are essentially zombies who act like ants, an idea that would have been hot stuff in, say, a 1932 issue of *Thrilling Wonder Stories*, but which today seems hackneyed and even dull.

The plot involves the Borg going back in time to take over the Earth and to stop warp drive from being invented. The Borg plan involves invading the *Enterprise* (which followed them back in time) and taking it over, deck by deck. Data (Brent Spiner), the android who wants to be human, is captured by the seductive Borg Queen (Alice Krige), who wants to make all humankind into machines. She looks at once elegant and greasy, and tries to seduce Data by, among other things, giving him hairy arms, then purring in his ear "Are you familiar with physical forms of pleasure?"

Star Trek: First Contact is the sort of story that might have been done as a two-part episode of *Star Trek: The Next Generation*. It is realized on a bigger scale, of course, and the dramatics are more intense, but it doesn't boldly go where no *Star Trek* has ever gone before. I wish they would, now that they're in features, but I don't think they ever will. But *First Contact* shows they can be familiar and fun.

John Carpenter's *Escape from L.A.* was anything but fun. Kurt Russell returns as Snake Plisskin, the Clint Eastwood–styled antihero of *Escape from New York* (1981), but he should have stayed away. When he first appeared, Plisskin had a slightly satirical edge, as if we weren't supposed to take him seriously. Though it falls apart toward the end, *Escape from New York* was one of Carpenter's better efforts, with colorful characters and a fast pace.

But this belated sequel is, unfortunately, one of Carpenter's worst films—crude, obvious, and dull. It has a jerky, clumsy pace, a routine story, and lame-brained attempts at satire and, worst of all, presents Snake Plisskin dead seriously as the last free man in a corrupt society. He's free all right—free of anything like a sense of responsibility to anyone else; he's selfish, self-centered, not bright, dishonest, and mean-spirited. As played by Russell again, he's a one-note clod with attitude and damned little else.

In the script by Carpenter, Russell, and coproducer Debra Hill, Plisskin, still a criminal, is forced by the fascistic government of the U.S. to enter Los Angeles, supposedly to rescue the daughter of the Reagan-styled president (Cliff Robertson) but really to retrieve a "Black Box" she's stolen. An earthquake has turned Los Angeles and Orange County into a series of islands, where people considered unfit for decent American society have been sent, and there are murderous gangs of several types. At the end, Plisskin learns the Black Box can shut off all sources of power on earth—and he pushes the button. This means that people under the sea drown, planes plunge to the earth, people on medical support die, babies in incubators are wiped out, and so forth. And this is the hero.

Carpenter, Russell, and Hill thought they were presenting some kind of libertarian viewpoint, but even real libertarians don't equate the right to wear furs with religious freedom, as this movie does. Here, the rights to smoke, to eat red meat, and to have as many guns as you like are all lumped in together. As biting policical satire, *Escape from L.A.* rates somewhat below the Three Stooges' *You Natzy Spy.*

Over the years, John Carpenter's films have become increasingly sour and bitter; his version of *Village of the Damned* wasn't just a misfire, it was shockingly bad and mean, besides. And the same is true of *Escape from L.A.* If this misanthropic nightmare is Carpenter's idea of a fun movie, he needs to take some time off and think things through.

I don't know what I was expecting with *The Island of Dr. Moreau,* the third movie version of H. G. Wells's 1896 novel (his second), but I'm pretty sure it wasn't this astonishing, shocking, funny, extravagant, and beautiful thriller. It was greeted with screams of outrage by critics, and though it opened well, the box office fell off rapidly, and the film barely turned a profit. But I enjoyed the hell out of it. From the impressive opening credits to the melancholy ending, it's nothing at all like the other two versions, *Island of Los Souls,* with Charles Laughton, and *Island of Dr. Moreau,* with Burt Lancaster.

One reason this movie drove some reviewers nuts is because Marlon Brando plays Dr. Moreau. I admit that the idea of Brando starring in a movie that climaxes with beast people in Jeeps roaring through a jungle blazing away with machine guns and blowing up buildings is a long way from *Last Tango in Paris.* But Brando is an eccentric, imaginative man, and had a grand time here. Some of the strangest ideas in the film came from him, and as bizarre as he gets, which is pretty damned bizarre, his interpretation of the character of Dr. Moreau is consistent, appropriate, and inventive. He uses an effete

British accent and tiny little buck teeth; he dresses in flowing robes, often in bright colors, often with extravagant headdresses of one sort or another, including, incredibly, an ice bucket. His Moreau is epicene, almost effeminate; his love for his creations is real, but it's actually self-love—he sees them as extensions of himself, and little else.

The story, though set in the future, is much the same as before: an outsider (David Thewlis), rescued from the sea by Moreau's drunken associate (Val Kilmer), is taken to Moreau's island, where he gradually discovers that Moreau is turning animals into human beings. Here, he's doing it through genetic manipulation rather than the vivisection the novel was attacking, but the results are the same: a tribe of half-human, half-animal creatures confused and bitter about their fate. Eventually, of course, all hell breaks loose.

Director John Frankenheimer didn't try to "transcend" the genre as some others have before him; he accepted the idea that this movie is in a particular genre—science fiction thriller—and went on from there, seeking to make it the best such film he could. The result is his best theatrical movie in twenty years, far superior to his earlier SF-monster movie, *Prophecy*.

Like Moreau, Robert Louis Stevenson's tale of Dr. Jekyll and Mr. Hyde keeps being reworked for new generations. Valerie Martin's novel *Mary Reilly* had a premise that sounded hopeless: the tale of Jekyll and Hyde told from the point of view of the wealthy Jekyll's maid, Mary Reilly. But it's an impressive book, well-researched, imaginative, and intelligent. It's obvious why someone would want to make a movie of it—but the material is far trickier than it seems at first, as the movie version shows. It's disappointing on almost every level except production design; the Stephen Frears–directed film is slow, uninvolving, and essentially pointless.

The main problem that Christopher Hampton faced in writing the script is that in the novel little happens, and what we learn about Mary (who tells the story in the book) comes from what she says in her writing, not from how she behaves toward other people, including Dr. Jekyll and Mr. Hyde. Hampton had to find ways to realize through action and dialogue concepts that Mary simply tells us in the novel—and he doesn't do this well.

Julia Roberts is surprisingly well-cast as Mary, but as Jekyll and

Hyde, John Malkovich produces a pair of annoyingly mannered performances that are completely unconvincing. It is crucial to the tale of Jekyll & Hyde that while we know that the same actor is playing both roles, the other characters in the film must not recognize them as the same person—but here the "two" characters look almost exactly alike. The transformation scene is silly: it looks like Hyde is a homunculus living inside Jekyll, so that at one point in the change, Malkovich has two heads and four arms. In the original by Stevenson (whose name doesn't appear in the credits of *Mary Reilly*), Jekyll was trying to free his darker self. That made Hyde intrinsically evil; some of that idea remains here with nothing to support it—even though Hyde emerges because Jekyll is trying to cure himself of a disease. Malkovich's Hyde is evil apparently just because he thinks it's cool.

Mary Reilly feels like a poorly adapted stage play, bound by its sets, limited in its aspirations, pretentious where it should have been simple, and thoroughly unimaginative. Its biggest crime, however, is that this fascinating story here has become sadly dull.

The other movie of 1996 derived, however distantly, from Stevenson's novella was radically different. This was Eddie Murphy's remake of Jerry Lewis's *The Nutty Professor,* and it turned out surprisingly well. It's not a top-notch comedy—there are big weaknesses and it runs down in the second half—but in Professor Sherman Klump, Eddie Murphy has found his most human, likable character to date. It's a genuinely sweet film, with a sense of real romance and personal discovery.

The story remains roughly the same, with a shy college professor, in love for the first time, using his own discovery to transform himself into what he thinks is a more attractive person. In Murphy's version, directed by Tom Shadyac, Prof. Sherman Klump weighs four hundred pounds—courtesy of great makeup and a "fat suit" from Rick Baker— but he's a sweet-natured genius, shy and burdened with powerful feelings of inferiority. When he transforms, it's into a slightly meaner version of Murphy's usual screen character, a weakness in what's otherwise a pretty good comedy.

Multiplicity was funny, the premise is novel and interesting, the special effects are excellent, and it's well directed by Harold Ramis. But there's something missing that keeps *Multiplicity* from being as memorable and worthwhile as Ramis's somewhat similar *Groundhog Day* of a few years ago.

Part of the problem is that the movie, written by Chris Miller & Mary Hale, and Lowell Ganz & Babaloo Mandel, doesn't view the basic premise from enough angles, but more important, while like *Groundhog Day* the movie is about a guy learning to value his life and himself, here he's OK from the start. Yes, at the end of *Multiplicity,* Michael Keaton's Doug Kinney is a better person, but he wasn't a bad person to begin with. The best story, someone said, is always about The Person Who Learns to Be Better; here, Doug Kinney already knows how to be better—he just doesn't know how to manage his time.

Happily married but overworked and inattentive, Doug meets a doctor who allows Doug to clone himself. This is just a gimmick, and the filmmakers know it: the cloning machine looks like a cross between a gynecological examining table and a Xerox machine. Eventually, Doug One clones himself again, and Dougs Two and Three clone Doug Two, resulting in a wacky, childlike Doug Four—a blurred copy. Complications ensue without many surprises, other than that at the end, all four Dougs are still around.

The value of *Multiplicity* lies in the basic situation, and in Keaton's inventive improvisation and occasional physical comedy—*Multiplicity* is not above indulging in slapstick. The movie is at times hilarious, it's always interesting, and Keaton does good work. But there are no big scenes in the movie, the premise is not examined as well as it should have been, and most people, while enjoying the movie, are likely to feel that something is missing. Maybe another Michael Keaton.

Though it wasn't intended as a comedy, taking it as one is really the only way to get through *Barb Wire,* adapted from a pretty bad comic book by Chris Warner. It was designed largely as a vehicle to turn pneumatic Pamela Anderson Lee (from TV's *Baywatch*) into a movie star—and spectacularly failed in the attempt. The surgically enhanced Lee plays the title role, a bounty hunter who runs a bar in the last "free area" of the twenty-first-century United States. Her former lover and his wife turn up, trying to get to Canada so the wife can lead a resistance movement. Barb has the necessary item to get them across the border. Will Barb do the right thing? Do you recognize this as the plot of *Casablanca*?

If *Barb Wire* had been better and had acknowledged swiping the plot of one of the most beloved movies ever made, nobody would have minded much. But the movie, written by Ilene Chaiken and Chuck Pfarrer, merely recycles *Casablanca's* plotline with a straight face, as if they assumed no one would notice the resemblances. And did it in the context of a turgid, uninvolving movie in which even the action scenes don't amount to much. Director David Hogan shows no flair for action here and little understanding of irony, tension, or characterization.

Barb Wire repeats the junk-apocalypse future we've seen so often by now. There's lots of rusting metal and everyone wears leather and drives either old motorcycles or refurbished cars. It's visually almost indistinguishable from *Escape from L.A.*—nihilism by rote. It's too self-consciously hip to be amusing camp, but too trashy to be anything else.

As noted earlier, 1996 was crowded with films that could be described as science fiction or fantasy, but which are now just part of Hollywood's standard output. Francis Ford Coppola, for example, directed Robin Williams in *Jack*, about a child who ages at four times the normal rate. Most critics didn't care for the movie, and audiences weren't drawn to it, either; but despite some failings, I found it intelligent and warmhearted.

Jack isn't just a comedy; at times it is very serious, because there's no way out for Jack; as he says at one point, "What do I want to be when I grow up? Alive." The script by James DeMonaco and Gary Nadeau deals with a central theme that Coppola has imaginatively, even lyrically, expanded upon: all our lives are fleeting, over in a flash. I realize that *Jack* is Coppola doing work for hire, but I believe that in years to come, the movie will find its place and Robin Williams's performance in the title role will be more appreciated.

Danny DeVito's career as a director has, so far, been best described as "promising," but perhaps he should have been directing children's films all along because *Matilda* is by far his best effort yet, a delight from beginning to end. There's not a wrong move in it, and at times DeVito demonstrates an almost uncanny understanding of what children love—and what really scares them. Screenwriters Nicholas Kazan and Robin Swicord adapted Roald Dahl's novel.

Matilda (Mara Wilson) is a brilliant, good-hearted little girl born into a family of jerks. While still very young, Matilda realizes she's an outsider and discovers the local library for herself. But when she insists on going to school, her parents dump her in Crunchem Hall, a private institution headed by the formidable Miss Trunchbull (Pam Ferris). This behemoth, stout of leg and back, broad of beam, with her oily hair bunched up in a hard little knot on her head, is a sadistic tyrant who loves her job. Things go badly for Matilda, until she discovers she has telekinetic powers and uses them to right wrongs, punish the guilty, and reward the innocent.

I was especially impressed by the wonderful control of tone that DeVito exhibits as a director, but *Matilda* suffered the fate of most of the good children's movies of recent years and died at the box office.

Another film with telekinesis as a side issue did much better; this was *Phenomenon*, starring John Travolta. George Malley, the character he plays, is so saintly that most actors would look pretty foolish in the role. But Travolta has tremendous screen presence and an innate likability; he keeps George rooted in the real world for almost the entire film.

George is a well-liked, easygoing guy who's ambling through life with no particular goal in mind, other than romancing Lace Pennamin (Kyra Sedgwick). One night, he sees a bright light which suddenly flares up in the sky; he falls to the street unconscious and unnoticed. When he awakes, he soon discovers his intelligence has greatly increased. Furthermore, he's become a kind of information sponge, staying up all night reading books and coming up with fabulous inventions that will help the world. And he can sense earthquakes, locate lost people via their thoughts, and use a trace of telekinesis. He, and we, assume the light in the sky had something to do with his increased abilities, but we learn at the end that the source is a brain tumor that will soon kill him. This comes from nowhere, and iritated audiences who liked the film otherwise.

Phenomenon is nowhere near as original as screenwriter Gerald DiPego seemed to think. The idea of an ordinary person becoming a super-genius has been used in the past, most notably in *Flowers for Algernon* by Daniel Keyes, which was turned into a TV drama, a movie, and a stage play. The pastoral setting is phony, and the ending is aggravating: George dies solely to make the hoary old carpe diem point once again.

And yet the film has a likability that cannot be ignored, largely thanks to John Travolta and director Jon Turteltaub. We end up caring about George because Travolta insists that this mild, unimportant guy really matters—not because he's become a super-genius but because he seems so damned real. Too bad the rest of the movie doesn't.

Unforgettable marks the studio debut of director John Dahl, whose independent films noir, *Red Rock West* and *The Last Seduction,* have won him a lot of deserved praise. But *Unforgettable,* written by TV producer Bill Geddie, is a synthetic thriller driven by—yet again—coincidences. Stars Ray Liotta and Linda Fiorentino are both quite good, but they're mired in an implausible story. Liotta plays a Seattle medical examiner, once suspected of his wife's murder, who discovers that Fiorentino has made a breakthrough. She's created a fluid that, when mixed with cerebral fluid from one person and injected into another, will give the second person vivid flashes of the memories of the first.

This is more than a little absurd, but it's about the only moderately original SF idea in any of the 1996 releases. It's too bad it's developed illogically and grafted onto a routine crime picture with an unnecessary ticking-clock plot element. (Using the fluid steadily increases the risk of heart attacks.) *Unforgettable* turned out to be anything but.

The oddest SF film, or sort-of SF, was undoubtedly *Mad Dog Time* (on video as *Trigger Happy*). Titles at the beginning announce that it is set on an alternate Earth where gangsters rule. An excellent cast, including Jeff Goldblum, Richard Dreyfuss, Gabriel Byrne, Diane Lane, and Henry Silva, is wasted in this overstylized flop. Goldblum is particularly good and a reason to see the film in and of himself. But the world wasn't ready for a movie inspired by Frank Sinatra's Rat Pack and French gangster films.

As the audience for movies has grown younger and predominantly male, the big-ticket movies have transmogrified into extravagant action epics. They've continued to increase in scale—and the increase in scale has meant that action pictures have adopted more science fiction themes. When the hero is a mass of rippling muscles like Arnold Schwarzenegger or Sylvester Stallone, it takes increasingly potent firepower to bring him down. And this, too, has begun to require science fiction elements. Indeed, many of the kids out their in Internet land who claim to be "science fiction fans" are really action-movie fans—it's just that action movies so often include SF concepts.

And 1996 was no different. Schwarzenegger's *Eraser,* directed by Charles (Chuck) Russell, has as its gimmick a ray gun that can see through walls, and people, and which uses electromagnetism to fire aluminum bolts at nearly the speed of light. Though no classic, it has enough amazing action sequences to be entertaining. Stallone's *Daylight,* directed by Rob Cohen, deals with a Manhattan-to-New Jersey auto tunnel sealed at both ends by an explosion—an idea that edges toward science fiction. The film itself is well-produced, but uneven. In *Chain Reaction,* Eddie Kasalivich (Keanu Reeves) and Paul Shannon (Morgan Freeman) are involved with a means of deriving power from the hydrogen in water, and we see a demonstration early on, but there's a big explosion, and our hero is soon on the run in a movie that tries to incorporate Hitchcockian elements. Despite direction by the reliable Andrew Davis, the movie is a waste of time and money. John Travolta is the villain in John Woo's hyperkinetic (and hyperillogical) *Broken Arrow,* about the theft of nuclear devices, one of which goes off beneath the southwestern desert. Though the plot is clumsy, Woo's experience made it the best action movie of 1996.

Although it's not at all science fiction, another movie deserves mention here—because it is about a writer whose works included science fiction: Robert E. Howard, creator of Conan the Barbarian. *The Whole Wide World* is based on *One Who Walked Alone,* a memoir by Novalyne Price, who almost became Howard's girlfriend during the year before he killed himself. Renee Zellweger plays Price, and Vincent D'Onofrio is Howard, making him both vital and shy; even though he's sunny, big-spirited, and full of braggadocio, there's a darkness within D'Onofrio's Howard, and he's easily wounded. The film is well worth seeing.

There were other science fiction movies released in 1996, such as the very lame spoof *Spy Hard,* but most of these went straight to videotape and/or laserdisc. For the record, these titles included *Alien Agenda: Endangered Species; Alien Vows; Chase Moran; Crossworlds; Deadly Contact; Dreammaster: The Erotic Invader; Invader; Memory Run; Nirvana; The Scourge That Never Dies; Shadow Warriors; The*

Silencers; Starlight (Willie Nelson's first SF film, if that's a distinction); and *Solo* (a killer cyborg goes straight).

Science fiction was once the province of low-budget movies, with the occasional "daring" movie that cost about as much as regular films do. But movies have become event entertainment; studios can easily spend $100 million on a spectacular film—and the chances are more than good that the movie will be science fiction. Will it be "good" science fiction? Probably not. But as has been true of Hollywood since there was a Hollywood, the big spectacular films are usually worth seeing once. Eventually, perhaps, they'll eventually be worth seeing more than once.

Five Fucks

Jonathan Lethem

Jonathan Lethem's first story appeared in 1989. That count was up to around forty stories by the time his first novel, *Gun, with Occasional Music,* appeared in 1994. The reviews were enthusiastic. *Science Fiction Age* wrote: "Call it tech noir if you must. . . . This is not an Orwellian future. Lethem allows the reader to inhale another blend of dystopia, a page from a book of Huxley's." When his second novel was published, *Newsweek* wrote: "An author to be reckoned with . . . A social critic, a sardonic satirist like the Walker Percy of *Love in the Ruins.* But with *Amnesia Moon,* Lethem slips out of the shadow of his predecessors to deliver a droll, downbeat vision that is both original and persuasive." Lethem's most recent books are the story collection *The Wall of the Sky, The Wall of the Eye,* which won the 1997 World Fantasy Award for Best Collection, and the novel *As She Climbed Across the Table.* His short fiction has appeared in *Interzone, New Pathways, Pulphouse, Isaac Asimov's Science Fiction Magazine, Universe, Journal Wired, Marion Zimmer Bradley's Fantasy Magazine,* and *Aboriginal SF.* He is the recipient of the IAFA Crawford Fantasy Award and the Locus Award.

About his work in general, he writes:

"It's probably obvious already that I'm engaged with 'genres' but not bound by them. Technology in my work is iconographic and metaphoric. I wouldn't know an extrapolation if it came bearing flowers. I write about myself and my friends; the thing is, we grew up in a misshapen future world called America. And we watched a lot of movies. And read a lot of SF."

About his short story "Five Fucks," he writes:

"Bruce Sterling said: 'Nobody ever has sex in a Lethem story without something bad happening. Just for once I'd like to see you write a story where the characters aren't punished for getting laid.'

"In response, I did the reverse and went as far in that direction as possible—sort of a Judo approach to criticism.

"Along the way I indulged in my other weakness, for homage and other forms of cribbing. Thanks therefore to George Herriman,

Cornell Woolrich, Alan Rudolph, Italo Calvino, Shelley Jackson, George Gissing, Thomas Berger, and the director of *I Wake Up Screaming,* whose name I can't seem to dig out of my reference shelf this morning."

1.

"I feel different from other people. Really different. Yet whenever I have a conversation with a new person it turns into a discussion of things we have in common. Work, places, feelings. Whatever. It's the way people talk, I know, I share the blame, I do it, too. But I want to stop and shout no, it's not like that, it's not the same for me. I feel different."

"I understand what you mean."

"That's not the right response."

"I mean what the fuck are you talking about."

"Right." Laughter.

She lit a cigarette while E. went on.

"The notion is like a linguistic virus. It makes any conversation go all pallid and reassuring. 'Oh, I know, it's like that for me, too.' But the virus isn't content just to eat conversations, it wants to destroy lives. It wants you to fall in love."

"There are worse things."

"Not for me."

"Famine, war, floods."

"Those never happened to me. Love did. Love is the worst thing that ever happened to me."

"That's fatuous."

"What's the worst thing that ever happened to you?"

She was silent for a full minute.

"But there, *that's* the first fatuous thing I've said. Asking you to consider *my* situation by consulting *your* experience. You see? The virus is loose again. I don't want you to agree that our lives are the same. They aren't. I just want you to listen to what I say seriously, to believe me."

"I believe you."

"Don't say it in that tone of voice. All breathy."

"Fuck you." She laughed again.

"Do you want another drink?"

"In a minute." She slurped at what was left in her glass, then said, "You know what's funny?"

"What?"

"Other people do feel the way you do, that they're apart from everyone else. It's the same as the way every time you fall in love it feels like something new, even though you do the exact same things over again. Feeling unique is what we all have in common, it's the thing that's always the same."

"No, I'm different. And falling in love is different for me each time, different things happen. Bad things."

"But you're still the same as you were before the first time. You just feel different."

"No, I've changed. I'm much worse."

"You're not bad."

"You should have seen me before. Do you want another drink?"

The laminated place mat on the table between them showed pictures of exotic drinks. "This one," she said. "A zombie." It was purple.

"You don't want that."

"Yes I do. I love zombies."

"No you don't. You've never had one. Anyway, this place makes a terrible zombie." He ordered two more margaritas.

"You're such an expert."

"Only on zombies."

"On zombies and love is bad."

"You're making fun of me. I thought you promised to take me seriously, believe me."

"I was lying. People always lie when they flirt."

"We're not flirting."

"Then what are we doing?"

"We're just drinking, drinking and talking. And I'm trying to warn you."

"And you're staring."

"You're beautiful. Oh, God."

"That reminds me of one. What's the worst thing about being an atheist?"

"I give up."

"No one to talk to when you come."

2.

Morning light seeped through the macramé curtain and freckled the rug. Motes seemed to boil from its surface. For a moment she thought the rug was somehow on the ceiling, then his cat ran across it, yowling at her. The cat looked starved. She was lying on her stomach in his loft bed, head over the side. He was gone. She lay tangled in the humid sheets, feeling her own body.

Lover—she thought.

She could barely remember.

She found her clothes, then went and rinsed her face in the kitchen sink. A film of shaved hairs lined the porcelain bowl. She swirled it out with hot water, watched as the slow drain gulped it away. The drain sighed.

The table was covered with unopened mail. On the back of an envelope was a note: *I don't want to see you again. Sorry. The door locks.* She read it twice, considering each word, working it out like another language. The cat crept into the kitchen. She dropped the envelope.

She put her hand down and the cat rubbed against it. Why was it so thin? It didn't look old. The fact of the note was still sinking in. She remembered the night only in flashes, visceral strobe. With her fingers she combed the tangles out of her hair. She stood up and the cat dashed away. She went out into the hall, undecided, but the weighted door latched behind her.

Fuck him.

The problem was, of course, that she wanted to.

It was raining. She treated herself to a cab on Eighth Avenue. In the backseat she closed her eyes. The potholes felt like mines, and the cab squeaked like rusty bedsprings. It was Sunday. Coffee, corn muffin, newspaper; she'd insulate herself with them, make a buffer between the night and the new day.

But there was something wrong with the doorman at her building.

"You're back!" he said.

She was led incredulous to her apartment full of dead houseplants and unopened mail, her answering machine full of calls from friends, clients, the police. There was a layer of dust on the answering machine. Her address book and laptop disks were gone; clues, the doorman explained.

"Clues to what?"

"Clues to your case. To what happened to you. Everyone was worried."

"Well, there's nothing to worry about. I'm fine."

"Everyone had theories. The whole building."

"I understand."

"The man in charge is a good man, Miss Rush. The building feels a great confidence in him."

"Good."

"I'm supposed to call him if something happens, like someone trying to get into your place, or you coming back. Do you want me to call?"

"Let me call."

The card he handed her was bent and worn from traveling in his pocket. CORNELL PUPKISS, MISSING PERSONS. And a phone number. She reached out her hand; there was dust on the telephone, too. "Please go," she said.

"Is there anything you need?"

"No." She thought of E.'s cat, for some reason.

"You can't tell me at least what happened?"

"No."   \

She remembered E.'s hands and mouth on her—a week ago? An hour?

Cornell Pupkiss was tall and drab and stolid, like a man built on the model of a tower of suitcases. He wore a hat and a trench coat, and shoes which were filigreed with a thousand tiny scratches, as though they'd been beset by phonograph needles. He seemed to absorb and deaden light.

On the telephone he had insisted on seeing her. He'd handed her the disks and the address book at the door. Now he stood just inside the door and smiled gently at her.

"I wanted to see you in the flesh," he said. "I've come to know you from photographs and people's descriptions. When I come to know a person in that manner I like to see them in the flesh if I can. It makes me feel I've completed my job, a rare enough illusion in my line."

There was nothing bright or animated in the way he spoke. His voice was like furniture with the varnish carefully sanded off. "But I haven't really completed my job until I understand what happened," he went on. "Whether a crime was committed. Whether you're in some sort of trouble with which I can help."

She shook her head.

"Where were you?" he said.

"I was with a man."

"I see. For almost two weeks?"

"Yes."

She was still holding the address book. He raised his large hand in its direction, without uncurling a finger to point. "We called every man you know."

"This—this was someone I just met. Are these questions necessary, Mr. Pupkiss?"

"If the time was spent voluntarily, no." His lips tensed, his whole expression deepened, like gravy jelling. "I'm sorry, Miss Rush."

Pupkiss in his solidity touched her somehow. Reassured her. If he went away, she saw now, she'd be alone with the questions. She wanted him to stay a little longer and voice the questions for her.

But now he was gently sarcastic. "You're answerable to no one, of course. I only suggest that in the future you might spare the concern of your neighbors, and the effort of my department—a single phone call would be sufficient."

"I didn't realize how much time had passed," she said. He couldn't know how truthful that was.

"I've heard it can be like that," he said, surprisingly bitter. "But it's not criminal to neglect the feelings of others; just adolescent."

You don't understand, she nearly cried out. But she saw that he would view it as one or the other, a menace or self-indulgence. If she convinced him of her distress, he'd want to protect her.

She couldn't let harm come to E. She wanted to comprehend what had happened, but Pupkiss was too blunt to be her investigatory tool.

Reflecting in this way, she said, "The things that happen to people don't always fit into such easy categories as that."

"I agree," he said, surprising her again. "But in my job it's best to keep from bogging down in ontology. Missing Persons is an extremely large and various category. Many people are lost in relatively simple ways, and those are generally the ones I can help. Good day, Miss Rush."

"Good day." She didn't object as he moved to the door. Suddenly she was eager to be free of this ponderous man, his leaden integrity. She wanted to be left alone to remember the night before, to think of the one who'd devoured her and left her reeling. That was what mattered.

E. had somehow caused two weeks to pass in one feverish night, but Pupkiss threatened to make the following morning feel like two weeks.

He shut the door behind him so carefully that there was only a little huff of displaced air and a tiny click as the bolt engaged.

"It's me," she said into the intercom.

There was only static. She pressed the button again. "Let me come up."

He didn't answer, but the buzzer at the door sounded. She went into the hall and upstairs to his door.

"It's open," he said.

E. was seated at the table, holding a drink. The cat was curled up on the pile of envelopes. The apartment was dark. Still, she saw what she hadn't before: he lived terribly, in rooms that were wrecked and provisional. The plaster was cracked everywhere. Cigarette stubs were bunched in the baseboard corners where, having still smoldered, they'd tanned the linoleum. The place smelled sour, in a way that made her think of the sourness she'd washed from her body in her own bath an hour before.

He tilted his head up but didn't meet her gaze. "Why are you here?"

"I wanted to see you."

"You shouldn't."

His voice was ragged; his expression had a crushed quality. His hand on the glass was tensed like a claw. But even diminished and bitter he seemed to her effervescent, make of light.

"We—something happened when we made love," she said. The words came tenderly. "We lost time."

"I warned you. Now leave."

"My life," she said, uncertain what she meant.

"Yes, it's yours," he shot back. "Take it and go."

"If I gave you two weeks, it seems the least you can do is look me in the eye," she said.

He did it, but his mouth trembled as though he were guilty or afraid. His face was beautiful to her.

"I want to know you," she said.

"I can't let that happen," he said. "You see why." He tipped his glass back and emptied it, grimacing.

"This is what always happens to you?"

"I can't answer your questions."

"If that happens, I don't care." She moved to him and put her hands in his hair.

He reached up and held them there.

3.

A woman has come into my life. I hardly know how to speak of it.

I was in the station, enduring the hectoring of Dell Armickle, the commander of the Vice Squad. He is insufferable, a toad from Hell. He follows the donut cart through the offices each afternoon, pinching the buttocks of the Jamaican woman who peddles the donuts and that concentrated urine others call coffee. This day he stopped at my desk to gibe at the headlines in my morning paper. "Union Boss Stung in Fat Farm Sex Ring—ha! Made you look, didn't I?"

"What?"

"Pupkiss, you're only pretending to be thick. How much you got hidden away in that Swedish bank account by now?"

"Sorry?" His gambits were incomprehensible.

"Whatsis?" he said, poking at my donut, ignoring his own blather better than I could ever hope to. "Cinnamon?"

"Whole wheat," I said.

Then she appeared. She somehow floated in without causing any fuss, and stood at the head of my desk. She was pale and hollow-eyed and beautiful, like Renée Falconetti in Dreyer's *Jeanne d'Arc*.

"Officer Pupkiss," she said. Is it ony in the light of what followed that I recall her speaking my name as though she knew me? At least she spoke it with certainty, not questioning whether she'd found her goal.

I'd never seen her before, though I can only prove it by tautology: I knew at that moment I was seeing a face I would never forget.

Armickle bugged his eyes and nostrils at me, imitating both clown and beast. "Speak to the lady, Cornell," he said, managing to impart to the syllables of my given name a childish ribaldry.

"I'm Pupkiss," I said awkwardly.

"I'd like to talk to you," she said. She looked only at me, as though Armickle didn't exist.

"I can take a hint," said Armickle. "Have fun, you two." He hurried after the donut cart.

"You work in Missing Persons," she said.

"No," I said. "Petty Violations."

"Before, you used to work in Missing Persons—"

"Never. They're a floor above us. I'll walk you to the elevator if you'd like."

"No." She shook her head curtly, impatiently. "Forget it. I want to talk to you. What are Petty Violations?"

"It's an umbrella term. But I'd sooner address your concerns than try your patience with my job description."

"Yes. Could we go somewhere?"

I led her to a booth in the coffee shop downstairs. I ordered a donut, to replace the one I'd left behind on my desk. She drank coffee, holding the cup with both hands to warm them. I found myself wanting to feed her, build her a nest.

"Cops really do like donuts," she said, smiling weakly.

"Or toruses," I said.

"Sorry? You mean the astrological symbol?"

"No, the geometric shape. A torus. A donut is in the shape of one. Like a life preserver, or a tire, or certain space stations. It's a little joke of mine: cops don't like donuts, they like toruses."

She looked at me oddly. I cursed myself for bringing it up. "Shouldn't the plural be *tori*?" she said.

I winced. "I'm sure you're right. Never mind. I don't mean to take up your time with my little japes."

"I've got plenty of time," she said, poignant again.

"Nevertheless. You wished to speak to me."

"You knew me once," she said.

I did my best to appear sympathetic, but I was baffled.

"Something happened to the world. Everything changed. Everyone that I know has disappeared."

"As an evocation of subjective truth—," I began.

"No. I'm talking about something real. I used to have friends."

"I've had few, myself."

"Listen to me. All the people I know have disappeared. My family, my friends, everyone I used to work with. They've all been replaced by strangers who don't know me. I have nowhere to go. I've been awake for two days looking for my life. I'm exhausted. You're the only person that looks the same as before and has the same name. The Missing Persons man, ironically."

"I'm not the Missing Persons man," I said.

"Cornell Pupkiss. I could never forget a name like that."

"It's been a burden."

"You don't remember coming to my apartment? You said you'd been looking for me. I was gone for two weeks."

I struggled against temptation. I could extend my time in her company by playing along, indulging the misunderstanding. In other words, by betraying what I knew to be the truth: that I had nothing at all to do with her unusual situation.

"No," I said. "I don't remember."

Her expression hardened. "Why should you?" she said bitterly.

"Your question's rhetorical," I said. "Permit me a rhetorical reply. That I don't know you from some earlier encounter we can both regret. However, I know you now. And I'd be pleased to have you consider me an ally."

"Thank you."

"How did you find me?"

"I called the station and asked if you still worked there."

"And there's no one else from your previous life?"

"No one—except him."

Ah.

"Tell me," I said.

She'd met the man she called E. in a bar, how long ago she couldn't explain. She described him as irresistible. I formed an impression of a skunk, a rat. She said he worked no deliberate charm on her, on the contrary seemed panicked when the mood between them grew intimate and full of promise. I envisioned a scoundrel with an act, a crafted diffidence that allured, a backpedaling attack.

He'd taken her home, of course.

"And?" I said.

"We fucked," she said. "It was good, I think. But I have trouble remembering."

The words stung. The one in particular. I tried not to be a child, swallowed my discomfort away. "You were drunk," I suggested.

"No. I mean, *yes*, but it was more than that. We weren't clumsy like drunks. We went into some kind of trance."

"He drugged you."

"No."

"How do you know?"

"What happened—it wasn't something he wanted."

"And what did happen?"

"Two weeks disappeared from my life overnight. When I got home I found I'd been considered missing. My friends and family had been searching for me. You'd been called in."

"I thought your friends and family had vanished themselves. That no one knew you."

"No. That was the *second* time."

"Second time?"

"The second time we fucked." Then she seemed to remember something, and dug in her pocket. "Here." She handed me a scuffed business card: CORNELL PUPKISS, MISSING PERSONS.

"I can't believe you live this way. It's like a prison." She referred to the seamless rows of book spines that faced her in each of my few rooms, including the bedroom where we now stood. "Is it all criminology?"

"I'm not a policeman in some cellular sense," I said, and then realized the pun. "I mean, not intrinsically. They're novels, first editions."

"Let me guess; mysteries."

"I detest mysteries. I would never bring one into my home."

"Well, you have, in me."

I blushed, I think, from head to toe. "That's different," I stammered. "Human lives exist to be experienced, or possibly endured, but not solved. They resemble any other novel more than they do mysteries. Westerns, even. It's that lie the mystery tells that I detest."

"Your reading is an antidote to the simplifications of your profession, then."

"I suppose. Let me show you where the clean towels are kept."

I handed her fresh towels and linen, and took for myself a set of sheets to cover the living-room sofa.

She saw that I was preparing the sofa and said, "The bed's big enough."

I didn't turn, but I felt the blood rush to the back of my neck as though specifically to meet her gaze. "It's four in the afternoon," I said. "I won't be going to bed for hours. Besides, I snore."

"Whatever," she said. "Looks uncomfortable, though. What's Barbara Pym? She sounds like a mystery writer, one of those stuffy English ones."

The moment passed, the blush faded from my scalp. I wondered later, though, whether this had been some crucial missed opportunity. A chance at the deeper intervention that was called for.

"Read it," I said, relieved at the change of subject. "Just be careful of the dust jacket."

"I may learn something, huh?" She took the book and climbed in between the covers.

"I hope you'll be entertained."

"And she doesn't snore, I guess. That was a joke, Mr. Pupkiss."

"So recorded. Sleep well. I have to return to the station. I'll lock the door."

"Back to Little Offenses?"

"Petty Violations."

"Oh, right." I could hear her voice fading. As I stood and watched, she fell soundly asleep. I took the Pym from her hands and replaced it on the shelf.

I wasn't going to the station. Using the information she'd given me, I went to find the tavern E. supposedly frequented.

I found him there, asleep in a booth, head resting on his folded arms. He looked terrible, his hair a thatch, drool leaking into his sweater arm, his eyes swollen like a fevered child's, just the picture of raffish haplessness a woman would find magnetic. Unmistakably the seedy vermin I'd projected and the idol of Miss Rush's nightmare.

I went to the bar and ordered an Irish coffee, and considered. Briefly indulging a fantasy of personal power, I rebuked myself for coming here and making him real, when he had only before been an absurd story, a neurotic symptom. Then I took out the card she'd given me and laid it on the bar top. CORNELL PUPKISS, MISSING PERSONS. No, I myself was the symptom. It is seldom as easy in practice as in principle to acknowledge one's own bystander status in incomprehensible matters.

I took my coffee to his booth and sat across from him. He roused and looked up at me.

"Rise and shine, buddy boy," I said, a little stiffly. I've never thrilled to the role of Bad Cop.

"What's the matter?"

"Your unshaven chin is scratching the table surface."

"Sorry." He rubbed his eyes.

"Got nowhere to go?"

"What are you, the house dick?"

"I'm in the employ of any taxpayer," I said. "The bartender happens to be one."

"He's never complained to me."

"Things change."

"You can say that again."

We stared at each other. I supposed he was nearly my age, though he was more boyishly pretty than I'd been even as an actual boy. I hated him for that, but I pitied him for the part I saw that was precociously old and bitter.

I thought of Miss Rush asleep in my bed. She'd been worn and disarrayed by their two encounters, but she didn't yet look this way. I wanted to keep her from it.

"Let me give you some advice," I said, as gruffly as I could manage. "Solve your problems."

"I hadn't thought of that."

"Don't get stuck in a rut." I was aware of the lameness of my words only as they emerged, too late to stop.

"Don't worry, I never do."

"Very well then," I said, somehow unnerved. "This interview is concluded." If he'd shown any sign of budging I might have leaned back in the booth, crossed my arms authoritatively, and stared him out the door. Since he remained planted in his seat, I stood up, feeling that my last spoken words needed reinforcement.

He laid his head back into the cradle of his arms, first sliding the laminated place mat underneath. "This will protect the table surface," he said.

"That's good, practical thinking," I heard myself say as I left the booth.

It wasn't the confrontation I'd been seeking.

On the way home I shopped for breakfast, bought orange juice, milk, bagels, fresh coffee beans. I took it upstairs and unpacked it as quietly as I could in the kitchen, then removed my shoes and crept in to have a look at Miss Rush. She was peaceably asleep. I closed the door and prepared my bed on the sofa. I read a few pages of the Penguin softcover edition of Muriel Spark's *The Bachelors* before dropping off.

Before dawn, the sky like blued steel, the city silent, I was woken by a sound in the apartment, at the front door. I put on my robe and went into the kitchen. The front door was unlocked, my key in the deadbolt. I went back through the apartment; Miss Rush was gone.

I write this at dawn. I am very frightened.

4.

In an alley which ran behind a lively commercial street there sat a pair of the large trash receptacles commonly known as Dumpsters. In them accumulated the waste produced by the shops whose rear entrances shared the alley; a framer's, a soup kitchen, an antique clothing store, a donut bakery, and a photocopyist's establishment, and by the offices above those storefronts. On this street and in this alley, each day had its seasons: Spring, when complaining morning shifts opened the shops, students and workers rushed to destinations, coffee sloshing in paper cups, and in the alley, the sanitation contractors emptied containers, sorted recyclables and waste like bees pollinating garbage-truck flowers; Summer, the ripened afternoons, when the workday slackened, shoppers stole long lunches from their employers, the cafés filled with students with highlighter pens, and the indigent beckoned for the change that jingled in incautious pockets, while in the alley new riches piled up; Autumn, the cooling evening, when half the shops closed, and the street was given over to prowlers and pacers, those who lingered in bookstores and dined alone in Chinese restaurants, and the indigent plundered the fatted Dumpsters for half-eaten paper-bag lunches, batches of botched donuts, wearable cardboard matting and unmatched socks, and burnable wood scraps; Winter, the selfish night, when even the cafés battened down iron gates through which night-watchmen fluorescents palely flickered, the indigent built their over-night camps in doorways and under sidestreet hedges, or in wrecked cars, and the street itself was an abandoned stage.

On the morning in question the sun shone brightly, yet the air was bitingly cold. Birds twittered resentfully. When the sanitation crew arrived to wheel the two Dumpsters out to be hydraulically lifted into their screeching, whining truck, they were met with cries of protest from within.

The men lifted the metal tops of the Dumpsters and discovered that an indigent person had lodged in each of them, a lady in one, a gentleman in the other.

"Geddoudadare," snarled the eldest sanitation engineer, a man with features like a spilled plate of stew.

The indigent lady rose from within the heap of refuse and stood blinking in the bright morning sun. She was an astonishing sight, a ruin. The colors of her skin and hair and clothes had all surrendered to gray; an archaelogist might have ventured an opinion as to their previous hue. She could have been anywhere between thirty and fifty years old, but speculation was absurd; her age had been taken from her and replaced with a timeless condition, a state. Her eyes were pitiable; horrified and horrifying; witnesses, victims, accusers.

"Where am I?" she said softly.

"Isedgeddoudadare," barked the garbage operative.

The indigent gentleman then raised himself from the other Dumpster. He was in every sense her match; to describe him would be to tax the reader's patience for things worn, drab, desolate, crestfallen, unfortunate, etc. He turned his head at the trashman's exhortation and saw his mate.

"What's the—," he began, then stopped.

"You," said the indigent lady, lifting an accusing finger at him from amidst her rags. "You did this to me."

"No," he said. "No."

"Yes!" she screamed.

"C'mon," said the burly sanitateur. He and his second began pushing the nearer container, which bore the lady, towards his truck.

She cursed at them and climbed out, with some difficulty. They only laughed at her and pushed the cart out to the street. The indigent man scrambled out of his Dumpster and brushed at his clothes, as though they could thereby be distinguished from the material in which he'd lain.

The lady flew at him, furious. "Look at us! Look what you did to me!" She whirled her limbs at him, trailing banners of rag.

He backed from her, and bumped into one of the garbagemen, who said, "Hey!"

"It's not my fault," said the indigent man.

"Yugoddagedoudahere!" said the stew-faced worker.

"What do you mean it's not your fault?" she shrieked.

Windows were sliding open in the offices above them. "Quiet down there," came a voice.

"It wouldn't happen without you," he said.

At that moment a policeman rounded the corner. He was a large man named Officer McPupkiss who even in the morning sun conveyed an aspect of night. His policeman's uniform was impeccably fitted, his brass polished, but his shoetops were exceptionally scuffed and dull. His presence stilled the combatants.

"What's the trouble?" he said.

They began talking all at once; the pair of indigents, the refuse handlers, and the disgruntled office worker leaning out of his window.

"Please," said McPupkiss, in a quiet voice which was nonetheless heard by all.

"He ruined my life!" said the indigent lady raggedly.

"Ah, yes. Shall we discuss it elsewhere?" He'd already grasped the situation. He held out his arms, almost as if he wanted to embrace the two tatterdemalions, and nodded at the disposal experts, who silently resumed their labors. The indigents followed McPupkiss out of the alley.

"He ruined my life," she said again when they were on the sidewalk.

"She ruined mine," answered the gentleman.

"I wish I could believe it was all so neat," said McPupkiss. "A life is simply *ruined;* credit for the destruction goes *here* or *here*. In my own experience things are more ambiguous."

"This is one of the exceptions," said the lady. "It's strange but not ambiguous. He fucked me over."

"She was warned," he said. "She made it happen."

"The two of you form a pretty picture," said McPupkiss. "You ought to be working together to improve your situation; instead you're obsessed with blame."

"We can't work together," she said. "Anytime we come together we create a disaster."

"Fine, go your separate ways," said the officer. "I've always thought 'We got ourselves into this mess and we can get ourselves out of it' was a laughable attitude. Many things are irreversible, and what matters is moving on. For example, a car can't reverse its progress over a cliff; it has to be abandoned by those who survive the fall, if any do."

But by the end of this speech the gray figures had fallen to blows and were no longer listening. They clutched one another like exhausted boxers, hissing and slapping, each trying to topple the other. McPupkiss chided himself for wasting his breath, grabbed them both by the back of their scruffy collars, and began smiting their hindquarters with his dingy shoes until they ran down the block and out of sight together, united again, McPupkiss thought, as they were so clearly meant to be.

5.

The village of Pupkinstein was nestled in a valley surrounded by steep woods. The villagers were a contented people except for the fear of the two monsters that lived in the woods and came into the village to fight their battles. Everyone knew that the village had been rebuilt many times after being half destroyed by the fighting of the monsters. No one living could remember the last of these battles, but that only intensified the suspicion that the next time would surely be soon.

Finally the citizens of Pupkinstein gathered in the town square to discuss the threat of the two monsters, and debate proposals for the prevention of their battles. A group of builders said, "Let us build a wall around the perimeter of the village, with a single gate which could be fortified by volunteer soldiers."

A group of priests began laughing, and one of them said, "Don't you know that the monsters have wings? They'll flap twice and be over your wall in no time."

Since none of the builders had ever seen the monsters, they had no reply.

Then the priests spoke up and said, "We should set up temples which can be filled with offerings: food, wine, burning candles, knitted scarves, and the like. The monsters will be appeased."

Now the builders laughed, saying, "These are monsters, not jealous gods. They don't care for our appeasements. They only want to crush each other, and we're in the way."

The priests had no answer, since their holy scriptures contained no accounts of the monsters' habits.

Then the Mayor of Pupkinstein, a large, somber man, said, "We should build our own monster here in the middle of the square, a scarecrow so huge and threatening that the monsters will see it and at once be frightened back into hiding."

This plan satisfied the builders, with their love of construction, and the priests, with their fondness for symbols. So the very next morning the citizens of Pupkinstein set about constructing a gigantic figure in the square. They began by demolishing their fountain. In its place they marked out the soles of two gigantic shoes, and the builders sank foundations for the towering legs that would extend from them. Then the carpenters built frames, and the seamstresses sewed canvases, and in less than a week the two shoes were complete, and the beginnings of ankles besides. Without being aware of it, the citizens had begun to model their monster on the Mayor, who was always present as a model, whereas no one had ever seen the two monsters.

The following night it rained. Tarpaulins were thrown over the half-constructed ankles that rose from the shoes. The Mayor and the villagers retired to an alehouse to toast their labors and be sheltered from the rain. But just as the proprietor was pouring their ale, someone said, "Listen!"

Between the crash of thunder and the crackle of lightning there came a hideous bellowing from the woods at either end of the valley.

"They're coming!" the citizens said. "Too soon—our monster's not finished!"

"How bitter," said one man. "We've had a generation of peace in which to build, and yet we only started a few days ago."

"We'll always know that we tried," said the Mayor philosophically.

"Perhaps the shoes will be enough to frighten them," said the proprietor, who had always been regarded as a fool.

No one answered him. Fearing for their lives, the villagers ran to their homes and barricaded themselves behind shutters and doors, hid their children in attics and potato cellars, and snuffed out candles and lanterns that might lead an attacker to their doors. No one dared even look at the naked, miserable things that came out of the woods and into the square; no one, that is, except the Mayor. He stood in the shadow of one of the enormous shoes, rain beating on his umbrella, only dimly sensing that he was watching another world being fucked away.

6.

I live in a shadowless pale blue sea.

I am a bright pink crablike thing, some child artist's idea of an invertebrate, so badly drawn as to be laughable.

Nevertheless, I have feelings.

More than feelings. I have a mission, an obsession.

I am building a wall.

Every day I move a grain of sand. The watercolor sea washes over my back, but I protect my accumulation. I fasten each grain to the wall with my comic-book feces. (Stink lines hover above my shit, also flies which look like bow ties, though I am supposed to be underwater.)

He is on the other side. My nemesis. Someday my wall will divide the ocean, someday it will reach the surface, or the top of the page, and be called a reef. He will be on the other side. He will not be able to get to me.

My ridiculous body moves only sideways, but it is enough.

I will divide the watercolor ocean, I will make it two. We must have a world for each of us.

I move a grain. When I come to my wall, paradoxically, I am nearest him. His little pink body, practically glowing. He is watching me, watching me build.

There was a time when he tried to help, when every day for a week he added a grain to my wall. I spent every day that week removing his grain, expelling it from the wall, and no progress was made until he stopped. He understands now. My wall must be my own. We can be together in nothing. Let him build his own wall. So he watches.

My wall will take me ten thousand years to complete. I live only for the day that it is complete.

The Pupfish floats by.

The Pupfish is a fish with the features of a mournful hound dog and a policeman's cap. The Pupfish is the only creature in the sea apart from me and my pink enemy.

The Pupfish, I know, would like to scoop me up in its oversized jaws and take me away. The Pupfish thinks it can solve my problem.

But no matter how far the Pupfish took me, I would still be in the same ocean with *him.* That cannot be. There must be two oceans. So I am building a wall.

I move a grain.

I rest.

I will be free.

Lifeboat on a Burning Sea

Bruce Holland Rogers

Bruce Holland Rogers has taught creative writing at the University of Colorado and the University of Illinois but is now writing full time. He writes a column for *Speculations* magazine, which is aptly titled "Staying Alive": it focuses on the psychological and spiritual challenges of a career in fiction. Rogers has been nominated for the Edgar Allan Poe Award by the Mystery Writers of America, and he is a past winner of the Jonny Cat Litter-ary Award, sponsored by the Cat Writers Association and a cat litter company. (Your editor isn't making this up.) His stories "These Shoes Strangers Have Died Of" and "Lifeboat on a Burning Sea" were both on this year's final Nebula ballot in the short story and novelette categories respectively.

About "Lifeboat on a Burning Sea," he writes:

"My wife is a social psychologist and one of her research areas is social networks. Maybe that helps explain how I came to write a story that examines death as a social phenomenon.

"In Hindu mythology, Indra's Net is a web of connected jewels. Each jewel reflects the image of every other jewel on the net so that every part contains the whole. Our social networks are a bit like this. Each of us constructs an impression of every other personality in the network. Unlike ordinary reflections, social ones are stored in our memories and become internalized as evolving aspects of our personalities. We don't just reflect everyone else on the net—we store a dynamic version of each person we meet.

"That's one sort of immortality.

"Ordinarily, we can't disconnect the social self from the 'unreflected' self. In part, the story is a thought experiment about doing just that."

Deserters.

When I can't see the next step, when I can't think clearly about the hardware changes that TOS needs in order to become the repository, the ark, the salvation of my soul, I think of deserters.

I think of men on the rail of a sinking tanker. For miles around, there are no lights, only water, black and icy. A lake of flame surrounds the ship. Beyond the edge of the burning oil slick, a man sits in the lifeboat looking at his comrades. The angle of the deck grows steeper. The men at the rail are waving their hands, but the one in the boat doesn't return. Instead, he puts his back into rowing, rowing away. To the men who still wave, who still hope, the flames seem to reach higher, but it's really the ship coming down to meet the burning sea.

Or this:

The arctic explorer wakes from dreams of ice and wind to a world of ice and wind. In the sleeping bag, his frostbite has thawed and it feels as though his hands and feet are on fire. It is almost more than he can endure, but he tells himself he's going to live. As long as his companion is fit enough to drive the sled, he's going to live. He hobbles from the tent, squints against the sunlight. When he finds the dogs and sled gone, he watches for a long time as the wind erases the tracks.

In these fantasies of mine, the dead bear witness.

From the bottom of the sea, dead sailors wave their arms.

Frozen into the ice, a leathery finger points, accuses.

There must have been a time when I wasn't aware of the relentless tick of every heartbeat, but I don't remember it. My earliest memory is of lying awake in my bed, eyes open in the blackness, imagining what it was like to be dead.

I had asked my father. He was a practical man.

"It's like this," he said. He showed me a watch that had belonged to my grandfather, an antique watch that ran on a coiled spring instead of a battery. He wound it up. "Listen," he said.

Tick, tick, tick, I heard.

"Our hearts are like that," he said, handing me the watch. "At last, they stop. That's death."

"And *then* what?"

"Then, nothing," he told me. "Then we're dead. We just aren't anymore—no thought, no feeling. Gone. Nothing."

He let me carry the watch around for a day. The next morning, the spring had run down. I put the watch to my ear, and heard *absence,* heard *nothing.*

Even back then, lying awake in the dark with my thoughts of the void, I was planning my escape.

Tick, tick, tick, went my heart, counting down to zero.

I wasn't alone. After my graduate work in neuronics, I found a university job and plenty of projects to work on, but research is a slow business.

Tick, tick, tick.

I was in a race, and by the time I was fifty-six, I knew I was falling behind. In fact, I felt lucky to have made it that far. We were living at the height of terrorist chic. The Agrarian Underground and Monetarists were in decline, but the generation of bombers that succeeded them was ten times as active, a hundred times as random in their selection of targets. Plastique, Flame, Implosion. . . . They gave themselves rock-bank names. And then there were the ordinary street criminals who would turn their splitter guns on you in the hope that your chip, once they dug it out of your skin, would show enough credit for a hit of whatever poison they craved.

Statistically, of course, it wasn't surprising that I was still alive. But whenever I tuned in to CNN Four, The Street Beat Source, the barrage of just-recorded carnage made me wonder that *anyone* was still alive.

Fifty-six. That's when I heard from Bierley's people. And after I had met Bierley, after I had started to work with Richardson, I began to believe that I would hit my stride in time, that Death might not be quite the distance runner he'd always been cracked up to be.

I had known who Bierley was, of course. Money like his bought a high profile, if you wanted it. And I had heard of Richardson. He was hot stuff in analog information.

Bierley and Richardson were my best hope. Bierley and Richardson were magicians at what they did. And Bierley and Richardson—I knew it from the start—were unreliable.

Bierley, with his money and political charm, would stay with the project only until it bored him. And Richardson, he had his own agenda. Even when we were working well together, when we were making progress, Richardson never really *believed.*

In Richardson's office, he and I watched a playback of Bierley's press conference. It had been our press conference, too, but we hadn't answered many questions. Even Richardson understood the importance of leaving that to Bierley.

"A multi-cameral multi-phasic analog information processor," Bierley said again on the screen, "but we prefer to call it TOS." He smiled warmly. "The Other Side."

From behind his desk, Richardson grumbled, "God. He makes what we've done sound like a séance."

"Come on," I said. "It's the whole point."

"Are you really so hot to live forever as a machine consciousness, if, fantasy of fantasies, it turns out to be possible?"

"Yes."

"Your problem," he said, pointing a finger, "is that you're too damned scared of death to be curious about it. That's not a very scientific attitude."

I almost told him he'd feel differently in another twenty years, but then I didn't. It might not be true. Since I had *always* seen death as the enemy, it was possible that someone like Richardson *never* would.

"Meanwhile," Richardson continued, "we've made a significant leap in machine intelligence. Isn't that worthy of attention in its own right without pretending that it's a step toward a synthesized afterlife?"

On the screen, Bierley was saying, "Of all the frontiers humanity has challenged, death was the one we least expected to conquer."

"As if, Christ, as if we'd already *done* it!"

Bierley peered out from the screen. He had allowed only one video camera for the conference so that he'd know when he was looking his viewers in the eye. "Some of you watching now will never die. That's the promise of this research. Pioneers of the infinite! Who doesn't long to see the march of the generations? What will my grandchild's grandchildren be like? What lies ahead in one hundred years? A thousand? A million?" After a pause and another grandfatherly smile, a whisper: "Some will live to know."

Richardson blew a raspberry at the screen.

"All right," I admitted. "He oversells. But that's Bierley. Everything he says is for effect, and the effect is *funding*!"

On the screen, the silver-haired Bierley was rephrasing questions as only he could, turning the more aggressive queries in on themselves.

Wasn't this a premature announcement *of a breakthrough bringing hope to millions?* Would Bierley himself turn a profit from this *conquest of humanity's oldest and cruelest foe?* Would he himself be among the first *to enter the possibly hazardous territory of eternity to make sure it was safe for others?*

Then he was introducing us, telling the reporters about my genius for hardware and Richardson's for analog information theory. We had sixty technicians and research assistants working with us, but Bierley made it sound like a two-man show. In some ways, it was. Neither of us could be replaced, not if you wanted the same synergy.

"Two great minds in a race for immortality," Bierley said, and then he gave them a version of what I'd told Bierley myself: Richardson was always two steps ahead of my designs, seeing applications that exceeded my intentions, making me run to keep up with him and propose new structures that would then propel him another two steps beyond me. I'd never worked with anyone who stimulated me in that way, who made me leap and stretch. It felt like flying.

What Bierley didn't say was that often we'd dash from thought to thought and finally look down to see empty air beneath us. Usually we discovered impracticalities in the wilder things we dreamed up together. Only rarely did we find outselves standing breathless on solid ground, looking back at the flawless bridge we had just built. Of course, when that happened, it was magnificent.

It also frightened me. I worried that Richardson was indispensable, that after making those conceptual leaps with him, I could never go back to my solitary plodding or to working with minds less electric than his. *All* minds were less electric than his, at least when he was at his best. The only difficulty was keeping him from straying into the Big Questions.

The camera had pulled back, and Richardson and I both looked rumpled and plain next to Bierley's polish. On screen I stammered and adjusted my glasses as I answered a question.

Richardson was no longer watching the press conference video, but had shifted his gaze to the flatscreen on his office wall. It showed a weather satellite image of the Western Hemisphere, time-lapsed so that the last seventy-two hours rolled by in three minutes. It was always running in Richardson's office, the only decoration there, unless you counted that little statue, the souvenir from India that he kept on his desk.

On the press conference tape, Richardson was answering a question. "We don't have any idea how we'd actually get a person's consciousness into the machine," he admitted. "We haven't even perfected the artificial mind that we've built. There's one significant glitch that keeps shutting us down for hours at a time."

At that point, Bierley's smile looked forced, but only for an instant.

"The best way to explain the problem," the recorded Richardson continued, "is to tell you that thoughts move through our hardware in patterns that are analogous to weather. Sometimes an information structure builds up like a tropical depression. If conditions are right, it becomes a hurricane. The processor continues to work, but at greatly reduced efficiency until the storm passes. So we're blacked out sometimes. We can't talk to . . ." He paused, looking at Bierley, sort of wincing, "to TOS, until the hurricane has spent its energy."

"You don't like the name," I said in Richardson's office.

Richardson snorted. "The Other Side." He leaned back in his chair. "You're right about the money, though. He charms the bucks out of Congress, and that's not easy these days."

On the tape, I was telling the reporters about the warning lights I had rigged in the I/O room: They ran up a scale from Small Craft Advisory to Gale Warning to Hurricane, with the appropriate nautical flags painted onto the display. I had hoped for a bigger laugh than I got.

"Can we interview the computer?" a reporter asked.

I had started to say something about how the I/O wasn't up to that yet, but that TOS itself was helping to design an appropriate interface to make itself as easy to talk to as any human being.

Bierley's image stepped forward in front of mine. "TOS is _not_ a computer," he said. "Let's make this clear. TOS is an information structure for machine intelligence. TOS is interfaced with computers, can access and manipulate digital data, but this is an analog machine. Eventually, it will be a repository for human consciousness. If you want another name for it, you could call it a Mind Bank."

"No one gets it," Richardson said, "and this press conference isn't going to help." He looked at me. "*You* don't get it, do you, Maas?"

"I don't even know what you're talking about."

"Trying to synthesize self-awareness is an interesting project. And putting human consciousness into a box would be a neat trick, instructive. I mean, I'm all for trying even if we fail. I expect to fail. Even if we succeed, even if we find a *technical* answer, it begs the bigger question."

"Which is?"

"What does it *mean* to live? What does it *mean* to die? Until you get a satisfactory answer to that, then what's the point of trying to live forever?"

"The point is that I don't want to die!" Then more quietly, I said, "Do you?"

Richardson didn't look at me. He picked up the Indian statue from his desk and leaned back in his chair to look at it. When he put it down again, he still hadn't answered.

The statue was a man dancing inside an arc of flames.

The next week, Bierley deserted us.

"Brain aneurism in his sleep," one of the old man's attorneys told me via video link.

There had been no provision in Bierley's will to keep seed money coming. If he went first, we were on our own. The attorney zapped me a copy of the will so I could see for myself.

"Makes you think," the attorney said, "doesn't it?" He meant the sudden death. I thought about that, of course. As strong as ever, I could hear my pulse in my throat. *Tick, tick, tick.* But I was also thinking something else:

Bastard. *Deserter.*

He had left me to die.

Weeks later in the I/O room, I said to Richardson, "We're in trouble."

He and a technician had been fiddling with TOS's voice, and he said, "TOS, what do you think of that?"

"I don't know what to think of it," said the machine voice. The tone was as meaningfully modulated as any human voice, but there was still something artificial about the sound—too artificial, still, for press exposure. "I don't know enough of what Dr. Maas means by 'trouble.' I'm unsure of just how inclusive 'we' is intended to be."

"My bet," Richardson said, "is that he's going to say our project has funding shortfalls up the yaya."

"Yaya?" said TOS.

"Wazoo," Richardson said.

"Oh." A pause. "I understand."

Richardson grinned at me. "English as she is spoke."

I waved off his joke. "There's talk of cutting our funding in Congress. I've been calling the reps that were in Bierley's pocket, but I can't talk to these people. Not like he could. And I sure as hell can't start a grass-roots groundswell."

"How about that lobbyist we hired?"

"She's great at phoning, full of enthusiasm, to tell me how bad things are. She says she's doing her best." I dropped into a chair. "Damn Bierley for dying." And for taking us with him, I thought. Didn't those bastards in Washington understand what the stakes were here? This wasn't basic science that you could throw away when budgets were tight. This was life and death!

Tick, tick, tick.

My life. *My* death!

Richardson said, "How desperate are we?"

"Plenty."

"Good." Richardson smiled. "I have a desperation play."

We played it close to the edge. Our funding was cut in a House vote, saved by the Senate, and lost again in conference committee. Two weeks later, we also lost an accountant who said he wouldn't go to jail for us, but by then we had figured out that the best way to float digital requisition forms and kite electronic funds transfers was with TOS. We couldn't stay ahead of the numbers forever, but TOS, with near-human guile and digital speed, bought us an extra week or two while the team from Hollywood installed the new imaging hardware.

The technicians and research assistants kept TOS busy with new data to absorb, to *think about,* and I worked to add "rooms" to the multicameral memory, trying to give TOS the ability to suppress the information hurricanes that still shut us down at unpredictable intervals. The first rooms had each been devoted to a specific function—sensory processing, pattern recognition, memory sorting—but these new ones were basically just memory modules. Meanwhile, Richardson paraded people who had known Bierley through the I/O room for interviews with TOS.

The day of the press conference, I deflected half a dozen calls from the Government Accounting Office. Even as the first reporters were filing into our pressroom, I kept expecting some suits and crew cuts to barge in, flash badges, and say, "FBI."

I also worried about hurricanes, but TOS's storm-warning lights stayed off all morning, and the only surprise of the press conference was the one Richardson and I had planned. While stragglers were still filing into the room—security-screening and bomb-sniffing that many people took some time—the video behind the podium flicked on.

"Bierley, regrettably, *is dead*," said Bierley's image. He was responding to the first question after his prepared statement. "There's no bringing him back, and I regret that." Warm smile.

The press corps laughed uncertainly.

"But you're his memories?" asked a reporter.

"Not in the sense that you mean it," Bierley said. "Nobody dumped Bierley's mind into a machine. We can't do that." Dramatic pause. "Yet." Smile. "What I am is a personality construct of *other* people's memories. Over one hundred of Bierley's closest associates were interviewed by TOS. Their impressions of Bierley, specific examples of things he had said and done, along with digital recordings of the man in action, were processed to create me. I may not be Jackson Bierley as he saw himself, but I'm Jackson Bierley as he was seen by others."

Bierley chose another reporter by name.

The reporter looked around herself, then at the screen. "Can you see me?" she said. "Can you see this room?"

"There's a micro camera," said the image, "top and center of this display panel. Really, though"—he flashed the grandfatherly Bierley smile—"that's a wasted question. You must have had a harder one in mind."

"Just this," she said. "Are you self-aware?"

"I certainly seem to be, don't I?" said the image. "There's liable to be some debate about that. I'm no expert, so I'll leave the final answer up to Doctors Maas and Richardson. But my opinion is that, no, I am not self-aware."

A ripple of laughter from the reporters who appreciated paradox.

"How do we know," said a man who hadn't laughed, "that this isn't some kind of fake?"

"How do you know I'm not *some incredibly talented actor who's wearing undetectable makeup and who studied Jackson Bierley's every move for years in order to be this convincing*?" Undetectably, unless you were looking for it, Bierley's pupils dilated a bit, and the effect was to broadcast warmth and openness. We had seen the real Bierley do that in recorded addresses. "I guess you have to make up your own mind."

Then he blinked. He smiled. Jackson Bierley didn't intend to make a fool of anyone, not even a rude reporter.

"What does Bierley's family think of all this?" asked someone else.

"You could ask them. I can tell you that they cooperated—they were among those interviewed by TOS. They have me back to an extent. I'll be here to meet those great-great-grandchildren I so longed to greet one day. Unfortunately . . ." and suddenly he looked sad. "Unfortunately, those kids will know Bierley, but Bierley won't know them. Only much more research can hold out the promise that one day, a construct like me really will be self-aware, will remember, will *be* the man or woman whose life he or she extends into eternity."

He didn't mention the licensing fee his family was charging us for the exclusive use of his image, any more than Bierley himself would have mentioned it.

"Are the Bierleys funding this project?"

"I know a billion sounds like a lot of money, but when it's divided up among as many heirs as I have . . ." He paused, letting the laughter die. "No. They are not. This project is more expensive than you can imagine. In the long run, it's going to take moon-shot money to get eternity up and running."

"And where's that money going to come from, now that your federal funds have been cut off?"

"Well, I can't really say much about that. But I'll tell you that it will be much easier for me to learn Japanese or Malay as a construct than it would have been for the real Jackson Bierley." He smiled, but there was a brief tremor to the smile, and it didn't take a genius to see that Jackson Bierley, personality construct or not, was one American who didn't want to hand yet another technological advantage across the Pacific.

"In these times, it's understandable that the American taxpayer wants his money spent on hiring police," Bierley went on. "Why think about eternal life when you're worried about getting home from work alive? It's too bad that *both* can't be a priority. Of course, with the appropriate hardware attached, a machine like TOS could be one hell of a security system—a very smart guard who never sleeps." As if a TOS system could one day be in everyone's home.

Richardson and I stepped to the podium then, and for once I was happy to have no public-speaking skills. The Bierley construct jumped in with damage control whenever I was about to say something I shouldn't. He made jokes when Richardson dryly admitted that in all honesty, the construct was closer to a collaborative oil painting than it was to the real Jackson Bierley. Of the three of us up on the platform, the one who seemed warmest, funniest, most human, was the one inside the video screen.

After the conference, we got calls from the Secretary of Commerce, the Speaker of the House, and both the Majority and Minority Leaders in the Senate. Even though they were falling all over themselves to offer support for funding, Richardson and I knew we could still screw it up, so we mostly listened in while the Bierley construct handled the calls.

It was Richardson who had pulled our fat out of the fire, but even I was caught up in the illusion. I felt grateful to *Bierley.*

Once we'd restored our funding, I expected things to return to normal. I thought Richardson would be eager to get back to work, but he wouldn't schedule meetings with me. Day after day, he hid out in his office to tie up what he said were "loose ends."

I tried to be patient, but finally I'd had enough.

"It's time you talked to me," I said as I jerked open his office door. I stormed up to his desk. "You've been stalling for two weeks. This project is supposed to be a collaboration!"

Without looking up from his phone screen, he said, "Come in," which was supposed to be funny.

"Richardson," I told him, not caring who he might be talking to, "you were brilliant. You pulled off a coup. Great! Now let's get back to work. I can sit in my office and dream up augmentations for TOS all day, but it doesn't mean squat if I'm not getting your feedback."

"Have a seat."

"I'd prefer to stand, damn it. We're funded. We're ready to go. Let's get something *done!*"

He looked up at last and said, "I'm not a careerist, Maas. I'm not motivated by impressing anyone."

"And I am?" I sat down, tried to catch his eye. "I want to get to work for my own reasons, all right? The Bierley construct is incredible. Now what can we do next?"

"What indeed?"

"Yes," said the voice of Jackson Bierley. "I'm going to be a pretty hard trick to top, especially once you've got me in 3-D." The phone screen was at an acute angle and hard for me to see, but now I noticed the silver hair.

"Is that it?" I said. "You spend your day on the phone, chatting with the construct?"

Richardson said, "Bye, Jackson," and disconnected. "The construct is interesting. This is a useful tool we've invented."

"It is," I agreed. "It's something we can build on."

"It's something lots of people can build on." He folded the phone screen down. "A week ago I got a call from a Hollywood agent. He wanted to talk to me about some ideas. Constructs for dead singers— they could not only do new recordings, but grant interviews. Dead actor constructs. TOS-generated films scripted by dead writers and directed by Hitchcock or Huston or Spielberg or any other dead director you'd care to name. TOS is getting so good at imaging, you'd never need to build a set or hire a vid crew."

"Is *that* what you've spent all this time on?"

"Of course not. It's a good idea from the agent's perspective—as he sees it, he'd represent all of the virtual talent and practically own Hollywood. But it sounds to me like a waste of resources."

"Good."

"I'm just pointing out that everybody who hears about what TOS can do will see it in terms of meeting his or her own needs. The agent sees dead stars. You see a stepping stone to immortality. I see a tool for making my own inquiries."

"What inquiries?"

"We've had that discussion." He pointed at his wall. "They've always had a better handle on it than we have."

I looked where he was pointing, but just saw the usual time-lapse satellite image of weather systems crossing the globe. Then I realized that something was different. The display wasn't of the Western Hemisphere, but of the Eastern.

Richardson picked up the statue on his desk. "Shiva," he said. "This arc of flames that surrounds him is life and death. Flames for life. Spaces between the flames for death. The one and the zero. Reincarnation."

For once it was my turn to be the skeptic. "You find that consoling? An afterlife that can't be verified? It's superstition, Richardson."

"It's religion," he said, "and I don't have any more faith than you do that I'll be reborn after I die. Maybe I don't *dis*believe it as much as you do. Since it can't be falsified, it's not subject to any scientific test. But as a metaphor, I find it fascinating."

"What are you talking about?"

"Maas, what if you really *knew* death? What if you and death were intimate?"

"I still don't follow you."

"You're so interested in synthetic consciousness. What about synthesized death? If you knew more about death, Maas, would you still have this unreasoning fear of it?"

I snapped, "What do you mean, 'unreasoning'?"

"Forget it. I guess it's not your cup of tea. Why don't you think about this instead: Could a TOS construct replace you?"

"Replace me?"

"The way we replaced Bierley. The Bierley construct works for us every bit as well as the original did. So what about you? If I built a Maas construct, could it work on augmenting TOS as well as you do? It could sound like you, it could interact with other people convincingly, but could it think like you, design like you?"

"I don't know," I said. "I doubt it. A construct mimics social impressions. The pattern of thought that produces the behavior in the construct isn't sequenced quite like the thought in our heads. But you know that. Hell, what are you asking me for? You're the information expert."

"Well, if the behavior is the same, if the behavior is the production of good ideas, then maybe all we'd have to do is teach the machine to go through the motions that produce that behavior. We'd get the construct to act out whatever it is that you do when you're producing a good idea. Maybe it would kick out quality results as a sort of by-product."

I chewed my lip. "I don't think so."

"Works with Bierley."

"That's social skills. Not the same."

"You doubt the machine intelligence is sufficiently sophisticated, right?" Richardson said. "You're investing all this hope in TOS as a repository of consciousness, but you're not sure that we can even *begin* to synthesize creative thinking.

"Bierley makes for some interesting speculation," he went on. "Don't you think so? The original is dead. Jackson Bierley, in that sense, is complete. What we're left with is our memories of him. That's what we keep revising. And isn't that always true?

"My father died fifteen years ago," he said, "and I still feel as though my relationship with him changes from year to year. A life is like a novel that burns as you read it. You read the last page, and it's complete. You think about it, then, reflect on the parts that puzzle you. You feel some loss because there aren't any pages left to turn. You can remember only so many of the pages. That's what the construct is good for—remembering pages."

He smiled. "And here's the metaphysics: While you're trying to remember the book that's gone, maybe the author is writing a new one."

He put the statue of Shiva down on his desk. "Give me some more time, Maas. I'm not sitting on my hands, I promise you that. I'm working on my perspective."

"Your perspective."

"That's what I said."

I exhaled sharply. "I've been thinking about your suggestion that we tie building security into TOS. I could do that. And I guess I could work on getting rid of the hurricanes once and for all. But that's not just a hardware problem."

"All right. I'll give you an hour a day on that. OK?"

I didn't tell him what I really thought. If I thoroughly pissed him off, who knew how long it would take for us to get back to our real work? I said, "Get your perspective straight in a week."

In a week, he was gone.

One of the research assistants, somewhat timidly, brought me the news. She had been watching CNN Four and saw a bombing story across town, and she was certain that she had seen Philip Richardson among the dead.

She followed me into my office, where I switched on the TV. CNN Four recycles its splatter stories every twenty minutes, so we didn't have long to wait.

The bomb had gone off in a subway station. Did Richardson ride the subway? I realized I didn't know where the man lived or how he got back and forth from work.

The station would have channeled the energy up through its blast vents—everything in the city was designed or redesigned these days with bombs in mind. But that saved structures, not people. Images of the station platform showed a tangle of twisted bodies. The color, as in all bomb-blast scenes, seemed wrong; the concussion turns the victims' skin slightly blue.

The camera panned across arms and legs, the faces turned toward the camera and away.

"Three terrorist groups, Under Deconstruction, Aftershock, and The Last Wave, have all claimed responsibility for the bombing," said the news reader.

There, at the end of the pan, was Philip Richardson, discolored like the rest. At the end of the story, I ran back the television's memory cache and replayed the images. I froze the one that showed Richardson.

"Get out," I told the research assistant. "Please."

I called the police.

"Are you family?" asked the desk sergeant when I told her what I wanted. "We can't make a verification like that until the next of kin have been notified."

"His goddamn face was just on the goddamn TV!"

"Rules are rules," she said. "Hang on." Her gaze shifted from the phone to another monitor as she keyed in the query. "No problem, anyway. This is cleared to go out. And, yeah, sorry. The list of fatalities includes your friend."

I broke the connection.

"He was no friend of mine."

Deserter.

At first I dismissed the thought of making a Richardson personality construct. It wasn't the personality I needed, but the mind. Substance, not surface.

But how different were they, really?

Maybe, Richardson had said, *all we'd have to do is teach the machine to go through the motions. Maybe it would kick out results as a by-product.*

I went to the I/O room where the hologram generator—Richardson's idea—had been installed. I called up Bierley.

"Hello, Maas," he said.

"Hi, Jackson."

"First names?" Bierley arched an eyebrow. "That's a first for you." Except for distortion flecks that were like a fine dust floating around him, Bierley was convincingly present.

"Well," I said, "let's be pals."

His laugh was ironic and embracing at the same time. "All right," he said. "Let's."

"Jackson, what's the product of 52,689 and 31,476?"

"My net worth?"

"No. Don't kid. What's the product?"

"What were those numbers again?"

"You're shading me, Jackson. You can't have forgotten."

About then, the Small Craft Advisory light came on, but I ignored it. Chaotic disturbances hardly ever built to hurricane force anymore. Sure enough, the light went out soon after it had come on.

"What's this about?" Bierley asked me.

"Did you calculate the product on the way to deciding how you'd respond to the question? Or did you just straight to an analysis of what Bierley would say?"

"*I* did neither," Bierley said. Which was true. There wasn't an "I" there, except as a grammatical convention. "Don't confuse me with your machine, Dr. Maas. You're the scientist. You know what I'm talking about." He brushed the lapel of his jacket. "I'm an elegant illusion."

"Would you give me some investment advice, Jackson?"

The hologram smiled. "My forte was always building companies," he said, "not trading stocks. Best advice that I could give you about stocks is some I got at my daddy's knee. He said you don't go marrying some gal just because another fool loves her."

I smiled, and then I wondered if Bierley's father had actually said that. If it sounded good, that's what would matter to the construct. But that's just what would have mattered to the real Bierley, too.

That is, what had mattered to the real Bierley and what mattered now to the construct was that the story have its effect. He had made me smile, made me think that Bierley the billionaire was just a regular guy.

What if a Richardson construct could work the same way? The effect that Richardson had produced, the one I wanted to duplicate, was an effect on me. I wanted to stretch my thinking. What if that depended more on the emotional state he generated in me than on his actual ideas?

No, I thought. That was ridiculous.

What decided me was the phone call.

"Are you Maas?" the woman said. Her hair was long and black, but disarrayed. Her eyes were red-rimmed. On her face was the blankness that comes after too many days of anger or grief or worry, when the muscles can't hold the form of feeling any longer but the feeling persists. "I'm Phillips," I thought she said. That is, I thought she was saying her name was Phillips. But she was only pausing to search for the next word.

"I'm Philip's . . . widow," she said.

I hadn't know Richardson was married. I wasn't the only one he had deserted.

"Yes," I said, and then again, more gently: "Yes, Mrs. Richardson. I'm Dr. Maas." An infant wailed in the background, and Mrs. Richardson seemed not to have noticed. "I'm Elliot Maas."

"Do you know where he is?" she asked.

Was she really asking what I thought she was? I opened, then closed, my mouth. What would I tell her? *He's dead, Mrs. Richardson. Death is not a location. Where is he? He isn't anywhere. Mrs. Richardson, he is not. Mrs. Richardson, your husband doesn't exist. Where he used to be, there is nothing. Mrs. Richardson . . .*

"I'm sorry," she said. "I'm not being very clear." She put her hand to her forehead and closed her eyes. "The ashes, Dr. Maas. Have the ashes been delivered to you?"

I stared stupidly at the screen.

"The coroner's office says they had the ashes delivered to me, but they didn't. I thought perhaps they had made a mistake and sent them to Philip's work address." She opened her eyes. "Did the coroner's office make a delivery?" In the background, the infant cried more lustily.

"I don't know," I said. "I could check, I suppose."

"They used to . . ." Her mouth trembled, and she pursed her lips. Her eyes glistened. "They used to let you make your own arrangements," she said. "But they don't do that anymore because there are so many bombs and so many . . . I never saw him. I never got to say good-bye and now they can't even find his ashes."

"I'll make inquiries."

"His mother's been here, trying to help out, but she . . ." Richardson's wife blinked, as if waking. "Oh, God. The baby. I'm so sorry."

The phone went black, then the screen showed the Ameritech logo and the dial tone began to drone.

I made sure that the ashes hadn't been delivered to us, and I called the coroner's office where they swore that the ashes had been processed and delivered to Richardson's home address days earlier. They had a computer record of it.

When I called Mrs. Richardson back, it was the other Mrs. Richardson—his mother—who answered. She looked worn-out, too. One more person that Richardson had abandoned.

But she would manage to get by in whatever way she had managed before. I was the one he had hurt the most. I was the one with the most to lose.

When Richardson's wife came to the phone, I told her that I'd struck out with the coroner. "But I think there is a way that I can help you," I said. I even admitted that it might be of some use to me, as well.

Who knows whether the construct brought Sharon Richardson any consolation? She came by from time to time as the construct evolved, and she usually brought the baby. That actually caused a problem the first time she did it—I had cleared her through the building's recognition system, but TOS didn't want to let Richardson's infant daughter, a stranger, inside without my authorization. The door refused to open. TOS-mediated security still needed some tinkering.

In the I/O room, Sharon Richardson told the construct, "We miss you."

"He loved you," the construct told her.

"We miss you," she said again.

"I'm not really him."

"I know."

"What do you want me to say?"

"I don't know. There's something that never got said, but I don't know what it is."

"Everything passes away. Nothing lasts," the construct said. "That's the thing he carried with him every moment. Nothing lasts, and that's the thing we have to hold on to. That's the thing we have to understand, that we're as transitory as thoughts. Butterflies or thoughts. When we really understand that, then we're beautiful."

Defeatist, I thought. *Deserter.*

"That's not it," she said. "I heard him say that. More than once."

"What do you want me to say?" the construct repeated.

She looked at me, self-conscious, then turned away.

"He was selfish," she said to the floor. "I want to hear him . . . I want you to say you're sorry."

The construct sighed. "Do you think he died on purpose?"

"Did he?" she said. "I *loved* him!"

"Nothing lasts."

"Say it!"

The image of Philip Richardson closed his eyes, hung his head, and said, "Death comes. Sooner or later, it comes."

Sharon Richardson didn't leave looking any more prepared for life without Philip than she had looked when she first called me, looking for his ashes.

I wasn't any more satisfied than she was. That the construct wasn't finished yet was the one thing that gave me hope. But not much.

Using the Bierley construct as the interviewer, TOS had talked to Sharon, to Richardson's mother, his brother, and his two sisters. The interviews took place in the I/O room where the hologram made Bierley more convincingly warm, caring, and real. He extracted insights, anecdotes, and honest appraisals from every technician who had worked with Richardson on TOS. I flew in Richardson's grad school peers and colleagues from his stints at MIT and Stanford. They all talked to Bierley, and Bierley interviewed me, too. I was as exhaustive and as honest as I could be in conveying my impressions of Richardson. Everything about him mattered—even whatever had irritated me. It was all part of the pattern that made him Philip Richardson. After the interviews, I'd stay in the I/O room talking to the construct as it developed. That made for late nights.

Irritatingly, TOS started to suffer again from hurricanes. Those chaos storms in the information flow started to shut down the Richardson construct around one in the morning, regularly.

"It's like you're too much contradiction for TOS to handle," I told the construct late one night. "A scientist and a mystic."

"No mystic," Richardson said. "I'm more scientist than you are, Maas. You're in a contest with the universe. You want to *beat* it. If someone gave you the fountain of youth, guaranteed to keep you alive forever with the proviso that you'd never understand how it worked, you'd jump at the chance. Science is a means to you. You want results. You're a mere technologist."

"I have a focus. You could never keep yourself on track."

"You have an obsession," the construct countered. "You're right that I can never resist the temptation of the more interesting questions. But that's what matters to me. What does all of this"—he swept his hand wide to encompass the universe with his gesture, and his hand came to rest on his own chest—"What does it all mean? That's my question, Maas. I never stop asking it."

"You sound like him. Sometimes I forget what you are."

"I'm a dead loss, that's what I am," the construct said with a smile. "I probably argue as well as Richardson, but when it comes to conceptualizing, I'm just TOS. Not that the machine is chopped liver, but you haven't resurrected Philip Richardson."

The Small Craft Advisory light had been on for an hour, but now the next light in the sequence came on. Gale Warning.

"We'd better talk fast," said Richardson. "I don't have much time." He smiled again. "Memento mori."

I said nothing, but stared at him. The hologram generator had been improved a bit recently, and for minutes at a time, I could detect no flaw in his appearance. The eye was so easy to fool.

This was the fifth night in a row with a hurricane. They always came after midnight. *Tick, tick, tick.* Like clockwork.

But TOS hurricanes were a function of chaos. Why would they suddenly behave so predictably?

And then I thought again, *The eye is so easy to fool.*

The ashes never *had* turned up.

"Son of a bitch!" I said aloud.

That's when the hurricane light came on and the hologram of Philip Richardson winked out.

I sat thinking for five minutes in the quiet building, the building that was down to just two overnight guards—a skeleton crew—since TOS oversaw security and controlled all the locks inside and out. A big, silent building. For five minutes, I considered what I needed to do. Then I went to the part of the building that housed the TOS memory.

The multi-cameral design of TOS made it relatively easy to isolate various functions from one another. I could pull all the sensory "rooms" off-line and make changes in them, and the rest of TOS wouldn't know what I was doing. It would be like slicing the corpus callosum in the human brain—the left hemisphere wouldn't know what the right was doing, wouldn't know that things were being monkeyed with in the other hemisphere. But TOS was self-programming, so I needed instructions from the left hemisphere to reprogram the right. Getting the job done without tripping whatever safeguards Richardson had programmed in meant pulling out one room at a time, giving it a function, downloading the result of the function as a digital record, then emptying the room of any traces of what it had just done before I connected it back to the whole. One room at a time, I captured the instructions that would let me generate false data for the sensory rooms.

The process would have taken thirty seconds if I could have just told TOS what I wanted to do, but it wouldn't have worked that way. Doing it the slow way took an hour.

I went back to the I/O room and said, "I'm going home." TOS started to process the words, and the phrase tugged at the tripwires I had just programmed.

To the rest of TOS, the sensory rooms sent sounds and images of my walking out of the room, closing the door, walking down the corridor, down the stairs, out of the building, and across the parking lot. TOS saw me get into my car and drive away.

And TOS didn't just see this. It heard, felt, and smelled it, too.

Meanwhile, the sensory rooms suppressed the data that was coming from the I/O room, data that said I was still there, at the back of the room, hiding behind file cabinets with the lights out. Otherwise, everything ran as it normally would.

The eye was easy to fool. Yes, and so was the ear. So was the motion detector. So was the air sampler.

He came in at about four o'clock. The hall lights at his back showed that he was dressed in something baggy. He said, "Lights," and the lights came on in the room. It was a sweat suit. A gray one. He said, "The one and the zero," his code, I suppose, for "System Restore," and the Hurricane, Gale Warning, and Small Craft Advisory lights clicked off in quick succession.

He called up the construct and said to it, in a flat voice, "Hello, Richardson."

And the construct answered, mimicking the tone, "Hello, Richardson." The construct shook his head. "You sound hollow." Then he smiled. "Death warmed over, eh?"

The man in the sweat suit sat down with his back to me and watched the construct without answering.

"So tell me what it's like," said the construct. "You give *me* some information for a change."

"It's more real than you could believe. He's more dead than you can imagine."

"Of course." Big smile. "I'm a construct. I only *seem* to imagine."

"Richardson is more dead than even Richardson could have imagined."

"Wasn't that the point of this exercise?"

The man in the sweat suit didn't answer.

"I don't understand why you're not excited. This is a break-through!"

"I suppose it is." He took a deep breath and let it out. "Give me Bierley."

"Cheer up," the construct said. "It's the great adventure. You'll make the journey with your memory intact."

"Shut your trap and give me Bierley."

The Richardson construct hesitated a moment longer. Then, without transition, it was Bierley in the hologram.

"Hi," Bierley said.

"Hi, Jackson."

"You don't look so good."

"So I've been told."

"Want to start with easy questions?" asked Bierley. "His favorite color, that sort of thing?"

"I'm through with the construct. It doesn't interest me anymore." He stood up. "I just came by to tell you that it's time for me to move on."

"That's enough," I said.

He jumped at the sound of my voice, but he didn't turn around.

"Richardson," I told him, "you are a son of a bitch."

"Richardson's dead."

"So you've told me," said Bierley.

"I was talking to Maas," he said, his voice still flat.

"Maas went home over an hour ago," said the construct.

"Turn the construct off," I told him. "I built a sensory barricade. TOS doesn't know I'm in the building, and won't know it until I leave this room."

"Clever."

"What is?" said Bierley.

I said, "No more clever than splicing yourself into the image bank at CNN Four. No more clever than hacking your way into records at the coroner's office and police department."

"TOS did most of the work."

"Most of what work?" said the construct.

"Turn it off," I said again.

"Bierley," he said, "give me Richardson again."

The hologram flipped immediately to the other man's image.

"You want Richardson? There he is. That's the closest anyone can get. Not the real thing, of course, but more Richardson than I am." But then he did shut the construct down. Again he said, "Richardson is dead."

"You used me. You planted the idea. You knew I'd build the construct."

"I'm not him. I'm the space in between. I'm the void." He edged toward the door as I stepped closer to him, close enough to see his profile. He still didn't turn to face me.

"I want to kick your living, breathing ass," I said. "We've lost a lot of time on this."

I nodded at the empty space above the hologram projector. I said, "So you've met him. You've had a chance to see yourself as others saw you. Was it worth it?"

He said nothing at first. "The curious thing," he said at last, "was that the construct wasn't surprised to meet me."

"Nothing much fazes you, Richardson. Why should your construct be any different?"

"I don't think that's it," he said. "I think it was something others knew about Richardson, that he would do anything to know . . ."

"What do you do during the day? Do you watch the building?"

He was silent.

"Have you seen your wife come here? Doesn't look good, does she? She paid a price for your little experiment, wouldn't you say? Have you been keeping up?"

"Every day," he said, "I'm aware of the zero where Richardson used to be. Every day, I'm face to face with his absence."

I clenched my fists. "Do you have any idea what it's been like for me to think that you were gone?"

"I know she . . ." For a moment, he was at a loss. "He loved her very much."

"What about me? I can't bring TOS to its potential on my own. You left me without hope!"

"Richardson did that," he said. And again, flatly: "Richardson is dead."

"Why did you have to do it like this? We could have made you a construct! Do you think you need to be dead for people to say what they really think of you?" I pounded my fist on the hologram console. "Damn it, I'd have done whatever you wanted me to. Whatever it takes, whatever you need. But it didn't have to be like this!"

"Richardson wanted to bring you along," he said. He took another sideways step toward the door. "He thought it would help you if you had a closer look at what you were afraid of."

I sat down. I tried to take the anger out of my voice. "Whatever you need," I said, "however strange, you just ask for it from now on. Understand? After we get this straightened out, assuming I can keep you out of prison, you tell me about how you want to use TOS, and we'll do that. Just so you give some attention to the things that *I* am interested in."

"I don't think you understand. You can't bring him back from the dead. The construct was for the bardo."

"The what?"

"The in-between time. Before its next life, the soul looks back, understands. Looks back, but there's no *going* back. There's only the next life, and forgetfulness."

He turned his face to me. His expression was blank, so blank that in truth he didn't look like himself.

"I'm the soul who doesn't forget. I'll have a new life, the life of a man who *understands* death. I have died. I am dead. And I will live again." He looked at his hands. "What a thing to long for."

He was right. I hadn't understood. I had thought this whole thing was like the story of the man who stages his own funeral so he can hear what the mourners will have to say about him. But there was more to it than that.

I said, "You're not going anywhere."

He stepped closer to the door. "I'll have another life."

"Got TOS to make an electronic funds transfer, did you? You're a rich man?"

"It's not like that. I'm going naked. I'm taking nothing along."

"I see. Taking no baggage but your worthless skin and your new-found wisdom."

"Memory."

"How about your wife, then? Did you and TOS arrange some little windfall for her?"

"Richardson's wife!" he shouted. "I'm not him! Richardson is dead!"

He ran, then. I followed him out of the I/O room, but I didn't bother to run.

As soon as I was out in the hallway, TOS did what I knew it would do. I had just materialized out of thin air, and TOS could only conclude, recognizing me or not, that some sort of security breach had taken place.

All over the building, doors locked. The alarm rang at the security guards' desks. Through the glass wall along the corridor, I could see one of the guards in the other wing looking up at the lights on our floor.

Richardson tried the stairwell door. It wouldn't budge.

"Richardson," I said gently as I approached. "Philip."

He ran down the side corridor, but was blocked by a fire door.

"It's over," I said when I had turned the corner. "Let it be over."

He whirled to face me. "I won't bring him back!" he said. "Forever is *your* obsession, not mine!" Then, pleading: "I *can't* bring him back! It can't be done!"

"Surely," I said, "you've seen whatever you needed to see. Surely you have come to understand whatever it is that you needed to understand."

"I won't help you!"

I grabbed the front of his sweatshirt. "When they arrest you, Philip, when the truth comes out . . ."

He masked his face with shaking hands and slumped against the fire door.

"When the truth comes out, I can help you or I can hurt you, Richardson."

"Dead," he said through his hands. "He's dead."

"You can get your life back. It's going to be a bit smashed up. It's going to take some piecing back together. But you can have it back."

He pressed his hands hard against his face.

Bierley saved his ass.

The construct was making calls to our politicos before the police had taken Richardson from the building, and before sunrise, there were thirty spin doctors in different parts of the country finding ways to put what Richardson had done in the best possible light.

The press verdict, basically, was genius stretched to the limit. He'd pushed himself too hard doing work vital to national interests. The courts ordered rest, lots of psychological evaluations, and release under his own recognizance. Eventually, he received a suspended sentence for data fraud.

And Sharon Richardson took him back. I wouldn't have, if he'd been replaceable. It was hard to imagine an infidelity worse than his. I had to welcome him back. But she chose to.

Deserters.

When the work is hard, I think of deserters. And the work is often hard. We've been at it again for months now, but Richardson and I don't throw off sparks the way we once did. We talk about technical problems with TOS, and we bounce ideas off each other, but something's gone.

No more conceptual leaps. No more flying from breakthrough to breakthrough.

I think of men on the rail of a sinking tanker. I think of the arctic explorer stranded on the ice.

I think of deserters. What are they afraid of?

Maybe they are afraid of the wrong thing.

The dead bear witness.

From the bottom of the sea, dead sailors wave their arms.

It's not that Richardson has gone dull. If anything, his mind has more edge than before. But we'll be arguing some point of memory structures and I'll happen to catch his eye and see . . .

There's someone else looking back.

"Philip Richardson," he likes to remind me, "is dead."

I'd be a damned fool to believe him.

There are a lot of damned fools in the world.

I still hear the *tick, tick, tick* of my heart, the one, one, one that counts down to zero. I still believe that there's a chance, just a chance, that I can find a door into eternity. When Richardson and I were at our best, there were days when I thought I had glimpsed that door.

But I don't work with the same focus I once did. Whatever I'm doing, there's something that flutters at the edge of my consciousness.

When, at quiet moments, I hear the blood rush in my ears, when I feel my heart thumping in my chest, it's not just the numbers counting down that I think of. It's also the numbers already counted. Bierley, gone. Richardson . . . different.

I am fifty-nine years old.

What if I succeed? What if I reside in TOS, eternal, separate, watching the living die and die and die?

Often, I think of the man in the lifeboat. He has rowed himself to safety, beyond the burning oil, beyond the fire's reach. Through the smoke and flames, he can see the others waving to him, holding out their arms. Do they think he'd row back across the fire in a wooden boat?

Crowded at the rail, the sailors wave and sink. Each drowns alone, but they sink together.

There's no comfort in a common grave, I tell myself.

But on days when I can't think clearly, I sit and look at my hands, the hands of a man who is rowing himself to safety, and I know that the sea around him is wide. And black. And cold. And empty.

Appendixes

About the Nebula Awards

Throughout every calendar year, the members of the Science-fiction and Fantasy Writers of America read and recommend novels and stories for the annual Nebula Awards. The editor of the "Nebula Awards Report" collects the recommendations and publishes them in the *SFWA Forum*. Near the end of the year, the NAR editor tallies the endorsements, draws up the preliminary ballot, and sends it to all active SFWA members. Under the current rules, each novel and story enjoys a one-year eligibility period from its date of publication. If the work fails to make the preliminary ballot during that interval, it is dropped from further Nebula consideration.

The NAR editor processes the results of the preliminary ballot and then compiles a final ballot listing the five most popular novels, novellas, novelettes, and short stories. For purposes of the Nebula Award, a novel is 40,000 words or more; a novella is 17,500 to 39,999 words; a novelette is 7,500 to 17,499 words; and a short story is 7,499 words or fewer. At the present time, SFWA impanels both a novel jury and a short-fiction jury to oversee the voting process and, in cases where a presumably worthy title was neglected by the membership at large, to supplement the five nominees with a sixth choice. Thus, the appearance of extra finalists in any category bespeaks two distinct processes: jury discretion and ties.

Founded in 1965 by Damon Knight, the Science Fiction Writers of America began with a charter membership of seventy-eight authors. Today it boasts about a thousand members and an augmented name. Early in his tenure, Lloyd Biggle Jr., SFWA's first secretary-treasurer, proposed that the organization periodically select and publish the year's best stories. This notion quickly evolved into the elaborate balloting process, an annual awards banquet, and a series of Nebula anthologies. Judith Ann Lawrence designed the trophy from a sketch by Kate Wilhelm. It is a block of Lucite containing a rock crystal and a spiral nebula made of metallic glitter. The prize is handmade, and no two are exactly alike.

The Grand Master Nebula Award goes to a living author for a lifetime of achievement. In accordance with SFWA's bylaws, the president nominates a candidate, normally after consulting with previous presidents and the board of directors. This nomination then goes before the officers; if a majority approves, the candidate becomes a Grand Master. Past recipients include Robert A. Heinlein (1974), Jack Williamson (1975), Clifford D. Simak (1976), L. Sprague de Camp (1978), Fritz Leiber (1980), Andre Norton (1983), Arthur C. Clarke (1985), Isaac Asimov (1986), Alfred Bester (1987), Ray Bradbury (1988), Lester del Rey (1990), Frederik Pohl (1992), Damon Knight (1994), and A. E. van Vogt (1995).

The thirty-second annual Nebula Awards banquet was held at the Holiday Inn Crown Plaza Hotel in Kansas City, Kansas, on April 19, 1997, where Nebula Awards were given in the categories of novel, novella, novelette, short story, and lifetime achievement (Grand Master). As part of a program to honor older writers who are no longer writing and publishing, Judith Merril was honored as SFWA's third Author Emeritus. Wilson Tucker was honored last year; Emil Petaja, honored in 1995, was the first.

Selected Titles from the
1996 Preliminary Nebula Ballot

NOVELS

Blindfold by Kevin J. Anderson (Warner/Aspect)
Feersum Endjinn by Iain M. Banks (Bantam)
The Transmigration of Souls by William Barton (Warner)
Sailing Bright Eternity by Gregory Benford (Bantam)
Headcrash by Bruce Bethke (Warner)
Brightness Reef by David Brin (Bantam)
Cetaganda by Lois McMaster Bujold (Baen)
Permutation City by Greg Egan (HarperPrism [UK: Millennium])
The Bones of Time by Kathleen Ann Goonan (Tor)
1968 by Joe Haldeman (Morrow)
Remnant Population by Elizabeth Moon (Baen)

Beowulf's Children by Larry Niven, Jerry Pournelle, and Steven
Barnes (Tor)
The Killing Star by Charles Pellegrino and George Zebrowski
(Morrow)
The Shattered Oath by Joseph Sherman (Baen)
Holy Fire by Bruce Sterling (Bantam)
Nobody's Son by Sean Stewart (Ace)
Whiteout by Sage Walker (Tor)

NOVELLAS

"Beauty and the Opera or the Phantom Beast" by Suzy McKee
Charnas (*Asimov's Science Fiction,* March 1996)
"Fault Lines" by Nancy Kress (*Asimov's Science Fiction,* August 1995)
"A Man of the People" by Ursula K. Le Guin (*Asimov's Science
Fiction,* May 1995)
"We Were Out of Our Minds with Joy" by David Marusek
(*Asimov's Science Fiction,* November 1995)
"Gas Fish" by Mary Rosenblum (*Asimov's Science Fiction,*
February 1996)
"The Doryman" by Mary Rosenblum (*Asimov's Science Fiction,*
December 1995)

NOVELETTES

"Age of Aquarius" by William Barton (*Asimov's Science Fiction,*
May 1996)
"A Worm in the Well" by Gregory Benford (*Analog,* November 1995)
"Simply Indispensable" by Michael Bishop (*Full Spectrum 5,* Bantam,
1995)
"Bulldog Drummond and the Grim Reaper" by Michael Coney
(*The Magazine of Fantasy & Science Fiction,* January 1996)
"El Hijo de Hernez" by Marcos Donnelly (*The Magazine of Fantasy
& Science Fiction,* April 1995)
"The First Law of Thermodynamics" by James Patrick Kelly
(*Intersections,* Tor, February 1996)
"Across the Darkness" by Geoffrey A. Landis (*Asimov's Science
Fiction,* June 1995)

"Of Silence and Slow Time" by Karawynn Long (*Full Spectrum 5,* Bantam, 1995)

"The Land of Nod" by Mike Resnick (*Asimov's Science Fiction,* June 1996)

"Survivor" by Dave Smeds (*Immortal Unicorn,* HarperPrism, 1995)

"Javier, Dying in the Land of Flowers" by Deborah Wheeler (*The Magazine of Fantasy & Science Fiction,* January 1996)

SHORT STORIES

"Life on the Moon" by Tony Daniel (*Asimov's Science Fiction,* April 1995)

"Ebb Tide" by Mary Soon Lee (*The Magazine of Fantasy & Science Fiction,* May 1995)

"The Dream of Houses" by Wil McCarthy (*Analog,* November 1995)

"Rhapsody" by Lyn Nichols (*Blood Muse,* Donald I. Fine, 1995)

"Stop-It-Now" by Jonathan V. Post (*Tomorrow SF,* June 1995)

"Count on Me" by Ray Vukcevich (*The Magazine of Fantasy & Science Fiction,* November 1995)

"Cool Zone" by Pat York (*Full Spectrum 5,* Bantam, 1995)

Past Nebula Award Winners

1965

Best Novel: *Dune* by Frank Herbert

Best Novella: "The Saliva Tree" by Brian W. Aldiss
    "He Who Shapes" by Roger Zelazny (tie)

Best Novelette: "The Doors of His Face, the Lamps of His Mouth" by Roger Zelazny

Best Short Story: "'Repent, Harlequin!' Said the Ticktockman" by Harlan Ellison

1966

Best Novel: *Flowers for Algernon* by Daniel Keyes
    Babel-17 by Samuel R. Delany (tie)

Best Novella: "The Last Castle" by Jack Vance

Best Novelette: "Call Him Lord" by Gordon R. Dickson
Best Short Story: "The Secret Place" by Richard McKenna

1967

Best Novel: *The Einstein Intersection* by Samuel R. Delany
Best Novella: "Behold the Man" by Michael Moorcock
Best Novelette: "Gonna Roll the Bones" by Fritz Leiber
Best Short Story: "Aye, and Gomorrah" by Samuel R. Delany

1968

Best Novel: *Rite of Passage* by Alexei Panshin
Best Novella: "Dragonrider" by Anne McCaffrey
Best Novelette: "Mother to the World" by Richard Wilson
Best Short Story: "The Planners" by Kate Wilhelm

1969

Best Novel: *The Left Hand of Darkness* by Ursula K. Le Guin
Best Novella: "A Boy and His Dog" by Harlan Ellison
Best Novelette: "Time Considered as a Helix of Semi-Precious
     Stones" by Samuel R. Delany
Best Short Story: "Passengers" by Robert Silverberg

1970

Best Novel: *Ringworld* by Larry Niven
Best Novella: "Ill Met in Lankhmar" by Fritz Leiber
Best Novelette: "Slow Sculpture" by Theodore Sturgeon
Best Short Story: no award

1971

Best Novel: *A Time of Changes* by Robert Silverberg
Best Novella: "The Missing Man" by Katherine MacLean
Best Novelette: "The Queen of Air and Darkness" by Poul Anderson
Best Short Story: "Good News from the Vatican" by Robert Silverberg

1972

Best Novel: *The Gods Themselves* by Isaac Asimov
Best Novella: "A Meeting with Medusa" by Arthur C. Clarke

Best Novelette: "Goat Song" by Poul Anderson
Best Short Story: "When It Changed" by Joanna Russ

1973

Best Novel: *Rendezvous with Rama* by Arthur C. Clarke
Best Novella: "The Death of Doctor Island" by Gene Wolfe
Best Novelette: "Of Mist, and Grass, and Sand" by Vonda N. McIntyre
Best Short Story: "Love Is the Plan, the Plan Is Death" by James
     Tiptree Jr.
Best Dramatic Presentation: *Soylent Green*
     Stanley R. Greenberg for screenplay (based on the novel *Make
     Room! Make Room!*)
     Harry Harrison for *Make Room! Make Room!*

1974

Best Novel: *The Dispossessed* by Ursula K. Le Guin
Best Novella: "Born with the Dead" by Robert Silverberg
Best Novelette: "If the Stars Are Gods" by Gordon Eklund and
     Gregory Benford
Best Short Story: "The Day Before the Revolution" by Ursula K.
     Le Guin
Best Dramatic Presentation: *Sleeper* by Woody Allen
Grand Master: Robert A. Heinlein

1975

Best Novel: *The Forever War* by Joe Haldeman
Best Novella: "Home Is the Hangman" by Roger Zelazny
Best Novelette: "San Diego Lightfoot Sue" by Tom Reamy
Best Short Story: "Catch That Zeppelin!" by Fritz Leiber
Best Dramatic Writing: Mel Brooks and Gene Wilder for *Young
     Frankenstein*
Grand Master: Jack Williamson

1976

Best Novel: *Man Plus* by Frederik Pohl
Best Novella: "Houston, Houston, Do You Read?" by James Tiptree Jr.
Best Novelette: "The Bicentennial Man" by Isaac Asimov

Best Short Story: "A Crowd of Shadows" by Charles L. Grant
Grand Master: Clifford D. Simak

1977

Best Novel: *Gateway* by Frederik Pohl
Best Novella: "Stardance" by Spider and Jeanne Robinson
Best Novelette: "The Screwfly Solution" by Raccoona Sheldon
Best Short Story: "Jeffty Is Five" by Harlan Ellison
Special Award: *Star Wars*

1978

Best Novel: *Dreamsnake* by Vonda N. McIntyre
Best Novella: "The Persistence of Vision" by John Varley
Best Novelette: "A Glow of Candles, a Unicorn's Eye" by Charles L.
    Grant
Best Short Story: "Stone" by Edward Bryant
Grand Master: L. Sprague de Camp

1979

Best Novel: *The Fountains of Paradise* by Arthur C. Clarke
Best Novella: "Enemy Mine" by Barry Longyear
Best Novelette: "Sandkings" by George R. R. Martin
Best Short Story: "giANTS" by Edward Bryant

1980

Best Novel: *Timescape* by Gregory Benford
Best Novella: "The Unicorn Tapestry" by Suzy McKee Charnas
Best Novelette: "The Ugly Chickens" by Howard Waldrop
Best Short Story: "Grotto of the Dancing Deer" by Clifford D. Simak
Grand Master: Fritz Leiber

1981

Best Novel: *The Claw of the Conciliator* by Gene Wolfe
Best Novella: "The Saturn Game" by Poul Anderson
Best Novelette: "The Quickening" by Michael Bishop
Best Short Story: "The Bone Flute" by Lisa Tuttle*

---

*This Nebula Award was declined by the author.

1982

Best Novel: *No Enemy But Time* by Michael Bishop
Best Novella: "Another Orphan" by John Kessel
Best Novelette: "Fire Watch" by Connie Willis
Best Short Story: "A Letter from the Clearys" by Connie Wilis

1983

Best Novel: *Startide Rising* by David Brin
Best Novella: "Hardfought" by Greg Bear
Best Novelette: "Blood Music" by Greg Bear
Best Short Story: "The Peacemaker" by Gardner Dozois
Grand Master: Andre Norton

1984

Best Novel: *Neuromancer* by William Gibson
Best Novella: "PRESS ENTER ■" by John Varley
Best Novelette: "Bloodchild" by Octavia E. Butler
Best Short Story: "Morning Child" by Gardner Dozois

1985

Best Novel: *Ender's Game* by Orson Scott Card
Best Novella: "Sailing to Byzantium" by Robert Silverberg
Best Novelette: "Portraits of His Children" by George R. R. Martin
Best Short Story: "Out of All Them Bright Stars" by Nancy Kress
Grand Master: Arthur C. Clarke

1986

Best Novel: *Speaker for the Dead* by Orson Scott Card
Best Novella: "R & R" by Lucius Shepard
Best Novelette: "The Girl Who Fell into the Sky" by Kate Wilhelm
Best Short Story: "Tangents" by Greg Bear
Grand Master: Isaac Asimov

1987

Best Novel: *The Falling Woman* by Pat Murphy
Best Novella: "The Blind Geometer" by Kim Stanley Robinson
Best Novelette: "Rachel in Love" by Pat Murphy

Best Short Story: "Forever Yours, Anna" by Kate Wilhelm
Grand Master: Alfred Bester

1988

Best Novel: *Falling Free* by Lois McMaster Bujold
Best Novella: "The Last of the Winnebagos" by Connie Willis
Best Novelette: "Schrödinger's Kitten" by George Alec Effinger
Best Short Story: "Bible Stories for Adults, No. 17: The Deluge" by
James Morrow
Grand Master: Ray Bradbury

1989

Best Novel: *The Healer's War* by Elizabeth Ann Scarborough
Best Novella: "The Mountains of Mourning" by Lois McMaster
Bujold
Best Novelette: "At the Rialto" by Connie Willis
Best Short Story: "Ripples in the Dirac Sea" by Geoffrey Landis

1990

Best Novel: *Tehanu: The Last Book of Earthsea* by Ursula K. Le Guin
Best Novella: "The Hemingway Hoax" by Joe Haldeman
Best Novelette: "Tower of Babylon" by Ted Chiang
Best Short Story: "Bears Discover Fire" by Terry Bisson
Grand Master: Lester del Rey

1991

Best Novel: *Stations of the Tide* by Michael Swanwick
Best Novella: "Beggars in Spain" by Nancy Kress
Best Novelette: "Guide Dog" by Mike Conner
Best Short Story: "Ma Qui" by Alan Brennert

1992

Best Novel: *Doomsday Book* by Connie Willis
Best Novella: "City of Truth" by James Morrow
Best Novelette: "Danny Goes to Mars" by Pamela Sargent
Best Short Story: "Even the Queen" by Connie Willis
Grand Master: Frederik Pohl

1993

Best Novel: *Red Mars* by Kim Stanley Robinson
Best Novella: "The Night We Buried Road Dog" by Jack Cady
Best Novelette: "Georgia on My Mind" by Charles Sheffield
Best Short Story: "Graves" by Joe Haldeman

1994

Best Novel: *Moving Mars* by Greg Bear
Best Novella: "Seven Views of Olduvai Gorge" by Mike Resnick
Best Novelette: "The Martian Child" by David Gerrold
Best Short Story: "A Defense of the Social Contracts" by Martha
    Soukup
Grand Master: Damon Knight

1995

Best Novel: *The Terminal Experiment* by Robert J. Sawyer
Best Novella: "Last Summer at Mars Hill" by Elizabeth Hand
Best Novelette: "Solitude" by Ursula K. Le Guin
Best Short Story: "Death and the Librarian" by Esther M. Friesner
Grand Master: A. E. van Vogt

Those who are interested in category-related awards should also con-
sult *A History of the Hugo, Nebula, and International Fantasy Awards*
by Donald Franson and Howard DeVore (Misfit Press, 1987). Periodically updated, the book is available from Howard DeVore, 4705 Wed-
del, Dearborn, Michigan 48125.

About the Science-fiction
and Fantasy Writers of America

The Science-fiction and Fantasy Writers of America, Incorporated, includes among its members most of the active writers of science fiction
and fantasy. According to the bylaws of the organization, its purpose
"shall be to promote the furtherance of the writing of science fiction,
fantasy, and related genres as a profession." SFWA informs writers on

professional matters, protects their interests, and helps them in dealings with agents, editors, anthologists, and producers of nonprint media. It also strives to encourage public interest in and appreciation of science fiction and fantasy.

Anyone may become an active member of SFWA after the acceptance of and payment for one professionally published novel, one professionally produced dramatic script, or three professionally published pieces of short fiction. Only science fiction, fantasy, and other prose fiction of a related genre, in English, shall be considered as qualifying for active membership. Beginning writers who do not yet qualify for active membership may join as associate members; other classes of membership include illustrator members (artists), affiliate members (editors, agents, reviewers, and anthologists), estate members (representatives of the estates of active members who have died), and institutional members (high schools, colleges, universities, libraries, broadcasters, film producers, futurist groups, and individuals associated with such an institution).

Anyone who is not a member of SFWA may subscribe to *The Bulletin of the Science Fiction and Fantasy Writers of America.* The magazine is published quarterly, and contains articles by well-known writers on all aspects of their profession. Subscriptions are $15 a year or $27 for two years. For information on how to subscribe to the *Bulletin,* or for more information about SFWA, write to:

SFWA, Inc.
532 La Guardia Place
Box 632
New York, NY 10012-1428

Readers are also invited to visit the SFWA site on the World Wide Web at the following address:

http://www.sfwa.org